The Keys of the Watchmen

Kathleen C. Perrin

Summary: During a tourist trip to Mont Saint Michel in Normandy, France, 17-year-old Katelyn Michaels is confronted by two unusual young men, one who insists she is there to save the mount, and the other who will stop at nothing, even murder, to prevent her from fulfilling her destiny.

1. Young Adult—Fiction. 2. Paranormal—Fiction. 3. Time Travel—Fiction. 4. Romance—Fiction. 5. Mont Saint Michel—Fiction. 6. France—Fiction. 7. Medieval History—Fiction.

To see photos of Mont Saint Michel, visit the author's website at:
www.kathleencperrin.com

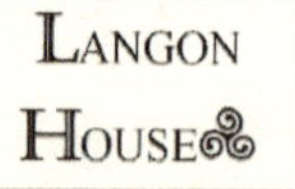

The Keys of the Watchmen / Kathleen C. Perrin. – 1st ed.
Watchmen Saga: Volume 1

Library of Congress Control Number: 2014922001
Published by Langon House, Salt Lake City, Utah

ISBN-13: 978-0692342855
ISBN-10: 0692342850

Printed in the United States of America by CreateSpace

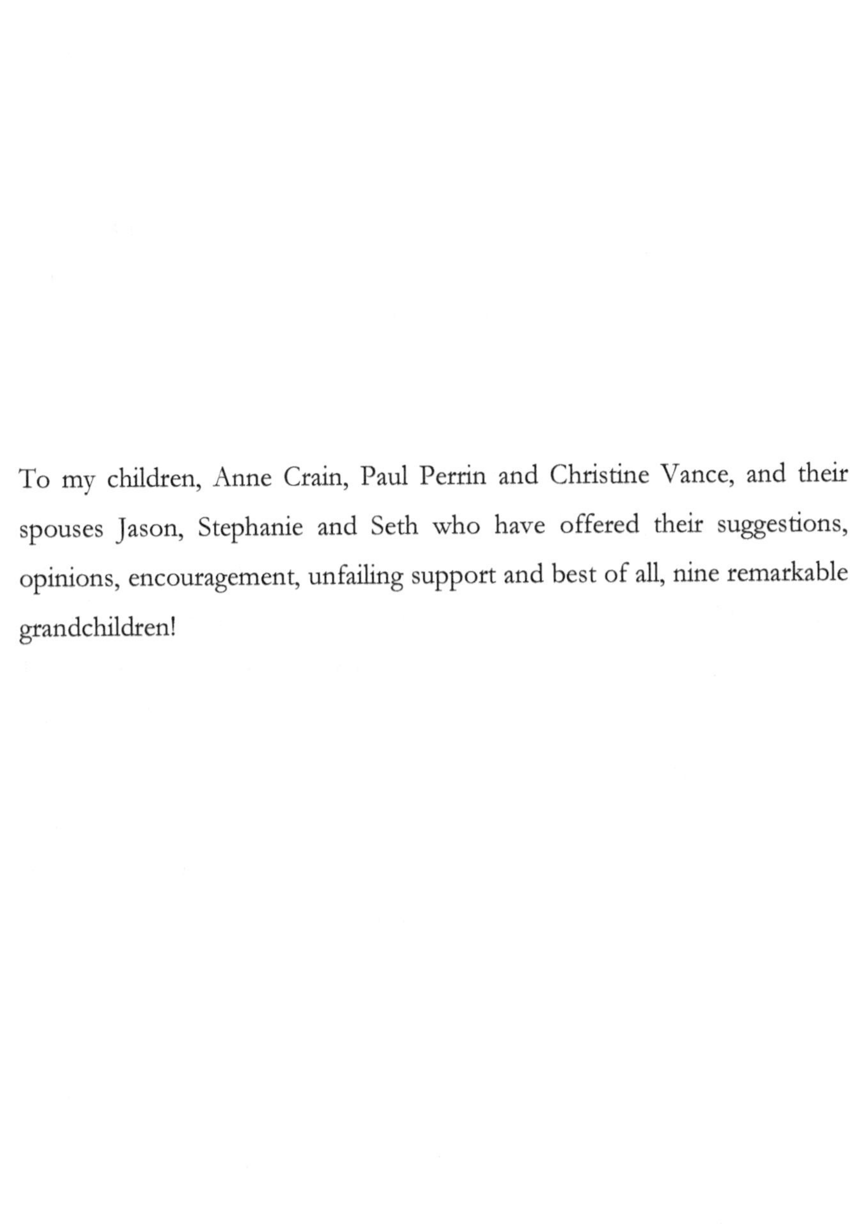

To my children, Anne Crain, Paul Perrin and Christine Vance, and their spouses Jason, Stephanie and Seth who have offered their suggestions, opinions, encouragement, unfailing support and best of all, nine remarkable grandchildren!

Acknowledgements

Thanks to my Breton husband who has not only supported me in my writing for years, encouraged me to keep going when I had all but given up, brainstormed with me countless times, but who also gave me the gift of my muse, *la Belle France.* Because of him, I have had the stones of Mont Saint Michel infused in my soul because I have had the opportunity of touching them and walking upon them too many times to count. Because of him, I have had the blessing of living within stone walls—erected by his ancestors—that inspire and motivate me to tell the stories of the tumultuous history and the breathtaking landscapes of France.

Thank you to Kristen Eliason, my friend and a talented writer and poet, for her helpful suggestions and her thoughtful edit of my manuscript.

And a very special thanks goes to my daughter Christine Vance who has acted as my motivator, cheerleader, psychiatrist, secretary, copy editor, agent, formatter, and cover designer. This project would never have come to fruition without her tireless work and the endless hours she has spent assisting me.

Prologue

BANISHED. THEY HAD been banished.

The stinging wind whistled its mocking censure and the beating rain hammered out its wrath upon the ill-protected flesh of the two fleeing refugees. There had been no time to prepare for their exodus, and inadequately clothed, they had been obliged to depart without delay.

The woman bent her head in sorrow, grieving at her forced relinquishment of the only earthly domicile she had ever known. Her impossible choice had led to this. Never again would she bask in the utopian abode lovingly prepared for her—with every imaginable luxury—by a doting father. So as not to attempt to return, that same father had arranged for her and her companion to be transported and abandoned in a distant land, far from familiar haunts. He had also warned them that guards had been placed around the domain's perimeter with explicit instructions not to allow them to re-enter.

The man who was now her husband attempted to shield her from the elements with his protective arms. Although she could not hear his voice above nature's howling fury, she heard his words in her heart. *You made the right decision. I love you.*

That knowledge gave her the strength to go on. The children she would bear him would understand. She had given up her life of ease and luxury for them. Knowing the consequences, she had willingly disobeyed her father. And he had been left with no choice but to punish her for that blatant transgression.

The sound of crashing waves heralded their approach to the sea, and the dreary sky above gave no sign of slowing its unrelenting chastisement. When the barbs of a large thistle caught in her wet hair, her companion removed it, drawing blood from his index finger. As if astonished at the scarlet droplets that fell to the sodden ground, he stopped in his tracks and stared. She pressed her hand around his finger to staunch the flow of the red liquid, and marveled at its warmth. Her flagging spirits were buoyed up by this reminder of his humanity.

In the distance, a single ray of light illuminated the rocky crags of a lone barren hill.

"I . . . know that place," the man uttered. "Come, we will find shelter there."

She thought the forest canopy would provide better protection from the rain, but she placed her trust in him. She had witnessed his exceptional goodness—his valiant fight against the evil that threatened the world. Her beloved father recognized it, but it had not prevented him from casting the man out of his presence.

And so, she followed as he picked up a large stick and whipped it through the thick undergrowth like a finely-honed steel blade, forging a pathway through the unyielding scrub brush that crowded around the trunks of the towering trees. When an all too familiar hissing sound broke the silence, she recoiled in horror, just out of range of a striking serpent's fangs.

A violent blow from her companion's stick caught the reptile in mid-air, and before she could even exhale, he had flung it away with firm deliberation.

He said nothing as silent tears spilled down her cheeks, but he took her hand and brought it to his lips. With renewed determination, she followed him to the foot of the hill and then side by side, the couple began their ascent, slipping and sliding on the rocky incline.

Her trust in him was rewarded when they found the entrance to a small cave nestled under the outcropping of granite that topped the hill.

"We will be safe here for the night," he said. "Tomorrow, we must move on and find food, but before we sleep, there is something we must do. Come."

He drew her out of the rudimentary shelter, and then assisted her to the highest point of the rocky hill. Even her immense fatigue and the pelting rain did not dampen the exhilaration she felt as she looked out upon the unobstructed vista. Before them lay a field of velvet green carpet, woven from the treetops of the forest they'd traversed. Behind them stretched the vastness of the ocean, boiling with the foam of its tempestuous waves, but also teeming with the hope of nourishing life. The world was full of possibilities. Although their struggle would not be without hardships and sorrows, they would survive.

Her companion pushed a large stone onto the center of their rocky platform, and with soothing tones, he gave her verbal instructions. Her body cried out in agony from the strenuous journey and exposure to the harsh elements. Her stomach clamored for sustenance, but for a moment, her mortal concerns were set aside for loftier purposes as she helped him gather and place the stones. She rubbed her bleeding hand across their roughness, appreciating the tactile sensation. She looked into his eyes as he brushed her cheek with the back of his swollen fingers. Then, with her hand interlocked with his, she knelt beside him at the make-shift structure.

She knew and accepted the consequences of their disobedience. She had been warned, yet she made the choice willingly, knowing the rewards outweighed the punishment. But as the parting clouds allowed the rain to soften to a gentle mist and light to break through, there was something she *didn't* know. At that moment, she did not know that their simple act of devotion under such difficult conditions would result in a well-kept secret that would impact them and their descendants for generations to come. And she did not know just how far others would go to discover that secret.

Part One

And there was war in heaven: Michael and his angels fought against the dragon . . .

The Book of Revelation 12: 7

Chapter 1

I THINK IT'S SAFE to say I wouldn't be here if it wasn't for Jackson. I fought coming, but Jackson fashions himself a budding "Renaissance Man" (his words, not mine), and so *he* was excited. He actually *wanted* to come to France. He begged to come. And Mom said he couldn't come alone. So here I am. Just so you know, I don't plan on enjoying it. Besides, what seventeen-year-old girl wants to hang out for the summer with her kid brother?

Oh don't get me wrong. It's not that I have anything against France, it's just that I refuse to like anything SHE likes. The Frenchwoman. The one who destroyed my family and nearly killed my mother. Oh okay, so maybe that's a bit extreme. Jackson tells me I'm *always* exaggerating. She didn't actually try to kill my mother, but what she did was nearly as bad. Thank heavens she's too '*fatiguée*' after the four-hour drive from Paris to visit the abbey. Thank heavens she finds her gazillion-dollar-a-night room Dad is paying for is just so 'bee-u-tee-ful' that she needs a 'lee-tle *sieste*.' Thank heavens for a few hours of peace. No more of her "Mont Saint Michel resisted zee English siege and France eez zee very best country een zee world."

But, I do have to admit that when I first saw the mount looming up out of the mist off the coast of Normandy, it *was* very 'bee-u-tee-ful.' It was as if it spoke to my soul. Almost as if I knew this place, and I was coming home. What do the French call it? *Déjà vu*? I know, I know. That sounds trite. A bit melodramatic, but I don't know how else to put it. I didn't get a B minus in 11th Grade English Composition for nothing: "Katelyn lacks originality, uses too many clichés, and needs to apply herself more. I'm still convinced there's some talent in there somewhere." That's a direct quote from my English teacher, Mrs. Hunter.

But of course, I won't let the Frenchwoman know that. I mean about Mont Saint Michel—Mount Saint Michael in English—speaking to my soul, not that I got a B minus in English Composition. I'll just keep my feelings about this place to myself. Maybe I'll tell Jackson. I don't know. It depends on how much of a jerk he's planning on being. And maybe I won't hate *everything* about being in France.

Anyway, with HER out of the way, Jackson and I have the entire afternoon to ourselves to explore the island. It's not an island, really, just more of a hunk of rock stranded out in the middle of a flat sandy bay. When the tide's in, it's surrounded by the sea because Jackson tells me they just ripped out the causeway that connected it to the mainland for decades and replaced it with a bridge. Jackson's been reading about Mont Saint Michel. He's got his nose in the guidebook right now.

"Remember those sheep we saw on the road right before the bridge?" he asks me.

"Yeah," I say. Duh. It was kind of hard to miss them since the shuttle had to stop to let a 'we're-not-afraid-of-anything' flock of sheep cross the road.

"Well, they're a special breed that feed only on the grass in the salt marshes along the coast of the Mont Saint Michel Bay."

"Guess *those* lamb chops are pre-salted," I say.

"Very funny," he says, but my sarcasm doesn't stop him.

He tells me the bay has an area of over a hundred thousand acres. I can't really conceive of how much that is, but it sounds big. It *looks* big.

"'Mont Saint Michel is a tidal island and is the site of one of the largest tides in the world,'" Jackson reads to me, as we sit on our twin beds in our hotel room. We have a cool view of the bay and nearby coastline. "It can go out eleven miles. Just think. Eleven miles of pure sand."

"Wow," I say, trying to display adequate appreciation for his skills as my private guide. "So, how do the tides here work? I mean, does the sea come in and out each day, or what?"

I don't really care about the tides. I'm forcing myself to show interest. It keeps the peace.

"It says here there are two high tides, and two low tides every twenty-four hours. Actually, it's more like twenty-five hours. There are about twelve hours and twenty-five minutes between the two high tides."

"So what does that mean exactly," I ask, not trying very hard to figure it out. I'll leave the figuring-out stuff to Jackson. It makes him happy to think he's so much smarter than me.

"Oh come on, Katie. You're not that dumb. It means that twice a day, the mount is surrounded by water, and twice a day the tide goes out eleven miles. The ocean is constantly moving from high tide to low tide, and then back to high tide. Cool, huh?"

"Yeah, cool," I say. Honestly, it's not that cool to me.

But he doesn't stop there. "And you know why they occur, don't you?"

"Why what occurs?" I ask, trying to push his buttons.

"I mean why there are tides in the first place?"

I know that the moon has something to do with tides, but I'm not going to play his game. "Uh," I say trying to think of some clever retort. "Of course I do. They're for the Fish Olympics. They have contests to see which fish can swim the fastest against strong currents."

"Yeah, like I'm so sure," Jackson says. From his sarcastic tone I can tell he's not amused at my poor attempt at being clever, but he is certainly anxious to show me just how clever *he* is. "The tides are caused by the gravitational attraction of the moon on the Earth. At full and new moons, or what they call dark moon, the gravitational pull of the moon and sun are combined, so you have extra high tides."

Thanks a lot, Smarty Pants. I've always wanted to know everything I possibly could about tides. While he's talking to me, I run my fingers through my heavy hair, damp from the cloying humidity. I decide to braid it to keep it from clinging to my neck. Now it thumps on my back like a knotted rope. I'm not sure which is worse.

"But, Katie," he continues, "get this: when the tide's out, there are areas that have quicksand. Unsuspecting tourists get swallowed up walking out there in the bay."

I don't know if that's true or not, but I don't plan on testing it. I'll stay on dry land. Besides, if those tourists don't get pulled under by the quicksand, they'll drown when the tide comes rushing back in as Jackson says "at the speed of a galloping horse." He informs me that equals one yard per second.

" 'There's a difference of fifty feet in depth between high and low tide,' " Jackson reads to me and then adds, "so unless you're Michael Phelps, you're in trouble."

I'm a good swimmer, but I'm no Michael Phelps. I wouldn't want to be out in that bay when the sea rushes in, so I don't think I'll be using my swim team skills any time soon.

"We can watch the tide come in tonight from the ramparts," Jackson continues.

It sounds kind of interesting, I guess. We'll see this evening. The tide is supposed to come in at around seven o'clock. Maybe we'll get to see some tourists drown.

Chapter 2

I LOADED MY BACKPACK with my camera gear, and at the last minute, the impression came to my mind: *take your computer.* So I decided to slip my laptop computer in the pack as well, along with my newest high-tech acquisition, a solar battery charger. They didn't add much weight to the pack and I wasn't so sure I trusted the old-fashioned lock on our door. If my computer or other electronic gear were stolen, my life—as I knew it—was over.

For some strange reason, I also threw in my travel kit and my small first aid kit. After all, you never know when you might need a toothbrush or a laptop! Or an iPhone, (or Dad's old iPod with some music I wanted to transfer). Or a pen drive. Or my cool little pop-up speakers. Or my headlamp. Or shampoo or Neosporin. Then I grabbed a navy bandana and tied it around one of the straps. That might come in handy too.

We left our room at the Du Guesclin Hotel with its incredible view to work our way along the walkway topping the ramparts, down several sets of narrow stone steps, and back to the entrance of the mount to begin our explorations. We had to fight counter-current against a group of tourists, with their own tons of camera gear, to once again step into the outer fortified courtyard, through which every person visiting the monument had to pass.

A single street in the village curved up from the causeway at the foot of the mount where the millions of tourists—who made this France's number two tourist destination after Paris—arrived by shuttle bus from the parking area on the mainland. We had planned on staying three nights, and out of the blue, I felt glad we were staying so long. Weird! Anyway, the Frenchwoman told us that at seven o'clock when the shops closed, most of the tourists would leave. Then we'd really be able to explore the mount in peace. I was looking forward to that, because even though it was a Monday and the weekend was over, the crowds were so thick, we could hardly make our way through the street. It wasn't a street really, more of a cobblestone walkway. There were no cars. There couldn't be. It was too narrow and there were simply too many people.

Earlier, when we'd been dragging our wheeled suitcases up the cobblestones on our way to check into the hotel, Jackson had been fascinated by an ancient-looking cannon standing like a sentinel in the outer courtyard in front of the drawbridge that served as a portal into the village. Now as we reached the cannon again, he flipped through his guidebook. I tried to snap a few candid shots of him leaning against it, but that proved to be a challenge as a mob of French school children emitting high-pitched whining sounds swarmed around him like a bunch of ants.

"Katie," he called. "Come over here. You won't believe what this is!"

As I pushed my way through the anthill, something rough brushed against my arm. It almost felt as if I'd been whipped by a stalk of stinging nettle and I wondered if I'd been stung by an insect. French ants maybe? There was a slight rashy-looking mark on my arm, but no tale-tell signs of insect bites. Had someone scratched me? I looked around but didn't see any guilty-looking assailant.

"Come see," Jackson insisted. "This is called a *Michelette.* It's an iron bombard left by the English in their siege of Mont Saint Michel during the Hundred Years' War. That's mad awesome!"

I didn't really care about the Hundred Years' War. I didn't even know what it was, or when it was, but as I touched the cannon or bombard, or whatever it's called, something bizarre happened. It was like an electric shock. And a flash of something in my mind, like I could actually see the cannon being used all those hundreds of years ago. Weird. I wasn't into history, so why would that happen? I had no idea, but it gave me the willies. Then, the hairs on my neck began to prickle. Someone was watching me!

Once again I looked around, and this time, I spotted a really strange-looking guy turning quickly away from my view. It wasn't his face that was strange-looking. I didn't actually see his face because it was covered by the cowl of a robe. One of those long monk-looking robes made out of some type of home-spun loosely woven wool.

Okay, it's the twenty-first century, and if you want to wear a long woolish robe in the middle of June, then you can wear a long woolish robe, and I'm not one to judge. Heck, there were some British kids two feet away from me with pink hair and giant gauges in their ears. And of course, the ubiquitous Goths. Dressed all in black, they lurked in corners, avoiding the sun as if its rays were poison darts. Even worse were your typical American tourists in Aloha shirts and dorky bucket hats, and the European men wearing socks with sandals. I mean, people can wear whatever they want.

Anything goes. But wool in June? Wool? Was he the one who'd brushed up against me? I tried to snap his picture, but by the time I got my camera up, he had disappeared into the crowd.

After I'd taken a few selfies of me and Jackson, we crossed over the drawbridge and through what he informed me was "The King's Portal." Even though I'd walked under the heavy stone archway before, this time a wave of panic washed over me. Instinctively, I looked straight above my head to see the rusted spikes of a metal gate that could be lowered down to the drawbridge.

"Jeez, a real live portcullis," *Smarty Pants* said. I guess Jackson saw me studying the spiked gate, which thanks to him, I now knew was a portcullis. But his words made my panic disappear as quickly as it had come. I am not normally a paranoid or jumpy person. I chalked it up to the Frenchwoman. She'd rocked my stable world and destroyed my sense of security. My anger and spite were just manifesting itself in odd ways.

I tried to focus on my surroundings. Ancient half-timbered structures crowded in upon us. Every inch of space on either side of the cobblestone pathway was filled with turrets, towers, quaint metal merchant signs, store fronts, and hawkers touting their wares.

"Ee gads, Hermione" Jackson said with a pretty good English accent. "I do believe we've found Diagon Alley."

"Yeah," I replied, "except we're in France and there's no magic."

To my left, two large windows and an opened door allowed passers-by to look into a well-stocked medieval-looking kitchen. Jackson and I stopped to watch two buxom girls dressed in period costumes beating eggs in copper bowls.

"That's *La Mère Poulard,"* Jackson informed me, as he referred to his guidebook. "The oldest and most famous eating establishment on the mount. They're whipping up omelets. The copper supposedly causes a chemical reaction to fluff up the eggs. People come from all over the world to sample those super-puffy creations."

Their wire whisks clicked out the well-rehearsed tempo together. *Clickity, clickity, clack* echoed through the crowded streets. I had never particularly liked eggs, but suddenly, I wanted nothing more than one of *La Mère Poulard's* omelets. We'd had an early lunch, and now I felt hunger pangs unlike any I'd ever experienced. I almost felt like I hadn't eaten in days. I was starving. A scrap of bread, a cracker. Anything. But most of all, an omelet.

My hunger pangs disappeared as I saw my reflection in the restaurant window. It wasn't my own face that startled me, but the face I saw reflected behind me. Mr. Woolrobe. His eyes were burning holes in my back. I forced myself not to turn, but instead, studied the face under the hood that I'd earlier been unable to see. I judged him to be about nineteen or twenty. Just a couple of years older than me. I could see some honey-colored hair—longish hair escaping from his cowl. Where my brownish-gold hair is straight and heavy, his goldish-blond hair twisted into springy curls. But it was his eyes that caught my attention. I couldn't tell exactly what color they were, but they were dark and piercing. The exact opposite of my own light blue eyes. And something else. His eyes were . . . earnest. I'm not sure I even know what earnest looks like, but that's the word that popped into my mind to describe those eyes. It was as if he were begging me for something. An unspoken request telegraphed by pleading eyes. And somehow, without ever having seen him before, I felt I could trust him.

I picked up my camera, and pretending to focus on the whisking '*Poulettes*,' I snapped Woolrobe's reflection, tilting my camera to avoid a glare. I know how to hold a camera for a shot like that. Photography is the one thing I'm better at than Jackson, and so he doesn't even try. He's the tour guide; I'm the photographer.

I adjusted to get a different angle and then felt, rather than saw, a scuffle break out behind me. I snapped another shot and then turned to see Woolrobe running up the street being chased by one of the Goths I'd seen earlier: a guy dressed all in black, with spiky, dyed-black hair and chains rattling from his tight pants.

"Come on, Katie. Let's get moving," Jackson said, punching me lightly in the arm. "We've still got the whole village to explore and the abbey to visit. Stop dawdling."

Now honestly, what twenty-first century kid in his right mind uses the word dawdle? Jackson—the self-proclaimed Renaissance Man—uses dawdle.

A handful of quaint shops lined either side of the street, but plenty of tacky ones crowded in as well. I wasn't interested in the shops. I'd never let Nicole—my best friend back home—hear me say that. But really, I don't need a gargoyle in every shape and size. Now if there'd been any of the famous French *haute couture* it'd be a different story, but kitschy abbey replicas and plastic swords aren't really my thing. Besides, I just wanted to see the abbey. There was something drawing me up to it. I couldn't quite figure it out.

"Hey," said Jackson still reading from his guidebook. "Did you know that Saint Michael is the archangel who fought with Satan and cast him out of heaven? That's him on the top of the church spire."

The golden spire that rose above the abbey at the top of the mount bore a statue of Saint Michael—Saint Michel in French—and thus the name Mont Saint Michel.

"Yeah, I know. Saint Michael is the dragon slayer. Whacked that nasty beast with his ginormous sword," I said as I picked up one of the many sword samples from the shop displays that spilled out into the street. "Satan is represented figuratively as a dragon somewhere in the Bible."

"Really?" Jackson asked as he began thumbing through his book.

I felt proud to know something Jackson didn't. But I'm kinda into the Bible, and he isn't. He always has his nose in a book, and it's no secret that my parents view him as "the smart one." I guess I'm the "pretty one," though. At least that's what Mom always tells me to appease me after making mounds of fuss over her *intelligent* child. Okay, I'm above average in the looks department, I guess. My hair is so thick that all my friends envy me. And I'm tall and skinny. I never appreciated that until my curvy friends (the ones all the boys loved in 6th Grade) started worrying about their weight. I never will be curvy, but then I never worry about my weight, either, and they hate that. I'm flat-chested, but I can eat anything I want and I never gain a pound. Yeah, they *really* hate me for that. But pretty? In all honesty, not really.

I feel like my parents don't appreciate me for my brains. I'm not "Mister-I-have-the-encyclopedia-memorized," but I'm not dumb, either. "Katelyn just needs to apply herself more," became their mantra after they read that comment from Mrs. Hunter.

But I am a closet techie. I keep it to myself, but I totally geek out with my computer and digital cameras, including a pretty chill movie camera with a built-in projector. And I'm a movie nerd. I love watching and making them and I decided I just might make a chill movie about Mont Saint Michel. I'm also a TV geek. I especially like the old television series. I mean, was there ever a better sit-com than *I Love Lucy?*

"Satan represented as a dragon in the Bible," I heard Jackson mumble to himself. "Yeah, it says that here in the introduction." He dashed up a staircase leading away from the principal street. "Come sit down. I gotta read this to you."

I extricated myself from the throngs of tourists and we climbed up several steps to sit in a dark passageway of stone worn smooth by centuries of foot traffic.

"It's in the Book of Revelation in the New Testament," he said. "Getta load of this: 'And there was war in heaven: Michael and his angels fought against the dragon: and the dragon fought and his angels, and prevailed not; neither was their place found any more in heaven. And the great dragon was cast out, that old serpent, called the Devil, and Satan, which deceiveth the whole world: he was cast out into the earth, and his angels were cast out with him.'"

"Sick," I said, as I opened my backpack. "This mount is named after Saint Michael. People in medieval times believed this is where that battle took place. The ultimate struggle between good and evil. This is where Satan was cast down. Guess that means he's out there in the bay somewhere." I have no idea where my off the wall explanation came from. It just came. But Jackson, who is definitely way too smart for a fourteen-year old, is also too easily spooked for his age, and I always do my part to add fuel to the fire.

"Creepy," he replied. "That's why there's quicksand."

He really believes me.

But that thought was cut short as I put my camera in my backpack and my hand touched something metallic. It was something metallic that didn't belong there. I rummaged in my bag to see what it was. At first I thought it was our bulky, metal room key, but then I remembered that Jackson had our key. It looked like some kind of medallion or pendant, and it was quite large. About the size of the palm of my hand.

"Jackson, did you put this in my backpack?" I asked as I started to pull out the object.

Before I got it out and before Jackson could reply, I felt pressure on my shoulder. Woolrobe was kneeling behind us. His breathing was rapid, and droplets of sweat were dripping from his forehead.

"Katelyn Michaels, the *enseigne* is yours," he whispered into my ear with a heavy French accent. "The evil ones have been waiting a very long time to prevent you from receiving it. Keep it safe. You will know what to do with it when the time comes. We have faith in you. Do not disappoint us. *Everything* depends upon you."

Before I had a chance to react, Woolrobe ran back up the narrow passageway and disappeared, but not before the Goth guy below on the street caught sight of him. And judging from his expression, he was a very angry Goth.

Chapter 3

I WAS PRETTY RATTLED by the brief encounter, but for some reason I didn't want to let Jackson know that. I'd spent my life trying to successfully torment my baby brother, and yet now, for some reason, I felt protective of him.

"What was that all about," he asked. "What did that guy say to you?"

"Nothing," I said as I jammed the odd metal item Woolrobe had called an "enseigne" back into the recesses of my backpack. "Just some weirdo getting kicks out of spooking tourists."

"He looked like *he* was the one who was spooked," Jackson said. "Did you see the way he was sweating? And did you see that Goth dude down below on the street? If looks could kill, we'd be dead."

"Those guys are probably working together to mess with tourists. You know, naïve American kids exploring medieval France, thinking we're all that. We must be so irritating to the French. I bet those guys set out at the beginning of the day to see how many of us they can freak out. Ooooo, ooooo," I said while waving my hands in his face, "the ghost of a medieval monk haunting the obnoxious visitors. For heaven's sake, Jackson, don't be so gullible."

Either he believed my explanation, or he didn't want me to continue to accuse him of being gullible—and the truth of the matter is that Jackson really is gullible—because he stood up, traipsed back down the steps to the main street, and gestured for me to follow.

The truth also is that I was rattled. Mr. Goth had looked like he was ready to kill someone, and Woolrobe had called me by name.

Could he have overheard Jackson say my name?

I dismissed that possibility pretty quickly. Jackson never calls me Katelyn, just Katie. Katelyn is for my English Composition Teacher and for my parents—when they're mad at me or lecturing me. None of my friends call me Katelyn. And yet Woolrobe had clearly called me Katelyn. And he'd used my last name. And someone had put that object in my backpack. It had to have been him down at the village entryway when we were looking at the cannon. That's when Woolrobe brushed against my arm with that coarse, home-spun fabric and scratched me.

What on earth had he meant? I'd know what to do with that metal thingy when the time came? And what was that business about he'd been waiting a very long time to give it to me? 'We have faith in you? Everything depends upon you?' Oh come on. Sounds like my parents: 'We have faith in you, Katelyn. We know you'll make the right decision about not going to the Charred Walls of the Damned concert next Saturday night. We're depending on you, Katelyn. You have to be an example for your brother, Katelyn.'"

But, this was more than just a lecture from my parents. And it was more than weird. This had no explanation. As we got to the last of the shops at the top of the village street, my eyes were drawn to a large sign in one of the windows: "*Cartes Postales, Souvenirs, Enseignes.*"

I pressed my back against the stone wall of the shop, and pulled my brother out of the oncoming foot traffic. I had a clear view both up and down the street.

"Jackson, do you know what this means?" I asked in what I hoped was a casual manner as I pointed to the word in question: *Enseignes.*

Jackson, unlike me, has studied French and is amazingly competent for never having been to France before. I know. It's annoying, because although I've taken Spanish for the past four years, the extent of my proficiency is basically '*¿dónde está el baño?*' and that isn't going to help me much in France. Unless I run into a Spaniard who happens to know where the restrooms are.

"Well," Jackson replied in his I'm-so-glad-you-asked tone, "*cartes postales* means post cards, and of course souvenirs is self-explanatory, and *enseignes* . . . Let's see, I don't know what that means, but I recall seeing that word in the guide."

I thrummed my fingers against the wall trying to disguise my anxiety.

"*Enseigne, enseigne* . . ." he muttered as he flipped to the index of his guidebook. "Yes, here it is. Hold on a sec." He turned to the correct page and ran his finger down the lines of text.

Thrum, thrum. Thankfully, there was no sign of my 'friends.' Jackson was silently reading through the text. "Okay, let me read this to you."

I felt the texture of the rough stone below my fingers as he read: " 'Even during the Hundred Years' War, pilgrims, called *Miquelots,* came flocking to Mont Saint Michel to plea for Saint Michael's protection against the wickedness and snares of the devil, to be miraculously healed from disease and illness, and to be granted pardons for their sins.' I guess they thought the mount had mystical healing properties, or something."

I listened patiently, wondering if I should pray for a miraculous healing of my own. Oh, not for me. For my father. Maybe he could be healed of his illness of incredible stupidity and of his disease of mid-life crisis that had torn apart our family. However, since I didn't have a whole lot of faith in *that* miraculous cure, I just kept listening patiently. And watching people. Watching to make sure I didn't see Woolrobe or Gothman.

" 'Most Miquelots,' " Jackson continued, " 'claimed they had been inexplicably called to the mount. They left everything behind to go. In the first half of the fourteenth century, a well-documented phenomenon occurred. Despite all the dangers involved, children traveling without their parents began banding together to go on pilgrimages to the mount. They were called shepherd lads and lasses.' "

He paused for a moment and said, "I guess that makes us shepherd lads and lasses. After all, we're here without our parents."

"And we certainly had to go through danger," I said. "Driving all the way from Paris with the most dangerous woman I've ever met."

"Yeah, well, I think their dangers were more life-threatening than ours," he insisted, obviously trying to keep me on the subject. After all, I had asked him about the curious word. "Like the plague, hunger, disease, bandits," he continued, "and then if they actually made it all the way to the Normandy coast, they didn't have a bridge to across the bay, like we had. They had to brave the quicksand, currents, and tides."

"Okay, I get your point. Their dangers were more life-threatening. But ours are worse."

"Worse than dying of the plague? Worse than getting pulled under by quicksand? Just think about it Katie," he said as he moved his hand lightly up my face, "being slowly sucked under and anyone trying to rescue you being pulled under with you. Feeling the sand enter your mouth, and then your nose, and then your eyes? Worse than that?"

His hand tickling my nostrils was giving me the creeps, and I pushed it away. "Okay, so you made a three-pointer, and I missed a free throw."

"And to make things even worse, most of those pilgrims, including the shepherd lads and lasses came during the Hundred Years' War, so they had to pass through enemy lines."

"Enemy lines?"

"Yeah, in the fourteenth and fifteenth centuries. At one point, the entire Normandy mainland was in English hands except Mont Saint Michel."

"Okay, so that's the war with the cannons?"

"Yeah. And as you can imagine, the war just added to the dangers for the pilgrims."

"You mean kind of like the war in our family added to our danger?"

He looked at me with steely eyes, and said. "Give it a rest, Katelyn." Jackson never called me Katelyn, so I knew he was mad. "Can't we forget about her for one hour?"

"You're right. It's not your fault our dad's a jerk. I'm sorry. Okay, cut to the chase. What on earth is an *enseigne*?"

"That's what I've been trying to tell you, but you keep interrupting me. I needed to paint the picture for you, but I think you've got it. It was a really tough deal for the *Miquelots* to get all the way here, and so they wanted to be able to prove to their peeps back home that they'd actually made it all the way to the abbey sanctuary."

"And so," I interrupted, "they bought a token of their trip. An enseigne. What were they exactly? Does it say what they looked like?"

"Let me see: 'they purchased medals made of lead, called enseignes, fabricated by the monks and villagers.' Blah, blah, blah," Jackson said as he continued scanning through the information.

Someone coming out of the shop brushed against me. I must have jumped a mile, but it was just a little girl skipping excitedly around her mother who was holding a large package.

"Okay, here's some more: 'The enseignes were engraved with an image of Saint Michael and the inscription in old French: *Aultre ne Veut* meaning No Other.' It doesn't say exactly what that's supposed to mean, though."

I was certain Jackson could hear the thump-thumping of my erratic heartbeat and so I turned away from him and examined the window display. I could see replicas of the metal enseignes he'd described. They were produced in all sizes, shapes and colors as pendants, key rings, pins and simple round medallions—all probably made in China.

My fingers were itching to pull out my enseigne to see if it matched Jackson's description. But then, even if it did, so what? What did it mean? Why had Woolrobe been so anxious for me to have it? Why had he seemed so afraid that Gothman would get it? Could this be some elaborate joke Jackson was pulling on me?

I was hopeful, but I was also rational. Jackson didn't know anyone in France besides my father and his wife, and least of all in Normandy. And he certainly hadn't had any time to arrange anything after our arrival. I'd been with him every second. Besides, although he was smart, he wasn't that smart.

Where was my father when I needed him? I could have used his advice about now. Oh, yeah. That's right. Dad gave up the right to give me advice when he left us for that Frenchwoman. I was on my own for this one.

And then it hit me. Maybe it was her! Could it be her? The Frenchwoman?

That was a question I couldn't answer. I knew absolutely nothing about her. I had avoided learning anything about her. But one would think she'd want to do everything she could to make us like her, not hate her. Wasn't that why she insisted on bringing us to Mont Saint Michel while Dad was working at his new job in Paris? But then again, maybe she was crazy.

Maybe she wanted to hurt us, or scare us away so we'd never come back to France again. Maybe she wanted to kill us and make it look like a terrible, unfortunate accident so she could have Dad all to herself. She certainly had some kind of crazy power to entice my devoted father to turn his back on twenty-three years of what I had thought was a great marriage. To leave his home, his children and his country. To give up everything he held dear to move to Paris for her.

It had to be her: some convoluted scheme to destroy not only my mother, but my mother's children as well. She wanted all of my father's affection for herself. She must have thought this was the perfect scheme. She'd brought us to this mystical place to slowly terrorize us. What she hadn't counted on was my ability to see the truth about her. I knew it all along. She was pure evil.

"Not gonna work," I said to myself, not realizing I'd said it out loud until Jackson replied "What's not gonna work?"

"Oh . . ." I adlibbed quickly, "I was thinking I'd buy one of those enseigne thingies for Nicole, but I don't think she'd like it."

"Yeah, not exactly her style," he agreed. "Besides, it wouldn't mean anything to her. After all, she didn't actually make it here to complete the pilgrimage, did she? She's not a true Miquelot like us."

Then I thought of an even better idea.

"Wait here a sec, Jackie. I'm going to buy some for us. Souvenirs of our pilgrimage. Besides, who wouldn't want some protection against the wickedness and snares of the devil?"

Jackson laughed. But my real motivation was that he hadn't actually seen the object I'd found in my backpack earlier and I didn't want to have to explain it to him. By buying an enseigne for him and pretending to buy one for myself, I could examine the thing without having to answer any of his nosey questions. He'd had enough of my hatred for the Frenchwoman, and this time, I wasn't about to make any claims I couldn't back up with hard proof.

"Let me come with you and choose it," he said.

"Nope," I insisted. "It's a gift from me to you, so I get to choose. Wait for me here."

I entered the shop and made my selection, finding a key ring enseigne for five euros that fit the description Jackson had read to me. Five euros was a small price to pay for the peace to examine my own enseigne. After taking the small paper bag from the salesgirl, I placed it along with my wallet into my backpack and slipped my enseigne into the bag with Jackson's.

"Let me see," Jackson said as I rejoined him outside the shop.

"Hold on. Let's wait 'til we're out of this crowd."

As we stepped back into the flow of foot traffic working its way up the street, we were carried along like flotsam, unable to break away from the motion of the human wave. When we reached the very top of the street, the cobblestone pavement gave way to a wide staircase leading up to the abbey, and the crowd thinned.

I looked all around me to see if Gothman and/or Woolrobe were following us, but I saw no one. Well, not actually 'no one.' There were dozens of exhausted tourists stopping to catch their breath as they made their way up the stone staircase. Others sat on the walls at the top of the staircase looking down on us. None of them seemed inordinately interested in me or Jackson.

As we reached the top of what I soon discovered was just one of several sets of stairs, I pulled Jackson along a pathway leading away from the abbey and out towards the ramparts encircling the village. When we'd found a quiet place under a tree, removed from the masses, I jumped up to sit on top of the stone wall. We had an unimpeded view across the sandy bay to the mainland of Normandy.

"Here," I said as I pulled out his gift from the paper bag, "I got one with a key ring for you. Thought that would be useful in a few years for when you start driving. I think you'll really need protection then. We'll all need protection! Anyway, it's just like the description you read to me. Mine's a bit different," I added, not knowing yet just how different it would prove to be as I pulled it out of the bag.

"Thanks, Katie. Seriously. That was nice of you to buy me a gift, especially one that protects me from evil." He laughed. "And besides, now I can prove to my friends—who will be completely uninterested, by the way—that I braved the quicksand and made it all the way to the abbey. Well, almost all the way."

"Yeah, well speaking of the abbey, why don't you tell me about it before we go up?"

As Jackson flipped through the guidebook deciding on what he was going to share with me, I examined my enseigne. Unlike his, my medallion looked old. It was made of a heavy grayish metal. Yikes, I thought to myself, I hope it isn't made of lead.

Could I get lead poisoning from this kind of metal? I had no idea. Maybe it was pewter. Yeah, it was probably a pewter replica of the medieval lead enseignes. There was no way the Frenchwoman would've paid to have a genuine antique. But I had to admit, she'd done a good job. It certainly looked like an antique to me.

" 'The first sanctuary was built in the eighth century after Saint Michael appeared to Aubert, the Bishop of Avranches, and instructed him to build a church on the rocky islet.' "

I pretended to be paying close attention, but in fact, I was studying my enseigne. Where Jackson's medallion was round, mine was slightly oblong with a link on the top through which a chain could be threaded. Although the metal appeared to have been rubbed by generations of fingers, I could clearly make out the image of the Archangel Michael holding his sword up high and the slain dragon lying at his feet. Below that image were the words Jackson had read to me: *Aultre ne Veut*. What had he said it meant? Oh yeah, 'no other.' But below those words, were two additional words: *Que* 'K' something or other. Que K----? I guessed from my high-school Spanish that the '*que*' meant 'that or than' and then a K-word. I looked closer. It wasn't a word. It was another letter after the K. It was an M. K and M. Two initials. And they happened to be my initials: Katelyn Michaels.

Though the initials appeared to have been etched into the metal, whereas the other words were embossed—probably as a result of hot metal having been poured into a mold—it didn't look like the etching had been done recently. You know, you can tell that kind of thing because of the raw, shiny edges. The etched initials had the same worn patina as the words above them. So what did it mean? *Aultre ne Veut* . . . *Que KM*. 'No other . . . than K.M.'

Boy, she was good. She was really good.

Jackson stopped reading. I rubbed the metal with my thumb, as if by doing so I could tell where it came from. None of those earlier flashes hit me now. I felt nothing but warm metal.

Jackson paraphrased: "it seems Aubert wasn't a very obedient guy because he repeatedly ignored the angel's instructions to build a church, and Saint Michael finally got serious. He touched the bishop's head with his finger of light, and it burned a hole that went clear through the poor dude's skull."

Another pause from Jackson. I turned the medallion over.

"Cray," he added, and for a moment I thought he was talking about my enseigne. But he was focused on his guidebook. "Early monks actually found a skull with a hole in it buried here on the mount and it's been an object of veneration ever since. It's in a church in Avranches, across the bay on the mainland over there," he pointed. "The St. Gervais Basilica. I'm putting in my request right now to visit that church. Imagine, a human skull touched by Saint Michael! And there's another place I want to see in Avranches," he added. "In medieval times, the abbey had one of the most magnificent libraries in all of Western Europe—illustrated manuscripts copied by hand by the monks that included the ancient writings of the Greeks and Romans, holy texts from the Bible, and works of early Christian scholars. Wow, good thing those manuscripts survived. Maybe we can go to Avranches tomorrow."

In the distance, I could see the town of Avranches hugging the coastline. But I wasn't seeing Avranches, I was seeing the oddly shaped symbol embossed in high relief on the back of my enseigne.

It was not a symbol I recognized. It looked like a squished square with one rounded corner. At first glance, it meant absolutely nothing to me, and yet as I rubbed my fingers across its highly raised surface, there was just the briefest flash of an image that tickled the deepest recesses of my consciousness. I saw myself pressing the metal symbol into a stone surface. And I felt—not heard—the word "key" come to my mind. Then the image was gone as quickly as it had come and I was left to wonder if it was just my imagination. Can you feel a word? I hadn't heard it spoken, and I hadn't seen it written in my mind's eye. I had simply felt it. My enseigne was a key. But to what?

I shook that thought from my head. After all, wasn't this just an elaborate joke meant to spook me? The Frenchwoman couldn't control my thoughts. She couldn't make me experience these odd flashes of recognition. Could she?

Jackson was still telling me about the abbey. ". . . so the abbey is a result of a thousand years of building. It's a mishmash of styles, stairs, corridors and chapels so complex even seasoned guides can get lost. Only a portion can be visited." He moved his finger down the page as he scanned the text.

My finger was repetitively running over the raised symbol on my enseigne, and the flashes returned just as suddenly. It was like I was scanning not a page of text but scrolling down a computer screen in my mind with images flashing by so quickly I couldn't focus on any one image, until . . . the scrolling stopped on a pair of eyes. Earnest eyes. Woolrobe's pleading eyes. I actually felt myself jump.

"It says that Aubert's original oratory built in 709 A.D. is gone, but you can actually see a wall from it through an opening in a crypt on the bottom level of the abbey. It's called *Notre-Dame-Sous-Terre.* That literally means: 'Our Lady Under Ground.' Cool. I hope we get to see it."

"Yeah, Jackson. That's cool. Our Lady Under Ground," I repeated, thinking not of a crypt but of eyes. However, I made an attempt to focus on his words, so I added, "Sounds kind of gloomy to me, but it must be pretty interesting. I hope we see it too." I had asked him to tell me about the abbey, so it wasn't fair that I wasn't giving him my full attention. But at that moment, I had no idea of just how important that crypt really was. To me . . . or to Woolrobe.

"Then came the Romanesque period," he continued excitedly, but I couldn't focus on his words about barrel vaults and Gothic flying buttresses. I determined to let go of my anger, hatred, and now my new emotion of anxiety, for the rest of the afternoon. I would forget about the Frenchwoman. I would forget about Woolrobe and Gothman. I'd forget the earnest eyes, the strange symbol, and the eerie flashes. For the next few hours, I would humor my brother and allow myself to be immersed in the medieval world around me.

". . . the front part of the church was destroyed in a fire in 1776 but instead of rebuilding that portion, they shortened the nave and added this neo-classical façade." He showed me the photo in his guide.

"Ugh," I said. "That doesn't fit the medieval church. How could they have ruined it like that?"

"It was the big thing at that time in France. Everything Greek or Roman was in."

"Yeah," I said, drawing on everything I'd learned in my Humanities class to impress my brother. "Napoleon had an artist paint his coronation in the cathedral of Notre Dame. They decked out the most famous Gothic cathedral in the world to look like a Roman villa, and Napoleon is dressed as a Roman emperor."

"That's just sick, Katie. I'm impressed. You're not as dumb as you look!"

Instead of punching him as I would normally have done, I looked at him and smiled. It could be a lot worse. I could have a little brother who was into drugs, torturing small helpless animals, addicted to video games, or trying to hook up with my friends. Besides, he was reasonably polite, didn't burp or make bathroom-humor jokes too often, and he was relatively un-cranky. Even if I was furious that Mom had made me come to France with him, it wasn't his fault I was angry. He didn't deserve to be the recipient of the wrath directed at my father and his trophy wife. I had been unfair to him. For one afternoon, I would actually try to be a good sister.

"Jackson," I said as I slipped the enseigne into the zippered pocket of my roll-up capris. "You know what? You're okay."

"Gee, Katie. What's the matter with you?" He looked at me with a puzzled expression.

"Nothing. I just think it's awesome you're interested in the world around you instead of dumb stuff like most kids your age. Let's go see the abbey."

His eyes actually lit up like it was Christmas morning and I marveled at how little it took to make my kid brother happy. I almost gave him a hug.

I should have.

Chapter 4

MY THIGHS WERE BURNING when after paying our entrance fee, we finally reached the top of the ninety or so stone steps wedged between the fifteenth-century abbot's lodgings and the abbey church.

"Wow," I panted to Jackson as I tried to catch my breath. "How can anyone over forty even make it up here? I'm exhausted, and I'm a swimmer."

"Yeah, well you're also carrying about twenty pounds of excess weight in that backpack of yours," Jackson said. "Whatever possessed you to bring every bit of electronic gear you own for a little afternoon outing?"

He had a point there. "I don't trust the French, if you know what I mean," I said sarcastically. He understood my double entendre.

At the top of the steps, we entered a covered entranceway where an exhibit of miniature replicas showed Mont Saint Michel's evolving sanctuaries.

"Look at these rad models," Jackson said, changing the subject. I knew it was an attempt to make me forget the Frenchwoman, if even for an afternoon.

The first model showed the granite hill surrounded by a vast forest of green trees. I read on the plaque below the model that thousands of years ago the mount was part of a large forest before erosion and rising sea levels turned it into a tidal island.

"Look at this," Jackson said pointing to the next exhibit showing strange rock formations on top of the mount. "In the Neolithic era the mount was already considered sacred and they think there were dolmens on the summit that lined up with menhirs in the surrounding hills."

"I have no idea what a dolmen or a menhir is," I said.

"You know, like Stonehenge," Mr. Know-it-All informed me. "In England?" He looked at me like I was the densest person he'd ever known.

"Yeah, I know. I've heard of Stonehenge," I said. "And I know it's in England."

"Well, this part of France is full of megalithic stones. Dolmens are the table-like formations found at Stonehenge and menhirs are single standing stones. When there's a group of them, they're called alignments."

"Okay, Mr. Anthropology, so what were they for?" I asked as I walked around the glass case that held the model and studied the odd stones. For some reason, I wanted to know more about them. Something about those stones intrigued me. I wanted to touch them, but of course, glass encased the model.

"I don't know all that much about Neolithic culture," Jackson admitted. "There've been some pretty crazy explanations, like alien visitors, but we don't really know. There are some links with astronomy. Like certain stones line up with the equinoxes or solstices. It could have helped them know when to plant crops, but astronomy doesn't answer all the questions about the stones. They could have been graves or monuments for worship."

I looked at that lone dolmen on the top of the otherwise empty mountain in the model, and the word Jackson used pressed itself into my mind. It was all about worship, but I couldn't picture exactly what kind of worship.

"Sweet," Jackson said with some excitement, pointing to another plaque, "look at what this says: 'The summit has produced strange luminous electrical phenomena which, according to legend, testify of mysterious powers here that link Heaven, Earth and the Underworld.' "

"Heaven and the Underworld? Yeah," I said sarcastically, "and they really expect us to believe that stuff?"

"Hey," said Jackson, "you're the one who told me this is where Michael fought Lucifer and cast him and his angels out of heaven."

I shivered.

"I guess that's what they mean by the Underworld," he continued. "Satan, man and God. All united in one place. But wait, I'm not done reading. Have you ever heard of the New Jerusalem that's supposed to be built in the last days?"

"Yeah, Jackson, I've heard of it. I think that also comes from the Book of Revelation. So what about it?"

"It seems that people in the Middle Ages believed Mont Saint Michel was the spot where the New Jerusalem would come down out of heaven. And you're right with your Bible facts, Katie. Here's the scripture from Revelation," he said as he pointed to a plaque. "'And I John saw the holy city, new Jerusalem, coming down from God out of heaven, prepared as a bride adorned for her husband.' So every time those natural luminous phenomena occurred, the people would probably freak out thinking the New Jerusalem was coming down. Cool huh? Wish we could see *that* tonight."

"Yeah, way cool."

"So here's a model of the infamous oratory Aubert finally built after getting his skull bonked," Jackson said, moving on to the next case. "What do you bet he used the stones from the megaliths to build it?" A tiny structure topped the otherwise barren mountain in the model. My eyes were drawn to the mount's first Christian edifice. It was small and simple, yet something about it said power to me.

Something told me that those stones held an incredible secret.

But what secret?

Chapter 5

AFTER STUDYING THE rest of the models showing the abbey throughout its impressive thousand years of architectural transformation, it was time to see the edifice in person.

And so Jackson and I walked out onto the stone-paved terrace where the abbey visit began. Before us stood the plain façade of the abbey church I'd seen in the guidebook. I was right. It didn't fit the medieval feel of the rest of the complex.

Behind us stretched the one hundred thousand acres of the sandy bay.

"Let's go look at the view for a minute," suggested Jackson.

I wanted to savor the panorama too. We walked up to the stone wall surrounding the ocean-side of the terrace, and then leaned against it. The wall was all that kept us from falling off the edge of the mountain. This was the backside of the island looking out towards the open ocean rather than the coastline view we had from our hotel room or from the ramparts. The sight was spectacular. For as far as the eye could see flat, wet sand shimmered in the afternoon light. I couldn't even see the ocean in the distance, and the only water visible was an occasional glint from areas where the sand was slightly depressed and water had pooled.

"This would be a good place to watch the tide come in," said Jackson. "You can see for miles. It's hard to believe that by tonight this mountain will be surrounded by water."

I had to admit, it was hard to believe. I drew in a deep breath of the fresh, slightly tangy air and flushed my system of the lingering tension. The magic of this place helped erode the memory of my earlier unsettling encounter.

From our vantage point, we looked down at the steep drop to the sand below us. There were no buildings below the abbey on this side of the mountain. Just craggy rock-outcroppings and fortified stone walls holding up the terrace. And then an unbidden dark thought entered my mind: this would be a good place to commit suicide . . . or murder.

I shuddered as I quickly stepped away from the wall, trying to shake off the presence of something dark and evil.

Jackson had made his way to the corner of the terrace, and he called out to me. "Come see this, Katie. There's a miniature church down there." He was peering out over the ledge. Then he flipped through his guidebook.

As I sauntered over to him, trying to act unaffected by the creepy unbidden thought I'd just experienced, I kept well away from the wall. When I reached him, he pointed down to a tiny granite chapel built on a stony islet attached to the main island by a narrow rock-covered beach. It was clear that at high tide, the little islet would be surrounded by water.

"That's weird," he said. "The guide said it's called Saint Aubert's chapel."

"I thought that was the first chapel built on the top of the mount. The one that's under all of this," I said as I turned and indicated the abbey church.

"Yeah, well I guess since it got all covered up someone decided Aubert should have something named after him that's visible."

He continued scanning through his guidebook. I was feeling a little freaked out by the view into the void. I've never been particularly afraid of heights, so it surprised me. And then as I studied the tiny edifice below us, I was filled with an overwhelming feeling of love and sacrifice. I instinctively knew that there was a heart-breaking story attached to the chapel below. I wanted to know that story.

"No," I said without even thinking. "That chapel was not built for Saint Aubert. What does the guide book say?"

"All it says is that the chapel was built in the fifteenth century on a rock, which according to legend, fell from the summit to the sea during construction work on the abbey."

I could visualize something falling, narrowly missing . . . what? A shiver started at the base of my spine and ran all the way up to my head. And then it was almost as if I could hear a cracking sound of stone on stone. A sense of great loss nearly brought tears to my eyes, and I somehow knew the chapel was built in honor of a cherished child who had died prematurely in that very spot below. I had no idea why such an idea came to my mind, but it did.

"Come on, Jackie," I said with forced cheerfulness. "Let's keep going."

As we headed across the terrace towards the church entrance, I noticed strange markings in the rectangular stone blocks that paved the terrace: one small symbol per stone. Something about the symbols intrigued me. My enseigne! I stopped Jackson as I pulled the medallion out of my pocket.

"Look at these markings," I said. "Do you know what they are?"

"No clue," he admitted.

As we looked closer, I could see that some of the markings resembled letters, numbers, or mathematical symbols, but others had no meaning to me. None of them matched the symbol on the back of my enseigne, but somehow I felt they were connected.

I א = M A 3 ◻ ꓶ 9 4

As I was clicking photos of the symbols, a group of what looked—and sounded—like American tourists approached us. I cringed at their loud obnoxiousness. So much for studying the marks in peace. They were accompanied by a guide who said to us in heavily accented English, "I see you are discovering the jobber's marks. May we join you?"

"Sure," I said. I was interested in hearing his expert explanation of the "jobber's marks." With his tall, lanky body, geeky t-shirt, and the know-it-all condescending expression on his face, the guide could have been the long-lost twin of Sheldon in *The Big Bang Theory*. I decided to listen to what he had to say, though I hoped it had nothing to do with string theory versus loop quantum gravity.

"Jackson," I whispered as I gestured towards the guide, "get a load of Sheldon!"

"No kidding," he whispered back.

"Have any of you read the novel *Pillars of the Earth* by the British author Ken Follett?" French Sheldon asked.

Not only had I never read the book, I'd never heard of it. But several of the people in the group raised their hands.

"I am recommending it to you to learn about the Gothic style and about the cathedral builders," French Sheldon told us, slaughtering the

English i-n-g ending. I think it's called the gerund. Or was it the present participle? Yeah, that was it.

Jackson pulled a pencil from his backpack and made a note in the margin of his guide.

"Those of you who have read the book are understanding the hierarchical organization of the craftsmen working at a medieval building site," French Sheldon continued with another present participle misapplication. American Sheldon's I.Q. would never have allowed him to make such fundamental linguistic errors. Furthermore, French Sheldon pronounced the word 'hierarchical' as 'he-arsh-ee-cal.'

It was annoying, and I had to concentrate to understand him. At least I could understand American Sheldon. Well, I could understand his words, but seldom his scientific subject matter. That would be Jackson's department. On the other hand, this guy was speaking my own language and I couldn't speak to him in French, so I just had to deal with it.

As he rattled of facts about medieval architects, I tried to send a telepathic message to French Sheldon: get to the point. I don't think I can stand the verb slaughter much longer.

"Next were the stonemasons. Medieval stonemasons were highly qualified and literate craftsmen. Every stonemason was choosing an individual jobber's mark."

There. He was finally talking about the marks.

"Each stone was engraved with the stonemason's personal mark, which was then allowing the architect to judge the quality of his work and pay him for each stone cut."

I looked again at the symbol on my enseigne. Was it a jobber's mark?

"Here on the West Terrace," French Sheldon continued, "you will be finding the largest concentration of visible jobber's marks, but you will also be seeing them throughout the abbey if you are looking carefully. Now, as we are entering the abbey church, I am wanting . ."

I am wanting to stop listening to you, Sheldon.

I grabbed Jackson's arm as he set off to follow the group and said "if we go with them, we'll have to tip Sheldon. Besides, I wanna show you something." I decided it was time to enlist his help, even though I didn't plan on telling the truth about how the medallion had happened to come into my possession.

Just as I lifted the enseigne to show him the symbol, a crushing blow hit me square on the back. Then everything went dark.

Chapter 6

I STRUGGLE TO OPEN my eyes. Why won't they open?

"Ka . . . tie," I hear someone calling from a million miles away. It's so faint I can barely make it out, but yes, I'm certain it's my name. It's as if someone is speaking underwater, as if the sound is being carried along by undulating waves of liquid.

"Ka . . . tie, come on. Wake up!" It sounds closer and louder.

I have no idea where I am or what has happened to me, but I do know my name is Katie, and I finally recognize the voice of my brother. That's right. My brother Jackson.

I want to speak to him, but I can't get my brain to tell my mouth how to form words. I try to wipe the cobwebs from my mind, but the sticky strands wrap tightly around my eyelids. And my hands—like my mouth—aren't cooperating. I feel a dull pain on the side of my head, but I can't touch it. There's also something else I have to do, but I can't quite remember what it is.

Someone pats my cheek gently but rapidly, and then another voice speaks to me in gobbledygook.

"Mademoiselle, mademoiselle, mademoiselle. *Etes-vous blessée? Ouvrez vos yeux, s'il vous plaît.*"

And then I feel light permeating the blackness. Someone has lifted my eyelid and is shining a beam in my eye. I'm finally able to react to what my brain is telling me to do. I shake my head and force the invading bright intrusion to retreat.

And then, my eyes finally obey and open. I am lying on a hard surface in the open air. A slight breeze cools my skin from the overhead sun pounding down on my face.

"Oh Katie, you freaked me out." I see a face peering at me. It's Jackson. "Are you okay?" he asks.

"I'm not sure," my brain says, but I don't hear my voice repeating it. Once again, I order my mouth to obey my brain, and then an eternity later I hear the words: "I'm . . . not . . . sure." And I'm not.

Then I move my limbs and try to lift my head to sit up. A powerful feeling of nausea overcomes me.

"Restez tranquille, mademoiselle," says the other male voice. *"Prenez votre temps."* My brain can't make any sense of the sounds.

And then I remember. Jackson and I are in France. The words are in French. That's why I can't understand him.

Then I see the face. Sheldon. No, French Sheldon. Suddenly, everything comes back to me. Jackson and I are at Mont Saint Michel, and French Sheldon is a tour guide. He just told us . . . something. I can't remember.

"Oh you poor girl," a woman with purple-gray hair says to me in English. Then I see the group of Sheldon's American tourists surrounding me.

It's humiliating. I don't like all the attention, so I try to sit up again. This time, I actually make it all the way. The nausea is still there, but I refuse to give in to it, and it subsides as I sit for a few moments.

"I'm okay, I'm okay," I insist, hoping that Sheldon will take his overly-solicitous Americans away. They paid to see the abbey, not Katelyn Michaels spread-eagled on the church's terrace just about ready to up-chuck.

"Are you certain," asks French Sheldon. "I can call the first-aid office for help."

"No, I'm fine." I don't feel fine, but I certainly don't want French Sheldon to know that. I just want him and his groupies to go away.

"Please, go ahead on your tour," I gesture with my hand. "I'll just sit here a bit with my brother. He'll stay with me."

"*Eh bien,* if that is what you are wanting."

Yes, Sheldon, that is what I am wanting, I think, but I say only "Yes."

Sheldon and his group leave us and I breathe a bit easier.

Jackson doesn't look too happy about being left alone with me. Because he's so smart, sometimes I forget that he's basically just a kid. Right now, he looks like a pretty scared kid. Who wouldn't be in his situation? After all, we're in a foreign country, neither of our parents is with us, and although he speaks some French, he's not exactly fluent. It would be scary for him if I had to go to the hospital, so in spite of how I really feel, I know I must make an effort.

"Really, Jackson. I'm okay. Just help me over there to the wall." There is a low stone wall next to a set of steps leading up to the abbey church. "Let me just sit there for a sec."

"Sure, Katie," he says as he picks up my backpack and with the other hand helps me stand. I rub my shoulder as we walk slowly to the wall.

"Give me your phone. I'll call . . ."

"No," I stop him before he says her name. Somehow in my mind, I think that if she doesn't have a name, then she doesn't really exist. I know. Pretty dumb, huh? But that's how I cope with my cheating father. Deny, deny, deny. Besides, isn't she trying to hurt me? Had she somehow arranged for me to . . . to what? I'm not even sure why I'd been lying on the terrace.

"What happened?" I'm finally able to ask.

"Some kids—some of those Goths we saw in the village—were running around on the terrace like a bunch of idiots, whipping a chain around, and one of them plowed right into you like he didn't even see you. You went flying like a rag doll."

"No wonder my head hurts," I say rubbing the side of my head. "I hit it on the stone paving."

"Oh, you didn't hit your head on the stones," Jackson says. "You hit it on the chest of that guy who *stopped* you from smashing it on the stones!"

"What are you talking about?"

"Well out of the blue, that monk guy we saw earlier was suddenly there and caught you before you hit the ground. But you hit him so hard, you lost consciousness."

Woolrobe!

"What happened to him," I ask with my heart pounding. Woolrobe had possibly saved my life.

"Heck, I don't know. I wasn't exactly paying attention to him. He laid you down on the ground and then I guess I . . . I kinda started yelling, and then the guide and his group came running back to help. He was suddenly there to catch you and then he was gone."

I scan the entire plaza to see if Woolrobe is anywhere to be seen. He isn't.

Then I ask, "So what about the guy that hit me? And his friends? The Goths? What happened to them?"

But before he can answer, I remember. The enseigne! Where is it? I'd been holding it in my hand when I was hit.

"My enseigne," I cry out. "Jackson, where's my enseigne? I had it in my hand. I was just about to show you . . . Go see if I dropped it out there on the terrace. Hurry, before someone else picks it up. Run!" I must sound totally hysterical, because Jackson is looking at me with saucer-sized eyes.

"Jeez, calm down," he says. "I didn't see it, but I'll go look. But what's the big deal. We can go back and buy another one. It's only a couple of euros."

"No," I say. "You don't get it. It was one of a kind. It had a mark on the back that looked like those jobber's marks, and I . . ." I what? What did I want to tell him? And then it just came to me. "They told me at the store that it was a . . . promotional dealie. I got it because yours was the thousandth enseigne they'd sold, and so I kinda won a prize. Well, almost. I'm supposed to find a mark matching the one on the back of my enseigne somewhere in the abbey . . . and if I find it and go back to the store with a photo of it, I'll win a prize of one thousand euros." Wow, I'm amazed at myself. After nearly cracking my skull open, I still manage to come up with a whopper of a story I know Jackson will believe.

"Why didn't you tell me that to begin with?" Jackson asks. "Like when you came out of the store? Let me go look." As he starts to jog out to where I fell, he turns and says, "Katie, maybe those Goths knew you'd won the enseigne and that's why they hit you. Maybe they stole it so they could get the prize themselves."

Yeah, that's exactly what I'm afraid of—that the Goths stole my enseigne—but I don't say that to Jackson. I also know it was the spiky-haired, chain-rattling Goth dressed all in black I'd seen chasing Woolrobe earlier—the same angry one who saw Woolrobe talking to me on the stairs—who plowed into me. Yeah, I'm sure he was the one who did it, but I don't say that to Jackson either.

The fact of the matter is that Gothman could have stolen my backpack if he'd simply been after money. My electronic gear in my backpack is easily worth more than the mythical one-thousand euro enseigne, but of course, I also instinctively know that my unfortunate encounter with Gothman has nothing to do with a simple theft. Either the Frenchwoman is trying to drive me crazy with her mysterious appearing and disappearing enseigne, or she has nothing to do with it and the enseigne really is a mystery. In either case, I have no idea what to do about it.

My accident has made it hard to make sense of the thoughts tumbling around in my head. I rub the tender spot right above my left ear and force myself to remember everything that has happened since Jackson and I first started on our 'pilgrimage' up the village street. Woolrobe's words come back to me: "The evil ones have been waiting a very long time to prevent you from receiving it. Keep it safe. You will know what to do with it when the time comes. We have faith in you. Do not disappoint us. *Everything* depends upon you."

I unconsciously place my hand on the cold stone of the wall on which I am sitting and twist my palm. Why did I do that? It felt like a tactile memory, just like when I open my padlock on my locker in gym. I don't think I can even say the numbers of my locker combination out loud. My fingers just turn it to where it needs to be.

And then I remember something else. Key! Yes, I had felt that word in my brain earlier. The enseigne is a key to something. I must place the raised symbol into the matching recessed symbol and turn. This is a frightening thought, because I suddenly realize that there's no way the Frenchwoman can make me feel this type of tactile memory. She can't make me experience emotions about an inanimate object. No way. It just makes everything all the more confusing. If she's not behind this, then what on earth is happening?

When Jackson comes back empty-handed and dejected-looking from his search, I know with certainty that Gothman stole my enseigne. I don't know why. I don't know what it means, but I do know one thing: I know that medallion is worth a lot more than a thousand euros. I also know that I've got to find the same symbol someplace in the abbey . . . and that I must recover my key.

Chapter 7

"WHAT DO YOU WANNA do?" Jackson asked me. "D'ya think we should call the police? I'm sure they'll remember you back at the store. You can tell them someone stole your enseigne. Maybe they'll give you another chance."

"No," I said trying to figure out how to enlist Jackson's help without uncovering my lie about the enseigne. "We've already paid to get into the abbey. If we went all the way back down to the store now, we'd just lose time and our entry fee. Besides, I don't have the energy after that fall to climb all the way back up here again today. I remember what the mark looks like," I added as I took out the spiral notebook I always kept in my backpack. "We're already here, so I think we should go ahead and visit the abbey and see if we can find the mark."

"Okay, then on our way back to the hotel, we'll stop at the store and tell them what happened," Jackson suggested.

"Yea, sure," I agreed. I'd cross that bridge when I came to it.

"We'll tell them not to give the prize to those Goths. Let's hope they don't beat us to it. They've already got a head start."

After finding a pen, I duplicated the symbol from my enseigne as exactly as I could. "Here," I said ripping out the page from my notebook. I handed it to Jackson. "This is what it looks like."

ם

"The Goths might have a head start," I insisted, "but they haven't searched the terrace, and this sure looks like a jobber's mark to me. I think we should cover the entire terrace before we try inside. You game?"

"You bet. Let's split up. You do the north side," he said as he indicated the section to my left, "and I'll do the south side. Walk in straight lines. "

"How do you even know which is north and south?" I asked. "We're a million miles from home and we're on an island!"

"Oh for heaven's sake, Katie. Just watch the sun. Besides the façades of medieval churches always face west, 'cuz the apse—that's the wall on the opposite side with the altar—always faces east. You know, when you enter a church, you go from west to east, which symbolizes going from the evil of the world to the glory of the New Jerusalem to come."

"How do you know stuff like that," I said. "That's just wrong on so many levels."

"Well, I guess *you're* feeling better," Jackson replied with a grin. "You're back to your usual sarcastic self."

We spent the next half hour checking every stone on the terrace, but we didn't have any luck. My mark was nowhere to be found. This was going to be a harder search than I'd anticipated. I was feeling achy and tired, but I couldn't let Jackson know that. I could sleep later, but now, I felt compelled to keep searching.

"Come on," I said. "Let's go inside. We'll skip the Gothic portion. The jobber's mark is from an earlier period." I have no idea why I knew that, but I did. "We'll have plenty of time to come back tomorrow or the next day and visit the parts of the abbey we miss today."

As we approached the entrance to the church, we both paused to look up. Looming high above was the church's slender spire, topped by a gilded statue of the dragon-slayer himself. It was the closest view we'd had of the Archangel Michael, and yet he was still probably a good hundred and fifty feet above us.

Because of the distance, it was hard to make out Michael's features but it didn't matter. I didn't need to see him up close to feel his impact. Michael ruled the island, towering above it like a guardian of truth and righteousness, as if he were watching for Lucifer's approach and was ready to slay him again if necessary. In fact, the winged statue was the highest point for miles around. We'd just made the drive from Paris, and there were only gentle hills that fed into the flatlands of the coast where the sea met the sky.

"That statue is twelve feet tall and weighs a thousand pounds! How on earth did they get it up there?"

I couldn't take my eyes off it. Jackson was right. I couldn't imagine how something so large could have been hoisted up that thin spire and fixed into place. It was an impossibility. Only the hand of God could do something like that.

And then my thoughts changed from 'how' to 'who.' Who was this Michael portrayed as a knight in medieval armor slaying a dragon? And I couldn't forget the wings. This knight happened to have wings. Was he just some allegorical figure in the Bible used as an example of mankind's struggle between good and evil? Our choice between Lucifer or God? Or did Michael exist? And surely angels didn't really have wings. Did I believe in such things as angels and dragons? Did I believe in the Bible? Did I believe in Lucifer? For that matter, did I believe in God?

I knew I could definitely answer the last question in the affirmative.

My faith in God was a gift given to me without my ever having had to do much to obtain it. I'd always considered myself a Christian, though neither of my parents were particularly religious and didn't go to any specific church. My spiritual journey had been mine alone. I'd been neither encouraged nor discouraged by anyone in my family. Occasionally, Jackson had agreed to come with me to visit a newly opened church in our town, and once or twice, I'd gone to church when invited by friends. I'd listened to pastors, priests and even a rabbi or two, but none had been able to satisfactorily answer my pointed questions, so I'd filed them all away and had continued the quest on my own. That's when I started reading the Bible. Although I wasn't certain whether some of its stories were allegorical—like Michael's story, or the story of Adam and Eve, or Job, or Jonah being swallowed by a big fish—I did believe it to be the word of God.

As I wondered about Michael, an overwhelming feeling of peace engulfed me assuring me that not only was Michael real, but that . . . well, it's silly really, but it almost felt like I knew him. Michael, I mean. I know. It sounds ridiculous. I wasn't a particularly impressionable teenager. Not like some of my friends who had absurd crushes on the current teen idols and somehow believed their dream crushes would be reciprocated. No, this wasn't like that. It was a feeling of profound respect and honor I felt at being in the presence of greatness. And a confirmation that I personally knew the great one.

And then it happened. As if I heard the words out loud, I felt the Archangel speaking to me, pressing into my mind a message similar to the one Woolrobe had given me earlier: "Katelyn, I've been waiting for you for a very long time. Everything depends upon you. You will know what to do when the time comes. Hurry now, come inside."

Chapter 8

AFTER HEARING THE bizarre message in my mind, I stopped dead in my tracks and looked all around me to see if someone had actually spoken to me.

"This place is getting to me," I said without realizing I'd verbalized my thoughts.

"What did you say?" Jackson asked. "You look like you've seen a ghost."

"I . . . a, well . . ." I shook my head and rubbed my hand over the lump behind my ear.

Now really. How could I tell my fourteen-year-old brother that I'd just communed with a statue—or an angel? Oh yeah, that's right. I couldn't. Because if I did, he'd do everything in his power to have me committed.

Maybe I should just go ahead and have myself committed first and save him the trouble.

It really had to be the fall, because I now knew the Frenchwoman couldn't cause me to hear voices. Hadn't Joan of Arc heard voices? And you know what happened to her. The English burned her at the stake. I wasn't about to give anyone the motivation to burn me at the stake, even if it was only a metaphorical burning.

"It's . . . it's nothing," I managed to stutter to Jackson. "Probably just the effects of the accident. I'm feeling kind of . . . kind of lightheaded."

"Katie, I think we should go back to the hotel. Forget about your stupid enseigne. It's not worth it. You've probably got a concussion. We need to get you to a doctor right away. Maybe you're having a brain hemorrhage!"

"For heaven's sake, it's not a brain hemorrhage. But, I think you might be right," I conceded, "I mean about the concussion." And I believed it. I had a concussion and it was causing me to hear voices. Still, that explanation didn't adequately account for the earlier odd feelings I'd experienced. After all, they'd occurred before I hit my head.

But in spite of my concerns, I couldn't turn away from the door to the church. It was as if a giant magnet were pulling me towards it. Whispering to me, lulling me to come. "The answers you seek are inside," it called to me.

"But like I said, it will be faster to get back to the village by way of the abbey than to go all the way back around and down the stairs," I said to Jackson. "Let's just walk through and then go back to our hotel."

"Look, just give me your cell phone." Jackson insisted. "I think we should call . . ."

"No!" I said before he could say the name of my father's trophy wife. I couldn't bear to hear that name spoken. But, I had to appease my worried brother, so I said, "We'll get back to the hotel just as quickly on our own, and then you can get her."

If I'd known then that I'd never see that hotel room again, I probably wouldn't have entered the church.

Chapter 9

WE TRY TO HURRY through the abbey church, but it's almost impossible for either one of us to ignore a thousand years of architectural history. Jackson points out how the heavy Romanesque barrel vault of the south transept is slowly flattening out, sagging under its own immense weight. It feels like I've seen the window before, but with stained glass in it.

While Jackson's looking up, I'm looking down at the immense flagstones under my feet, searching for jobber's marks. I'm also looking all around me for Gothman or Woolrobe. The floor of the church has been worn smooth by the feet that have polished its surface over a thousand years, and no jobber's marks are to be seen. However, I sense the presence of someone watching us, and I turn quickly. I see no sign of either Gothman or Woolrobe, but my stomach is churning. The clammy dankness of the church suddenly feels suffocating. My skin is crawling and the hair on my neck is standing up. I feel the presence of evil.

I'm startled by the sound of wings flapping perilously close to my ears and I jump about a mile. For a brief instant, I think it's actually the sound of angel wings or more likely, dragon wings—not that I know what they sound like. I've been thinking too much about angels and dragons, but the flapping sound turns out to be a panicked bird that's found its way into the church through the open door on the side. My heart races as I watch the bird circle around fruitlessly in search of freedom. It's trapped, and as I silently pray for it to find the exit, I feel the walls closing in around me, trying to trap me as well. I begin to hyperventilate. As I turn, I see a flash of black in one of the chapels, but then it's gone.

"Let's go," I call to Jackson, who reluctantly but loyally responds. I know he wants to get me back to the hotel, but he's torn by his duty to me and his desire to study this place.

We follow the arrows from the church into the abbey cloister. The shift in scale is remarkable. Where the space inside the church is vast, this space is small and intimate. I feel liberated. There's a roof over the square walkway, but the center green space is open to the sky. The north side of the cloister opens out onto the sea, and the view is breathtaking. I inhale the tangy air and my breathing starts to slow down. Jackson is looking around in amazement. Since I've never really seen a cloister, I'm not certain what one is supposed to look like, but this is not what I expected. I instinctively know this cloister is unusual, and I want to know more about it.

At the opposite end, I spot French Sheldon with his American groupies, and it is almost as if seeing him makes me feel safe. Safe from what, I'm not certain, but where earlier I felt annoyed by his group of tourists, now I feel there is safety in numbers.

"Come on, Jackson. Let's go listen."

"Are you sure Katie? Don't you think we should get you back?" my brother says, though his eyes tell me he wants nothing more than to soak in everything French Sheldon has to say.

"Honestly, I'm feeling better. This cloister is amazing."

"Because of the space issue on the top of this mount," we pick out Sheldon's words, "you will be noticing that this cloister is built on a much smaller scale than most medieval cloisters. The dimensions of the human body are reflected in the height of the double row of staggered columns."

Sheldon pauses as he sees us, and then says, "Ah mademoiselle, you are looking much better. Please, join us, if you are feeling . . . how do you Americans say? Up to it?"

The groupies gesture warmly for us to join them and then pat me on the back and whisper polite platitudes in my ear. I welcome their close proximity. Even their touches.

We crowd in to hear French Sheldon's further explanation.

"The foliage on the frieze above the columns represents the Garden of Eden, as does the actual garden area in the center of the cloister. The monks cultivated every kind of flower known to grow in this climate in an attempt to replicate the first garden God placed on the earth."

The Garden of Eden. Yes, there is something peaceful and comforting about this place. I feel it deeply. Adam and Eve must have felt these same sentiments in their lush garden paradise, before they'd been driven out into the lone and dreary world. And then with his next words, French Sheldon, mentally drives me out of this garden paradise as well.

"However," he continues, "during the 1423-24 siege of Mont Saint Michel in the Hundred Years' War, the monks used every bit of this garden space to grow food. Because the English could not conquer the island, they attempted to starve its inhabitants. They had the island entirely closed off from the coast, and they did not willingly allow a single morsel of food to cross through their ranks to get to the *Montois*. That's what we call the inhabitants of Mont Saint Michel."

Like earlier in the day, an unbearable hunger pang hits me. It's as if I have total empathy for the Montois. I feel their hunger. I feel their despair. But I also feel their determination. A sense of reverence overcomes me and I stoop to touch the tiny leaves of the boxwood hedge that encloses the dark green blades of carefully tended grass in the garden square.

"What happened?" I hear the woman with purple-gray hair ask. "Were the English successful with their blockade?"

"No," confirms Sheldon with gusto, displaying visible pride. "Though many of the valiant inhabitants of this mount were actually dying of starvation or disease, they never capitulated. Every patch of soil on the mount was used for cultivating food. By cover of darkness, the men of the mount were attempting to cross the treacherous quicksands of the bay to procure food from the mainland. Some were pulled into the sands and perished. Others were lost at sea. Because all the sailing vessels had been captured and destroyed by the English, when the tide was in at night, the men were setting off in makeshift rafts—fashioned of broken-down furniture or structural beams—to fish in the bay. Their vessels were not sea-worthy, and the strong currents were capsizing their rafts. But the Montois never gave in.

"This is the only spot of ground along the entire coast of Normandy that did not succumb to the English during that war. To us, the mount is a symbol of freedom. It is a symbol of fortitude and determination. Unfortunately, we were not having that same determination when the Nazis invaded our shores five hundred years later."

I am mesmerized by his narrative, and I even overlook his verb slaughter because his tale captures my attention. I feel the Montois' pain. I sense their willingness to give all they have, even their very lives, to protect their mount from the enemy. In the whistle of the brisk ocean breeze, I hear the resonating echoes of their cries of bravery and despair. In the white puffs of cotton clouds dancing across the indigo fields of the sky, I see manifestations of both their strengths and weaknesses combining into a tapestry of valiant determination and unbearable heartache. In the healing balm of the sunbeams that shine through the columned arcades, I feel the warmth of their hearts and spirits. But I also feel the coldness of their dwellings, their fireplaces having long since been devoid of any kind of fuel.

"Let us continue around the cloister," says Sheldon, drawing me from my private reverie. "It is not only Garden of Eden imagery you are finding here. If you start at this point and study the friezes, you will find representations beginning with the creation through the stories of the Old Testament, through the events of the New Testament, and finally to the ultimate creation of New Jerusalem in the last days. The Montois were believing this mountain to be the spot designated by God for his holy city. So in this enclosed garden suspended in the sky are represented the origins and the end of God's earthly creation, summarizing in its completeness the perfection of His Divine work, from Alpha to Omega."

The Garden of Eden, New Jerusalem. The beginning spot and the end spot. Alpha and Omega. It is almost too much to process as my mind tries to make sense of Sheldon's commentary.

I am startled back to reality when someone jostles me, and my contemplation is immediately replaced by anxiety. I turn, fully anticipating seeing someone dressed in black, but it is only one of the American women losing her balance as she tries to snap a photo through the double row of columns. She has an artistic eye, and I remember I haven't taken any photos. It's a fascinating perspective she's trying to capture, and I decide to do the same. I raise my camera, adjust the lens to focus on the far columns, and then freeze when through the viewfinder—as clearly as if he is standing right in front of me—I see Gothman at the end of the row of columns. He's looking straight at me and I see hatred in his eyes. And something else . . . fear. In spite of his physical superiority, in spite of the fact that he just knocked me out and stole my enseigne, Gothman is afraid of me. I quickly snap a photo, but when I lower my camera, he is gone, having disappeared through a large doorway.

"Jackson," I whisper, "I just saw the Goth who knocked me down. What should we do?"

My little brother is not one to pick a fight or invite confrontation, but I see a fire in his eyes that surprises me.

"We're going after him. That's what we're going to do."

I'm caught off guard. I'm not sure I really want to pursue Gothman. In fact, I'm afraid to pursue him but thoughts of my stolen enseigne overcome my reluctance. That and the conviction that Gothman is more afraid of me than I am of him. I can't imagine why that would be true, but I know it is.

"I'm not gonna let him get away with what he did to you," Jackson continues. "Which way did he go?"

I point towards the door on the opposite side of the cloister, and Jackson bolts off in hot pursuit. I'm left with little choice but to follow my brother as he attempts to defend my honor. Something about his reaction touches a tender chord in my heart. I realize with a clarity that astonishes me that not only does my brother love me, but that he's trying his best to make up for the fact that the only other male figure in our family betrayed and hurt us in the worst possible way. By this one small action, I recognize that Jackson has assumed a new role as 'man of the house.' I am touched. I need to support him in this new role, and so against my better judgment, I run after him. French Sheldon and his group look on in surprise.

The door from the cloister leads into a long room with rows of tables on either side. This must be where the monks ate their meals. A sign on the wall calls it the Refectory. The hall is filled with an unusual amount of natural light, and yet there are only two windows on the narrow wall at the opposite end. I wonder how there is so much light. There's just one other exit from the room near the entryway from the cloister, but I somehow know Gothman didn't go that way. But he is nowhere to be seen. Where could he have gone?

There are several tourists admiring the vaulted wooden roof that looks like the inversed hull of a ship, and then I see a woman disappear from my sight, melding into the wall and then reappearing. What is going on? As I approach the first table, I see that the sunlight is being admitted into the room by dozens of narrow lancet windows inserted into deep alcoves along both sides of the nave. From the end of the hall, where we entered, we saw only flat walls adorned with what appear to be evenly spaced half-columns, but as we move forward, the architectural magic of the hidden alcoves reveals itself.

I point out the first alcove to Jackson, and place my index finger over my mouth. He understands. Gothman is hiding in one of these narrow embrasures, but they're on both sides of the hall. In order to find him, Jackson will have to take one side, and I must take the other. I'm not certain I'm up to it but I'm motivated by the desire to reclaim my enseigne. I know it's the key to this entire mystery. Jackson gestures for me to take the left side.

Slowly, step by step, we move forward, keeping pace with each other on either side of the hall. My heart is racing, and I can hear the swooshing of blood in my ears. Gothman has already attacked once, and I know he won't hesitate to do it again. The only thing that keeps me going is knowing he's also afraid. For some reason, he believes I have some power over him.

I don't understand it, but I accept it. I have no other choice than to accept it because I'm compelled to find some answers.

And then I feel firm pressure on my shoulder. It doesn't frighten me. In fact it reassures me. I feel the same warmth from those fingers pressing into my flesh as I felt in the cloister when the sun illuminated my mind. I know it's Woolrobe and I know he is my ally, not my enemy. I trust him and there is more. I know him. Not like I know Mr. Benson at the corner grocery store, or Jeff Fitzgerald, the kid who lives two houses down from us. No, I really know him. I know his soul and it is pure. I know his heart and I . . . Okay, this is getting ridiculous.

"Stay here," he whispers to me in his heavily accented English as he pushes me against the wall. "We shall reclaim your enseigne."

He signals to Jackson to continue the careful advance, and surprisingly, Jackson doesn't flinch at seeing Woolrobe take over my role. Obviously Jackson also believes Woolrobe is on our side. After all, hadn't he been the one to cushion my fall on the terrace when Gothman attacked me?

My two protectors keep pace with each other until they've covered three-quarters of the long nave. Although I watch with my heart in my mouth, fully prepared for something to happen, I'm still startled when Gothman shoots out from the top of one of the alcoves like a cannonball, completely clearing Jackson's head. I immediately run to block the second exit door, and though I know Gothman has already succeeded once in head-butting me into unconsciousness, this time I know he's coming. And he's coming at top speed followed closely by Jackson and Woolrobe. I also know that French Sheldon and the Americans are approaching the entryway from the cloister because I can hear them.

"Don't let him out," I shout at Sheldon's group as they crowd into the cloister entrance, creating a haphazard barrier of American tourists, but a barrier nonetheless. "He stole my . . . pendant."

Gothman pulls up short when he realizes the exits are blocked. We have him trapped, and he knows it. Just before Jackson reaches him, Gothman whips out a lethal-looking length of chain from the depths of his baggy pants and slashes a vicious circle in the air around him. Woolrobe grabs Jackson, restraining my little brother, who appears hell-bent on revenge. I am amazed to see this side of Jackson that I've never seen before. My nerdy little brother is defending my honor. A flash of heat rushes through me, part fear for his safety and part emotion at his bravery on my behalf. Who knew?

Gothman's eyes dart rapidly back and forth between Woolrobe, Jackson, and my little group and then he hisses out something in French. "*Ne vous approchez pas. Je n'ai pas peur de tuer!*"

I don't understand the words he's saying, but there's something about his voice that makes me shudder. It's a unique voice, and I can't put my finger on what it is that sends chills through me. Perhaps I subconsciously understand his words. I look to Jackson for a translation, and he looks scared out of his gourd. That's more like the Jackson I know and love. Whatever this crazy dude said, it must be pretty bad. Gothman continues to whip the chain defensively as he backs into the corner of the refectory nearest the exits as the stunned Americans now press through the entryway from the cloister to get a better look at him. Great. Just what I need now. A bunch of lookie loos, but at least they are blocking that exit. I start to panic again as I realize that I am alone to defend the other exit from the refectory, and that fact is not lost on Gothman or Woolrobe, but my defender doesn't seem anxious to approach Gothman, and patiently holds his position.

"*Restez calme,*" Woolrobe says as he very gently edges closer. Those words were easy enough to understand. He wants Gothman to remain calm. Heck, I want me to remain calm.

"Rendez-moi la clef, et nous vous laisserons partir sans vous faire de mal," Woolrobe adds, as he continues to inch forward. And then as if for my benefit, he repeats what I assume is the same phrase in English. "Return the key, and we will let you depart unharmed."

For a fraction of a second, my thoughts stray from the dangerous situation in which I find myself to focus on one word Woolrobe just uttered: 'key.' He called my enseigne a key. I'd been right earlier. It is a key, but I still have no idea what it opens.

Without taking his eyes off of any of us, Gothman continues to whip the chain with his right hand as he now moves towards me using the wall behind him as protection. His eyes are terrifying. I can hardly bear to look at him, but I can't turn away. Then he holds up my enseigne in his other hand. "You will have to come for it yourself," he seethes at me in English.

I cringe at the sound of his voice and the evil in his eyes as they lock on mine, but surprisingly, I stand my ground. I don't know where this unexpected courage is coming from, but I am determined to do whatever it takes to retrieve my enseigne. From the corner of my eye, I see an almost imperceptible nod from Woolrobe to Jackson, and then Woolrobe dives at Gothman's feet in an attempt to avoid the thrashing chain. In the instant it takes Gothman to react, both Jackson and I join in the melee. I go straight for the hand with the enseigne, and Jackson goes for the hand with the chain. Unfortunately, Jackson gets the worse end of the deal because the end of the slackened chain succeeds in nicking my brother's chin. Where his flesh has been split open, I see blood spurting out and dripping down his shirt.

As Woolrobe succeeds in getting Gothman spread-eagled on the ground, I stomp on my attacker's left hand until his black-nailed fingers finally uncurl and release the 'key.' With a sense of utter relief, I secure the enseigne in my zippered pocket and then turn to assist my brother, as he falls backwards onto the stone floor and brings his hands to his chin. When Woolrobe—also distracted by Jackson's injury—unwittingly lightens the pressure on Gothman's body, the figure in black manages to writhe away and jump to his feet, and then sprints through the now-empty doorway.

Before he leaves the refectory, Gothman turns one last time and looks at me with the hatred I've already seen in his eyes. "Katelyn Michaels," he says. "You had better watch your back, because eventually . . . I *will* kill you."

With that chilling message, he turns and runs.

And I feel like throwing up.

Chapter 10

ALTHOUGH I WAS IN shock at the unfathomable words that had just been directed at me, it didn't take any thinking on my part to untie the navy bandana from my backpack and begin applying direct pressure to Jackson's chin. He was bravely trying to keep from crying to add more salt to his wound, which looked to me as if it required some stitches. I couldn't believe my brother had gotten injured 'defending my honor,' and I certainly couldn't grasp what had occurred to us in the past few hours.

French Sheldon and his groupies gathered around Jackson in their now-familiar solicitous manner. "Oh you poor boy," purple-haired lady said. "Who on earth was that evil man?"

I wish I knew the answer to her question, I thought, as I pulled Jackson to his feet, and he took over the job of holding the bandana to his chin.

"I'm fine, I'm fine," he insisted, although I knew from the paleness of his face that he very definitely wasn't fine. He was in shock, and unfortunately, so was I.

"Katelyn, *venez*, come. We must hurry," Woolrobe said to me quietly, grabbing my arm and attempting to pull me through the group of zealous Americans.

"He will return with . . . others. You must go down to the chapel, to Notre-Dame-Sous-Terre."

"Just hold on a minute," I said while pushing Woolrobe's hand off my arm. "You can't expect me to leave my brother like this. We've got to call the police. They'll protect us from that lunatic!"

"You better believe she's not going anywhere with you," piped up Jackson, with some color rushing back into his face. He continued to firmly hold the bandana against his chin.

"At least not until you've answered some questions! For starters, how do you and that Goth guy know my sister's name? And what's so special about that freakin' enseigne that he would be willing to kill for? It's gotta be worth more than a thousand euros!"

I wondered the same thing, but I was so surprised at this new take-charge brother of mine that I decided to let him ask the questions. I noticed how he was trying to make his voice—which had been changing for the past few months—sound lower than usual.

"Dear, are you all right?" Mrs. Purple-Gray hair asked me. "This just hasn't been your day, has it?"

Sheldon started speaking heatedly with Woolrobe in French, and it was all too much for me. My head was pounding and my heart was still racing. I needed to get out of the refectory and back into the fresh air of the cloister immediately, so I turned and pushed my way through the crowd while

Jackson, Woolrobe, and Sheldon worked out their testosterone issues without my interference. They didn't even seem to realize I was leaving.

With my head spinning, and the nausea hitting, I felt close to passing out. I needed to sit down and put my head between my legs. Since there was no place to sit in the cloister, I headed towards a wide set of stairs that led down to the lower levels of the abbey, and the continuation of the self-guided visit. I walked down a few steps so as not to be seen from the cloister. No sense in being a target for more of Gothman's attacks. Then, after lowering my head between my legs, I took ten deep breaths until the nausea and light-headedness passed.

Without even realizing it, I removed the enseigne from my pocket. I felt my fingernails digging into my palm and realized I was clutching it as if I would never let it go. I opened my hand and saw the deep marks left by my fingernails. And by the enseigne . . . the key. Its raised surface had left an imprint on my palm. There was nothing I would've liked more than to fling it away. It had been the focal point of this entire fiasco and I wasn't particularly interested in having more 'evil ones' chasing after me.

However, as much as I would've liked to give it back to Woolrobe and go along my merry way, that now seemed impossible. I was in too deeply. Besides, the enseigne hadn't caused me to experience flashes of recognition for places I'd never been. The enseigne hadn't caused me to hear voices—from angels, no less. The enseigne hadn't whispered my name to Woolrobe or Gothman. It wasn't the cause of what had been happening to me. It was a by-product. Throwing it away wouldn't solve the dilemma I was in or answer my questions. Too much had happened, and I couldn't make it all disappear by making the enseigne disappear. And as much as I would've liked to blame this all on the Frenchwoman, I couldn't even do that. This was something that had to do with me, not her. I had to figure out this whole situation on my own. And even Jackson and his bleeding chin would have to wait.

It was now late afternoon. From the dark recesses of the underground crypts, I felt a rush of cold air coming up the staircase. After setting the enseigne on the step, I pulled my windbreaker out of my backpack and put it on. The enseigne's gray metal melded into the grayness of the time-worn steps. Both had developed patinas of their own and I felt that both had witnessed centuries of untold events.

With reluctance but knowing it was unavoidable, I picked up the key to some unknown lock and stood up. What had Woolrobe said back in the refectory? 'You must go down to . . . Notre-Dame-Sous-Terre.' I'd heard those French words before Woolrobe said them. Yes, now I remembered. Jackson had translated them for me earlier, when we'd been sitting on the wall outside the abbey where I had given him the enseigne I'd bought in the souvenir shop. Notre-Dame-Sous-Terre: Our Lady Under Ground. But there was something else. What had Jackson said about it? I couldn't remember. I hadn't really been paying attention. But right now, I knew one thing. For some reason, I had to get to Notre-Dame-Sous-Terre. That was where I'd find answers.

I heard a commotion erupt in the refectory. More yelling and running feet. Jackson calling my name, and Woolrobe screaming at the top of his lungs: "Run Katelyn. *Allez.*" Although I felt like I couldn't abandon my brother, the words formed in my brain: 'no further harm will come to your brother. He will be fine. He is not involved. But you, Katelyn Michaels, must fulfill your destiny.' More voices speaking to me. This time, I didn't stop to analyze that implausibility. It didn't take more than an instant to understand the message. I had to run, and I had to run now.

Leaping down the steps three at a time, I just barely made it to the bottom and around a dark corner before I heard the noise of multiple sets of feet following me.

I inwardly cursed myself for not having taken one of the free maps distributed at the ticket booth for myself. When I'd paid our entrance fee, they'd given me only one map, and I'd turned it over to Jackson. The only saving grace was that every room in the abbey was identified with lettering in both French and English on clear acrylic panels. If I could find the darned chapel, at least I'd know it. Besides, I hardly had the time to stop and consult a map.

As I ran through the corridor and then through a variety of dimly-lit chapels and empty chambers, I immediately noted the difference in the scale and feel of the lower levels of the abbey. Where the Gothic portions above were light in terms of both weight and illumination, I was now in a dark and austere labyrinth that felt oppressive. I had no idea which way to go, but I did know I had to go down. I passed several astonished tourists, but I didn't take the time to ask for directions since I knew I was just barely ahead of my pursuers. Echoing steps on the stone floors let me know that. I was grateful for the tennis shoes I was wearing. They hardly made a sound except for an occasional squeak.

When I finally spotted a staircase going down, I didn't let the fact that it had a chain across it and a sign that said "no entry" stop me. I bounded over the chain and continued down into the bowels of the labyrinth. The light was growing dimmer as I reached a landing where the direction of the staircase changed. I hesitated for only a second, even though I could see no source of light ahead. I felt my way down the set of steps only to find a solid wooden door at the bottom. It was almost pitch black. I pushed in the stem of my watch, which lit its face, and used that sliver of light to locate an ancient latch on the door. Praying it would open, I lifted the lever and felt it respond. Then I pushed against the worn timbers of the door. It didn't budge. With all of my body weight, I pushed again, and felt it begin to move. I was more than happy to see light in the inch of space that had opened up.

Above me, the echoes of running feet were my sole motivator. In my biology class, we'd studied the fight or flight mechanism that sometimes gave people super-human abilities to survive in life-threatening circumstances. I didn't know if that's what I was experiencing, but all of the sudden, the door gave way, and I burst through into another dimly-lit corridor. In front of me was a room with ginormous pillars. I ran towards it, glancing at the sign: *"Crypte des Gros Piliers."* In English below, I read "Crypt of the Massive Pillars."

"Oh really?" I actually mumbled out loud. "As if I couldn't tell these were huge pillars." It wasn't Notre-Dame-Sous-Terre, but it actually cheered me up that my sarcasm hadn't deserted me. I spotted a young couple kissing in the darkness of one of the crypt's alcoves, and beyond embarrassment at my intrusion, I said in my very best French (actually it was my only French): *"Pardonnez-moi, s'il vous plaît. Parlez-vous anglais?"*

"Yes, a lee-tel," smoocher-guy replied, clearly annoyed at the interruption. Smoocher-girl was way more annoyed than smoocher-guy. She recoiled from me as if I were a leper. Dressed in a little black dress with spaghetti straps and of all things, stiletto heels, she looked more like she should be on a Parisian runway than in a chilly Norman abbey. Well, maybe I didn't know what the hot French girls were wearing this season, but really. She had no reason to act like I might contaminate her superior Frenchness.

'Notre-Dame-Sous-Terre," I said slowly, trying to pronounce each word correctly. "Do you know where it is? Please, it is very important." Smoocher-girl looked at me and rolled her eyes.

I'm not after your boyfriend, I thought but didn't say, so just cool your jets. I didn't have time to sit and play I'm-cooler-than-you games with 'Her Frenchness.'

"Oui," he finally said. "Eet is through zat co-ree-dor. You pass through several *chapelles*, and then *voilà*. You are zere."

"Merci beaucoup," I said to him. 'Thanks for nothing' was the message I telepathically sent to Her Frenchness. I don't think she got the message though, because unlike me, she probably didn't hear voices in her head.

As an afterthought, I turned to smoocher-guy and added, "if someone asks if you've seen me, please don't tell them where I went." Then I improvised, "I'm in an American television show. You know, *The Amazing Race,* and I'm racing for a million dollars. So help me out, okay?"

"*Certainement,*" he replied, but I wasn't sure if he understood me. Her Frenchness continued to shoot daggers at me but I really didn't care, and without any further telepathic message-sending, I turned and ran down the corridor that her kinder and gentler friend had shown me.

The ruckus behind me let me know that my pursuers hadn't given up the chase, but I didn't hear footsteps in the corridor. Perhaps smoocher-guy had humored me by sending them on a wild-goose chase. I hoped so.

I continued to run as fast as I could, stopping only briefly to check out the names on the acrylic signs. The gloominess of the thick walls and heavy barrel vaults weighed down upon me and I felt as if the tons of stone above me were slowly crushing me to death. Sucking the life out of me. What on earth was I doing running around in some medieval monastery as if my life depended on it? And yet, the nagging words in my mind wouldn't go away: 'your life does depend upon it.'

Jeez, that's certainly comforting.

I prayed that the voice or impression or whatever it was telling me that Jackson would be safe was correct. I could never forgive myself if something happened to him. My mother would never forgive me. I couldn't have cared less about what my father would think. He'd already let his family members know how little he cared about us. He was the king of abandonment.

I'd heard it said that before you die (or before you almost die), thousands of reels of life's films play through your mind in an instant. In those next few instants, I learned it was true. I saw my mother's smile as three-year old me finally dared to venture down the backyard slippery slide without holding on to the sides. A tiny baby boy screaming at the top of his lungs, taking all of my mother's attention. My jealousy transforming into joy as that same baby, now a toddler, took his first steps as I encouraged him. My father's embarrassment when I asked him where babies came from.

My father teaching me to kick in the neighbor's swimming pool, and later, helping me perfect my butterfly stroke in the community rec center. Obviously, that was back when I still adored my father.

My first crush and even my first kiss from my geeky next-door neighbor: the kiss I hadn't even dared tell my best friend Nicole about because it was too gross, but also just a little bit exciting.

The day I swam my fastest time ever in the 100 meter medley and took first place by a mile.

My first date.

My first real kiss.

The look, feel and smell of that aqua feather-light tulle and satin dress I wore to the Junior Prom: the one Mom had splurged on because I'd finally come home with a report card without a single C or D.

The smell of her home-made lemon bars and her Chicken Divine.

Driving on the freeway that first terrifying time and praying I wouldn't kill someone, myself included.

The crushing pain in my heart when my first-ever boyfriend broke up with me, telling me I was way too skinny.

The pain I felt when I found out one of my friends had betrayed our friendship by telling lies about me.

The even more crushing pain when Dad told us he was leaving. That was the one pain that had never gone away and it felt a lot like the pain I now felt in my chest as I pushed myself to run faster.

All of those scenes, with their corresponding emotions, smells and sounds flashed through my mind in a matter of seconds as I raced blindly through the underground passages of the thousand-year-old abbey. A thousand scenes. A thousand smells, a thousand feelings that made up the short seventeen years of my life.

And then I prayed to be able to live another seventeen years, and then another, and another. A lifetime of seventeen years.

Please God, please help me know where to go and what to do.

And then I was there. I didn't need to read the acrylic sign to confirm what I already knew. I'd finally reached Notre-Dame-Sous-Terre. The starting place.

Chapter 11

MY BREATHING SLOWS, and I feel safe. I am alone in the crypt. No tourists here to interrupt my privacy. I look around and oddly enough, I feel at home. I've never been here, and yet somehow, I know this place as well as I know each corner of my bedroom. It is my sanctuary. I know every stone and every semi-circular arch. I know the crypt's parallel naves—divided by a thick wall pierced by two barrel-vaulted arcades—with a chancel on each end. I know the simple stone altars in each chancel. They hide electric lights that artistically illuminate the intimate space. Other lights are hidden in a trio of niches cut into the crypt's walls. Four simple wooden benches sit in the right nave, ready for those who would worship at the altars of this chapel.

Although I'm tired and the benches call out to me, I choose to sit on a low stone wall below one of the illuminated niches. I am close enough to touch the altar. It is made of small roughly-hewn rubble stones but it appears to be a replica of an ancient altar. To my right, the largest niche of the entire crypt reveals a wall of stones that appear to be haphazardly piled on top of each other without the benefit, at least not the visible benefit, of medieval mortar. It looks as if this niche has been cut out to reveal a wall of stones placed there by nature herself. And yet, as I study the wall, I see an attempt at order. A hint of being man-made rather than nature-made.

Then I remember Jackson's words, as if he were speaking them to me now. I remember each word as if they were being dictated into my mind: *It says here that Aubert's original oratory built in 709 A.D. is gone, but you can actually see a wall from it through an opening in a crypt on the bottom level of the abbey. It's called Notre-Dame-Sous-Terre. That literally means: "Our Lady Under Ground. Cool, huh! I hope we get to see it.*

"Jackson," I say out loud. "I'm seeing it right now. I wish you were with me. I hope I'll get to show it to you. I hope you know how grateful I am to you for standing up for me. And please, forgive me for abandoning you with that injury. Hopefully, I will be able to explain it all to you later."

I picture Jackson's face, with blood running down his chin. Then I remember what Jackson told me about Aubert. He was the bishop of Avranches and he was commanded by the Archangel Michael to build a sanctuary on the mount. Aubert had been stubborn, and the archangel had visited him several times with the message, and then finally, had burned the message into his head with a single touch. That finger of light had burned a hole right through Aubert's skull. It had sounded like nonsense when Jackson had told me the story, and yet now . . . I can't put it into words. I don't know how to explain it. But I know that many things that would've seemed nonsensical to me yesterday are a reality today. Today, I suspend any judgment the normally sane Katelyn Michaels would make. Today, I am mystical Katelyn. Today, I am Katelyn who hears voices, who sees visions, and who is being pursued by two strange guys. Today, I am the Katelyn who has been spoken to by the Archangel Michael. Today, I am like Aubert, Bishop of Avranches, and I'd better listen to what the angel has to say, because I don't want to have a hole burned into *my* skull.

Today, the angel compels me through unspoken words to touch the stones of Aubert's sanctuary, and so I obey. I stand and rub my hands across the rough surface of the rocks, starting at the top. In a logical sequence, I touch every visible stone. I also search for jobber's marks, although I don't expect to find them on these ancient stones. These stones do not come from the stonecutters. These are not the stones of the cathedral builders. What had Jackson said earlier? Something about Aubert using the megalithic stones to build his sanctuary. But though I will not see the jobber's mark on these stones, I still seek something. I don't know what I'm looking for. Perhaps it's just to commune with the Bishop of Avranches who lived more than a thousand years ago. Perhaps it's to tell him that I too have heard the words of the Archangel. No. I seek something that is secret. Something secret . . . and sacred about these stones. I had felt it earlier while looking at the model of the ancient dolmen.

And then when I reach the lower left corner, it's as if I feel a surge of power penetrating my body. It's as if I have touched a live electrical wire. In fact, for an instant, I think that's exactly what I've done, and I look carefully to see if there is an exposed wire hidden among the stones. But there is nothing. I touch again, and this time, I feel nothing. I must have imagined it. The culmination of a day of imagined sensations. And yet, I know that's not true. I didn't imagine Woolrobe. I didn't imagine his earnest eyes and his pure soul. I didn't imagine Gothman, or that in contrast to Woolrobe, he was pure evil. I didn't imagine the enseigne. It is still clutched in my left hand. They are tangible evidence that my intangible feelings are real.

The sound of someone running tears me from my reverie and without conscious thought, I sit back down on my original perch beneath the niche. I place my right hand next to me on the stone surface and feel an indentation in the otherwise smooth texture. Like the acrylic sign identifying the crypt as Notre-Dame-Sous-Terre, I don't need to look at the indentation to know what it is. I know the feel of that indentation. It is my jobber's mark. As if in a trance, I transfer the enseigne—the key—from my left hand to my right. I place it so that the raised jobber's mark on the metal surface fits exactly into the indentation in the stone. And just as I hear the sound of approaching steps ready to break into the silence of my sanctuary, I instinctively twist my palm to the right. With that tiny twist of the hand, my whole world instantly changes.

Part Two

I have set watchmen upon thy walls, O Jerusalem,
which shall never hold their peace day nor night:

Isaiah 62: 6

Chapter 12

THE OLD MAN GENTLY stirred the ashes in the stone fireplace. The two weeks were up and Nicolas would be returning soon. He would be hungry. There was hardly any wood left for fuel on the mount, and the stonecutter hoped there would be enough heat for the watery soup to boil. The cabbage had been half rotten and he felt it wouldn't taste quite so horrid if it boiled. Unfortunately, the last of the grain had been used. There would be no more bread until the next harvest.

Maybe he'll bring some food back with him. I hope so.

The man didn't care about himself, even though his ribs jutted out like the flying buttresses of the abbey church he was helping to build. The agonizing pain from the constant hunger had finally left him, and for that he was grateful. But he no longer had the energy to carry out his duties. It didn't matter. His life was nearly over. He had served for so many years in such difficult circumstances that he'd finally come to the decision that he couldn't do it any longer. He didn't want to do it any longer. And thankfully, his replacement had come. He would make no more trips to the abbey. No more trips to the sacred chapel. He actually looked forward to the day when he could peacefully close his eyes and return to his maker. He would be able to report that he had carried out his duties to the very best of his ability.

He wasn't making the soup for himself. It was for Nicolas. He was worried about the young man who had come to take his place. Fortunately, young Nicolas hadn't experienced the years of penury. They'd begun when the English king had conquered Normandy fifteen years earlier at the battle of Agincourt. Except for the tiny Mont Saint Michel. The mount had defied the English, but the cost had been high. Nicolas hadn't suffered the full effects of the siege that had been going on for over a year. Nicolas—who'd slipped through the English blockade—had arrived from Brittany a few short months ago, with his robust health and rosy cheeks, seeking the old man, Jean le Vieux. The Montois—who always had a moniker for everyone—named him Nicolas le Breton. And those were the initials Jean had found on the lad's key: N.B. The key he'd been waiting to give his replacement for years.

Jean's early years, before he became Jean le Vieux, had been years of heartache, years of joy, and years of unspeakable events, like the Black Death. The only constant was the on-going construction of the abbey. Jean's skills as a stonecutter had been valued, but there were always the inevitable questions. Every so often, he'd have to concoct stories, disguise himself, or leave the mount. He was never far away though. He never shirked his duty. He was always vigilant, always watchful.

There were times when his frustration with the abbots and monks had been keen. There had been iniquity and false teachings. So much they misunderstood. So much they got wrong, and so many teachings of man that had entered the liturgy. And so much that had been lost. Like the story of Michael. They had built an edifice to him here on this mountain, and yet they didn't even know who he was. If only Jean could explain to them.

If only they understood the writings they *did* have. Every day, a group of monks sat in the scriptorium where they meticulously copied the words of the ancient prophets, the apostles, and the Savior himself. With elaborate embellishments, they illustrated those sacred texts, and yet they did not understand them. Mont Saint Michel was the 'City of Books.' Hundreds of volumes of those beautiful illuminated manuscripts were to be found in the abbey library, as well as other works of antiquity. And yet they had twisted the basic truths to such a degree that it was impossible for them to understand. If only he could teach them.

But that wasn't his stewardship. His was not to instruct, but to protect. To watch and protect. The monks viewed him as a stonemason. A stonemason who'd been granted free passage to all parts of the abbey, including the library, but a stonemason, nonetheless. They didn't know he could read the texts in Greek, or that Latin was second nature to him. Although they knew he spoke German and the language of their English enemies—because that had been indispensable in recent years—they didn't know he had heaven-taught tutors. And so, they wouldn't have listened, even if he had been allowed to teach.

Besides, he couldn't impose his will on anyone. Free will had always been the key, just as Nicolas was learning. It wasn't easy to let others make such foolish mistakes. But that was the plan and he'd valiantly fought for that plan. And because of his unfailing support, he'd been chosen. He—and a small group of others—to protect this sacred place. Now it was time for the youngsters to take over. They would choose how long they would serve. It would be their choice and their choice alone. Jean would not try to influence them.

He wondered about the girl. What would she be like? Would she even come? He'd read the prophecies about the last days. Though he couldn't imagine exactly what it was like, he knew it was a corrupt, selfish world where people thought only of their own base desires. It was a world of self-gratification, a world of lust for power, money and carnal pleasure. He was glad Nicolas had gone for her, but he prayed the lad would not be tempted by a world where Lucifer reigned virtually unchecked.

Although the Watchmen had been successful and had never allowed Lucifer and his fallen angels to discover the secret of the stones, the evil one had still managed to manipulate, corrupt and destroy so many of God's precious children that sometimes Jean felt the Son of the Morning was also winning the day. He'd certainly won the night.

"How art thou fallen from heaven, O Lucifer, son of the morning!" he muttered out loud, quoting the Prophet Isaiah's words.

Ultimately, God would prevail and Lucifer and his minions would be bound. They would not always have power over mortal men. They would not always have the bodies of mortals to inhabit. They would never have bodies of their own, either mortal or immortal. Never. And that is what they wanted above all else—something they could never have. And that was why the secret had to be protected.

His thoughts turned again to the girl . . . Katelyn. Katelyn Michaels. How appropriate that her surname was Michaels. It was not a coincidence. Her birth had been prepared for generations to come into a family whose surname was Michaels.

I'll find out soon enough if she will come. But if she doesn't, it shall be to Nicolas to find a solution. I have taught him well.

He thought of the past months of careful instruction he'd given Nicolas. He'd taught him everything he needed to know, even the English language. And then, they'd learned about the girl: the girl from the future who was needed to perform a task neither Jean nor Nicolas could perform. It had been shocking when they'd learned it was to be a woman. Jean hadn't known of any female Watchmen before. But she wasn't even a woman. Just a girl, really. A girl just past her seventeenth birthday. His own Marie hadn't been much older, but then, she hadn't been a Watchman. How was it possible that a girl with so little life experience could perform something they couldn't? How could she possibly defeat the English when the armies of France had been unsuccessful?

In all the years he'd served, Jean had never been called upon to use his enseigne, but he knew what to do. He knew about preparing the keyholes, but he no longer had the strength to cut the stone. Though Nicolas was just an apprentice, he'd already mastered the craft. He'd been noticed and praised by the head stonemason. He had gifted hands. And like Jean, Nicolas had been granted free passage to all parts of the abbey. So together, knowing how evil her world would be, how many distractions might tear her away from her duty, Jean and Nicolas had chosen the placement of her keyhole to be in the holy chapel itself. There where she would feel the power of her calling the most, and Nicolas had performed the work.

Jean wished he had something to offer the girl to eat upon her arrival, but that was why she'd been summoned. There was no food because of the siege, and she'd been summoned to end the siege, to end the threat to the abbey. Nicolas and Jean could not do it without her. And so she had to come. If she was one of the chosen few, then she'd been one of the valiant ones. Yes, she'd hear the summons and she would come. And Nicolas would be her teacher. Jean hoped he'd be allowed to tutor her for a short time as well, for it had been such a delight to be the tutor of the eager, young Breton.

In fact, the past months with Nicolas in the small half-timbered house on the hamlet's cobblestone street had been among the happiest of Jean's long life. Except for the years of his marriage. He contemplated those interminable years of solitude before his marriage and after the loss of Marie. He'd witnessed kings and queens, pilgrims and popes making the pilgrimage to the holy sanctuary, but he had been alone. He'd been alone for so long—fighting the battle alone—that he cherished every minute spent with the young man. Perhaps his own son would have been like Nicolas—with that same inquisitive mind, the willingness to learn, the irrepressible enthusiasm—if he hadn't died at such a young age. But his son's death had changed everything.

Watchmen were allowed to marry, to have children. It had never been forbidden. On the contrary. Marriage and children were all part of the plan of a loving God and a Watchman's family was entitled to the same blessings as the Watchman himself. He remembered those days when he'd courted Marie.

Marie was a *Miquelot*, a pilgrim who traveled to pay homage to Saint Michael. In fact, she was one of the shepherd lasses who came with the largest group of children that had ever come. Jean met her on the mount and he knew immediately. She was the one for whom he had waited so long. After they met and were getting to know each other, he asked about her pilgrimage and she told him her tale.

He closed his eyes as he thought of the beautiful young Marie and he heard her words as if she had spoken them yesterday. He pictured himself sitting on the Grand Degré staircase next to her. He remembered how the sun picked up the glints of red in her wheat-colored hair and how she smiled at him coyly. And he remembered her tears.

"I heard a voice," she explained. "All of us who came heard the voice. It wasn't a subtle voice, and yet neither was it a voice speaking words. It was a voice that spoke thoughts to our minds. It filled us with light and purpose. That purpose was as clear as the April showers after the cleansing rains, and it was as warm as the August sun. It was unlike anything I've ever experienced."

Jean knew about voices that spoke thoughts to one's mind, so this was nothing surprising.

"My family lives in Alsace," she continued, "far to the east of Normandy. The voice beckoned us to come, to launch our crusade to western lands. To Normandy. Here to the holy mount. It was a crusade of children to honor Saint Michel. I was washing my family's laundry in the stream by our farm. I had no idea where Normandy was or how far it was. I only knew I had to come."

"Did you say goodbye to your family?" Jean asked. "Did you explain to them?" He'd tried to explain to his own family, but they had not understood. It had been agonizing to leave them knowing he'd never go home again. They'd raised him to be a God-fearing son and yet they could not understand.

"No. It is one of my regrets," Marie told him. "Especially since I've been gone for so long. And especially because of . . . my brother," she paused and cleared her throat. Jean saw a shadow cross her bright blue eyes. He heard the emotion in her voice. "But I cannot change the past. When the call came, it was so strong I had no other choice but to obey. I folded the washing and left it in the basket by the stream and I started walking. I didn't even take the time to prepare a satchel of food or change into more suitable shoes or clothing for the journey. And you must understand, Jean, I love my family. But on that day, I realized I also loved God and I wanted to be obedient. What I did is inexplicable, and yet it is the truth."

"I understand," Jean said. And he did. Perfectly. His calling had required that same type of obedience and sacrifice.

"However, I wasn't alone," she continued her story. "As I approached the town, I heard my brother, Michel, calling out to me. He'd heard the voice as well. I was so happy to be with him. And then in the town, there were others. Children, I mean. Most were much younger than me. I was in my seventeenth year but my brother was only thirteen. And there were others even younger: eight, nine, ten and twelve years of age. And all of them, like Michel and me, came without their parents. They came from Germany and Italy and other countries as well. Places I'd never heard of before. Some of the children spoke in unfamiliar tongues, but they'd been called like us. Being from Alsace, my brother and I spoke German as well as French so we could communicate with the German children. They were happy I was with them and because I was older, I was like a mother to them."

Jean remembered every detail of her story. He knew how Marie took many of the younger children under her wing and became responsible for finding them food. He knew how some of the older boys made effigies of Saint Michel and led the procession carrying those figures along with standards bearing the coats of arms of their local gentry.

He knew how the ragtag procession inspired compassion among the townsfolk and villagers along the way, for these children had left their homes without any means of support. He knew that throughout their two-year journey they were provided with food and drink. However, he also knew of the journey's heavy toll. The children suffered from fatigue, insufficient protection from the harsh elements—including two long winters—illness and disease and a general lack of adequate nutrition for their growing bodies. Many did not make it.

"We had almost reached Chartres," she recounted. "It was one of the most important stages of our pilgrimage. We planned to stop at Notre Dame de Chartres and pray to the Holy Virgin to bless the rest of our journey. We could see the spires of that magnificent cathedral in the distance when we stopped for the night. That was the night my brother fell ill. We found shelter under a covered marketplace in a small town to the east of Chartres and a kind woman brought us bread and fruit. Michel had been limping for several days, but he'd pressed on. When I'd asked him about it the day before, he told me his foot hurt a bit but that he'd be fine. I guess he felt he had no choice but to keep going. I wish I . . ." She stopped and wiped a tear from her eye.

"It must have been hard," Jean said to her tenderly. "You were traveling as a large group, and he probably felt he couldn't fall behind or he would be lost."

"I would have stayed behind with him. I told him that, but he tried so hard to be brave. If only I had checked his foot earlier."

"Regret cannot change anything, Marie. It can only cause more pain. You did the best you could."

Jean spoke from personal experience. He felt complete and total empathy for this beautiful young woman. He knew what it was like to watch people die. He knew what it was like to feel completely and utterly helpless. He had watched the Black Death decimate the citizens of Avranches and wreak havoc in the villages of the surrounding coastline. He had witnessed the audacity of that merciless killer when it had invaded the mountain sanctuary.

Some said it was Divine Punishment. Some said it was the fault of the monks themselves, that their unrighteous acts had called down the wrath of God. It was true about the monks. There were times when some of the followers of Saint Benedict forgot to walk in the paths of virtuous light, when they forgot their vows of poverty, chastity and humility. Jean was personally aware of their iniquity.

However, there were also times when the abbot himself was the transgressor, and unless the monks rebelled or there was outside intervention, the abbot's offenses went unchecked and unpunished. If the abbot's actions threatened the security of the mountain, the Watchmen had divine authority to intervene when so instructed. Jean had just recently been forced to mount a successful rebellion against the treasonous abbot Robert Jolivet who had attempted to deliver the abbey into the hands of the enemy. Jolivet had thrown in his lot with the English Duke of Bedford, and even now still acted as Bedford's counselor on the mainland. Jolivet had been forced to flee Mont Saint Michel when the monks would no longer support their treasonous abbot.

Regardless of the evil acts that had occurred on the mountain, Jean did not believe the Black Death was the work of God, for the God Jean knew would never make his children suffer. God allowed men to suffer the consequences of their choices and he allowed the innocent to suffer the natural consequences of mortality, for that was the plan. But God did not cause the suffering, and the Black Death had been beyond anything Jean had ever witnessed before or since.

The stonecutter had tended to the strange black swellings in the armpits and groins of the unfortunate victims of that devilish plague. The egg-sized lumps oozed foul-smelling pus and then gave birth to boils and black splotches. Then, the fever engulfed the afflicted and they began spitting up blood. One of every three had died during those dark days. The elderly and children had been especially susceptible. It had been devastating to witness their suffering. Jean and the uninfected monks had tended to the ill, but they'd been helpless to stop the ravaging swath of death that had cut through all of France.

Afterwards, when the pestilence had run its course and moved on to other lands, Jean had lain awake for hours trying to forget the sounds of the victims screaming out in pain and anguish. Even with his eyes closed, he could not block the vision of that 'face of death' that set upon the visages of the suffering in the hours before they expired. He never wondered why he'd not been taken, because he knew it was not God's will for him to die before his replacement came. But there were days and nights when he wished he had been taken because the images seared into his mind were worse than death.

Yes, he could understand Marie's suffering, but he could not speak to her of his. Not yet.

"Jean, I failed him," continued Marie, speaking of her brother's illness. "I was his older sister and I did not care for him properly. If I'd done something earlier, he would not have . . . died. He'd be with me now, sitting here in the sunlight with us."

"Marie, I know it is hard to speak of this, but tell me what happened." He knew that speaking of the unspeakable would help her come to terms with her loss. There had been so many times he'd wished he had someone in whom he could confide.

"That night after we stopped, Michel felt feverish. I called upon Marguerite, a healer among us. There was a stream nearby and she said we needed to rinse Michel's foot. As we unwrapped the rags that replaced his worn shoes, I realized he must have stepped on something that punctured his heel. It was festering and bright red streaks ran up his leg. We cleaned the wound in the stream and then Marguerite applied leeches to let his blood. After they dropped off, she made a poultice of herbs and rewrapped his foot but that night, Michel's fever became worse. We tried to keep him comfortable and offer hope, but he lost his mind. He thought he was back in Alsace . . . on our farm. He kept calling for Maman and Papa. It was terrible."

As she told her sad tale, Jean dared to take her hand in his for a brief second and then he brushed away the tears that coursed down her cheeks.

"By sunrise, he could no longer open his eyes. I sent one of the boys to find the parish priest to perform the final sacraments, and then Michel expired. My only consolation is that he went quickly. His suffering was but a short time. The priest agreed to bury him in the parish cemetery. I left my brother behind. It was the hardest thing I've ever done."

Jean would have taken Marie into his arms if they hadn't been sitting in a public place. That was the instant he knew she was the one for whom he had waited so long. She was the one who had been prepared to accept his life. She was to be the love of his life.

The Miquelots came and went, but Marie stayed. The shepherd lads and lasses returned to their distant lands, but Marie did not go. Instead, she took employment in the village. When Jean finally explained his role on the mount, she was stunned. She understood why she'd come. Why she'd been called to make impossible sacrifices and endure unbearable heartache. She also came to accept the fact she would never make the trek back to her home. This was now her home. It took time, but she finally agreed to become his wife. She told him: "you are now my family. You are my mother and my father and my brother. You are my love, my heart, and my soul."

She agreed to live the life that was his, but a slow sadness built in Marie when their union was not blessed with children. It wasn't until many years after their marriage that a child was finally born. A son and of course, they named him Michel in honor of her lost brother and in honor of the Archangel. Their joy was full. Until that autumn day so many years ago that had changed everything.

The watery soup slowly began to bubble, and Jean's mind returned to the present. He stirred the hot liquid carefully. It was the best he had to offer his guest.

"I hope she has had a good meal," he said out loud. "She has need of all the strength she can muster."

With those audible words, Jean abruptly stopped stirring. His ponderings about Marie brought to mind something he and Nicolas had not considered. Perhaps the girl had been summoned for Nicolas, just as Marie had been summoned for him. He pondered the words from the creation story: *And the LORD God said, It is not good that the man should be alone; I will make him an help meet for him.* Maybe Katelyn Michaels' role was to be a helpmeet for Nicolas. Maybe with her by his side, Nicolas would be given the strength to conquer their foes.

But it still didn't make sense. Why would she be from the future? Surely, there was an abundance of suitable women in France in the year fourteen hundred and twenty-four from which to choose a proper spouse? No, there was something special about Katelyn Michaels. Although Jean still believed the fact she was female was significant for Nicolas, there was some specific skill she brought from the future that would allow her to assist Nicolas in fulfilling his role as the new Watchman.

For just the fraction of an instant, Jean reconsidered his decision. This latest development almost gave him a new zest for living. But the page had been turned. He only hoped he would be allowed to see a portion of the writing on the next page.

Chapter 13

IT'S ALMOST IMPOSSIBLE to describe the sensation that hits me as I turn my key in the jobber's mark. I don't feel it turn. Not like a secret mechanism or anything, but the minute I twist my hand, it's as if all the air is sucked from my lungs and breathing is no longer necessary. It isn't exactly painful, but it is a shock to my system. Immediately, I'm surrounded by intense light spinning around me and although I know I'm not breathing, I understand that the light is breathing for me, infusing my body with life-giving oxygen.

I don't feel motion but I know I'm moving because every color of the rainbow, even colors I've never seen, are streaming past me in the most beautiful patterns I can't even begin to describe. Feathery soft, the colors kiss my skin with warmth. All is light and beauty, warmth and reassurance. Even though I've never experienced anything like this, I'm not afraid. I feel the light pierce my body and fill my soul with perfect peace and I close my eyes. I don't know what's happening. I don't know where I'm going, but I know I'll be okay.

Then after the spinning light comes to a stop, I have a strange thought. Am I dead? I open my eyes. Judging by the fact that I'm still sitting on the cold stone in the crypt of Notre-Dame-Sous-Terre, I must be alive. I don't think this is what heaven looks like. But then since I've never been there—to heaven, I mean—I guess I could be wrong. Still, I'm pretty sure I'm alive and not in heaven.

And I'm all alone. No Grandpa Michaels or Nana Suzie to greet me. Isn't that what's supposed to happen when you go towards the light? Aren't your deceased relatives supposed to greet you and squelch your desire to go back into your mortal body with indescribable feelings of love and happiness? It's not that I don't feel happy, but it's not exactly what I'd call overwhelming happiness. And I don't feel any overwhelming love either. I decide to test myself. Nope, it's still there. I still hate the Frenchwoman. Okay, either I'm in hell or I'm still alive. Except for hating the Frenchwoman, I don't think I've really done anything to truly merit the hell business, so I must still be mortal. But something's different.

I look around the chapel for a clue. I can't put my finger on it but something has changed. I still see the niche opening in the wall to the right of me revealing Saint Aubert's original oratory, but it's kind of hard to make out. My eyes have a hard time adjusting to the dim light. It's much darker but of course, I've just been immersed in an aura of light, so it's probably just the absence of that light that makes the chapel seem so dark now.

For a second, I panic. My backpack is gone. Someone has stolen my backpack! But then, I slowly realize that my arms, although a bit numb, are still looped through its straps. I stand and take it off, setting it on the stone by my enseigne, still placed in the jobber's mark.

I inspect my tingling body, first turning my hands over, and then looking down at my legs and feet. Nope, nothing different there. I'm still dressed in my capris. I'm still wearing my tennis shoes. Then my body involuntarily shivers. That's it! It's really cold in here. It wasn't nearly that cold when I first came into the chapel. In fact, it's practically freezing. I unsnap the tabs on my capris and roll them down to make long pants. I'm already wearing my windbreaker and I have nothing warmer to put on.

I rifle through my bag to make sure nothing's been taken. Nope. It's all there: my camera gear, laptop, iPod, cell phone. Even the solar battery charger, which any computer thief would love. It means I don't have to rely on electricity. As long as the sun still exists, that is. And right now, I'm not so sure about that.

And it really is dark. No, I mean really, really dark. Yes. That's another thing that's changed. The chapel had been artfully illuminated by that carefully-camouflaged electric lighting, but now those lights have been extinguished. The only light comes from a single candle placed on the altar in front of me. Who turned off the lights and put the candle on the altar? Someone's been in this chapel since I sat down. It's a spooky thought. Could the action of turning the enseigne have caused me to fall asleep and it's now the middle of the night?

Then I look at the altar more carefully. This altar looks completely different. It's much simpler. Much older. Much starker. Now I'm convinced it's not the same altar I had seen earlier. And yet how can that possibly be? It's one thing to turn off the lights and bring in a candle. How do you change a stone altar? I don't think so. That's not possible. My heart starts to pound.

I pick up my enseigne and pull it to my pounding heart. It's warm and almost has a beat of its own. As if it is alive. I know that sounds ridiculous but I can't help the thoughts rattling around in my mind. Besides, I've got musical altars to worry about and that's a bit more incredible than a beating medallion. I unzip the pocket in my capris and place my enseigne there, carefully zipping the pocket closed. I have no desire to have it knocked out of my hand again by Gothman. Another thing I know for certain is that I must keep the enseigne . . . the key . . . safe.

Then I hear another sound and it's neither my beating heart nor my beating enseigne. It's footsteps I hear. Well, they're not really footsteps, they're footruns. Okay, so I know that's not a word but that's my best description. Someone's coming towards me and they're running. I don't know whether to be happy or afraid: happy because those footruns might bring someone who can answer my questions, or afraid because it could be Gothman and he's pretty much got me cornered.

I try to think of what I can use as a weapon and I quickly remove the small tripod from my backpack. It's not much, but I figure I can get a good head-whack in if I need to. But then again, I've never hit any living creature unless you count the jabs I've exchanged with Jackson (always, always in self-defense), and I'm not sure I can really do it. No that's wrong. I stomped Gothman's hand without any sense of reluctance, didn't I? If it's him coming, I can whack his head after all.

I zip up my windbreaker, put my arms through my backpack straps again and try to remember how the Karate Kid in the movie Jackson once made me see with him makes his defensive stance. But I'm not the Karate Kid and I'm not versed in any of the martial arts, so it's pretty pointless. I'm a swimmer and I don't think the butterfly stroke is going to help me much in this situation. So I stand with my tripod hidden behind me and wait. I can't see that I really have any other choice. Besides, my body doesn't seem to be responding to the message my mind is sending with a growing sense of urgency: "Run for your life!"

Chapter 14

NICOLAS USED HIS KEY to return and as he anxiously ran towards Notre-Dame-Sous-Terre, he tried to process everything that had happened to him in the past two weeks since he had gone to wait for Katelyn. Although he knew from Jean le Vieux that in bygone days, the village streets had been swarming with tradesmen, innkeepers, and Miquelots, the English siege had put an end to that and so Nicolas wasn't familiar with the village in those circumstances.

The Miquelots' desire for tokens of their pilgrimages had resulted in the rise of commerce over the past few centuries. The Watchmen's enseignes had been fashioned to reflect that fact. Besides the enseignes, Jean had told him of other trinkets that were sold including shells, pendants, effigies of Saint Michel, and containers for collecting samples of the sacred sands of the Mont Saint Michel Bay.

Nicolas knew that before the siege, the abbey could not accommodate all of the Miquelots. The abbot hosted the important pilgrims, and provisions had been made for the monks to take in the most destitute, but a large group of pilgrims remained. And so in exchange for goods or payment, the Montois had begun to open up their homes to the visitors. This eventually resulted in innkeepers plying their trade in the village.

However, Nicolas couldn't begin to imagine that those days spoken of by Jean could equal the chaos and cacophony of the village in Katelyn Michael's day. And the desecration of the abbey! It was abominable. The image of Christ driving the moneychangers from the temple flashed through his mind. He wanted to cleanse the cobblestone streets of those dregs of society who had turned this sacred place into a hideous commercial enterprise and to clear the abbey of the noisy, unhallowed visitors who cared little that this was a place of worship, of refuge. But that was not his role.

And then there was the manner of dress of these hordes of future humanity. Especially the women. Their wanton lack of modesty! It was veritably shocking. He had seen more of the female body by simply walking up the village cobblestone street than he had seen in the past nineteen years of his life. He blushed to think of bosoms practically tumbling out of tight-fitting sleeveless corsets. It was as if the female pilgrims were walking around in an abbreviated version of their underclothing. And their legs! He'd seen women wearing male trousers, which was a shock in itself, but even more shocking was that some of those trousers had been cut off clear up to the . . . He cringed to think of reporting it to Jean.

Furthermore, the way both the men and women fashioned their hair was indescribable. There were men with long hair and others with shaved heads (yet surely not from any religious motivation or due to a lack of hair follicles). Some even had designs shaved into their hair. Then there were those with hair sticking up in spikes, which reminded him of the portcullis. They were the ones dressed all in black. Even their fingernails were painted black. Chains hung from their clothing and iron nails pierced their noses or ears. Or their eyelids. Or their lips. It was no wonder their old adversary Abdon had chosen one of those mortal bodies to inhabit. No, that had not been a surprise.

And the women's hair was no better. Although he'd seen some with flowing curls and neat braids, not unlike the braids his little sister wore, others strutted about with shortly cropped hair like men. And the colors! Some hair was blond on top and black underneath. Vibrant manes in every shade of red were abundant. But even stranger was the lass with bright pink locks. Others had strands in every color of the rainbow mixed in with their normally-hued tresses. He knew of no dyes in his time that could produce such startling colors. But then, of course, he could not imagine any lass or lady of his era wanting such startling tresses.

He'd seen unusual body marking and painting as well. There were bare-armed men with detailed images seared into their skin, as if they'd been branded like common stock animals. However, the patterns were sophisticated and colorful. Some even had brandings on their necks or faces and there were even women with brandings. But most of the women just had paint around their eyes and on their lips: all colors and hues. And the black-clothed males and females painted their lips and eyes black as well. They were like frightening apparitions. Surely these were the last days spoken of by the prophets in the ancient writings.

Nicolas was likewise shocked at the behavior of the females. The flaunting of their sexuality with their face paint, bangles, baubles and unholy raiment. Their open seduction of the males with their intimate gestures and wanton eyes. It brought to mind the prophet Isaiah's words: *the daughters of*

Zion are haughty, and walk with stretched forth necks and wanton eyes, walking and mincing as they go, and making a tinkling with their feet.

But the people were not the only strange things he'd seen during the past two weeks. There were mysterious wagons outside the fortified walls of the village. From the ramparts, he saw people traveling in long enclosed carriages to cross a bridge that had been built to connect the mainland to the island. There were no beasts pulling the carriages, no visible means of locomotion, and yet they moved forward so quickly, it was beyond reason. At the foot of the mount, dozens of pilgrims exited the contraptions and then the strange carriages turned around and gathered up other pilgrims on the opposite side of the road to return them to the mainland. This shocking means of accessing the sacred mount went on all day long. No crossing of the sands. No waiting for the tides. No sacrifice to pay homage to Michael. It was no wonder there were so many pilgrims. This was not the arduous journey of Nicolas's day. No, these pilgrims traveled to Normandy in smaller, fast-moving carriages and when they reached the coastline opposite the mount, they left their smaller carriages in vast flat fields and simply climbed aboard the long carriages and crossed via the road built above the reaches of the sea.

Desecration: tying the sanctuary to the coast! If that scenario existed in his day, the fight to prevent the onslaught of the invaders would be impossible. The deadly sands and surrounding sea provided an added level of protection against the enemy. Of course those natural barriers also made it possible for the English to enforce their blockade.

The enemy was brilliant, really. They used the mount's own strength against its inhabitants. When the English realized the citadel—surrounded by its fortified ramparts and the sea—was impregnable, they decided to starve out the inhabitants. Or to wait until they died. They set up the blockade to prevent any foodstuffs from entering the mount. They were tenacious adversaries, refusing to abandon their long siege because Mont Saint Michel was the only part of Normandy that had not capitulated. Nicolas knew that it wasn't the number of Montois that was important to the English, nor was it the small piece of rocky mountain itself. It wasn't even the riches they would glean from the abbey's coffers and library. No, the English understood the Normans. They knew the mount would be used as a rallying cry for widespread rebellion and resistance if the Montois succeeded in repelling the English. And so the Montois must be defeated, the island fortress must be conquered.

Yet the English had not been prepared for the resolve, tenacity, and ingenuity of the Montois, including the monks and a small garrison of French soldiers. The resistant Montois had found ways to slip through the blockade and supplies had trickled in.

So the English increased their troops, assembling them all along the shores of the bay. In response, the Montois planted crops in every spot of island soil. They collected every drop of rain, which along with the miraculous waters of Saint Aubert's Spring, supplied their drinking water. Chickens were allowed free range to find every possible insect and morsel of nourishment so they would continue to produce eggs, and omelets—whipped up in copper bowls to give the illusion of being more consistent than they really were—sustained the people for some time. The Montois learned to cooperate and share with the weaker villagers. Michel watched over his children and the mount held strong.

Then the English built a massive fort in the village of Ardevon. The Montois mockingly called it 'La Bastille,' but they continued to find ways to foil the Bastille and the blockade.

Nonetheless, the siege had taken a heavy toll. The English had effectively destroyed the small fleet of Montois fishing boats. Timbers from homes or planks from furniture (which were also desperately needed for fuel) were used to fashion makeshift rafts and boats. Men were killed trying to slip through the blockade at night to fish or to make it to more distant shores. Desperate Montois, including women and children, drowned in the rising tide or were sucked into the deadly quicksands while trying to cross to the mainland at night. The Montois were getting physically weak. They were more subject to illness and death because their malnourished bodies were unable to fight off disease. The suckling babes were dying because their nursing mothers could not produce enough milk. The resolve of the valiant Montois was unraveling like a poorly woven cape.

And then the final blow had been delivered by the enemy. A flotilla of English ships arrived to complete the blockade on the mount's seaside. It was now virtually impossible for anyone on the mount to pass through the blockade by sea. For sustenance, the Montois were left with only what they could capture, cultivate or gather. Up until now, there'd been a remarkable display of civility and unselfishness among the citizenry, but starvation caused desperate people to do desperate things. Jean and Nicolas were concerned that the Montois would start in-fighting for survival . . . or that they would capitulate.

But the situation was much more serious than the Montois, soldiers, monks, or even Abbot Jolivet himself knew. It was not just a war for political advantage. Nicolas knew the Evil One's plan and it had nothing to do with claiming the island for England. It had nothing to do with enriching the conquering Duke of Bedford, the brother of England's King Henry V.

No, the results of defeat would be much more devastating. By inhabiting the mortal bodies of some of the key English combatants, Satan's legions hoped to finally gain control of the mount and learn its secret. And to do it, they would stop at nothing. It had been their influence that led to the blockade in the first place. They would do all in their power to kill all of the Montois so they could finally have free access to all parts of the holy mount. They knew that even the Watchmen were subject to disease, starvation and death. Then the armies of darkness would desecrate the abbey, take it apart stone by sacred stone, burn the village and decimate any reminder of the Archangel's victory at this sacred place: the place where they and their master had been cast out of heaven.

These were among the blackest days in the entire history of the mount. The Montois were losing their will to fight. It appeared that Lucifer could be victorious. And so another Watchman had been summoned. A Watchman from the future: the girl, Katelyn Michaels. And Nicolas had been sent to bring her back.

Nicolas hadn't known what to expect but it certainly wasn't the actual Katelyn Michaels. He'd come early to the mount to become familiar with his surroundings, to make certain the keyholes were prepared, and to search for Abdon. After seeing the assortment of females in this strange age, he was both relieved and shocked when he first saw the girl. He was relieved because in appearance, Katelyn Michaels was not outrageous like some of the other twenty-first century females. She was tall and much too thin but Nicolas had to admit she had a certain simple beauty about her. Although dressed in rolled up men's trousers, she had no bosoms hanging out of corsets, no bare legs . . . although half her arms and ankles *were* exposed. But clothing was not a critical element. Clothing could be camouflaged and he'd come prepared with an extra robe. There were other things that would have been more problematic. Katelyn Michaels' braided hair was not pink. Her scalp was not shaved. She had no nails through her lips.

Truly, how could I take a lass back to the fifteenth century with pink hair? he thought.

His shock was because she was so young and appeared so naïve and vulnerable. But also, un-invested, ambivalent and—he had to voice it to himself if not to Jean—so seemingly incapable of greatness. She appeared uninterested in anything of consequence and incapable of analytical thinking. After watching her and her younger brother in those minutes before Nicolas made the initial contact, it was clear she was neither a warrior nor an intellect. In fact, if anything, it was the younger brother who seemed more capable than his older sister. Jackson Michaels was intelligent and more importantly, keenly interested in the mount.

His sister was sarcastic and flippant. She was certainly unobservant. She'd been totally unaware of the fact that he had been watching her from the moment she set foot on the mount. She'd been oblivious of Abdon following her and intentionally crashing into her on the West Terrace.

Of course Nicolas himself had been guilty of negligence. He should never have allowed that to happen, especially after realizing Abdon's identity. But Nicolas had been taken by surprise that Abdon knew *his* identity. Nicolas didn't know the evil one knew him by sight. They'd never come face to face in his time. But from the instant Abdon's twenty-first century host had spotted Nicolas, the man in black had attacked him and tried to stop his mission. But Nicolas should have anticipated Abdon's bold attack on Katelyn. It meant that now, in Nicolas's time, Abdon would come to know who both Nicolas and Katelyn Michaels were. It meant that Abdon had waited centuries to stop the girl.

The fallen angels, unlike the Watchmen, did not have the capacity to travel through time. They did not have the keys. They were forced to continually change mortal hosts. After their hosts died, they had to start over each and every time. And it was extremely difficult to cultivate their hosts for there was a seed of goodness in every mortal man and woman: the light of Christ that helped mortals fight against darkness.

Yes, in spite of the great evil the Master of Evil himself had introduced to the earth, it was still a constant battle for Lucifer and his followers to successfully inhabit mortal bodies. And even if successful, they never had complete control of their hosts. That was why they were so anxious to learn the secret of the mountain. Their dependence on humankind was a curse they would do anything to overcome. All they wanted were their own immortal bodies. That was their desire. Their quest. It had been so since time immemorial, since Michel and his army had cast them out of heaven for rejecting God's plan. They were thus excluded from coming to earth to obtain bodies of their own.

Ironically, the presence of Abdon in the future world was the one bright hope to which Nicolas clung. It was counter-intuitive, but it was the truth. If the evil one was trying to stop Katelyn from returning to the past, then surely she would be successful at whatever it was she had been summoned back here to do. Abdon had learned of her and Nicolas's identities and hoped to change the past by changing the future. He had waited for generations to stop Katelyn Michaels and to stop Nicolas from escorting her back in time. He'd done everything possible to stop the Watchmen. Except for murdering them, of course. Abdon could not force his human hosts to commit murder. Unless it was in the host's nature to commit that sin, it was the one act of evil it was almost impossible to force a mortal host to do. Nicolas was grateful that in spite of the appearance of the young man clothed in black, bound in chains and painted in shades of darkness, and in spite of his own declaration that he was willing to kill, Abdon's host still obviously had regard for human life. He could have killed Katelyn on the West Terrace, but he hadn't.

For that matter Abdon's host could have killed me, thought Nicolas.

Nicolas also felt a glimmer of hope because of what he'd seen of Katelyn in the refectory, when he and Jackson had been stalking Abdon. Katelyn had been intent on recovering her enseigne, and surely she would not have felt that strongly about it had she not understood that it was more than just a mere pilgrim's trinket. She must have had some preparation.

Nicolas's keyhole was located in an inconspicuous corner of the Guest Hall and now as he hurried through the dark corridors of the abbey's underground network towards Notre-Dame-Sous-Terre, he was relieved to find them empty. It was dark and the sound of chanting from above permeated the lower reaches of the abbey. The monks were at prayer. It must be *Complines*, the end-of-the-day prayers. Nicolas offered his own prayer at the end of this difficult and trying day. The most unusual day of his life. His prayer was that Katelyn had been successful. That she had found her keyhole. That she had found it before Abdon had caught up to her, and that she had been alone in the chapel. Soon he would learn if his prayer was to be answered. But if she *was* there, he still had no idea what he was going to say to her.

Katelyn Michaels. The girl from the future. She was a complete enigma. How could anyone so young and ambivalent have any skills to turn the tide against an army of soldiers led by the evil Abdon? The Montois couldn't wait long for her to be tutored by Jean. They couldn't wait for her to grow up. Nicolas prayed that he and Jean had not gotten it wrong. He prayed it wasn't all a big mistake. But the voices had been clear. Katelyn Michaels from the twenty-first century was somehow going to save Mont Saint Michel.

Chapter 15

I DIDN'T KNOW WHAT to do. Should I run from the chapel? Try to hide someplace? Yet I couldn't do either because my idiotic body wasn't responding to my brain's order to move. I remained completely paralyzed, as if I were stuck to the stone floor with superglue.

What happened to the adrenaline rush I'd felt earlier? The fight or flight mechanism that allowed me to make it to the chapel in the first place? Clearly I had no fight or flight left. I was a sitting duck waiting for someone or something to attack me. Thoughts came to my mind of my poor mother reading the headline: "American Teen Killed by Mysterious Goth Cult in Gothic French Abbey."

Yet still I stood there rooted to the ground. Not even the image of my devastated mother who'd lost her husband to a Frenchwoman and now her daughter to a French cult could get me to move.

Oh don't get me wrong. I was scared, all right. My heart was pounding and I felt like I was going to throw up. I just couldn't do anything about it. I was frozen like a forehead with too much Botox.

And then Woolrobe's voice, paired with the sounds of him running, called out my name softly. It was surprising that I recognized a voice I'd heard only a few times and yet I knew it was him. It was not Gothman. I exhaled a million molecules of relief, not that I could put into words what a million molecules felt like, but that's how I felt. At least a million.

"Woolrobe?" I called out. "Is that you?"

Wow, that was completely ridiculous. I knew his name wasn't Woolrobe but since I didn't know what his actual name was, it just kind of slipped out. He must have thought I was a real idiot. I felt like a real idiot. But I also felt like a safe idiot.

Woolrobe came bolting around the corner and that's when my fight or flight mechanism kicked in—once I was out of danger. Go figure. I could move again and I moved myself right into Woolrobe's arms. Heck, I was so relieved to see a familiar face and a friendly face—for I instinctively knew he was friendly—that I didn't even think of how forward I was being by practically throwing myself at him.

My Women's Studies teacher, Ms. (emphasis on the *Ms.*) Carson would be disgusted. I was being the kind of pathetic female she detested: totally helpless Katelyn waiting for Prince Charming to save her from danger because she wasn't capable of saving herself. Well, Ms. Carson, I'd like to see how you'd react in this creepy place, hearing voices, being delivered disturbing messages and a strange medallion, and being physically attacked by Goths. And then to top it off, having some type of out-of-body experience in an ancient chapel. You might not be any braver than me.

Anyway, I felt Woolrobe stiffen as I practically smothered the life out of him with my hug, so I pulled away. And then as if to let me know he was not completely disgusted by my audacity, he touched his hand to my chin and lifted my face. His eyes searched mine with an intensity that now made *me* uncomfortable.

"Katelyn Michaels," he said. "You are . . . uninjured?" I could tell he was searching to find the English words.

"I'm okay," I assured him.

"Okay?" he asked. "I offer my apologies. I do not comprehend that word." His English was stilted and old-fashioned.

Now I know I'm not the most cosmopolitan teen around. I haven't traveled all over the world. I don't speak a dozen languages, but I'm pretty darn sure that okay has become an international term. I mean everyone understands okay. O.K.! Where on earth had Woolrobe been hiding for his entire life that he didn't understand okay?"

"Okay," I said again as I made the accompanying hand gesture. "It means, I'm fine. I am . . ." I couldn't think of how to explain it other than to say that I was okay. I wasn't great. I wasn't fabulous, but I wasn't horrible, either. So, we'd do it his way. "I am uninjured."

"*Heureusement.* You must to cover yourself with this," Woolrobe said as from under his robe, he pulled out a very large bag made from the same homespun fabric. The word knapsack came to mind. I don't know if that's what it's called, but it was bulging. From it, he removed a hooded robe like his own. "Hurry, we must to make haste."

Make haste? Who on earth was Woolrobe's English teacher? Obviously a very old geezer.

He enveloped me in his extra wool robe. Now I was Woolrobe Two! I'd made fun of his wool in June but it certainly didn't feel like June in the bowels of the abbey. I pulled the rough material over my head, adjusted it, and then allowed him to pull the hood up over my head. He stuffed my hair back into the depths of the hood so it didn't show.

"The enseigne?" he said. "Have you it?"

"Oui," I replied using one of my ten French vocabulary words said in an attempt to squelch my desire to reply, 'Yes, I *it* have.' This was really no time to be mocking his English. There were more important things at stake than syntax errors. And besides, I told myself, he speaks more English than you speak French, so get a life.

"In my pocket," I said out loud, and patted my pocket through the robe.

"C'est bon." He looked at me intensely and then took my hand and began to pull me.

I remembered what Jackson had said just a few minutes before, up in the refectory. He'd told Woolrobe I wasn't going anywhere with him unless he answered some questions. He was right. I was allowing myself to be hoodwinked, both literally and figuratively.

"Stop," I said. "I'm not going anywhere with you until you tell me what's going on. Who are you anyway? And what on earth happened to me when I turned the enseigne in the jobber's mark? And what's the deal with this chapel? It's different than when I came in. It's darker and colder. And who is that creepy Goth guy chasing me?" My questions tumbled out at about ninety miles an hour before I could even give him a chance to respond.

He looked like he didn't fully understand what I was saying, but he got the gist of it.

"Katelyn, we have not the time to discuss now. You must to come with me, and Jean will to explain."

Syntax *and* infinitive problems. I'd better learn French, I thought. Actually, I knew I was focusing on his English mistakes to keep my mind off the real issue: I had just experienced the most bizarre day of my life and it obviously wasn't close to being over.

"You know, you don't have to use "to" in front of every English verb," I said, being about as obnoxious as I could. I knew about infinitives from studying Spanish. "And who on earth is Jean, anyway?"

"I will . . . take you to him now. To the village."

"The village? Who are you? Why should I go with you?"

"My name is Nicolas. You must to come . . . or rather, you must come, because you are one of us." I could see him struggling to find the words to explain, and he finished in French. *"Comme moi et Jean."*

I had no idea what he was trying to explain but I'd learned one thing. Woolrobe's name was Nicolas. It didn't answer any of my other questions but somehow just knowing his name gave me a sense of calm . . . and a feeling of comfort. I'm not sure why, but it did. Nicolas, Nicolas. His name was familiar to me and yet I'd never known anyone with that name. Had I?

Then another thought brought me back to reality. "What about my brother? Where is he? I can't leave Jackson. I think he needs stitches." I could just imagine how furious my mother would be about my abandoning my brother when he needed medical attention.

"You brother will be . . . okay," he said with a grin, accompanying his facial expression with the proper hand gesture. "You see? I learn your new word. I ensured he shall receive the appropriate care."

Could he ensure my mother wouldn't kill me for leaving Jackson? I don't think so.

As I tried to make sense of my dilemma, I heard a humming noise coming from above. As I focused on the sound, I recognized the distinctive melodic pattern of a Gregorian chant.

It must be music piped into the abbey to add to the ambiance. Yet it didn't sound like a recording. It sounded like real monks and real chanting. I knew the abbey was a historical monument owned by the French government. It was not a working monastery. Far from it. There were like a million tourists, but I hadn't seen any monks—unless you counted Nicolas. So how could a thousand waves of vibrating tones be permeating my body like a jackhammer? And then it finally made sense. The chanting. The darkness and the extraordinary cold in the middle of a June afternoon. The change in the chapel altar. This was a dream. A nightmare, really. Or more likely, a brain injury. It had all started when Gothman pushed me down on the West Terrace. I was in a dream state—or a coma—induced by head trauma.

"Okay, okay," I said as I reached out to stop the dream figure who called himself Nicolas. "I get it now. This isn't real. I'm in a coma or something. Let's see, what do they call it? Traumatic Brain Injury? TBI? You're just a figment of my imagination. I'm really lying up there on the terrace unconscious."

The figment looked genuinely puzzled at my words. And he felt pretty darn real as he shook me and said, "Katelyn Michaels. You know who you are. You know why you are here. Your . . . dreams. Your . . . voices." Nicolas was trying hard to communicate something to me.

I shook my head and even slapped my own face. That felt pretty real too. My eyes were definitely open, but anything was possible with brain trauma. It all felt so darn real. As Jackson would say, "cray-cray."

"Okay," I conceded. "I guess the only thing I can do is play along with you until I wake up."

"Come," Nicolas said and I followed.

And though the coma or dream scenario made total sense, I somehow knew with that one word 'come' pronounced by Nicolas that this wasn't a dream. I didn't know why or how these bizarre things were happening, but they were real. I thought of Jackson. I even thought briefly of the Frenchwoman asleep in her hotel room, and for once, prayed that she would be there for Jackson. But with that simple command, I knew I had to go with Nicolas. I also knew that by following him, I would be leaving everything about my life, my family, my brother, my mother, my friends—and even the father I resented but now thought of lovingly—behind. I knew Nicolas expected me to leave everything I had known for an entire lifetime and follow him into . . . into what?

Chapter 16

JEAN JUMPED TO HIS feet when he heard Nicolas's characteristic knock on the heavy wooden door. The boy was back. Now the stonecutter would learn whether or not his apprentice had brought the girl.

The old man shuffled as quickly as his frail legs would carry him. He struggled to pull back the rusted bolt and then he pulled the door inward.

"*Nous sommes arrivés. Elle est venue avec moi,*" Nicolas said as Jean moved to allow the two robed figures inside. The girl had come.

"Mademoiselle Michaels, please come in," Jean said slowly in English. She looked about her with an expression that could only be called frantic. "My name is Jean and I have been waiting for you." He extended his hand and drew her into the small salon, lit only by a candle and the weak flames in the fireplace.

"Just what in the heck is going on?" the girl said in a type of English that Jean could barely comprehend.

"I know this must seem very strange to you, but we shall explain it all in due time."

"Aaaaaaaa, I don't think so! You'd better explain it all to me right now, or I'm headed right back to that chapel place to see if that enseigne thingy Nicolas gave me will make you and all of this disappear, 'cuz I'm pretty darn sure that I'm not in Kansas anymore!"

"Je ne comprends rien de ce qu'elle dit," Nicolas managed to say before the girl started spouting off again.

"Stop speaking in French! I don't understand a thing you're saying."

"Mademoiselle, that is exactly the observation Nicolas just made to me," Jean tried to explain to her with a smile. "This is difficult for all of us. We do not understand your accent or your vocabulary. It is vastly different from the English we have learned and you do not speak French, so we are struggling for mutual comprehension. I propose that you try to calm yourself and speak to us very slowly."

"Okay," she started and then stopped. "Oh yeah, you don't even understand that word, do you?" She mumbled to herself, and then finally said slowly and succinctly: "Where am I?"

"This is my home in the hamlet of Mont Saint Michel."

"Yeah, I . . . even though there were no lights on, I could pretty much make out the fact that your buddy here was leading me out of the abbey to the village," she said in that quick unintelligible slur. Then she slowed down and said, "but everything is changed. Everything is different. And it's the middle of the night. It was early afternoon when I entered the chapel. And who on earth was that Goth guy chasing me?"

"Yes, mademoiselle," Jean said, not understanding her question about the 'Goth guy.' "Everything must seem very different for you. Nicolas was sent to fetch you and bring you here."

"Yeah, I got that much, but I still don't get where 'here' is." She looked around the sparsely furnished room and threw out her hands. "And I sure as heck don't know why I got 'fetched' to begin with. Who are you anyway? And why is it so stinking cold? It's the middle of June, for heaven's sake."

Then she lifted up the heavy robe, pulled her arms from the sleeves and wriggled out of her strapped knapsack. She set it on the floor briefly as she shivered and then worked her arms back into the sleeves of the robe.

"It's absolutely freezing in here," the girl said as she picked up her knapsack and pulled it to her tightly as if it could somehow emanate heat. "This has gotta be a dream . . . or a coma!" She rubbed a spot on her head behind her ear. Then she shook her head back and forth with ferocity.

Jean could see she was getting more, rather than less, agitated. The small flame flickering below the pot of broth in the fireplace produced little warmth but it was the only source of heat in the chilled room, so he calmly took her by the hand and didn't hesitate as he escorted her to the wooden chair placed near the fireplace. He had fabricated the intricately-carved chair himself for his beloved Marie. This was the first time since Marie's death that another female would sit in her place. In fact, he was quite certain that no one had sat in the chair since Marie's death. Nicolas, knowing the chair was an emblem of Jean's undying adoration for his deceased spouse, never dared to sit there. Nicolas looked at Jean now with such astonishment that the old man had to place a hand on the younger man's shoulder to calm him.

He whispered in French to the perturbed young man, "The time has come, Nicolas. Do not trouble yourself about this. We must do our duty."

It was as if by the simple act of inviting Katelyn to sit in Marie's chair, Jean was turning the last page in his tattered book of life. He knew it and he knew that Nicolas knew it. But their duty precluded any other course of action.

To make matters worse, the bilious young woman plopped down onto the chair with such force that Jean swore he could hear the inanimate object cry out in protest. A chorus of wood fibers screaming out their displeasure. Praise be to God that she didn't break it.

Jean squelched his natural instinct to yank her out of the chair and shake some sense into her, but his years of watching others suffer had given him the genuine empathy and compassion required to overlook a multitude of sins. The girl was frightened and confused and who wouldn't be in her situation? His primary role was to provide her with a feeling of safety and reassurance. Everything depended upon his careful handling of the situation because she very well could return to Notre-Dame-Sous-Terre, as she had threatened, and then . . . all would be lost.

The Watchmen, like every other being born into mortality, had been given complete agency. No one could force them to do anything. No one could force the impetuous young lass to fulfill her destiny. Only she could make that choice. He prayed that the fact she'd come in the first place meant she understood her calling, but he had little way of knowing how much preparation she had received. And so that is where the tired old man began. Nicolas helped him pull out the hand-hewn bench from the table and both sat down facing the girl.

"Mademoiselle," Jean began in slow, deliberate English, "I know this is all very confusing for you, but I need to know one thing. Were you prepared to come here to us?"

"What do you mean was I prepared? I don't get what you're asking."

"Let me put it in the clearest manner I can. Did you hear his voice? Did the Archangel speak to you?"

Jean could see the girl hesitate before she opened her mouth to reply. The shadow engulfing her face could not hide the glint of light her eyes emitted.

"Ummm, what do you mean, exactly?"

So, he had spoken to her, Jean concluded, but she had not understood what was happening.

"It is different from me sitting here before you speaking audible words, which you hear with your ears. When *he* speaks, he speaks thoughts, images and perhaps even words to your mind. Did that happen to you?"

"I . . . I." She stopped, and a flicker of light from the fire pirouetted across her cheeks like a troop of miniature minstrels.

"Please mademoiselle, continue. We shall not find anything you say strange. We understand for the Archangel speaks to us as well."

"Well," she said as she shifted in her seat, "when I first saw Mont Saint Michel from the coastline, when we were driving here, you know with my stepmother and my brother, I . . . It was as if I knew it, the mount I mean, as if it were drawing me to come. I felt I was coming home and yet, I'd never seen it before. That was the first odd experience I had."

"Yes, mademoiselle, you do know the mount. Go on, please."

"Well, I just kept having these feelings that I'd been here before and that I was familiar with things, like when I touched the cannon—I think you call it a *Michelette*—and when I walked through the drawbridge."

A Michelette? He did not know what she was speaking about, but he didn't want to stop her to ask.

"And then Nicolas here put the enseigne in my backpack and when I touched it, I seemed to know it was a key. I'm still not sure what I opened when I used it, but I know it's a key. You're going to have to enlighten me on that one."

"Yes, we shall speak of the key later, but go on. Was there anything else?"

"Yeah, that creepy Goth guy following us. For some reason, he felt really familiar to me, like I knew him, but I've never set foot in France before and frankly, Goths aren't exactly my thing. I don't know how I could possibly know that jerk."

"Je pense qu'elle parle d'Abdon," Nicolas said and then explained to Jean how he had recognized Abdon in Katelyn's world, even though his mortal host was new. *"Et Abdon m'a reconnu aussi,"* the young man added.

It was not good news that Abdon had recognized the young Nicolas. Jean had done everything in his power to protect the lad. The old man had never wanted Abdon to know that his replacement had come.

"Well mademoiselle, it seems you have met our mortal enemy, Abdon. I assume he tried to stop you from coming to us?"

"Ahhh—yeah. He knocked me out and stole my enseigne. Nicolas helped me get it back or I wouldn't be here. Wherever here is," she said looking around with her eyes knit together. "Who on earth was that guy anyway?"

"I will tell you about Abdon in due time, but back to your preparation. What about voices? Did you hear a voice?"

"Well," she hesitated as if considering just how much she wanted to say, "I guess you could say that. When I was standing in front of the abbey church, I looked up at the statue of Michael, of the Archangel and well, I guess I kinda heard him talking to me. Just like you said. I heard words in my mind?"

"May I ask what those words were?" Jean asked leaning forward slightly. Nicolas sat quietly beside him without saying a word but he was also watching the girl intently.

"Ummm, well . . ." Jean could see she was reluctant to share but this time, he just sat and waited for her to continue.

"Yeah, so well, he said . . ." well I don't know if he said it or if I was just replaying in my mind the words that Nicolas had said to me earlier. "You know, it was kind of a repeat of what he," she indicated Nicolas, "said when I found the key in my backpack."

"Which was . . ." Jean knew exactly what Nicolas had said to Katelyn. The two had carefully rehearsed those words together so that Nicolas would get them right in English.

"Well, I heard the words in my mind. I was looking up at the statue on the spire of the church and . . . it was as if Michael were speaking to me. The words that came to me were: 'Katelyn, I've been waiting for you for a very long time. Everything depends upon you. You will know what to do when the time comes. Hurry now, come inside.'"

"So. You received your calling," Jean said.

"What do you mean, my calling? I have no idea what you're talking about."

"Mademoiselle Michaels, Nicolas and I are Watchmen. We watch over this holy mount. This was the site of very special events at the beginning of time. At the beginning of mortal time, that is. And certain valiant individuals have been chosen to watch over this sacred place. You are one of those individuals."

"Okay, you're completely insane," the girl said. "Just what's so valiant about me, huh? For heaven's sake, I'm only seventeen and I don't know anything about anything, least of all this holy—or whatever you call it—mount. I'm just a regular American teenager. And my mom's waiting for me back in the States so you can't possibly think I'm going to stay here with you guys and do any kind of watching!"

Although Jean didn't understand many of her words, he understood the overall meaning. She was having trouble comprehending that she had been called as a Watchman. In all honesty, so was Jean. How could this impudent girl possibly be chosen to do anything? But his was not to judge. Nicolas had been so different. The boy had immediately understood and accepted his calling. He had processed the mysteries of the mount without difficulty. Yes, it had been so easy with Nicolas. This girl from the future was definitely a contrast. And not in a good way.

"I don't know exactly what your role is," Jean admitted. "However, there is something special about you, something only you can do for us here that has brought you back."

"Brought me back?" What do you mean, brought me back?"

Jean instantly regretted his choice of words. He had been too hasty. She was not yet prepared for the reality of traveling back in time. In spite of the chill in the room, beads of sweat broke out across his forehead. One of them ran unimpeded into his eye, the salty liquid stinging him as a reminder of his mortality. Mortality. It was . . . so difficult to broach the subject with this new resentful pupil. He could tell that Nicolas was anxious to jump into the conversation but Jean placed his withered hand upon the lad's leg and shook his head in the negative.

"Mademoiselle . . . may I call you Katelyn?"

"Ah, yeah, no problem," she answered. "Might as well be on a first-name basis with my hallucination, don't you think? After all, it's so 'last month' to be addressed as Mademoiselle Michaels. And I'll just call my little nightmares Jean and Nicolas, then. What could be more civilized?"

Jean assumed this was her way of giving him permission to use her given name, but he wasn't altogether certain.

"Mademoiselle Katelyn," he said her name with precision, as if by saying it, he was acknowledging her role. "I know you have many questions, and they will all be answered, but let us go back to your first question. You asked me where you were and I told you in my home in the hamlet. What you didn't ask me is perhaps the more important question: when are you?"

"When am I?" she asked. "You mean like in the TV show *Lost?*' She wrinkled her brow together and looked at him questioningly. "Just exactly what do you mean?"

He had no idea what she meant by 'the lost TV show' but he tried to answer her question. "You said that everything has changed, everything is different. And you are right. Everything *is* different because although you are in the same place as you were before you turned your key, you are not in the same time."

"I know, I know. That's what I've been trying to tell you. It's like midnight outside," she said. "Where did all those hours go? My brother's probably freaking out."

"No, my dear," he said. "It is not later. It is earlier. Much earlier."

"Okay, now you're freaking me out," she said. "What do you mean?"

The girl set her knapsack on the floor and pulled her legs up onto the chair, and though she was covered in the heavy wool robe, she hugged her arms around her bent limbs. Jean had never seen a young woman sit in such an inappropriate manner and he shook his head in disbelief. However, he continued his attempt to enlighten the audacious child, regardless of her ill-mannered behavior.

"You asked about your key—the enseigne. You asked what kind of a key it is. Katelyn, it is a key to turn time backward or forward. You used it to go back in time."

"What?" she cried. "What did you say? Are you saying it's a key that changes time? That I've come back in time?"

"Yes, mademoiselle. That is what I said."

Without a hint of a warning, the girl launched herself from her chair to the door of the abode. Before young Nicolas could catch her, she wrenched open the door and ran out onto the rough cobblestones of the hamlet's only street. And then, with no regard for the sleeping villagers whose lives were already filled with abominable trauma, Katelyn Michaels began to shriek at the top of her lungs.

Chapter 17

AS QUICKLY AS HE could, Nicolas reached the hysterical girl who was running her hands across the rough walls and windows of the hamlet's edifices. She was like a rabid animal, screaming and kicking but fortunately she stopped short of biting. He wrapped her tightly in his arms but tried to communicate through his gentle pressure that he was not a threat. He had never had an interaction with a female like this.

"Katelyn, you must be quiet" he whispered into her ear. "The villagers will wake and there will be questions."

"Questions!" she screamed. "Ya think? How about *my* questions?"

"Come back inside," he coaxed. "Jean will explain."

Her frantic movements slowed and then her tears came. Nicolas felt totally helpless. The only first-hand experience he'd had with the female gender was his stoic mother who never cried, and his little sister, who cried incessantly. However, this girl from the future, Katelyn Michaels, was not a nine-year-old like his sister.

How can this hysterical girl possibly save the mount? he thought.

He escorted her back into the house, amazed that no one had been awakened by her screaming. At least no one had come out of their homes. The Montois were so exhausted and worn-down from hunger that sleep was their only haven of peace.

When the sobbing girl was once again seated before the fireplace, Jean took her hand in his and said, "T'is difficult to accept, I know, but if you reach down into your soul, you will come to understand."

Katelyn looked up at him and then wiped the black streaks of her dissolving eye-paint onto the sleeve of her borrowed robe.

Bravo, thought Nicolas. *Twenty-first century grime on my robe.*

"How can this possibly be?" she asked. "How can I possibly have traveled back in time?"

"Is it any more incredible than communing with the Archangel?" Jean asked her. "You have come to accept the fact that you have done that."

"I . . . I just can't believe this is happening," she replied. "This has to be a dream. A nightmare. A coma. I'm sure I'll be fine when I wake up."

"I wish I could tell you that it is so," the old man said, "but when you wake up you will find me and Nicolas here just as we are now. And it will still be fourteen hundred and twenty-four. And we will still be hoping you can perform a miracle."

"1424?" she asked. "You mean like ONE FOUR TWO FOUR?"

"Yes, Mademoiselle. Nicolas brought you back to the year 1424."

"You've got to be kidding me!" she cried. "Why on earth did you bring me back to 1424? And you expect me to help you do something here? You think I can even survive in 1424? Ya got running water? A bathtub? A toilet? I don't think so. Heck, I'd even settle for a Walmart!"

Nicolas was getting more and more furious by the minute. The entire mount was starving to death trying to hold off the enemy, and here was this screaming, coddled creature thinking only of herself. He did not need this. He needed to concentrate all of his strength on defeating Abdon. He could not believe the restraint Jean was exhibiting. For his part, Nicolas felt like wringing her neck.

"Mademoiselle, please calm down," Jean implored. "Let us explain."

"Calm down? CALM DOWN? You rip me away from my brother and leave him all alone in the future and no one ever hears another word from me? How do you think my mother's gonna cope with this, huh? She's already lost her husband, and now she's going to lose her only daughter? And you want me to calm down?"

"I can only imagine how confused you must feel, but you need to understand that you will be able to return to your time after your assignment is completed. You will go back to the exact time and place. Your family will not suffer. They will never know you were gone."

Those words seemed to calm her momentarily, for the shrieking stopped. Nicolas breathed a sigh of relief, but it was short-lived.

"And just what on earth is my assignment supposed to be?"

"The mount is under siege by the English," explained Jean, "and the Montois cannot hold out any longer. Without your help, the mount and more importantly, the abbey, will be lost."

Nicolas watched her face as Jean provided his explanation. Where Katelyn had cried hysterically before, she now began to laugh hysterically. Nicolas was certain that a grave mistake had been made. Surely they had been deceived about Katelyn Michaels.

"Oh this is rich," she sputtered. "Katelyn Michaels has been whisked through time to save Mont Saint Michel from the wicked English. Yeah, Katelyn is such a military genius. And you know the worst part about it?

Katelyn Michaels doesn't give a hoot about protecting France from the English. Let them come! Who cares? If anything, I'd be on the side of the English. After all, England is the mother country of America. At least I speak their language. And at least England is still an ally to America. The English, as you call them, haven't stabbed America in the back like the French. Besides both France and England are just second-class powers in my world. America is the last bastion of freedom in the world."

Nicolas hadn't understood all of her words but he could not restrain himself any longer. He jumped in before Jean could stop him and pulled Katelyn to her feet.

"You, Mademoiselle Michaels, are the most ill-mannered, over-indulged female I have ever had the misfortune to meet and I will happily deliver you back to Notre-Dame-Sous-Terre without any further delay. It will be my pleasure to dispatch you right back to where you belong."

"Nicolas, calmes-toi aussi. Tu n'aides pas," Jean said as he stood and wrenched Nicolas away from her with surprising strength. *"Mets-toi a sa place, et essaies de comprendre un peu."* Nicolas regretted his rash reaction but this girl was just so incredibly aggravating.

He stepped back and took a deep breath as Katelyn sat back down. For a few seconds no one said a word. Nicolas bowed his head and placed his hands over his eyes. He tried his best to put himself in the girl's place as Jean had asked him to do.

Yes, it must be very frightening for her, Nicolas finally admitted to himself. *Even though I had to leave my home to come here, I was still in the same time period, with the same culture and the same language. Jean is right. I must try harder to understand her.*

Nicolas had seen Katelyn's world, if only briefly, and there was no doubt the contrast must be shocking. He had been shocked when he went to her world, fully knowing he would soon return to his own time. But he could not keep down that bubble of anger pushing against his chest, threatening to strangle him. He'd given up his family and his entire life to come to the mount. He had willingly left everything behind, including his parents and siblings, all of whom he adored. All they were asking of Katelyn Michaels was a few days, maybe a few weeks of her time, and then she could go merrily back upon her way to her absurd, meaningless life in the twenty-first century. Honestly, was that too much to ask of her?

"I am sorry, mademoiselle," Nicolas said grudgingly, but only to appease Jean. He didn't care about Katelyn's feelings. "I wish you to stay. We have need of you here." She looked up at him, but he refused to be moved by the single tear working its way down her cheek. It was purely histrionics.

"Mademoiselle," Jean said. "It is late and you are understandably confused and probably very tired and hungry." Jean looked at Nicolas with piercing eyes, and Nicolas understood the message clearly: keep quiet and keep your feelings to yourself.

"I am going to ask just one thing of you. Stay with us here for twenty-four hours. I have made up a bed for you in a private bedchamber upstairs and I promise you will be safe. Let us speak tomorrow in the light of day and then you can make your decision. Are you able to do that?"

"Well it doesn't seem like I have any choice," she answered.

"You always have a choice, my dear. But please, let us sup together. I have some hot broth on the fire," Jean said, looking at Nicolas again. This time his look was a question, not a command.

"And I have brought additional sustenance for us to share," Nicolas said, going to his bulging knapsack and pulling out the foodstuffs he'd managed to gather from the future hamlet. Nicolas couldn't even determine what all of the items were he had brought back. Some were in round metallic containers with pictures of the type of food he assumed was inside. He found this twenty-first century alimentation to be quite bizarre.

He explained in French to Jean how he had taken the few trinkets and coins Jean had given him and traded them for food, and about how he'd actually scavenged some of the food from the refuse barrels that dotted the village.

"There is so much waste in your world," he said to Katelyn, as if she were personally responsible for it.

And his fury at her rose as he lined up his treasures on the table. These goods brought from the twenty-first century could help feed the villagers for a week and yet here he was sacrificing them as a peace offering for their self-centered guest. He picked up a container with a picture of what looked like meat. He examined it carefully, trying to figure out how to open it. It had a little key on the side secured by a piece of metal.

"Corned-beef," mumbled Katelyn as she took the container from him and using the key, split the metal apart. "That's what keys are for. To open things. Not to whisk you away from everything you know and everyone you love," she said with what Nicolas found to be a carefully calculated touch of sadness in her voice.

The histrionics won't work, so now she's going straight for the heart. She's already figured out that Jean has a tender spot, thought Nicolas.

However, as much as he wanted to shake her, Nicolas remained silent, waiting to see how his mentor would respond to the girl's latest approach.

"Ah, your key definitely opened something, Katelyn," Jean said calmly. "But just like this odd little container from your world, one never really knows what a key might unlock or what's inside the container. You may think your key has opened Pandora's Box. But perhaps, just perhaps, you opened up hope, instead of all the evils of the world."

Nicolas had no idea what Pandora's Box was, but he carefully watched Katelyn Michael's reaction to his mentor's words. She seemed contrite, but he'd given up trying to read her true feelings.

"Okay," said Katelyn as she handed the aromatic meat to Jean who emptied it into the broth cooking over the flame. "I'll stay the night if you promise me that I can return without my brother knowing I've been gone. And I guess I am pretty hungry. I've hardly eaten anything all day."

You do not even know what 'hardly eaten anything' means! Nicolas thought.

"You will go back to the future to the exact time you left," Jean assured her as he stirred up his now much heartier stew. "You could stay a year and he would not know you were gone. But we shall commence with twenty-four hours."

"A year?" she said in clear dismay. "A whole year. Yeah, I'd love to see the shock in his eyes when I show up only a few minutes later for him but a year later for me and my hair has grown a foot. Just how would I explain that one, huh?"

Jean laughed, and said, "Well, if you do stay a year, I guess we must be certain to cut your hair before you return to the future."

"Great," she said as she picked up Jean's knife sitting on the table, "I bet you guys don't even own a pair of scissors?"

"Scissors?" Jean repeated. "I'm afraid I don't know that word."

"Never mind," Katelyn said, shaking her head slightly. "Twenty-four hours. I'll agree to twenty-four hours."

"That will do," Jean said. "We cannot ask more of you and we cannot force you to stay."

"Well," she said in a calmer manner as she assisted Nicolas in setting out their simple pewter mugs and bowls on the table, "this ought to help me get an A in European Medieval History next year at least. Heck, this could be worth several papers. Maybe I'll stay a couple of days after all and have a good look around."

Nicolas didn't know what she meant about the 'A' in European Medieval History and the 'papers,' but he jumped on her last phrase. Even though he didn't like this abrasive young woman, he trusted the Archangel and he hoped that with a bit more time, they could all figure out why Katelyn Michaels had been summoned here at this specific point in history. He would do anything to help alleviate the Montois' suffering and to defeat the English, even if it meant tolerating this irritating female from the future.

"*D'accord,* mademoiselle," Nicolas said in what he hoped passed for a pleasant tone of voice. "I shall be pleased to assist you in 'looking around' but I fear we can go no further abroad than the banks of our little isle."

"Well if your little isle here is free of all the tourist traps I saw in the twenty-first century, it just might be worth seeing."

"I don't know what your tourist traps are, but the English have certainly set up their own *pièges,*" Nicolas said using the French word for traps, "all around the island. I fear we are encumbered with great trials here and as we make our inspection, perhaps it will come to you how you may assist."

"I honestly don't have a clue as to that," she said without any evident sarcasm. "I think your archangel made a big mistake. I still have more questions than answers." Then she let out the oddest snicker and said, "but at least I've had one question answered."

"And that would be?" Jean asked, as he removed the pot from the fire and began dishing out small portions of the stew into the pewter bowls lined up on the table. Nicolas poured some of their precious cider—made from the few apples they had managed to harvest that year—into their assortment of pewter mugs.

"Why Nicolas had never heard the word 'okay.' " She looked at Nicolas and smiled, and as angry as he was at her, he couldn't refrain from smiling back. An odd sensation filled his chest and he quickly looked away.

"I think you both better learn the word because I can hardly speak a sentence without using it," she said as with Jean's worn knife she cut some slices off the crusty baguette Nicolas had scavenged from her world.

And so as the three of them shared their glorious meal from the twenty-first century, Katelyn Michaels tried to explain the proper utilization of the word 'okay.' Evidently, she found her cider to be 'not okay' because she spewed it out all over the table. Perhaps she wasn't expecting the sweet liquid to be quite so fermented. But that was 'okay.' It just meant more for them.

Chapter 18

AFTER JEAN AND NICOLAS escorted Katelyn to her upstairs sleeping chamber, leaving her with a single precious candle, they returned to the fireside downstairs. Nicolas resented that candle. If truth be told, he resented everything about Katelyn Michaels. The coddled maiden would probably let the candle burn down until it was no more, taking no heed of its value in these difficult times. He'd almost lost control of his anger when he'd produced the chamber pot—which he had personally and thoroughly washed in the cleansing ocean waters—and she had once again crumbled into a mass of utter hysteria.

The lass was thoroughly worthless. He didn't know much about the twenty-first century, except for what he'd seen in his two weeks there, but Nicolas had immediately recognized it as a self-indulgent society where immediate gratification was the order of the day. He'd seen enough to get a feel for the luxurious furnishings of the eating and boarding establishments in the village. After exchanging a gold coin for two weeks of room and board in one of the village inns, he was astonished to learn about the sweet-smelling indoor facilities for private needs: large porcelain chairs full of water that cleaned waste away. He'd had to ask the chamber maid who escorted him to his room what its purpose was. She had been just as astonished as he when she showed him how it and the bathing facilities functioned. They were truly astonishing. Clearly *Princess* Katelyn had never relieved herself in nature.

After everything he and Jean had done to make her comfortable in their humble abode, he was incensed that she was so incredibly ungrateful. The two men had done their best: firstly, to provide her with a degree of privacy, and secondly, to equip the chamber with the finest furnishings they could still find or trade for in the village. Jean le Vieux had insisted on this.

"She will be frightened," he'd explained to Nicolas, "after exchanging her loved ones and the security of her twenty-first century life for the insecurity of a village under siege from a heartless enemy. But she will be even more frightened at the prospect of being under the same roof as two single men. She will certainly find it inappropriate. We must do our best to make her feel as safe and as comfortable as we can. She must feel she has some measure of privacy."

Nicolas had resisted, maintaining they had neither the time nor the means for such frivolous things. But Jean had been adamant. A door to the bed chamber, which had earlier been used to build a raft was replaced. Precious food had been traded for it and for the fresh straw tick on which *Her Highness* now slept. Jean had even sacrificed his marriage bed board, a timber frame through which he had looped cured-leather straps to support the tick.

The curtains installed around her bed had been kindly donated by the Widow Mercier, their neighbor who had taken a fancy to Nicolas. Since his arrival in the village, he had assisted her with many odd jobs and she had insisted they take the heavy velvet curtains as payment for his services.

"Besides," she'd remarked with a sly smile after Jean had explained why they were on a cleaning frenzy. "I have no need of them. And nothing is too good for our Nicolas. I applaud anyone who can capture a moment of joy in these vile times."

Now, as the two Watchmen sat together in the glow of the dying embers, Nicolas felt emboldened to make a request of his mentor.

"Papa," Nicolas whispered in French, using the term of endearment he generally used when addressing his beloved tutor, "I have done as I was instructed. I brought this girl from the future. I cannot imagine what she can possibly do to help us but I have tried to be patient and contain my wrath towards her. However, I would like to make just one request of you. You know I have never asked for anything."

"What is it my boy?" asked the kindly old man who had used up every ounce of his mortality in the service of the Archangel.

"I wish you to make an oath with me. I know you are the master and I am the student, but this is of the utmost importance."

"I cannot make an oath without knowing what it is," Jean said as he rubbed his rheumy eyes with his crippled fingers. "Please explain your desire and then I will decide the judiciousness of entering into an oath." The skin on the back of Jean's hands was paper-thin and mottled with age spots.

Those hands have seen more sorrow and hardship than a hundred lifetimes of hands, thought Nicolas. *I must be more thoughtful of him, for I don't think he shall last much longer.*

"Papa, please listen to me. I am concerned about the tutoring you will be giving Katelyn Michaels. She is not one of us. You know that as well as I do. You can sense it and feel it. I know you can. She won't be staying here on the mount. She will be returning to her world in the future. I am asking you not to tell her the secret of the mount. I don't trust her with that knowledge."

"Nicolas, if she has been chosen as a Watchman then she must know where her duty lies. And perhaps she will protect the mount in the future, in her own time. We do not know or understand what her destiny is. She must know the secret."

"Papa, I have been thinking about it. All she really needs to know is that her duty is to prevent the English from conquering the mount—from destroying the abbey." Nicolas rubbed his hands together to warm his fingers.

"But what if her mission requires her to stay here for an extended period of time? Then she will need to know."

"I don't think that will be the case," Nicolas replied with as much conviction as he could muster. "The Archangel's message was clear. She is needed at *this* point in history to perform a specific task that no one else can perform. I don't think it is something that will take years. Papa, you and I both know the Montois cannot survive for years. They can barely survive for months, or even weeks. No, her task here will not take long. And then after it is completed, she will go back to her life. She will not need to know about . . ."

Nicolas didn't even dare pronounce the words aloud. The girl claimed she didn't speak French, but who knew for certain? She could be at that very moment listening to them through the floorboards. Abdon had taught Nicolas that one could never be too careful.

"She does not need to know," Nicolas repeated. "Can you imagine what might happen in her world if she lets out the secret? As I told you, I saw Abdon in her future world. He is there. With a small army of wretched mortals. He is still trying to ascertain the secret of the mount. We cannot entrust the secret to her. Even if she does prove to be trustworthy, I don't think she is strong enough to withstand Abdon."

"Hmmm," Jean said as he rubbed his whiskers. "I must ponder this. I must seek guidance on the matter."

"Papa, you know how the Archangel speaks to mortal men. He does not command in all things. He allows us to act of our own volition, to use our God-given talents. He will not answer you on this subject. He expects us to use wisdom. If he commanded in all things, don't you think he would have told us exactly what Katelyn Michaels is supposed to do here? Don't you think he would have told her? No. It is always the same message: 'You are needed. You will know what to do when the time comes.'"

"But surely she will instinctively know that she is here to protect something of vital importance. She will ask questions."

"I have thought about that as well. We will answer her questions. We will tell her that the future of her world depends upon France winning this war. That if we do not succeed in vanquishing the English from our shores, the fate of her world will be at stake. That is what we will tell her."

"But what if France does not win the war?" Jean asked. "What if in her world Mont Saint Michel *was* conquered by the English? We do not know what is to happen in the future. But she will know. And if France does not win, she will know we are lying."

"Yes we do know, Papa. I know. The Mont belongs to France in the future. I saw it with my own eyes, and France will win this war because otherwise the abbey would have been destroyed. Abdon would not be there in the future still trying to destroy it. The village and abbey would not have been there for Katelyn to visit because they would have been destroyed. But the abbey is there, Papa. I visited it. I walked through its corridors, I visited its chapels. True, there have been changes and additions, including the marvelous chancel in the church, the one we are working on to replace the collapsed apse. And the sacred chapel is still there, just as it is in our day. Katelyn Michaels came to us from Notre-Dame-Sous-Terre."

"And Abdon? You're certain it was him?"

"Yes. He must have had hundreds of hosts since our time, but it wasn't difficult to recognize him. Evil like that is not hard to miss. It was Abdon. And he knew me. He even called me by name, so he knew who I was—in the future. He had been waiting all those years for Katelyn Michaels to visit the mount so that he could stop her from performing whatever task she is here to perform now. He tried everything he could to stop Katelyn from coming back with me, because he knew that whatever she came to do, she was successful. I mean, she will be successful. If Abdon tried so hard to stop her in the future, it was because he knew what she would do in the past."

Nicolas paused for a moment and pondered what he had just said. It was confusing to think about the ramifications of time. But it all made sense. And he had to accept the fact that Katelyn was the key, and that she would succeed in her mission. In spite of her completely irrational behavior and seeming lack of ability, there was something she would do to save Mont Saint Michel.

"The blessing," Jean said, "is that unlike you, Abdon cannot travel back and forth in time. He knows who she is in the future because he comes in contact with her and you in our present. He learns you are both Watchmen. Then he must wait for six hundred years to stop her from coming back. Or stop you from bringing her back. But right now, in our time, he does not know who you are or who she is, and he does not know what her mission will be. We must take advantage of that fact now."

"Yes, and another blessing," Nicolas added, "is that he was not able to manipulate his host in the future to kill either her or me. Even though he threatened to kill Katelyn, he didn't. Even when he had the opportunity to do so. To injure, yes. But not to kill. Quite different from his current host."

"And that means," Jean said, "that in the twenty-first century the evil ones still have not perfected their abilities to control the human soul. That is why they are so desperate to learn our secret, so they do not have to keep changing human hosts and so they can fully and entirely control their hosts."

"My brief journey to the future has taught us many things, Papa. Abdon is on the mount in that future world, and he has access to the abbey, but he does not know the secret. He still does not know. He does not know what he is looking for, and because of that, he still believes he must destroy the mount to find it. In the future, the entire mount is protected by the French State. To destroy it would be next to impossible unless another war is part of the future after Katelyn's time. For now, we have only to concern ourselves with this war. If we can win this war, we know that in six hundred years, the abbey will still be standing."

"But I'm not convinced that Katelyn Michaels will be content with your explanation," Jean insisted. "That she is here only to help us be victorious. She will ask why. Surely she will wonder why it is so critical for France to win this battle. I already told her that this was the site of very special events at the beginning of mortal time and that she was one of the valiant individuals chosen to watch over this sacred place. Surely, she will ask for further explanation."

"We must approach it from her perspective, Papa. I have thought of an idea. She spoke of being from a country I have never heard of. Do you remember what she called it?"

"Amer . . . something," Jean said. "I remember that part because I remember thinking it was the French word for bitter: *amer*. Ironic, the name of her country begins with a root that is bitter."

"Yes, Amer-something," Nicolas repeated. "And did you hear what she said about France and England—that they were second-class powers in her world? This country of hers—where they speak the strange English—must be a very powerful country to be more powerful than both France and England. And what else did she say? I could not understand all of her words."

"She said that England was the mother country to her country and that her country was the last bastion of freedom in her world."

"Yes. It is perfect," Nicolas jumped in hastily. "This will be our approach. We shall tell her that if France does not win this war, her country will never come into existence. That her entire future world will be non-existent. That her Amer-country, the last bastion of freedom, will never be created. I believe that will be a powerful incentive. A powerful motivator. I do not think she will have any other questions."

"But how do you explain away what I already told her about the abbey?" Jean asked, his utter weariness easily readable from the slowness of his hand movements. "About it being sacred ground, the spot where sacred events took place and about her being called to watch over it?"

"Don't you see Papa? It all fits. This is sacred ground because this is where Satan and his dark angels fought to defeat God's plan for mortal man to have agency. To have freedom of choice in mortality. Mont Saint Michel is a bastion of freedom. We are fighting to protect our freedom from an enemy invader. We are fighting for freedom over tyranny. That is our battle cry. That is why all of France is heralding our achievements, why Frenchmen everywhere are encouraged to keep up the fight. To regain our freedom and kick out the *Godons.*" Nicolas used the derogatory term for the English employed by the Normans.

"And free choice is important to Katelyn Michaels," Jean said with a hint of enthusiasm. His voice was a bit stronger. "I myself told her she had the freedom to choose if she stays or leaves. That is what finally calmed her down: knowing that she could leave if she wanted, that she was not being held against her will. You may be right, Nicolas. I have tutored you well. You have magnified your calling."

"Then we are agreed: Freedom will be our banner. Freedom will be our rallying cry. Freedom will be the reason Katelyn Michaels returned to us from the future. We will tell her that Mont Saint Michel is a sacred place because it is the ultimate bastion of freedom from tyranny, that its role is to preserve freedom in the world and that the destiny of the world is for her Amer-country to become the all-powerful bastion of freedom in the future. That is what we will tell her. She will ask no other questions."

"But surely she will find it illogical to fight for the enemy of the country that spawns her own land."

"Not if we convince her that only through a French victory will her own country come into existence." Nicolas paused as a myriad of thoughts raced through his brain and slowly the argument formed in his mind, as if a million letters aligned themselves onto a page of perfect snow-white paper and organized themselves into perfect words and perfect sentences. And then, he could see the words written in his mind. It seemed like an eternity that he read and pondered the words and sentences, but in reality, it was but an instant.

"Papa, the inspiration has been given to me." Nicolas looked up into the weary man's eyes. "I have had an epiphany. The Archangel has assisted us. I now know this truth: Katelyn's country comes into existence because it breaks away from the tyranny of England. It comes into existence in defiance of England, and it does so with the help of France, with the help of French thought and French philosophy. And even with the help of a handful of valiant Frenchmen. That is clear to me now. France must not be invaded by the English. France must not become a larger territory of England. France must be victorious in this war or Katelyn Michael's country will never come into existence. And Papa, that is not just an argument I came up with to appease a self-indulgent girl from the twenty-first century. It is the truth."

"And if Katelyn Michael's country does not exist," Jean said with a lilt in his weak voice, "Katelyn Michaels herself will not exist—at least not as she is now. And the brother and mother about whom she seems so concerned will not exist either. Nicolas, I think it is fair to say that you have not only found a way to keep the secret of the abbey safe, but that you have also found the perfect motivation for her to stay and fulfill her destiny here. Well done, my son."

Jean patted Nicolas's leg with such love and affection that Nicolas could almost taste the love. He could feel it and smell it and he knew at what cost it had been accorded. Jean had lost his only son, and in those four words 'well done, my son' and that one pat upon his leg, Nicolas felt Jean's complete acceptance of Nicolas as his son. And it was more than that. With that phrase and gesture, Jean sealed the transference of power. The tutor had become the student, and the student the tutor.

Then as if hearing Nicolas's own thoughts, Jean quoted from the sacred manuscript he himself had hand-copied, a manuscript the two men studied daily: *'Well done, thou good and faithful servant; thou hast been faithful over a few things, I will make thee ruler over many things: enter thou into the joy of thy lord."*

Nicolas wept, knowing it was the pronouncement of both a beginning and an end. But his tears were tempered with the uncomfortable thought of how Katelyn Michaels was going to react when she heard the story Jean had concocted to explain to the Montois how and why this girl had suddenly appeared on the mount, slipping through the English blockade. And that explanation certainly did not include time travel! Battle lines would be drawn when she learned of the fabricated explanation and Nicolas hoped and prayed he would not be on the losing side of that coming battle.

Chapter 19

SURPRISINGLY, I SLEPT last night. I mean, who knew that a lumpy pallet full of who-knows-what-kind-of-stuffing would send me into la-la land after the day from hell I'd just survived. But nonetheless it did, after I figured out how to use the chamber pot (yuck)! Thank heavens I had tissue in my backpack. I guess there's something to be said for the power of shock and awe to send a body into survival mode.

Anyway, I don't even remember dreaming. Of course when I woke up, I had that inevitable moment of thinking I was dreaming. But no. It was all true. I had somehow traveled back in time to 1424 and I was sleeping in a poor excuse of a bed in an unheated house in Mont Saint Michel's medieval village. Only this really was medieval. Alas, no modern bathroom here. Honestly, I think that reality was harder than dealing with the fact that I'd magically time-traveled. I mean, it's all fine and good when the movies portray time travel in such a romantic and nostalgic way, but guess what guys? There's no bathroom! Nothing romantic about that. I don't want to be graphic, but let's be honest, shall we?

When I woke up, I pulled back the heavy curtains from around my bed and had a staring contest with the chamber pot. Frankly, the contest didn't last that long. The chamber pot won. I didn't see that I had much choice in the matter.

After that battle was over, I pulled out my travel toothbrush and toothpaste and did my best to brush away six hundred years of gunk from my mouth with saliva as my only aid. I say six hundred years because the last time I brushed my teeth was yesterday morning, and wasn't that nearly six hundred years away? Okay, so maybe that's a bit of an exaggeration. It hadn't really been six hundred years since I'd brushed my teeth, but it sure felt like it. They'd mysteriously grown a velvet covering. Hey, just like my bed curtains.

I had no idea what time it was but the hints of brightness breaking through the slits in the window shutters were enough to give light to the room and let me know it was morning. I also had no idea what month it was, but it definitely wasn't summer because it was cold, but not cold enough to see my breath.

I pulled my shoes and socks on because the wooden floorboards were not only freezing, but I didn't trust them not to have slivers. I tiptoed to the window, trying to avoid making the floorboards squeak because I wasn't ready to face my . . . let's see what should I call them? "Hosts" sounds so lovely and civilized, like being invited to stay at a Victorian manor for the weekend à la Jane Austen. But this wasn't exactly Netherfield and I wasn't Elizabeth Bennet. The word "captors" didn't fit either so I decided to go ahead and refer to them as Watchmen. That's who they said they were.

Anyway, I wasn't ready to face the two Watchmen below so I tried to be as quiet as possible.

I pulled open the heavy shutters and was surprised to see two tall narrow casement windows that actually had glass windowpanes. I'd never really thought about windows before. I mean, who really needs to know if there are glass windows in the fifteenth century? People from the twenty-first century who travel back to the fifteenth century, that's who. After trying to wipe away the condensation on the panes, I finally gave up and managed to figure out how to open them. They opened outward.

Leaning over the sill, I peered out over the ramparts towards the coast of Normandy. It was just like the view Jackson and I had from our hotel room the day before, except there was no road across the bay. It was a misty day and I couldn't make out the coastline—or the English soldiers who were supposedly out there somewhere. However, I could make out the shadows of two of the mount's defenders walking along the ramparts and looking out to sea. I had never experienced war and seeing them sent a shock of electricity through my body. This was not my brother's *Stratego* board game. This was the real thing. I wondered if my responsibilities as a Watchman (or was it Watchwoman in my case?) included rampart duty.

The brisk morning air was eerily still. No sounds of dogs barking, birds singing or neighbors calling out in greetings penetrated the soupy fog. The hustle and bustle of the busy twenty-first century village was non-existent. The toll of a bell shattered the silence like a rock hitting a window and scattering the glass into a thousand pieces. The sound reverberated as if the mist were a solid object sending back a piercing echo. I counted nine bells. Nine o'clock in the morning. I adjusted my watch. At least I now had a modern-day reference point in my new world.

I looked down below me. Although I'd only gone up one flight of stairs from the ground floor of Jean's house, with its front door that opened onto the village street, from the back of the house, I was actually several stories up. Straight below I could see a very small walled-in plot of ground squeezed in between the back of the house and the beginning of the system of stone walls that made up the ramparts. A large tree was firmly rooted in that tiny plot of ground and its branches nearly reached my window. The branches were all but bare and the few remaining leaves were golden red, telling me it was autumn—late autumn.

Great, it's almost winter. It's going to get even colder.

And then, just as the sun was straining to break through the gray mists to warm my skin, I hit my head with my palm as if to interrupt the flow of unbidden thoughts. Why on earth did I care if it was autumn or winter, summer or spring? It made absolutely no difference to me because I would be leaving by the end of the day to go back to my world. Back to Jackson and our lovely room in the Du Guesclin hotel with its lovely bathroom and its lovely hot water and its lovely fluffy towels. Yes, I was even willing to go back to the Frenchwoman. Yep, that's how bad it was. Not that I actually wanted to see her but I was choosing to be with her twenty-first century dishonorableness rather than with the honorable fifteenth century Watchmen.

Then another unbidden message pounded its way into my head like a jackhammer attacking a cement pad: Da-da da da-da-da-da. You cannot abandon us. Da-da-da-da-da-da-da. You cannot abandon us.

"Ya think? Heck if I can't abandon you," I said out loud, trying to interrupt the pounding in my head. "I don't care about your fight. I don't care about your time, and I don't care about you." But the pounding continued.

Below, I saw the figure of a frail old woman coming out of a door into the tiny plot of ground next door and as if she'd heard my ranting, she turned around and looked up at me.

What an idiot I am! I'm ranting in English, I thought to myself.

According to everything I'd learned the day before, the English were the despised enemy. What an idiot I was to be speaking English. Or even worse, ranting in English. The woman was several stories down and about a hundred pounds too light to actually do me harm, but the next person I met on the mount might not be so infirm. They'd probably just as soon kill me first and ask questions later as give me the benefit of the doubt. No, I'd have to be careful in the next few hours not to let anyone on the mount hear me speak English.

And then the oddest thing happened. The wizened creature smiled up at me and started waving with enthusiasm. Then she called to me in a surprisingly robust voice: "*Bonjour, madame. Vous êtes arrivées. Bienvenue.*"

Of course I couldn't understand what she said except the "*bonjour madame*" part, but to say I was surprised would be an understatement. Especially with the "madame" bit. Surely I didn't look old enough to be a madame. But then she was old and probably couldn't see me very well. And she had called up to me as if she had fully expected to see an English-ranting twenty-first century girl leaning her head out of her neighbor's window. Odd. Not knowing what else to do, I waved back and said in my very best French accent (which isn't saying much), "*Bonjour madame.*"

Then I pulled my head back into the room, and shut the window, confused and perplexed. It was time to face the Watchmen and ask some questions.

Chapter 20

AS I SIT AT THE hand-hewn table where Jean presents me a breakfast of stale bread and the corned-beef slop from last night, I begin to get the picture of conditions here. Nicolas is nowhere to be seen but I'm not ready to see him yet, and so I'm relieved. Frankly, I'm not ready to speak to Jean either and so I simply say *"merci."*

I have some thinking to do. He must understand my wish to be alone because he exits the room through a side door leading to who-knows-where. But thankfully, he leaves me by myself.

I don't eat the cold liquid with bits of congealed fat. I can hardly look at it in spite of the fact that my stomach's growling. Last night in the dark and when the stew was hot, I was able to get it down. But not this morning. At least not yet. But I pull the hard bread apart into small pieces and try to swallow them with only saliva as a chaser. No freshly-squeezed orange juice for Katelyn Michaels. I'm thirsty. And hungry. And I desperately want a shower. And an omelet: one of *La Mere Poulard's* omelets, and for an instant I have hope her establishment exists in 1424. I remember watching the *Poulettes* whipping up their fluffy omelets the day before and now I understand why I wanted one so badly. But *La Mere Poulard* isn't here and I don't think there are any eggs.

I sit at the table and lower my head into my hands, thinking of what Jackson and French Sheldon had said yesterday about the siege. Because the English could not conquer the island, they were attempting to starve out its inhabitants. They had the island virtually closed off from the coast and did not knowingly allow a single morsel of food to get to the Montois.

I remember the unbearable hunger pangs that hit me as Sheldon had spoken about it. I remember the feelings of empathy and respect I felt for the Montois and I suddenly realize something very frightening. The kind of hunger pangs I felt yesterday in the cloisters of the abbey don't come from twenty-four hours of slim pickings. They don't come from eating stale bread and watery gruel. They come from days and days of sustained deprivation. As I look down at Jean's concoction of corned-beef and cabbage slop, it doesn't seem quite so unappealing. I even manage to swallow a few spoonsful without gagging.

I also remember the feeling I experienced when from the Normandy coast, I first saw the silhouette of Mount Saint Michel rising from the sea and sands; the feelings of déjà vu that persisted throughout the day as I touched the English canon, as I passed under the rusted spikes of the portcullis, as I walked through the village streets, as I explored the West Terrace, as I touched the abbey stones.

Suddenly, I realize it *was* "déjà vu" in the true sense of the word. I know the French term means 'already seen.' Before I arrived yesterday, I had not only already seen Mont Saint Michel, but I had lived on Mont Saint

Michel! My feelings yesterday were a reminder of things I had seen, feelings I had already experienced. It is now clear to me, and it's troubling, because the realization only confirms that what Jean told me last night is true. I have already been here, but six hundred years earlier than my twenty-first century life. And yet yesterday, those experiences were not in the past, but still in my future. The dichotomy of it twists my mind into knots that cannot be untied. It wrenches my stomach into kinks of pain and panic. Because the message is clear. Even though I can't decipher the enigma of the time puzzle, my own déjà vu is telling me that I will be staying here for far longer than twenty-four hours. And I haven't the slightest idea of why. Why would I choose to stay, when Jean made it very clear that I have the choice to leave? I have no explanation. It's time to start asking questions.

I hope Nicolas is not in the house because I want to speak to Jean alone. I'm not blind. Nicolas's disapproval of me last night was thick enough to cut with a knife. No, it was even stronger than that. It was actual disdain. He thinks I'm a hysterical brat. Actually, I was pretty hysterical last night. But time travel? He expects me to just accept it without hysteria? Really? And even worse, he somehow believes that an average girl from the twenty-first century who has no skills in fifteenth century warfare can swoop in and save the day? Hey, I have pretty good self-esteem but I can't imagine what I can possibly do here. But the truth is, I know for some reason I'm going to stay so I better learn how to get along with these Watchmen. And they're trying to make me believe that I'm a Watchwoman? Really? Yeah, I've got plenty of questions.

"Jean," I whisper, not wanting Nicolas to hear if he's around. I stand up and go to the door from which he exited the room and I knock lightly. "Jean? Are you there?"

"Oui, mademoiselle. I am here." He opens the door and I can see he's in a storeroom. It looks like he's been taking inventory because food and tools are laid out in neat rows.

"Jean," I address him, and then think that may be presumptuous of me to call him by his first name. I know the French are very polite and very formal. "Monsieur Jean," I amend, since I have no idea of what his last name is or even if he has a last name. Anyway, I think Monsieur Jean sounds better than Monsieur Watchman, so after that little adjustment, I continue: "I have a lot of questions. Can we talk?"

"*Bien sûr, mademoiselle.* I have been waiting for you to ask."

I sit down on the crude bench and Jean takes a seat across from me. I look him straight in the eyes and get right to the heart of the matter: "Why should I stay?"

"Mademoiselle," he says. "I can only imagine how confusing this is for you. It is confusing for me and Nicolas as well. As I told you, you were chosen to come back in time to perform something that neither I nor Nicolas can do to save Mont Saint Michel. I do not know what it is but Nicolas is convinced you will be successful because the mount still exists in the future."

"But what on earth can I do? What skills could I possibly have that could help you?"

"I cannot answer your question, mademoiselle. We will have to find that out together, but whatever it is, you will be successful."

"I asked you last night to call me Katelyn. Okay? Not Mademoiselle Katelyn, not Katelyn Michaels. Just Katelyn."

He smiles at me and says "okay."

Good, he can now use the word "okay" properly in a sentence. I have taught him well.

"I'm going to ask you again. Why should I stay? I'm sorry to tell you this, but I have no interest in you or Nicolas. I have no interest in Mont Saint Michel or its sacred abbey. I have no interest in being a Watchman." Actually, that's not entirely true, because I am really, I mean really interested in everything that has happened to me. I have just come whistling back through six hundred years of time, and I find that pretty darn interesting, but I'm not going to let him know that, and so I say: "I just want to get back to my time and to my brother. What can you tell me that could possibly convince me otherwise?"

"Mademoi . . ." he starts and then quickly corrects himself. "Katelyn, what I have to say to you is very important." He stops and appears to be choosing his words carefully. I don't know if it's because he's searching for the words in English or because he doesn't know what to say. But for once, I wait patiently without saying anything

"It will be hard for you to understand," he says, "and it may be very painful, but you must listen."

Okay, he has my attention but I'm not going to roll over and play dead. At least not yet!

"This mount, this island, this abbey . . . they are sacred. They represent freedom. It is vital that the mount survives the onslaught of the English."

"Why?" I ask. "Why on earth should I care about whether Mont Saint Michel falls into English hands or not? Why would I not choose to go back tonight?"

"Because you may not have anything to go back to."

Now he really has my attention. "What on earth are you talking about?" He looks at me, and although the skin around his eyes is wrinkled and saggy, his eyes are clear, and they pierce my soul.

"Nicolas and I were just as puzzled that a girl from the twenty-first century would be called back to help us. Then," he pauses, "let me be completely honest, when we met you last night, we were even more perplexed. It was evident that you did not want to be here. We talked about it last night. We could not understand why you were chosen to be a Watchman. After all, just as you say, you have no interest in us or in this mount. You have no interest in whether the French or the English prevail in this long war. So we asked ourselves why was it you?"

"And?" I ask.

"And . . . I think it was you for two reasons. The first, of course, is what I've already said. There are some skills you have that will help us be victorious. These skills must come from something you've learned in your time, or someone from our time period would have been called."

"Okay, even if I don't agree with that possibility, I'll agree to consider it," I say, "but what's the second reason?"

"The second reason is that you will be highly motivated to help us."

"Okay, see that's where you're wrong," I say almost pounding my fist on the table, but stopping short of making a loud noise. "I'm not highly motivated to do anything. Like I say, I just wanna go back. So what do you mean when you say there might not be anything to go back to?"

"Allow me to ask you a few questions and then I will answer yours. Katelyn, last night you spoke of your country. It is not a country Nicolas or I know. What is it called?"

"America. The United States of America." The words sound strange in this setting. They almost taste foreign in my own mouth.

"America," he says, and then repeats it again. "America. Tell me about your country. Where is it? How long has it existed?"

"How is this relevant?" I ask, frustrated that he's not answering my questions.

"I promise you that everything about your country is relevant to our discussion," he says. "Stop kicking against the pricks, Katelyn, and just answer my question."

I have no idea what he means when he says kicking against the pricks, but it doesn't sound pleasant so I decide I will appease him. He promised he'd get to my questions if I answered his. "Well, it's across the ocean from here," I say. "Far to the west."

"By England?" he asks.

"No, much further west than England. It's on a continent far across the ocean that your time doesn't even know about," I say and then think about it a bit longer. I mutter to myself: "Columbus sailed the ocean blue in fourteen hundred ninety-two. Yeah," I say, "my land will not be discovered until 1492 by an Italian named Christopher Columbus. There's a whole continent—well two continents actually—North and South America to the west across the ocean. Hundreds and hundreds of miles from here." I have no idea how far the American continent is from France, but I do know it's far. He probably doesn't know what a mile is anyway.

He looks at me with his eyes squinted and his lips pursed. He seems to be very focused on what I'm saying. "When it was—is," I say confused about how to speak about something that will happen in his future, but my past, "when it is discovered by Columbus, it will be called the New World."

"I do not understand your words: continent, miles," he says.

"It's a giant piece of land," I say trying to put it in words he will understand, "like France, Germany, Italy, and Spain all combined. Even bigger. And it's a long ways away. Many days traveling by boat. Maybe many months."

Heck, I have no idea how long it takes to go from Europe to America on a sailing ship. Guess I didn't pay much attention to the old Niña, Pinta and Santa Maria. Then I think about Leif Ericson. Wasn't he a Viking?

When did he live? It had to be long before Columbus. "Well, maybe some of the Scandinavians know about it—you know, like the Vikings? I think they sailed there before Columbus, but he's the one who gets the credit for discovering the New World."

"Scandinavia? Vikings?" he says trying to mimic my pronunciation exactly. "I don't know these words either."

I think some more. Where was Leif Ericson from? I don't know. I take a stab in the dark. "Do you know Norway?" I ask.

"Norway?" he replies. "The Norsemen?"

"Yeah, that's it. A Norseman by the name of Leif Ericson has already discovered the New World . . . I think."

"The Norsemen are the ones who gave *this* land its name," says Jean, making a half-circle gesture with his hands. "Norsemen invaded our shores many hundreds of years ago and some of them stayed. It came to be called *la Normandie*. There are many tales of the exploits of the Norsemen. I have heard legends about the great sailors who found land to the west. I thought they were just that—legends."

"Nope. They really did discover land," I say, actually feeling some enthusiasm for the conversation. Surprisingly, Jean is easy to talk to in spite of our language barrier. "They discovered my land. At least part of it is my land. There are many countries in this New World, but my country is the largest." *Is it?* I wonder. I'm not sure. Canada is pretty big, and so is Brazil, but I guess it's not like Jean is going to know if I'm wrong, so I continue. "And it is the most powerful. In fact, in my time, in the future, it becomes the most powerful country in the world. Although China and Russia have given us a run for our money. Well, it's certainly the most powerful democracy." Then I realize Jean probably can't understand what I'm saying, so I start over. "My country is a land where we have no king. We elect our leaders, and every man and woman has a vote. So we are the most powerful land of freedom in my time."

"Yes," he says. "That makes perfect sense. A land of freedom. But how is it that you speak English? Didn't your ancestors have their own language in that faraway land? I mean before they were discovered, as you say, by the Norsemen and then the Italian?"

"Well, the people who originally lived there—who live there now," I amend, once again getting bogged down by the time element, "have their own language. Many languages in fact. They are from many different tribes," I don't know if he will understand that word, and so I change it. "From many different groups. But they are not my ancestors. My ancestors came—will come—from Europe. Okay," I finally say. "I'm getting myself all confused. So even though this will happen in the future, it is in my past, so I'm going to use the past tense. Is that okay?" I ask.

"Okay," he says, using the hand signal.

"Okay," I answer back and actually smile at him before I realize what I'm doing. "Anyway, when the Europeans came—the people from your lands here—they found an indigenous" (yes, Mrs. Hunter, I do know some big words) "people whose civilization was not as advanced. Columbus named them Indians, because he thought he had sailed clear around the world to a country called India. He didn't realize he'd discovered a new land, because, well, the earth, this world is round," I try to explain, not knowing what he understands about the earth.

"The earth is round?"

"Yes," I say. "Like a ball." Jeez, I don't even know if they have balls in the fifteenth century, so I spread out the fingers of both hands and curve them around to touch each other, forming the best ball I can make. "Like a round stone," I amend. "If you start at the coast of France here, you can sail all around the world on the oceans, sailing around the land masses. You can go all the way around."

I can see he has many questions, but I don't want to get bogged down in these details. "We can talk of that later and I'll try to explain it better, but back to my country. Many Europeans wanted to live in the New World. Some wanted to get away from war, like you are experiencing here, some wanted to escape the tyranny of kings, but most wanted to go to a place where they could practice their religion without persecution. So they sailed across the ocean and made European settlements and then cities in the new land. The French went, the Spaniards went and the English went. And others. But most of the settlers in my country, in America, came from England."

"And what about the indigenous peoples. The Indians?" Jean asked.

It was not a pleasant topic, but I answered his question truthfully. "The Indians were not powerful enough to fight against these new settlers. Many of them were killed, or they died from diseases brought by the Europeans. Their descendants still exist in my country, but the dominant culture became the European settlers. And for America, that was the English. Most of my ancestors came from the British Isles," I say, but then realize he probably doesn't know that term. "From England," I amend. "That's why we speak English in America. But because these settlers were so far away from England for so long, our English is different from what they speak. I have a completely different accent and vocabulary than the English from England. And, then of course, there's another six hundred years of language evolution."

"And so the settlers from England made a new country?" Jean asks. He's completely focused on me, obviously concentrating on understanding.

"Yes, but it wasn't right away. The early settlers were considered English and the New World colonies belonged to England, but then the colonists revolted against England and fought a war in the 1700s to gain freedom from England. They did not like the English King taxing them and telling them what to do, especially when they lived so far away. They wanted to be free. Independent. They wanted to have a country where the people made their own rules and voted for their own leaders." There, I have given a five-minute lecture about democracy and the creation of the American Republic.

"Yes, Katelyn. Now I understand more fully. It makes perfect sense," Jean said.

"What makes sense?" I ask. "I can't see how any of this is relevant, how anything about my country can be important to this discussion."

"No, it *is* relevant, Katelyn. For your country, America, to break free of England in the future, your freedom fighters have need of France. You need France to be independent of England. Is that correct?"

"What do you mean is that correct?" I ask puzzled.

"You must know the history of your own country. Did France help America break free of England?" Jean asks.

I have to admit. He has me stumped. I'm not Jackson. I'm not a Renaissance woman. I don't know everything about everything. American History was in tenth grade and I didn't get an A. "I can't remember. I don't think so," I say. "France didn't have anything to do with it."

"Katelyn, are you certain?" he asks, pushing me to reconsider. "Maybe it wasn't the French rulers or soldiers. Maybe it was French culture or thinking that had an impact on your revolutionaries."

"Let me see," I say, digging as deep as I possibly can into my tenth grade memory. I seem to remember something about the Founding Fathers being influenced by a growing movement in France to do away with their monarchy. Or was it the other way around? Was it American independence that influenced the French Revolution? Then bits and pieces start to nibble around the shadowy recesses of my mind.

"Yeah. I think that's it," I say. "It started with philosophy. The men who founded my country were influenced by a movement called the Enlightenment, which was spread by French writers and philosophers. The new way of thinking influenced those who founded my country to break away from old forms of government. And now, I remember. At least one of the founding fathers, a man by the name of Benjamin Franklin, traveled to France to drum up support during the Revolutionary War—America's war with England. The French saw it as a way to weaken its long-time enemy, so they sided with the Americans."

"So even in the 1700s, France and England are still enemies," Jean interjects.

"Yeah, it's not until World War I that they become allies," I say and then regret opening up another can of worms. Besides, I'm not sure just when France and England stopped hating each other. Maybe it was long before World War I. On the other hand, maybe they still hate each other. I don't know. That's what Jackson's for.

"Just forget that," I say. "Yeah, in the 1700s, France and England continued to fight for superiority. They were each trying to build the strongest and most powerful empire—to control colonies they founded all over the globe—the earth. Yeah, I think the French sided with the Americans just to go against England. Did France give money or troops to the Americans? I don't know. I'm sorry," I say and then remember one more thing. "Hey, I know there was a French nobleman named Lafayette, who came and fought alongside the Americans. And I think there were others. But that's all I can think of. Whether or not the French support was enough to help the Americans win the war, I can't tell you."

"I think it must have been, Katelyn." The old man places his hand over mine and squeezes it gently.

"Why do you think that?" I ask, still wondering what this has to do with my dilemma.

"You asked me why I thought you were chosen to come back in time, and I told you that one of the reasons was that you would be highly motivated to do what you were called to do here. The reason you will be motivated is that you need France to be independent from England for America to be born. If we fail here, if we fail to repel the English invasion of Mont Saint Michel, I believe all of France will fall to England. Mont Saint Michel is a powerful symbol for France. If we fall, the rest of France will give up hope. There will be no France as we know it. It will all be part of England. And without France, I don't believe your country will be born."

"That's ridiculous," I say. But I'm not sure if it's ridiculous or not. I wish I'd paid more attention in History. "And even if you're right, what does it mean for me?"

"Katelyn," he says, looking at me with piercing eyes. "You can leave tonight to go back to the future, but if you do not succeed in helping us, your future may not be the same one you left. You may not even be an American. You may not even have your same family. Your brother may not exist. It is a distinct possibility that everything will be changed. Are you willing to take that chance?"

His words take my breath away. I pull my hand away from him gasping. "No, it's not possible! If I was there on the mount when Nicolas came to get me, then I would go back to the same place because I was already there!"

"Katelyn," Jean says slowly in a soft voice, as if by controlling his volume he can control my level of panic, "you were there because you succeeded in your mission six hundred years before you were born.

However, your future is not written in stone. If you choose not to perform your mission now, or if you go back before it is complete, you will change not only your future, but perhaps the world's future. Again, I ask you: are you willing to take that chance?"

"I can't wrap my mind around what you're saying." I shake my head and put my hands over my ears, trying to control the rising panic. None of what he says makes sense. It simply isn't possible. He sits and watches me patiently as I take five deep breaths and then I say, "If it has already happened in my past, then . . ." But I can't articulate my complete confusion.

"It is difficult to comprehend," says Jean. "because the mortal mind cannot conceive of time the way God sees time. For Him, time is not linear, the way we think of it. It is relative, eternal, ever-present. The past, present and future are one. Do not try to understand, just know this truth. Katelyn Michaels, if you do not do exactly what you were called to do here in 1424, I cannot guarantee that your future will be the same."

I'm stunned. I don't know whether to believe him or not. He may be trying to use scare tactics to convince me to stay, but the reality is this: do I dare take the chance of going back even if he isn't right? I don't think I do. And so I'd better figure out just what I—seventeen-year-old Katelyn Michaels, a better-than-average-student, but certainly not much more than that—can possibly do to defeat the English army in Normandy. And I better do it as quickly as I can, because I'm getting really hungry.

Chapter 21

WHEN NICOLAS ENTERED the house with his large bundle, he was pleased to see Jean speaking with the girl. Hopefully, his wise old mentor had convinced Katelyn Michaels to stay and Nicolas would not have to join in the difficult conversation. He'd left early that morning to avoid facing Katelyn when she awoke. He'd been so furious with her last night, but then his dreams had been filled with her. That braid hanging down her back like a hangman's noose. Her belligerent eyes. That strident way of walking and incomprehensible way of talking. And yet the dream had not been a nightmare. Far from it. It was confusing and troubling. Why couldn't things just stay the same? Just him and Jean. Why did the girl have to come?

"Ah, mon fils. Tu es de retour enfin," Jean said, then quickly changed to English. "You are back. Please join us. We have just had a discussion and I think Mademoiselle Katelyn has decided to stay with us."

The man's a miracle worker, thought Nicolas, but he didn't say anything out loud. He just sat, feeling more and more uncomfortable as the girl looked at him with her air of superiority. The girl didn't say a word either.

"So, I hope you found what you needed," Jean said breaking the thick silence as he looked from Nicolas to Katelyn. His brows were knit together as if he were puzzled and he drummed his fingers lightly on the table.

"Oui," replied Nicolas. *"Madame Mercier a été très gentille."*

"English please, Nicolas. Remember our . . . guest."

Jean clearly doesn't know how to label Katelyn either, thought Nicolas. *Is she a guest or a pest? A Watchman or an enemy who needs watching?*

"Hadn't you better give your . . . your acquisitions to Mademoiselle Michaels?" Jean prodded.

"It's Katelyn," the girl said with that exasperated tone in her voice. "Jeez, can't you guys get the message? Katelyn, plain and simple!" She slapped her hand on the table and Nicolas hoped it hurt.

Great, Nicolas seethed. *I can see that Jean's sacrifice to provide her with the most comfortable bed possible did little to improve her disposition. Too bad we did not force her to sleep on the floor. That's what she deserves! I'm ready to take Widow Mercier's bed curtains and wring her scrawny little neck with them.*

"You must excuse us, Katelyn," Jean interjected. "We are not used to being on such informal terms with such a lovely young lady as you and in our culture, it is almost an insult to address you without using the appropriate title. We cannot restrain ourselves. I fear there will be many more slips of the tongue, so I hope you will forgive us in advance."

What does she have to forgive us *for?* Nicolas thought with rising anger. *She is the one who should be asking for* our *forgiveness. For her intolerable behavior. The impudent little weasel. We've done everything we could possibly do to make her comfortable here. Who does she think she is? The Queen of France?*

"I'm sorry," she said, shocking Nicolas to the point where he almost gasped out loud. Almost, but not quite. "I overreacted," she continued. "I understand this is hard for you as well. In my world, we address each other by our given names and I'm not used to this formality. I realize you're showing respect. I'll try to adjust. It's okay if you call me Mademoiselle Katelyn."

Her words pricked Nicolas like the sting of the honey bee in the stone quarry last month, when he'd been trying to extract honey from its hive. It was almost as if Katelyn had read his thoughts and just to spite him, chose to envelope her words in the sweetness of honey. It caught him completely off guard and made him even more uncomfortable. And even madder.

"Well, Nicolas. Are you going to show us your treasures?" Jean asked.

Nicolas swallowed and laid the bundle on the table, unwrapping it carefully.

"Our kind neighbor has provided appropriate clothing for you," Nicolas said in a voice that didn't even remotely sound like his own. It was high-pitched and clumsy. He cleared his throat and continued, hardly daring to look Katelyn in the eyes. "These garments belonged to her deceased daughter and she has sent them for your use while you are here."

He pulled out a beautifully-crafted brocade gown with bits of golden threading and displayed it reverently across his arm. It was attire worn in better times. It had been a true gift of the heart for their kind neighbor to offer these treasures. They were her last connection to her only daughter, a beautiful young maiden who had died many years ago of the bloody flux, just a week after her betrothal. The Widow Mercier had never recovered from the loss. It was incredibly generous of her to allow Nicolas to borrow the precious apparel.

"Are you kidding me," the vixen answered. "You actually expect me to wear this?"

"Mademoiselle," Jean chimed in immediately. "Remember your circumstances. There will be many questions about your presence here. You must do your best to fit into our time and our culture to prevent speculative rumors."

"Oh my heavens," the girl groaned as she pawed at the beautiful gown. "How do you expect me to function in this? Not only will I be unable to figure out how I'm going to help you, but I won't even be able to walk!"

"You are right, my dear. That may be a bit restrictive," Jean said, as Nicolas looked on in dismay. Surely Jean was not going to be a traitor. "Keep searching." he continued. "I'm certain you will find something that will be acceptable to both the Montois and to you."

Nicolas watched with horror as she placed garment after garment into what he knew was her 'unacceptable' pile until finally she settled on a plain muslin gown with wide long sleeves and gathering just under the breast. It looked more like an undergarment than acceptable day wear.

"Okay, I guess I can settle on this," she said, "but I'll have you know it's not gonna be easy! And I'm not, I mean NOT giving up my sneakers."

Nicolas had no idea what sneakers were and quite frankly, he had little inclination to find out. He was so angry he could hardly focus.

"Here, you can take these back to your sweet," she said the word 'sweet' like the hissing of a snake, "neighbor." She stood and shoved the pile towards him, taking no heed of the possibility of snagging delicate threads on the rough surface of the table.

"And tell her . . ." The girl stopped in mid-sentence, sat down and did the most unexpected thing of all. She started crying.

"I'm sorry," she said again. "I'm just so doggone mad and confused and hungry and I just want to go home, only I can't go home because you tell me that there may be no home to go home to, and I'm just so mixed-up. And I desperately want a shower!"

Nicolas didn't understand much of her diatribe and he didn't care. He was not interested in her petty grievances. He was disgusted to see Jean stand up, walk around the table, and enfold the girl in his arms. Surprisingly, she collapsed against Jean's feeble chest and continued to sob as the old man gently patted her back and comforted her with whispered words and tender gestures. It was positively disgusting, and yet there was a part of Nicolas that wished he had thought of taking Katelyn Michaels into his arms.

His feelings were utterly out of control. They vacillated about as much as that wine-bibber of an abbot, Robert Jolivet, when he had to choose his favorite ale. Nicolas had no idea of what was happening to him. He was furious with Katelyn Michaels and envious of Jean all in the same instant. He wanted to scream at the ungrateful shrew and yet he also wanted to smooth her tangled locks and dry her tears as Jean was doing. He had many things still to learn from his mentor and perhaps the most important of all was how to deal with Katelyn Michaels. Jean le Vieux seemed completely able to quench her tears and calm her fears. And Nicolas was . . . well quite frankly, he was jealous. Jean clearly had a skill he hadn't yet shared with his pupil.

The vexed young man sat down in frustration and kept his mouth firmly shut.

"Now, now Mademoiselle," he overheard Jean whisper, "Everything is going to be . . . okay."

Oh, the disgust of it all. She even has the old man using her twenty-first century words.

Nicolas was fighting a battle he couldn't win and he was a poor loser. A very poor loser. He picked up the pile of clothing, carefully wrapped the gowns back up in their neat bundle, and stomped out the door in disgust. And neither Jean nor Katelyn did anything to stop him.

By the time he knocked on Madame Mercier's door, he had gained control of his outward emotions, but he was still fuming on the inside.

"Nicolas," the Widow Mercier said with surprise as she looked at the bundle. "*Qu'est-ce qu'il y a?* What is the matter? Does the clothing not fit? Is it not pleasing to her?"

"No, no, *ma chère Madame.* It is very pleasing to her," he lied, quickly trying to think of how he was going to handle the situation. Finally an idea came to him. "But she cannot bring herself to don such elegant apparel. She has no desire to flaunt herself when the *Montois* have so little. And she knows how precious these garments are to you and although she has practically no raiment left to speak of, she prefers to dress in men's clothing. She dressed as a man on our journey here because we deemed it to be safer for us both. However, she selected one simple muslin gown to borrow. Just for the celebration."

"Oh, my poor dear girl," the frail wisp of a woman said. She wiped at what seemed to Nicolas to be an imaginary tear. "How she must have suffered to breach the enemy lines to come with you. And how unselfish and thoughtful she is. She is thinking not only of me, but of the poor women in this cursed village who cover themselves with nothing but rags. Truly you have found a treasure, Nicolas. A gem among gems. To think that so as not to offend us, she chooses to wear men's pantaloons and shirts rather than these luxurious gowns, it is almost too much to believe. I saw her in the window, lad, and she is truly as beautiful as she is good and kind."

Yes, thought Nicolas, *she is about as good and kind as the killing sands of the great bay. She pulls you in with her beguiling ways and then smothers you until you die gasping for breath!*

"Yes," he said out loud, "she is unusual in her kindness."

Very unusual, indeed. In fact, her kindness is so unusual, it is impossible to put into words!

"I shall look forward to having her call upon me at the first opportunity she has to venture beyond the security of your home," the widow said. "She must be suffering from the ill-effects of her long and dangerous voyage here. And certainly she is disoriented and must find this place strange, especially as she does not speak our language. And of course, the most amazing part is that she has accepted the grimness of our situation, the penury of food and supplies, and that she is willing to fight alongside us as we battle our common enemy."

"Yes, she has agreed to that, and I can assure you that she is just as anxious to meet you, *chère* Madame, as you are to meet her. She has already expressed her great appreciation for the beautiful bed curtains you so kindly donated to our cause."

Those curtains I want to strangle her with!

"Well, if she shan't accept the clothing, at least I can contribute in a small way with the curtains. Offer a bit of privacy, you know. It is but a small token of my esteem for you, Nicolas. We have made plans for the celebration to be held the day after tomorrow. I hope that will allow her enough time to sufficiently recover from her ordeal."

"I hope that will be the case," said Nicolas, "But I beg for you and the other women to be patient with her. She suffers from bouts of terror, not only from the difficult journey, but from the unspeakable horrors and atrocities she saw perpetrated by the English soldiers in her village. When this happens, she can break out into fits of folly," Nicolas said, anticipating more of the shrew's untenable outbursts. "In fact, you may have heard her screaming last night. It was all I could do to assure her that she was safe, that we were finally here, but alas, one cannot always predict the ways in which a tender heart might twist reality."

Tender heart indeed!

"The poor, brave child," Madame Mercier said and this time, Nicolas actually saw a tear on her cheek. "We shall love and embrace her as one of our own."

"Thank you, dearest neighbor. I am hoping that with time, she will come to feel safe here among us, but she has suffered greatly from her ordeal. And I fear she will suffer even more when she learns the extent of this abominable siege."

And from learning she is my wife!

Chapter 22

JEAN WAS SO TIRED. Tired of the suffering, the violence, the disease, the hunger, the crying babes whose mothers' dried up breasts could not keep them from starvation. It wasn't his own suffering he could not endure. It was the suffering of others. He was tired of mortality. Jean wanted to close his eyes and pass into the next glorious phase of existence. He was ready to be greeted by Marie's welcoming smile and the warm embrace of his beloved son Michel.

He had given everything to his calling and served with every ounce of physical and emotional strength, and he could do no more. And yet, as if his physical body were an entity of its own, it would not allow him to go. And here he was now acting as an arbiter between his two young charges who acted like they had never said a civil word to a member of the opposite sex.

The Montois had neither the time nor the strength to wait for these two dueling adolescents to resolve their differences and so with a sigh, Jean prepared himself for another day, another week, perhaps another month. He understood his duty. He had to shape and mold the girl, and he had to do it as quickly as possible. And while he was doing that, he had to remind Nicolas of his destiny as well.

With a sigh, the old man pulled up Marie's chair and gently lowered Katelyn Michaels onto it.

"Sit down, mademoiselle," he said with as much authority and firmness as he could muster. "I can only begin to imagine the shock and sense of disorientation you must feel. Conditions here are not like your world. I understand that. But this is our reality and you are here to help us, not condemn us. Villagers are dying of starvation as we speak. And you sit there with heartier food before you than they have seen in months," he said as he pointed to her uneaten stew, "and yet you treat it with disdain."

As he looked into her eyes, he wondered if he had been too harsh. He could see the tears forming again in her eyes, and a single droplet spilled over her eyelid and worked its way down her cheek. She brushed it away and then wiped her eyes with her flat palms.

"Monsieur Jean," she replied with control of her voice. "I'm sorry. I really am. I'm not a bad person. I'm not a spoiled brat as you both probably think, but I've just never been placed in a situation like this, and everything is so . . . different. I keep thinking I'm going to wake up from a horrible nightmare and yet, I'm still here. It's going to take some time for me to adjust."

"Unfortunately, mademoiselle, we do not have the luxury of time on our side. We cannot wait for you to make adjustments."

"I'm sorry," she said again, and this time Jean saw the pleading in her eyes and the sincerity in her voice.

He softened his tone and said, "I hope you understand, Katelyn. You and Nicolas have more important things to do than to foment discord. You say you want to return to your time, but if that is so, then you must learn to bridle your anger, to temper your emotions. There will be many things more significant than the manner of dress that you will find distasteful about our circumstances, but those things cannot be changed. You and Nicolas must learn to work together or we shall never succeed. A Kingdom divided against itself shall be brought to desolation and a house divided against itself shall not stand."

"I've never had the fate of the world resting on my shoulders," she said. "At least not the fate of America." Her voice was soft, but steady, and there were no more tears. "You know, it's kind of a heavy burden for an average seventeen-year-old girl who's never had to worry about where her next meal is coming from. I've been faced with the challenge of adjusting to difficult circumstances before, and I'm afraid I've been a dismal failure. That's why I can't imagine why I've been 'called' as you say to be a Watchman. Someone got it wrong. Really wrong."

As he looked at her, Jean read profound sadness in her eyes. He'd misjudged her. He'd thought she had never known tribulation, but he could see he'd been woefully mistaken. This girl had a deep scar in her heart. She knew sorrow. He instantly regretted his harsh outburst.

"Will you tell me about it?" he asked. "About your difficult circumstances."

"It will seem insignificant to you. No one died. No one is starving to death. It's my family. My mother and my brother. The reason I'm so anxious to get back to my time is because I am responsible for my mother and my brother. I've got to get back to them. They need me."

"What do you mean? You mean they depend upon you for sustenance?"

"No, that's not what I mean. They depend upon me emotionally. My father left us. He abandoned us. He left my mother for another woman, a Frenchwoman. A despicable Frenchwoman. He lives in Paris now and my mother is in America—all alone. With complete unselfishness she sent us off to France to visit our father. Her last words to me were: 'Be safe Katelyn, and take care of your brother. Both of you come back to me.' If I don't return, she'll die of a broken heart. She won't survive. And my brother. He tries so hard to act mature and grown up, but I know he's dying inside. I have to get back to them. I have to take care of them."

"But you speak of having failed in difficult circumstances. You have not failed them, my dear. You will return to them."

"Oh no, I've failed all right. My father made that very clear to me. You see, I've failed to adjust to my new reality. My shattered family. When Dad left, he told me I needed to change my thinking from what my accepted point of view of what a family is to a new point of view. He called it a paradigm shift. When we got to Paris, and I let my feelings out about his new wife, he told me how disappointed he was in me that I couldn't make the paradigm shift. Well, I guess this," she said, spreading her arms apart to indicate the room in which they sat, "is just about the biggest paradigm shift I'll ever have to make, and I'll probably fail here as well. The irony of it all is that if I don't succeed here, I just might zap away my Dad . . . and his new wife. It's almost worth thinking about. Starting all over with a new family and a new reality. But I could never do that to my mother or brother. Never."

"Well, my dear, thank you for sharing that with me. And contrary to what you might think, you have only strengthened my conviction that you *are* the right one to be called." Jean thought of his beloved Marie. And his son. The helplessness he'd felt at not being able to prevent Michel's death.

The sorrow he felt when Marie chose another path. He and Katelyn Michaels were not so different, after all. Family was everything to them.

"Why would you possibly think that?" she asked. "I can't forgive my father and I hate my stepmother. There's nothing praiseworthy about that."

"Yes, that's true. Being unable to forgive is a canker that destroys souls. You must learn to forgive them but that discussion is for another day. But seeing the sense of responsibility you feel towards your mother and brother shows me the depth of your character. You may hide behind your age and inexperience but in many ways, you are wise beyond your years. Katelyn, you are not responsible for your brother or your mother. It is the other way around. Your mother and father are responsible for you and your brother, and yet you, seeing your mother's grief, have willingly taken on the role of protector. Without being asked. You are not being asked to do anything different now. It is just on a larger scale. Here, you are being called upon to be the protector of these people, the Montois. And protector of the mount. But, my dear, you are not alone. You have help and you must learn to trust that help. You must trust me and Nicolas."

"Okay," she said. "I give you my word that I'll do my best. I can't promise that I won't lose it from time to time, but I swear I'll try my hardest."

Jean didn't know what 'lose it,' meant, but he understood the context. The girl was ready to assume her role as a Watchman. He was glad he'd had the opportunity to have this discussion in Nicolas's absence. He would continue to respect the young man's wishes and refrain from revealing the true nature of the Watchmen's responsibilities to Katelyn Michaels. Nicolas himself would have to make the decision to tell her at some future point. For the present, Jean would tutor her as he had tutored Nicolas, and a renewed feeling of purpose strengthened his weak body. It illuminated his mind and rekindled the warmth that had nearly been extinguished in his heart.

For a brief instant, he wished he could be there to watch Katelyn Michaels fill the measure of her creation, but the lot had been cast and it was too late to turn back. He could be there to mold the soft clay, to suggest to the artist a method, but Nicolas would be the master sculptor. He would be the one to remove the blemishes, smooth the stone, and add the final touches. Jean suspected that the finished work would be a masterpiece.

"Good," Jean said. "We cannot afford to waste another day. The truth is that I am weak and my days are numbered, but I must prepare you for your assignment and we will begin now. We must begin your preparation now. Remain here, Katelyn. I will find Nicolas. He should be here with us."

As he opened the door and looked back at her, he added, "And besides, he has something very important to tell you."

Part Three

Set up the standard upon the walls . . .
Make the watch strong, set up the watchmen,
Prepare the ambushes:

Jeremiah 51:12

Chapter 23

AND SO IT BEGAN. The French lessons. The training. Along with my attempts to keep my cool and the less successful attempts made by Nicolas to refrain from killing me.

But first we had to handle some basic operating business. Like the wife stuff.

I deserve a lot of credit for the 'keeping my cool' part. I mean, A lot of credit! I actually managed to keep from screaming out loud when Nicolas informed me that I was his beloved bride. Yes, I'm a child bride and it seems this sort of thing is okay around here. Some girls get married here at age twelve. Twelve! So seventeen is more than okay. And Nicolas is nineteen. He's practically over the hill. Heck, it's a cause for celebration. The Montois want to kill the fatted calf for the bride and bridegroom. Except there's no fatted calf, just the Widow Mercier's bed curtains. And of course all of her daughter's gowns that I just refused to wear. That one brocade number alone that Nicolas tried to get me to wear must have weighed at least a hundred pounds. Can't you just see Katelyn dashing about fighting the English with an extra person draped around her body?

But hey, I ended up a winner from that little wardrobe fiasco. Nicolas told me that by refusing to wear 'those exquisite gowns,' I had managed to endear myself even more to Madame Mercier and the rest of the village women because it seems the widow spread the word quickly about 'Sainte Katelyn,' Nicolas's young bride, who preferred to suffer the indignity of wearing men's clothing rather than flaunt her youthful figure in linen and brocade gowns when the village women had nothing in comparison. They had only threadbare rags. Yeah, good old Sainte Katelyn.

But heck, it was all worth it because now I can get away with wearing my capris (well, my rolled-down capris), t-shirt, and windbreaker. And am I ever glad they're made of that nyloney stuff that you can wash and dry in a matter of minutes. Wow, can you imagine trying to keep brocade or velvet clean without a washing machine or a drycleaners? Nope, give me twenty-first century fabric any day. Oh, and I get to wear my tennis shoes as well. Nicolas has warned everyone about my strange Breton *sabots*. That's the French word for clogs.

And yes, that's the second part. It seems I am from Brittany. After all, there had to be an explanation for the mysterious young woman who suddenly appeared on the island and so I am now *la Bretonne*, and a bride. I don't know much about Brittany but from what they've told me, it's a pretty good cover story. Brittany is the westernmost region of France that juts out into the Atlantic Ocean. It's what Jean calls a duchy and he explained that in his time, it has gone back and forth in its alliances between England and France. Right now, the Bretons are siding with the French. So, the English are a common enemy of the Normans and Bretons.

I remember the drive from Paris when the Frenchwoman told us about the Couesnon River that empties into the Saint Michel Bay and provides a natural border between Normandy and Brittany. I even remember her explaining the centuries-old feud between the two regions over possession of Mont Saint Michel. She told me and Jackson that the mount used to be in Brittany, but a violent storm in medieval times actually changed the course of the river.

I can actually hear her voice saying: "Every French school child knows zee couplet: *'Le Couesnon en sa folie, mit le Mont en Normandie.'* Zat means: 'Zee Couesnon's madness placed zee Mount in Normandy.'"

I know the mount is in Normandy now, so I guess that storm has already happened. I haven't had a chance yet to ask Jean if he lived through it, but it had to be one heck of a storm.

But I am not just a Bretonne from across the river. No, I am from what they call *La Bretagne Profonde*. You see, that's where Nicolas is from. I've learned that the Montois call him 'Nicolas le Breton.' The good news is that very few of the peasants from the heart of Brittany speak French. They speak Breton, a Celtic language, like Welsh. So the fact that I don't speak French is easily explained. I'm a simple Bretonne peasant. Yep, a peasant. But hey, it works. Nicolas informed me that because English is such a guttural language like the Celtic languages, no one around here will be able to tell if I'm speaking English or Breton. That's a relief, since I don't want to be shot first and have questions asked later. But then, I don't even know if they have guns in 1424. I don't think they do. But they have cannons. I mean, I know the English have cannons, because I've seen one of them. In the future.

Anyway, here's the story Jean and Nicolas concocted to explain my sudden appearance on the mount. I was Nicolas's childhood sweetheart and when he left on his pilgrimage to Mont Saint Michel, he vowed to return for me, but the war had made it impossible. Finally, he could bear it no longer. He would brave any danger to claim his bride. What a beautiful story: two star-crossed lovers separated from each other by an enemy army and miles of tortuous territory. Actually we were separated by *lieues,* the French version of an English league. I learned from Jean that one *lieue* is about ten thousand feet, so that's roughly two miles. I wonder if that little bit of trivia will help me get that A on my Medieval France paper I'm planning on writing.

Back to the cover story: after so many months of being separated, Nicolas devised a plan to escape the island to find me, working his way through a myriad of dangers the entire way. You know, kind of like the Cliffs of Insanity and the Pit of Despair in my favorite classic movie, *The Princess Bride.* And of course, because he could not abandon the Montois in their hour of need, he vowed to return with me, his one true love. So I guess that makes me Buttercup and him Westley. And yes, he found me, because as Westley said, 'I will always come for you.' So together, we braved the Fire Swamp, avoiding the flame spurt, fighting the R.O.U.S.'s (Rodents Of Unusual Size), and navigating the lightning sands to return to our kingdom. Hey, we did have to deal with Abdon and his Gothmen, didn't we? So it's not that far-fetched. And it fits me perfectly. Whenever I had to get through a difficult challenge or survive an impossible swimming workout, I always referred to it as crossing the 'Fire Swamp.' So, this is perfect. It's a lovely little story in which I am portrayed as the heroine. Anything else would be inconceivable, and I mean it. (Anybody want a peanut?)

It is, in fact, a miraculous story, since no one has made it through enemy lines in months, but apparently, the Montois have a lot of faith in Nicolas. And now they have a lot of faith in me as well, as I learned when Nicolas presented his bride to the village matriarchs, gathered at Madame

Mercier's home. That's when I heard the news about our upcoming wedding. I think Nicolas did that on purpose. I mean breaking the news to me in front of the admiring onlookers. So I couldn't back out on my promise to Jean, and find a knife.

You see, after Nicolas informed the population that we had been married in a simple ceremony before leaving Brittany, the parish priest insisted we hold a Norman ceremony and celebration for the entire village. Nicolas tried to convince him that it wasn't necessary, but it was a hopeless cause. After all, there are few occasions to celebrate on Mont Saint Michel.

It must have been after his discussion with the priest that Nicolas decided to break the news to me at Madame Mercier's. After all, it was one thing to tell everyone we were married, but it was a totally different thing to actually get married! I would have been afraid of me if I'd been him. But he calculated his risks carefully. He figured I'd try to control myself in front of others. And those others would be a group of helpless, starving old women. I'd have to be completely crazy and heartless to lose it in front of them.

But I think he did have a moment of fear. The blood drained from my face when, in both languages, he made the big announcement of our wedding, and everyone saw it happen. The room went silent and they all looked frightened that I might go ballistic. They kept their distance, watching my face go from pallid chalk to blotchy red. At that point, Nicolas said something to them in French, and the crisis must have passed, because they all surrounded me with very solicitous gestures.

"What did you say," I asked him.

"I told them you were suffering from the ordeal we've been through and the thought of planning a wedding was just too much for you."

"That's all you said?" I probed, pretty certain there was more to it than that.

"Well that and the fact that you occasionally have fits of folly."

"Great, so they think I'm a psycho?"

"I do not understand what that means, but it is probably accurate!" He whispered that in my ear sarcastically and then brushed his lips along my cheek for the benefit of the women. I had a really hard time not wiping off his germs, but the show must go on. And I had to remind myself that these were starving women.

They all spoke to me at once at the speed of lightning in their high-pitched voices. It sounded like the singing birds in the Tiki Room. Only without music. And without birds. I turned to Nicolas for translation.

"Madame Katelyn. We will take care of all the details. You are not to worry. You just come and look beautiful," he translated.

Oh double great. Now they actually expect me to look beautiful? And to look adoringly at my husband? Could it possibly get any worse? Yeah, I'm now a madame instead of a mademoiselle, and in my world, that doesn't sound too good.

Madame Mercier and her cronies were happy to plan everything. Of course, there would be no feast, because there was no food but everything else would be taken care of for the poor, unfortunate bride who was suffering from post-traumatic stress syndrome.

"I've never seen them so happy," Nicolas said. "And nothing will lift the Montois' spirits more than a wedding, especially when it is considered to be a marriage of love," he added with a wink.

After we left Madame Mercier's home, I made it very clear to Nicolas that this was a marriage in name only and he didn't fight me on that point. I figured that by the time I got back to the twenty-first century, he'd be long dead so I wouldn't even have to worry about a quickie divorce. But Love? A marriage of love? Not.

We'd be lucky if we survived the ceremony without killing each other.

Chapter 24

SO TOMORROW, I AM to be married—at least in the eyes of the Holy Roman Catholic Church. I don't even scream out loud when Nicolas and I return to Jean's home—or should I call it the 'fantasy suite'—to spread the great news.

Nicolas tells me our marriage will take place at the village church, not the abbey church, which is reserved for the rich and the noble. It seems an abbot doesn't waste his time with mere peasants. Besides, Nicolas tells me, the abbot, a man named Robert Jolivet, has deserted his post and thrown in his lot with the English. He is currently advising the English Duke of Bedford who has controlled Normandy for nearly ten years now. The abbot is considered a traitor by the monks and the Montois.

But the village priest is happy to officiate in our mockery of a marriage in exchange for a rotting cabbage. So that's about the truth of what I'm worth around here—one rotting cabbage.

After Nicolas leaves us alone to post the banns with the priest, I ask Jean just exactly what that entails.

He explains to me that a notice must be posted on the door of the church to ensure that there are no grounds for prohibiting the marriage. No impediments. Like an existing wife or consanguinity. You know, like being cousins. Yuck. Or if either Nicolas or I have taken religious vows. I wish!

"The banns have to be posted even when they think we're already married?" I ask.

"Well, this is merely a formality since the priest does believe you are married. But he wants to make certain. Just in case. The Norman clergy don't trust the Breton clergy. For centuries, they've accused each other of heresy. I've seen that attitude at the Abbey. We once had a Breton abbot appointed and there was a wide-spread rebellion among the monks. So the priest just wants to confirm the authenticity of the ceremony. But even so, he has made some concessions. Technically, banns are supposed to be posted by the priests of both parties and on three consecutive Holy Days. That requirement has been waived."

"So the truth is, the priest just wants to make sure our marriage is legal in case Nicolas lied."

"Yes," Jean admits.

"Which he did," I add, so exasperated I can hardly contain my anger. I hit my fist on the table. I seemed to be doing that a lot lately.

"Yes. I'm sorry Katelyn," Jean says as he takes my hand and looks into my eyes. He seems to be doing that a lot lately, too. I can tell he's attempting to gauge my level of rage.

"We thought our story was foolproof," he continued. "I did not expect this to happen, and now I do not see any way out of it. If we protest, the priest will know we lied. And it is not appropriate for two young people to co-habit without the sanction of marriage. It would not be acceptable."

"Why didn't you just make up a story about my being his sister?" I ask, pulling my hand away.

"We thought of that, but it just did not make sense that he would make that dangerous journey for his little sister or that he would want to bring her back here. No, it could only be justified for a bride."

He looks so tired and frail and I feel guilty for raking him over the coals. I should be doing that to Nicolas, not Jean. But I don't think Nicolas would survive my interrogation if I had to face him right now, in spite of my promise to Jean. I'm just so incredibly mad.

Then I tell him what Nicolas said at Madame Mercier's. When he used the 'L' word.

"Honestly," I say. "You should be proud of me. When he said it was a marriage of love, I bit my tongue so hard I drew blood. I'm doing my best to keep my promise not to lose it, but why did he have to say that? Couldn't he just leave me a tiny bit of dignity? Did he have to rub my nose in it?"

"Katelyn, allow me to explain why this is perceived as a reason to celebrate. Especially for the women."

"Go ahead," I say, but I don't really want to know.

"I do not know your marriage customs," Jean begins. "Why do people get married in your time?"

"They get married because they fall in love," I answer sharply. "At least in most of the world. In France. In England. In America."

"Then why are you so offended that Nicolas calls this a marriage of love?"

"Because it isn't," I answer just as sharply.

"In our time, it is very rare for a couple to marry for love. Most marriages are arranged by the families, based on the benefits the bride and groom bring to the union. Mostly based on what the bride brings, actually. Most women have no say in who they marry. Many of them do not even know their future husbands."

"Oh, you mean like . . . me?" I ask, not willing to pass up an opportunity to get in my two-cents worth.

"Justified," said Jean. "But you have to realize that you would be considered a poor choice as a bride. You bring no land, no cattle, no goods, no dowry."

"That's right, I'm just a pathetic Breton peasant."

"Yes, but don't you see? That is what makes your story so compelling to the women. To them, you are a woman for whom a man has made every sacrifice. You have no dowry and yet Nicolas braved the dangers of the journey to bring you back. He was willing to lose his very life to marry you and love was his only motivation. You are a heroine for the women who often feel like chattel, bought and sold to the highest bidder. It is no wonder they wish to celebrate. They perceive your story to be what legends are made of, like the *Romans Courtois"*

"The what?"

"They are tales of courtly love. They are written in verse. Perhaps some of these tales have endured to your time. Tristan and Iseut, the *Roman de la Rose,* the Tales of Arthur?"

"Arthur? You mean like King Arthur? You know about King Arthur here in Normandy?"

"Of course. It was a French poet, Chrétien de Troyes, who wrote of Arthur and Lancelot, and of their love for Guinevere. T'was many years ago. Centuries even. But these tales have been told and retold for generations. Before the mount was under siege, troubadours sang these stories of love in the village. Everyone knows them, even though the people are illiterate. For the women, you are their living, breathing Guinevere. A woman so loved that no sacrifice is too great."

"Well, things haven't really changed much in six hundred years," I concede. "In my time, women love the same kinds of stories. Maybe the settings have changed, but the feelings are just the same."

"And so you understand," he says.

"And so I understand," I say.

I am their Guinevere and yet, not really. It's all a sham, and these poor, wretched women are victims just like me. Besides, as I recall, things didn't work out too well for Guinevere. And although Nicolas did make a dangerous voyage to bring me back, it certainly wasn't because of love. It was out of duty. And even though I don't know these women, I suddenly care about them. I don't want to disappoint them. Their lives are so bleak. They deserve a moment of happiness, if only for a day.

"What can I do to help you prepare for tomorrow. Surely you do not wish to attend your wedding dressed like that?" Jean looks at my modern attire and frowns.

"What I really want is a shower," I say. "How on earth do the women here stand not being able to wash their hair?"

"A shower?"

"A bath—you know, to bathe and wash my body. And my hair. With hot water?"

"Alas, t'is not possible, Mademoiselle. What little sweet water we have is reserved for drinking purposes. For everything else, we rely on seawater."

"You've got to be kidding," I moan.

"Kidding?" he asks.

"You know, teasing, joking?" I say. "Not telling me the truth," I amend, when I see his look of confusion. I've got to learn to choose my words more carefully because explaining every single thing I say is getting old real fast.

"No, I assure you Katelyn, I am telling you the truth. If you desire to bathe, it will have to be in the ocean. But I cannot conceive you would want to do that. It is too cold outside. And too dangerous with the English patrolling the waters. In normal times, those who wish to bathe, do so in the summertime—when it is warm."

I'm not about to wait eight months for a bath, but I'm also not sure I want to wash my hair in the ocean. That sounds disgusting. Jackson and I saw how sandy the water is. Salt and sand in my hair? Maybe I'll just settle for washing my body and living with dirty hair until I can find another solution. I'm going to be praying for rain.

"Okay," I answer. "Just how do you propose I bathe in the ocean?"

"Late tonight, the tide will be in. If you are willing to wait that long, we shall lower a bucket over the ramparts, and then you can bathe in the privacy of your bedchamber."

"In a bucket? Are you kidding," I say once again, forgetting my resolution to watch my vocabulary and keep my cool. "No, I want to immerse myself in the water. You know, my entire body in the water."

My travel kit has soap, bath gel, shampoo and conditioner. I also have a shower pouf and suddenly I'm obsessed with the idea of scrubbing my body until it's red and tingling, as if I can somehow scrub away the injustice of my new reality. I even have a razor to shave my legs, but seeing as how this is a marriage of convenience, I don't want to shave my legs. I certainly don't want to give Nicolas any reason to touch smooth, silky legs. But the hair business bothers me. Not because I care about what Nicolas or the Montois think, but because I just can't stand having dirty, smelly hair.

"But that is impossible, mademoiselle," Jean says with animation, drawing my attention back to the conversation. "If anyone dares to broach the city gates at high tide, the English will attack. They do not knowingly allow anyone to get near the sea, for if we are successful at doing that, we can fish and assuage our hunger. No, you will have to be content with a bucket of water."

Content I will not be.

"Never mind," I say to him. But I don't mean it.

The rest of the afternoon, Jean educates me in earnest. I am grateful that Nicolas leaves us in peace. I don't think I could concentrate with my future husband sneering at me.

After my French lesson, he gives me a lesson in history, explaining this decades-long war between the French and English for control of the French monarchy. I can proudly inform him the war is known as the Hundred Years' War in my history books. Not that I would've known that off the top of my head. I'd never heard about the Hundred Years' War before Jackson told me about it yesterday (or actually in about two hundred and fifteen thousand tomorrows). Anyway, I'm not so proud of myself after I see the impact the name of the conflict has on Jean, because now he realizes this war is far from over.

He tells me about the French King, Charles VI, visiting the abbey in 1386. He tells me the king was mad. I guess by 'mad' he means crazy, but I don't stop him to ask. I mean, I'm mad, but I'm not crazy, (at least I don't think so). I hope I don't go crazy!

Jean was a much younger man in 1386, and he speaks to me of the great Pierre le Roi, who was appointed abbot of Mont Saint Michel by the mad Charles.

"He was a great scholar and an astute man," he says speaking of the abbot as if he knew him personally. His next statement confirms that he did. "I miss him very much, particularly as his successor turned out to be a traitor."

"Yes," I say. "That must be Jolivet. Nicolas told me about him."

"Yes, well what Jolivet now tries to offer as a gift to the Duke of Bedford, namely Mont Saint Michel, Pierre le Roi made it very difficult for him to do."

"What do you mean?"

"When le Roi became abbot, he sensed an impending English attack and immediately began to fortify the abbey and village. I participated in the vast building project myself. It included the abbot's living quarters on the south side of the abbey. I will show them to you one day," he says, and I can see his mind is wandering. But then he comes back to reality.

"But more importantly, towers and defensive courtyards were erected, and the ramparts were reinforced and strengthened. If we have repelled the English so far, it is because of Abbot le Roi's vision. With proper guarding, our ramparts are impenetrable."

I ask him about the men I saw this morning guarding the ramparts.

"Is that what my job is going to be?" I ask. "Are they Watchmen?"

"No," he answers. "They are not Watchmen. They are French soldiers who have not abandoned us. They have thrown in their lot with us. Some are Norman knights who were dispossessed of their lands by the English and sought refuge with us. They remain faithful to our cause. The rest are a remnant of the garrison assigned by King Charles to protect the mount."

Jean tells me that the mad king is now dead and that the English are attempting to usurp his throne. After defeating Charles' superior army at the town of Agincourt nine years ago, the English king, Henry V, took Charles' daughter Catherine as his wife as part of the treaty agreements. The English now claim that Henry and Catherine's son (and Charles' grandson), Henry VI, is the rightful heir to the throne of France. I seem to remember Shakespeare writing a play about Henry V. Maybe when I get home—if I get home, I'll read it. It suddenly seems more interesting to me.

Anyway, Jean tells me that the mad Charles also had a son, the Dauphin. I learn that "dauphin" means the crown-prince and heir to the throne. Today (and when I say today, I mean 1424), that son, who is also named Charles, is twenty-one years old. Jean speaks of him with contempt even though he is the legal heir and the symbol of French victory. But he tells me that Charles has failed to stand up to the English and claim what is rightfully his: the throne of France as Charles VII. It seems the gutless Dauphin must travel through English-held territory to get to a city in northern France called Reims, and he's afraid to do it. Evidently Reims is where all the kings of France must be crowned to be considered legitimate. I don't know why Charles can't be crowned in Notre Dame de Paris, but Jean says that just won't work. You know, tradition and all.

So that's the current state of affairs. Two contenders for the throne of France: one French and one English, who is actually half-French. Jean explains that the ruling families of France and England have been intertwined for generations. This is a war between relatives. A war of a hundred years between cousins. It kind of helps me understand why so much of France has sided with the English.

Still, I'm not too invested in all the political intrigues that have caused this siege but I try to listen patiently. You never know when a morsel of information might come in handy. And since I'm here to save the mount, I have to be on my best student behavior.

Jean then explains the current state of affairs on the mount, without withholding anything. I pay more careful attention. Most of the monks and the Montois—except for the infirm and the very young—have survived the summer and fall because of their ability to grow just about anything, in just about anything. They have even planted crops in the village cemetery, the abbey grounds and the cloister. Yeah, I remember that from French Sheldon. Their diet of grains, fruits and vegetables has been supplemented by dried fish, caught and cured before the English entirely surrounded the mount with their ships. And the shellfish they gather at low tide.

But the crops have all been harvested and nearly all eaten, and the fish have all been consumed. The Montois have resorted to eating their domesticated animals: dogs and cats. And any bird that dares to land on the island. I remember how silent it was this morning when I opened my bedroom window. Now I know why.

"We did have two or three milk cows on the mount," Jean tells me, but since we turned their grazing plots into gardens, and without being able to procure alfalfa from the mainland, we could not sustain them. They have all been slaughtered and their meat cured. We still have some laying hens and roosters, but it's the same challenge: providing feed for them. They too will disappear one by one as they stop laying eggs."

And then he tells me of all those who have died—the mothers in child-birth, the babies who've starved to death. The children and elderly who have no defenses left.

I listen to him but don't say anything. There is really nothing to say. Either I succeed in whatever it is I'm supposed to do here, or everyone on this island dies. Or surrenders. But from the way Jean speaks, surrender is not an option. The Montois would give up their lives before giving up their mount. I'm not sure I've ever seen such dedication to such a hopeless cause. It's a heavy weight to carry on my shoulders. Too heavy.

"Soon," Jean continues, "the men will be so desperate to feed their families that they will attempt to reach the mainland by crossing the sands at low tide. They run the risk of falling prey to the English—or the quicksand. And even if they get to the mainland, it is no guarantee, for they will have to find food in territory controlled by the enemy and then manage to get it back to the mount. T'will be virtually impossible. Others will continue to try fishing from the island's shores or will fabricate makeshift rafts to get out to sea at night through the blockade."

His words are sobering. As he speaks, I try to think of how I can possibly turn the tide here and I can't come up with anything. Thankfully, he doesn't press me. He just patiently teaches me, although I know he's hoping that some bit of information he shares will fire my imagination. But it doesn't. I feel more and more helpless. But I can't give up. If I give up, these people will die and I will be unable to go home. At least not to the life I knew.

Then I ask him about Gothman. Abdon, I think they call him. My questions are numerous and I don't give him a chance to answer one before I ask another. "Who is he? How come you know about him here when he was in my time? Can he travel in time like me and Nicolas? Why was he trying to stop me from coming back?"

Jean hesitates. "Katelyn," he says, "there are forces that do not wish you to succeed in your mission. I mean forces besides the English"

"What kind of forces?" I ask. I'm not certain I want to hear the answer.

"Do you know of the Apostle John," he asks me.

"Yes, Christ's apostle," I reply. "John the Beloved. He's also known as John the Revelator. I guess because he wrote the Book of Revelation."

"Yes. That is good my dear. You have read the ancient writings."

"If you mean the Bible, yeah, I have. I don't understand it all, but I've read it."

"Have you read the apostle's account of the war in heaven? A war between Michael and Lucifer?"

"Yeah," I say, surprised at the direction this discussion is taking. "Jackson—my little brother—just read that passage to me when we got here to Mont Saint Michel. It's about Michael and his army fighting against

Lucifer and his army, and Lucifer and his angels being cast out of heaven. It was all there in Jackson's guide book. The stuff about people in medieval times believing that Mont Saint Michel is where that battle took place. Is it true? Is that what you're trying to tell me? Is this where Satan and his angels were cast out of heaven? What was the war about, anyway?"

"It is very complicated, my dear. The answers to your questions will all be part of your training. I do not have time to explain all of it to you now, but let me just say that it is true that Lucifer and his angels were cast out of heaven. They were prevented from ever obtaining physical bodies and so they try to inhabit the bodies of mortals to entice them to do evil, to thwart God's great plan. The only happiness they get is from causing man to sin, to turn from God. Their goal is to make man miserable."

I was completely baffled. "What is God's great plan?" I ask.

"His plan is for men and women to come to earth and make choices of their own free will to follow Him. To choose between good and evil so that He can reward them in heaven for their choices. Freedom of choice is the key to God's plan. Lucifer wants to take away the agency of man, just to spite God. He does not want man to be able to choose. Especially not to choose good. And so he and his angels do all they can do to force men to do evil. Some even inhabit the mortal bodies of vulnerable individuals."

"You mean like the evil or unclean spirits we read about in the New Testament? The ones Jesus cast out of the man into the herd of swine?"

"Yes, that is exactly right," Jean says. "Abdon is one of those unclean spirits, one of Lucifer's fallen angels who was chosen by the Prince of Darkness to destroy this mount, this symbol of freedom."

He pauses for a moment, and I have the distinct impression that he is choosing his words carefully.

"Lucifer hates freedom," he continues, "and so he wants this mount to fail in its battle against tyranny. He knows that freedom is power. Power over darkness. He does not want countries such as yours to come into existence. And so Abdon has tried through all the ages to destroy this mount by inhabiting the bodies of the weak."

"And Michael protects the mount?" I ask. "That is what we as Watchmen are called to do by the Archangel? To protect this mount against Lucifer and his fallen angels?"

"That is correct, my dear."

"But how can a handful of us fight against Lucifer and all his fallen angels?" I ask.

"Lucifer and his angels have the entire world to infiltrate," he explains. "Lucifer's power here is limited to Abdon, and perhaps a few others. I cannot tell you how many they are in number, but because they do not have mortal bodies, they have a distinct disadvantage."

"I would think it would be easier for them not to have bodies." I say. "They could influence more people at the same time."

"That is where you are wrong," he says. "It is very difficult for them to influence mortals, because mortals are inherently good, not evil, in spite of what some religious leaders would have the people believe. Katelyn, we are sons and daughters of God, and God is good. The fallen ones try to tempt man to choose evil but they are most successful when they can inhabit a mortal's physical body. But it takes years of cultivation and practice for them to do that. Just because a man chooses evil does not mean he is inhabited by an evil spirit. He may be tempted by the evil ones, but not inhabited. In fact, it happens very, very rarely. Abdon is one of the few who has been successful at it."

"So did he travel through time to stop me from coming back?" I ask again.

"No, Katelyn. The evil ones cannot do that. They are forced to abide by the time restraints of mortal men. If Abdon was in the future trying to stop you from coming back to us, it is because he somehow learns of your true identity in this, our time of 1424, and he has waited for six hundred years to stop you. In your time, he cultivated a human host to try to stop you—the mortal body you called . . . Now what was it again?"

"Gothman," I say.

"Yes, Gothman. You see, without a host body, Abdon cannot hurt you. He cannot stop you. Unless you intentionally allow it, he cannot even influence you. And even with a host body, Abdon does not have complete control. It is rare for the host to go against his or her natural inclinations. Nicolas told me that Abdon's host knocked you down, but he did not kill you. The host would not allow Abdon to kill you, even though he threatened to kill you."

The realization hits me: I may have escaped Gothman, but I haven't escaped Abdon.

"And so he's here now?" I ask. "Abdon's here in another host?"

"Yes, he is here. However, you must draw comfort in knowing that as of right now, he does not know who you are. And we will do everything to keep it that way. Also, you should know that although he has had the opportunity for many years to have his various hosts kill me, he has never succeeded. As you can see, I am still very much alive. He has never been able to obtain total control over his hosts. But, I must be honest. His current host is the most dangerous I've known. He attempted to kill me, but didn't succeed."

"So where is he," I ask with mounting panic. "Or better yet, who is he? Who is his host? Don't you think you should've told me this part a little sooner?" I am now more than panicked. I am furious. I feel that Nicolas and Jean have lied to me. They failed to prepare me for the reality of my situation. Not only do I have the English trying to destroy me, I have one of Lucifer's fallen angels trying to destroy me.

"Katelyn, if I had told you about Abdon earlier, what would you have done?"

"I would have turned around and run back to Notre-Dame-Sous-Terre and tried to get back to my own time and as far away from Mont Saint Michel as possible."

"Exactly. And then we would have failed. You would have failed. You would have gone back to who knows what."

I see his point, but I don't know how to respond. But at least now, I can begin to prepare.

"So who is his host?" I ask again.

"His host is the English commander of the company laying siege to the mount. His name is Collins. Constable Richard Collins."

"So now I get why the English soldiers won't give up and leave," I say.

"Yes. Their commander will never stop trying to conquer and destroy Mont Saint Michel. At least not as long as he is Abdon's host. That is why Nicolas came to get you, my dear. Someway, somehow, you have got to find a way to outwit Collins and get the English to abandon this cause."

By now, dusk is falling and my brain is so muddled, I can't handle another ounce of information. Especially such frightening information. I still have so many questions, and I sense that Jean has not told me everything. He's still holding back. Something doesn't sit right with me but I don't have the capacity to fit one more piece into the puzzle of my new existence. I'm afraid if I try, the pieces will scatter into the infinite moments of time, and I'll have to start finding them and fitting them together all over again. And so, I don't ask any more questions. At least not now. Now, I feel like I'm a soda can on a shooting range, getting pelted with bullets until I explode.

And so I look at him and say. "Enough. I can't do anymore today."

"Of course not, my dear," he says. "I am sorry to have burdened you with so much. You must be very tired, and you need plenty of rest for your big day tomorrow."

There is no more talk of a bath. A bath seems pretty insignificant compared to Abdon wanting to stop me, perhaps kill me. It seems trivial compared to the fact that tomorrow, I will not only be Abdon's target, but I will be a married target, at that! I want to cry thinking about my fate and about what is to take place tomorrow, but my self-pity is tempered by the tales Jean has told me of the starving Montois.

He lights a candle and putters about to prepare a meal. I help him place the pewter bowls on the table, wondering how they were cleaned from our earlier meals. Sandy seawater, I assume. But I find it doesn't matter.

I don't complain as he ladles up yet another serving of the cold corned-beef stew and dry bread. There is not enough fuel to justify serving the stew hot. I realize that even cold, it's a luxury compared to what the rest of the Montois are eating tonight. I think of the children and I eat every bite, every drop. There is a bit of water to drink, which he informs me comes from Saint Aubert's spring. The water is rationed and of course, every drop of rain water that can be captured adds to the meager supply.

I am grateful that Nicolas has had the decency to stay away. It will be hard enough for me to face him tomorrow. I wonder what he'll eat tonight, and I'm surprised that I care. But I do, and I find that odd.

I tell Jean I'm going to retire early. I look at my watch, glad I have the feature that lights up the watch face, because it is now completely dark in the room except for the tiny flame from the candle. It casts shadows about the room that remind me of dancing ogres. I hope they are not dancing for my demise. I'd rather have them dance for a wedding than a funeral.

Actually, I wouldn't mind them dancing for Constable Richard Collins' funeral.

It's eight o'clock. I bid goodnight to Jean and walk up his worn wooden stairs to my room like a robot, programmed for self-survival but without emotion.

As I prepare myself for bed, the emotions begin to build and then leak out. My wedding will take place in sixteen hours. I don't feel like a bride on the eve of her wedding. Instead, I feel tired and hungry. I feel sad. I feel frightened. I feel angry. I feel like I've almost lost my zest for life, like I've given up, but I can't give up. Too many people are depending on me. Perhaps I will feel better in the morning.

I can't feel much worse.

And there is a question I haven't had the courage to face. But even if I haven't asked it out loud, or even if I haven't asked it in my mind, the separate letters of it are all there, darting in and out of the dark corners of my being trying to come together to form themselves into words, and then into a sentence. I fight that coming together, because I cannot bear its implications. But it is inevitable. It's as if a giant magnet is passing over my body, pulling the letters and words together in the correct sequence until I can no longer ignore them.

Like a neon sign, the words flash before me, unrepentant and unforgiving at the same time.

I close my eyes, trying to block them out. But they flash in my mind. They can no longer be blocked out. They are unreasonable words, abhorrent words, and yet they are the words of my new reality. I have the fate of many lives in my hands through no choice of my own, and I have a responsibility to do whatever is necessary to preserve them. And it isn't just the fate of the Montois. Perhaps it's the fate of my entire country. The United States of America.

This is a time of war, and I know my life will be sought—by the English soldiers, and most probably by one Constable Richard Collins. And so the looming question is finally verbalized.

"Katelyn Michaels," I say out loud. "If necessary to complete your mission, are you capable of taking a human life?"

I don't know and I desperately hope that the fate of Mont Saint Michel and perhaps the modern world as I know it does not depend upon the answer.

Chapter 25

A NOISE STARTLES ME awake. At first, I think there's someone in my room. I hold my breath and listen carefully, but there's only the sound of the wind scraping the tree branches against the wall below my window. That must be the sound that woke me.

I look at my watch. It's twenty minutes past midnight. Less than twelve hours until my wedding. I'm wide awake. My heart is racing and as I close my eyes to try to go back to sleep, I realize it's a lost cause. Kind of like Mont Saint Michel.

Suddenly, I want that bath I told Jean about. I want to bathe more than anything in the world. I am compelled to bathe. I am going to have a bath if it kills me, and according to what Jean told me yesterday, it very well could.

It makes no sense, but I quietly get out of bed, pushing aside Madame Mercier's heat-giving bed curtains. It's chilly in the room, but not as chilly as the previous night.

I tiptoe to my backpack sitting on top of a blanket chest and rummage through it using my hands as eyes. I feel the outline of my enseigne, placed inside a zippered pouch. I pray it will remain safe. It is my key to return home. Literally. Finally, I find what I'm looking for. My travel kit. In a little net bag with a drawstring, I stuff my shower pouf, soap, bath gel and shampoo. And my headlamp.

I remove all my clothes, fold them neatly, and place them in my backpack. Then I cover my naked body with the robe Nicolas gave me in Notre-Dame-Sous-Terre. He never asked for it back, and I'm happy to have it now. Even though it scratches my skin, it's heavy and warm. It's the closest thing I have to a bathrobe. I place my treasured bath items and headlamp in one of its deep pockets.

I slip on my shoes and slowly open my bedroom door, cursing the squeakiness that threatens my plan. I wait to see if I've disturbed Jean or Nicolas. Actually, I don't even know if Nicolas is in the house. I never heard him come in, but then as soon as my head hit the pallet, I fell into a deep sleep of oblivion. Much needed after such a trying day.

When the door is finally opened far enough for me to slip through, I carefully move each foot forward so as not to cause any more squeaking. If they catch me now, my bath is history. Actually, if they catch me now, I'll have a hard time justifying my actions. They'll think I'm trying to escape my duties as a Watchman—and wife. And I'm not sure I can convince them otherwise. After all, I've never had to put my life in jeopardy to take a bath. It doesn't seem like a credible explanation for my nocturnal wanderings. But it's the truth.

By the time I finally make it down the stairs and out the front door, I'm exhausted from the effort to remain silent. The night is misty and yet the light of a full moon helps me navigate the rough cobblestones of the village street. I don't need my headlamp. It'll be for an emergency only because just how will I explain this magical object to villagers in 1424? They'll probably think I'm a witch and burn me at the stake. Yeah, I'll be a regular Kate of Arc.

For a few seconds, I panic, wondering if the tide has already gone out. In the afternoon—I guess it would be considered yesterday afternoon, since it is now past midnight—as I spoke to Jean, he told me high tide would be late that night, but I wasn't certain how late he meant. Will the water still be in? I'm not sure. Does it remain stationary before it starts going back out? I try to remember everything Jackson told me about tides. He said the ocean was constantly moving between high and low tides. And he told me something else. Yes, he said that at full and new moon, the tides are higher. Something about the sun combining with the gravitational pull of the moon on the earth. Since there's a full moon tonight, I think the chances are pretty good I'll find water.

Then I think of another problem. I remember I'll have to cross over a drawbridge with a portcullis to exit the village. And it's only logical that the drawbridge will be up and the portcullis down. Just how in heaven's name am I going to get around those obstacles? Especially if there're soldiers guarding the entrance?

I have no idea, but I keep creeping down the street, closer and closer to the village entrance. I hear no sounds, and for just a second, I'm glad the Montois have eaten their dogs. They would've warned the villagers and soldiers of my presence.

And then I remember something. Something I noticed when the Frenchwoman was leading me and Jackson into the village from the parking lot. I'd seen a handful of store clerks disappear around a stone abutment on the outside of the village ramparts. Then, when we got inside the village, past the moat and drawbridge, my suitcase had gotten a rock caught in its wheel. I'd pulled it over into an alcove in the stone wall to fix it, out of the way of the pressing crowd. In a dark recessed corner of the alcove, a well-dressed woman had suddenly materialized. At first she startled me, and then I realized she'd come through a camouflaged wooden door built right into the stone wall. It appeared there was an entrance tunneling through the thick rampart walls. The employees of the mount's restaurants, inns and souvenir shops could completely circumvent the main entrance with its mobs of anxious tourists. If that camouflaged entrance exists in the 1424 ramparts, I just might be in luck.

I press my body against the buildings and work my way down towards the entrance with as little noise as possible. At least if anyone looks up or down the cobblestoned passageway in the misty moonlight, they won't see my silhouette in the middle of the street. The hoot of an owl startles me, and I stumble to my knees. The owl better quiet down or a hungry Montois will be owl hunting.

By the time I reach the alcove, I've broken out into a sweat, in spite of the cold night. I can hear soldiers laughing ahead in the darkness, but I can't see them. I'm not sure just what they have to laugh about, but I'm grateful they can still find humor in this bleak situation. I slip into the alcove, hoping no one is hiding or sleeping in the niche and praying the doorway exists.

Without the light from the moon, it's pitch black. With my hands, I work my way around the curved surface of the stone, and then feel icy metal. It's the door, but instead of the wooden door I saw in my time, this is an iron door. And it feels heavy. I feel a system of dead bolts, but they are massive. There's absolutely no way I'm going to be able to open this door without making a horrific noise.

And then a commotion breaks out among the guards. I don't understand their words, but they are shouting at each other. I instinctively know they're fighting with each other—probably over a game of chance—not announcing an attack. But I don't know why I know that. Just as instinctively, I push and pull the heavy bolts, hoping the screeching sound of metal on metal will be hidden by their brawl. I feel as if my life depends upon their not hearing me, but that's ridiculous. I just want to take a bath and yet somehow, I know it's more than that. I'm being guided. Of that I'm now certain. I haven't heard a voice, I haven't seen a vision, but for the first time since coming back six hundred years in time, I begin to feel hope. The Archangel is with me. Somehow he'll help me understand what to do, so I let go of my fear and follow my instinct.

The men are still fighting when I succeed in releasing the bolts. It's as if I've been given added strength. The massive door glides open with surprising ease. Someone has kept the hinges well-oiled. I pull it shut behind me, praying that no one will re-bolt it from the inside. But there's no turning back now.

As I slip into a tunnel on the other side of the door, the overwhelming smell of urine and mildew overcomes me and I gag, nearly losing my inadequate supper of corned-beef stew. But I don't have time to be sick, I have another door to get through. I reach it on the other end of the short tunnel and find it to be narrow and placed at an odd angle. Then I remember the people I'd seen disappear through the stone abutment on the outside of the mount's ramparts back in the twenty-first century. The door is camouflaged by a wall of stone. These bolts are easier to manage and like the first door, this one pulls inward.

No moonlit night greets me, but then I realize there are a series of overlapping stone walls with only a narrow slit allowing one to pass through. Unless you actually approach and touch the wall from the outside, you'd never know the opening is there. And if you did discover it, you wouldn't be able to open the metal door from the outside of the ramparts because it is bolted from the inside. It's an ingenious design. Jean told me he'd helped on the rampart fortification project instigated by the former abbot, Pierre le Roi. This remarkable tunnel has Jean's name all over it and I know it has been built for me. Just for this moment. It is my destiny.

Chapter 26

I WAS RELIEVED THE tide hadn't gone out yet. Aided by the light of the full moon, I worked my way around the rampart walls until I found the perfect spot on a narrow strip of stony beach. It was hidden from the ramparts above by a large tree growing up along the wall, its roots clinging to a tiny ledge of soil out of reach of the lapping seawater. I looked out to sea and saw no sign of a sailing vessel and no lights along the coast. There was a section of water where the tree above blocked out the bright moonlight. The tree not only protected me from detection above, but it would also allow me to bathe in total darkness. I felt safe.

I removed my watch and placed it in the robe pocket with my headlamp. Then after securing my bath items in the drawstring net bag that hung from my wrist, I removed my robe and sneakers and slipped into the shallow water. Rather than finding it unbearably cold, I found it refreshingly welcome. The stress of my jaunt through the village and tunnel had left beads of perspiration running down my body.

I undid my heavy braid and floated on my back in the water, allowing the sea to engulf my hair. It tickled my shoulders like a thin layer of silk. Ignoring the sand and salt, I imagined myself in a pool of pristine water gently washing away my stress. I must have stayed there allowing the sea to lull me into a false sense of calm for a full five minutes. Then while sitting on the sandy sea bottom, I lathered up my hair and scrubbed my scalp until it tingled and my fingertips were raw. It was invigorating. After rinsing my hair over and over again, I stood up. The water came up only to my knees, and so I moved out a little further to scrub my body so I wouldn't have to stand completely naked out of the water. I kept moving until the water was waist deep.

As I used my shower pouf to work up a lather on the upper half of my body, I closed my eyes and imagined I was in my shower at home. Mother was humming her favorite Beatles' tune, and Jackson's CD player belted out Handel's *Water Music*. A paradox I know, but hey, that's my family. As the water lapped around me, I adjusted my footing and without realizing it, slipped out of the shadow into the moonlight.

That was all it took.

It was as if some giant sea creature enveloped me in its cavernous mouth, swallowed me whole, and then squeezed me until I stopped breathing.

Chapter 27

WHEN I REGAIN CONSCIOUSNESS, I'm disoriented. It's dark, and I'm lying on my side with my hands tied behind my back. My feet are also bound. I don't know where I am or *when* I am. So much has happened in the past few days that I've started questioning each new reality. I think of a movie I saw in my old life. It was about dreams, and dreams within dreams. So many layers of dreams that the dreamer has no sense of what is real. That's how I feel. I don't know what is real and what is a dream.

Then I feel a gentle rolling motion and I remember floating in the ocean outside the Mont Saint Michel ramparts. Yes, where I'd gone to bathe in some distant past. But I'm not in water now. There's something heavy on top of me, but I know it's not liquid. My head is covered in a loosely-woven and very itchy fabric—like a gunny sack. Although I feel claustrophobic, I can breath. And I can hear.

Someone is talking nearby and for once, I can understand some of the words. They are in English. But it's an odd and stilted English. I only understand about every third word. Slowly, like a camera lens, I zoom in and focus on what my reality is. It's 1424 and I believe I've been captured by the English. They are not my friends. They're my enemies.

Immediately, I remember that I'd been naked when I was bathing, and I begin to panic. I want to scream out, but I restrain myself. With my bound hands, I feel my body and I'm relieved that there's some sort of cotton fabric covering me. I panic, wondering if I've been sexually assaulted. After all, I am a young female and I've fallen into enemy hands. However, other than a general sense of achiness and a few tender spots on my arms, I don't feel any injuries.

I now realize it was completely foolhardy of me to leave the security of Jean's home in the middle of the night in the middle of a war. Jean warned me not to do it. And then I remember how I felt compelled to bathe in spite of the dangers. And I remember thinking I was guided there by the Archangel, that it was all part of my destiny. There's a reason I'm here, and I better find out what it is quickly, before I get hurt. Or worse. I must keep my wits about me. It's time for me to begin the process of saving Mont Saint Michel. I pray for protection.

Surprisingly, when I complete my silent prayer, my panic subsides and is replaced with a clarity of mind. First and foremost, I must not let them know I speak English. Secondly, I must learn everything and anything I can from them, while still protecting myself. Thirdly, I must find a way to escape and return to Nicolas. He will think I've abandoned him because of the marriage. He'll think I've betrayed him—and the Montois. My thoughts start swirling around in my head like the sands of the bay at the retreating tide. I must stop the flow of my sand thoughts, or at least sift through them. Why would I think of getting back to Nicolas instead of Jean? I hated Nicolas, didn't I? I hold on to a single grain of sand. His eyes.

Then I remember when I first saw Nicolas in the village—in my time. I remember his curly, honey-colored hair. But most of all, I remember his dark and piercing eyes. And thinking his eyes were earnest. He was begging me for something then, and without ever having seen him before, I felt I could trust him. At this moment, I *know* I can trust him. Regardless of how he feels about me, I can trust Nicolas. Another tiny grain drops into the mounting pile of the sand that is now filling my mind. And I know. He will come for me, just as Westley always comes for Buttercup. Nicolas knows I haven't abandoned them. He knows I've been captured by the English, and if I don't escape first, he'll put his life in danger to rescue me. And that thought makes me very, very motivated.

I strain to listen, being careful not to move. I don't want the soldiers to know I'm awake. As long as they think I'm unconscious, they probably won't bother me. As I force my brain to adapt to the cadence and intonation of their voices, I start to understand more of what they're saying. With concentration, I can follow their conversation and distinguish their voices. There are three men in the cabin, or at least three who are talking. One has a high-pitched nasally tone, another's voice is low and raspy, and the third has a lisp, more of a whistle, as if he's missing his front teeth. Given the lack of dental care in the fifteenth century, that wouldn't be unusual. It sounds like the men are playing cards. Do they have face cards in the fifteenth century? I don't know, but they're slapping something down on the table.

". . . her to Constable Collins as quickly as possible." Toothless says. "Where is he?"

"At the fort in Ardevon. But we are stranded here until the tide goes back in," says Nasal Dude.

I have no idea what or where Ardevon is, but it must be on the mainland of Normandy. I'm in a ship and the tide is out, so they can't get me back to shore yet. That's a good thing. How grateful I feel that Jean told me about Abdon and his human host, Constable Collins. Now I know exactly who I'm facing and I definitely prefer being at the mercy of these buffoons than in Abdon's hands.

". . . didn't touch her," says Raspy-Voice. "I certainly wanted to, but you know Collins."

"Naturally, he will want her all to himself," snickers Toothless.

"But why should we not be allowed to have a taste of her sweetness before we surrender her to him?" Nasal Dude asks.

I'm disgusted, but more furious than frightened. They're speaking of my body as if I'm an animal, a piece of property. I remember what Jean told me about the women on the mount feeling like chattel. Now I understand. I will never, never allow them to touch me.

"The orders are clear, mate," says Raspy-Voice. "He wants to personally interrogate and examine anyone captured from the mount. He wants to assess their condition, see their level of deterioration and starvation and then torture them for information."

"So, why not begin the torture session early?" Nasal Dude asks. "Please?"

"I fear that with the degree of pluck that little vixen exhibited earlier," says Raspy-Voice, "we might be forced to injure or kill her before we can have our way with her. And you know how clever and ruthless Collins is. He would ascertain the cause of her demise and kill us. T'is not worth the risk for the momentary pleasure."

All three of them laugh. I can hardly keep my anger contained, but I also appreciate knowing that I fought my captors. Good for me! I don't remember any of it. I'm not surprised to learn about Richard Collins' character. He's ruthless, cruel and sadistic, and he's not afraid to kill. It seems Abdon has found a worthy host.

"Is that why you saw fit to cover her nakedness?" asks Nasal Dude.

"Exactly, my man," Raspy-Voice replies. "I didn't want to start a riot among the crew that could have resulted in her death."

"I say the waste of a good shirt, sir," cackles Toothless.

"No, t'is actually the vile shirt worn by Mr. Thompson. I ordered the doctor to dress her in it."

More chortling from them and a desire to squirm for me. Who is Mr. Thompson and just why is his shirt, which I am apparently wearing, so vile?

"Brilliant," says Nasal Dude. "Let's hope she passes on the bloody flux to Constable Collins." I have no idea what the 'bloody flux' is, but I'm pretty certain it isn't a good thing.

"Yes. T'would serve the devil right," Raspy-Voice replies. "Dare I say it aloud? The man is evil personified." They have no idea of just how evil he really is.

"I don't mind Collins dying of the flux, but I for one would prefer the woman alive," says Toothless. "T'is possible that after he has examined her and had his fill of her, he will return her to us as a reward. After all, she's the first female from the mount to be captured alive. He could motivate his troops if the word is passed along that the constable shares the spoils. Besides, she will be but a momentary distraction for him. I hear the commander's desires are not easily assuaged. He craves variety and . . . quantity."

My horrible opinion of Collins just gets worse, if that is even possible.

"Let us hope, then, that she's still alive after he has finished with her." Nasal Dude chimes in. "But t'will not be the bloody flux that kills her. He is violent with his wenches."

I feel like vomiting.

"Did you have the opportunity to peruse our . . . guest?" pipes up Raspy-Voice. They all laugh at his use of the term. "She's quite a beauty. True, I prefer my women a pinch more voluptuous, but t'is not surprising considering her circumstances. However, in spite of her scrawniness, she doesn't seem to be suffering from starvation. T'was evident from her brute strength. In fact, she seems a healthy specimen. The Montois must have considerable more food than the constable estimates."

"Yes, and did you see her teeth?" adds Toothless. "I've never seen teeth like hers. They are perfectly aligned and as white and shiny as pearls. T'is quite extraordinary."

Thank you Toothless, I think. I'll pass on your compliments to my orthodontist. Oh, and by the way, I'd like to show you just how extraordinary my teeth really are. You come near me, and I'll bite your hand off!

"Your appetites will soon be satisfied. We will find more specimens like her when we invade the village. Enough to go around," says Nasal Dude.

Their raucous laughing curdles my stomach, but I set aside my personal distaste to focus on the information I've just heard. Constable Collins is planning an invasion of the mount. I silently plead with them to reveal more.

"But alas, my fine fellows," says Raspy-Voice, "for that we must wait until the next new moon. I was hoping for some tender flesh a bit sooner."

Bingo! The invasion will come at the time of the new moon. Of course. It makes sense. I remember how much light was given out by the full moon. I didn't even need my headlamp. The attack will happen when the moon gives no light, at new moon or what did Jackson call it? Dark moon. When is that? In a month? No that can't be right. Where is Jackson when I need him? In a month, it will be another full moon, won't it? Isn't that how the moon cycles work? Every twenty-nine days or so? No, dark moon will be in about two weeks' time. And the English will choose to come at high tide. Thanks to Jackson, I know that the tides are highest at full and dark moons.

"I win," I hear Raspy-Voice proclaim. "This is all mine, mates," he adds and I hear the scrape of metal coins on the table. "Now, shall we go up and see if we can't get the boatswain to move this lumbering vessel along a little faster. I'm hoping our dear Constable Collins will add more gold to our coffers."

I hear the chairs scraping across the wooden planks as they get up. Good, they're going to leave me alone.

But I'm not that lucky. I hear—and smell—one of them approaching my bunk, and I order my body to stay still and my eyes to remain closed. However, I don't have to worry about my eyes, because he doesn't bother to remove my hood. No, he just savagely punches me in the leg, and it is all I can do to keep from reacting. From screaming.

"Still unconscious," my assailant says. It's Toothless. I wish I could remove the rest of his teeth. One by one and without any anesthesia and then I'm horrified at my vicious thoughts. But I still wish it.

"Are you certain she's unconscious?" asks Nasal Dude. "Perhaps she has expired. That was some blow you gave her."

"No, she's alive," insists Toothless. "I can see her chest rising. She is still breathing."

He's standing over me, and I can hardly bear this degree of proximity.

"Are you certain?" asks Raspy-Voice. "Refrain from prodding her, Phillip. You might kill her, and I for one would not look upon that kindly, for then we would receive nothing for our trouble."

If Raspy-Voice calls that sucker punch from Toothless a prod, I'd certainly hate to feel a full out assault.

"Fear not, sir. I hear her breathing," Toothless (whose name I now know is Phillip), says as he lowers his head next to mine. I can hardly stomach the stench of his putrid breath burning my skin like acid.

"Come along," insists Raspy-Voice. "Leave her be." I hear a door close behind them as they exit, and I allow myself two seconds of self-pity groaning. I'll have a hefty bruise on my right thigh, but the bone isn't broken.

I consider my situation. I try to remember everything Jackson told me about the tides of Mont Saint Michel. There is a high tide roughly every twelve hours. That means a low tide every twelve hours. My captors were probably in a small rowboat when they grabbed me. I would've seen a large ship. Then, since the tide was going out when they snatched me, they had to get me back to their ship, which followed the tide out to sea. If high tide was around midnight last night, then low tide is around six in the morning. By noon, this ship will be back on the shores of Normandy.

Thank you, thank you, Jackson for all that trivia.

Now, I've got to get back to warn the Montois. And I need to know what time it is. But my hands are tied.

Then I remember: I left my watch in the pocket of my robe—Nicolas's robe—back on the beach. I hope whoever finds the robe will have the good sense to get it back to Nicolas and Jean. The Montois will recognize my 'Breton sabots.' They will know the shoes are mine. But if they find the modern gadgets—my watch and headlamp—in the robe pocket, Jean and Nicolas will have "some 'splainin' to do, Lucy."

But at least they'll know I didn't desert them. Jean knew I wanted a bath. They'll think I was either captured or drowned. I don't know why it's so important to me for them not to think I abandoned them. And then I realize. Because I actually care. I care about them all. But most of all, I care about Jean—and Nicolas. It's difficult to sort through my feelings about

Nicolas, but now is not the time to try. Now, it's time for me to figure out how I'm going to escape. And I've got to escape before Richard Collins, a.k.a. Abdon, gets his hands on me. Because if he does, I'm toast.

Chapter 28

I WAS SURPRISED AT how unbelievably stupid my captors were. First of all, they'd spoken openly in my presence about Constable Collins' plans to invade the mount and secondly, although my hands and feet were bound, they hadn't secured me to the bunk. I guess they weren't used to females who actually fought for their lives—or their honor. When I managed to sit up and shake the unattached hood from off my head, I saw that I was in what was probably the captain's quarters. One of those three fools actually had to be the captain of this ship. And England was winning this war?

Although there was no artificial light source in the room, enough sunlight filtered in through the port-hole for me to see. The night was over, and that meant the tide was heading back in. I had no time to lose.

I gagged as I looked at the soiled muslin shirt on me, which hit about mid-thigh. It was disgusting enough to think those gorillas had seen me naked, but it was even more disgusting to be wearing the filthy garment that had belonged to someone who had died of the bloody flux. My first order of business was to cut through my bindings so I could find something less repulsive to wear.

Raspy-Voice was probably the captain. He'd spoken with the most authority, and Toothless Phillip had addressed him as 'sir.' Yeah, I wasn't real thrilled to exchange Mr. Thompson's shirt for a garment belonging to Raspy-Voice, but it was better than being naked. And it was better than the bloody flux. I had no time to waste before the captain or one of his flunkies came to check on me.

I hopped over to the table where they'd been playing cards. There was nothing on it except a heavy pewter candlestick, so Captain Raspy-Voice had obviously scooped up the cards and his winnings and hidden them somewhere. I looked around and saw several built-in drawers. It was awkward, but even with my hands and feet bound, it wasn't that hard to open the captain's drawers. At least the unlocked drawers.

In the first drawer I opened, I actually found the net bag with my shower pouf, shampoo and soap intact. It wasn't what I was looking for, but I was glad to reclaim it. It only took me about five minutes more to find what I was really looking for. Actually, it was calling my name: "Katelyn, Katelyn, I'm in here."

And there it was: a razor-sharp dagger with a decorative silver hilt, shoved in a drawer with what looked like log books. The knife was probably war booty because I didn't think Raspy-Voice could afford such a piece. Museum-quality. It was now *my* museum-quality piece, taken as payment for that sucker punch from Toothless!

I heard scuffling above me, and my heart dropped to my feet but I didn't stop sawing away at the cords. After another few minutes, I had both my hands and legs freed. Then I searched the cabin, looking for something moderately clean to wear. Finally, I found a drawer full of folded linens, inner garments that appeared to be freshly laundered. Or as laundered as things could be in the fifteenth century.

As much as I despised putting on anything that had touched Raspy-Voice's body, I pulled out a clean linen shirt. I immediately removed the soiled shirt trying to touch it as little as possible. Then I folded it with the very tips of my index fingers and thumbs. I got a great deal of satisfaction from placing it in the bottom of Raspy-Voice's underwear drawer. The deceased Mr. Thompson was also happy to return the favor.

Before pulling on the shirt, I cut its sleeves with the dagger so they'd hit the middle of my upper arms, and then I ripped about a foot of fabric off the bottom. I didn't want to expose too much of my body, but I knew I'd need to move without restriction. The truth was that I'd very probably be swimming for my life. The entire ship started creaking and I began to sway back and forth as the ship's speed picked up. I had to hurry.

Then, I found a pair of short linen breeches with a drawstring: Raspy-Voice's undergarments, but I couldn't think of that gruesome possibility. At least they were clean, and I could secure them around my waist. I placed the rest of the garments neatly back in the captain's drawer on top of the sleeves I had ripped off and the soiled shirt. I hoped he wouldn't realize the disgusting rag was there for a long, long time. I shut the drawer, not wanting him to know I'd raided his clothing.

Since the sharp knife was too large and unwieldy to fit into my net bag, I ripped the strip of linen I'd cut from the bottom of the shirt into two pieces, and then wrapped each strip several times around my right calf and secured them tightly. I'd seen scuba divers with knives strapped to their legs, and I hoped my makeshift knife 'holster' would work. I tested it out, and it seemed dependable, but for now, I needed the dagger in my hands.

Once I was dressed, with my net bag secured around my wrist, I breathed a sigh of relief. At least now if someone came to check on me, I was both clothed and armed. However, the thought was sobering. I'd never had to defend my virtue or my life and I wasn't certain I was capable of doing it. Then I thought about what the men had said about Constable Collins and it became very clear in my mind. I couldn't allow myself to fall into his hands, and I would do whatever it took to prevent that from happening, even if it meant taking a human life. Surely God would forgive me for protecting myself—especially since the lives of innocent people on the mount depended on me. It was nearly impossible to come to terms with how much my life had changed in the past few days. But I had no choice. It was either kill or be killed.

I quickly crept back to the bunk, wrapped some of the blankets to look like I was still on the pallet, and then tiptoed across the room to look out the port window. I could see no land from this vantage point, but the ship was definitely riding the tide in toward the coast.

My plan was to find a hiding place near the back of the ship and then just before it reached the mount, to slip into the water and swim for my life. I counted on that galloping-horse tide to carry me in to the mount, making it difficult for the ship to come back if they discovered my flight. I knew what the dangers of the waters were. Jackson had made them relatively clear. But I'd rather die swimming, or even sucked up by quicksand, than in the hands of Abdon.

I drew some comfort from the fact that Nicolas had found me in the future. Although the time issues still made no sense to me, Jean had assured me that I would succeed. Otherwise, I wouldn't have been in the future. However, I knew I was living the present reality, and a misstep would change everything here and now, including the future.

When I reached the cabin door, I found it locked from the outside. I had to get out of this cabin, and get out fast, so I frantically started prying away at the wooden doorframe with the dagger to break through the lock. The wood was damp and a bit rotted, but I didn't know if I'd be able to get the door opened before someone came to check on me. I also knew that once the broken lock was spotted, the alarm would be sounded and I would lose the element of surprise.

Then I heard a noise in the hallway. Someone was coming, and faced with the reality of actually having to stab someone, I realized I couldn't do it. At least not yet. But I could smack someone on the head. I shoved the knife into my leg-holster and dashed to the table to grab the heavy candlestick. My heart nearly stopped beating as I heard the noise of a key fumbling in the lock. And then I heard the tumbler fall. I had only an instant to decide whether to hide behind the door and hope to remain out of sight, or to stand to the side of the door and go right for the head. Not knowing whether my visitor was alone or not (but probably because I was still afraid to confront anyone), I opted to hide behind the door.

After several unsuccessful attempts to push the door open because of the damage I'd inflicted to the frame, and some pretty foul Middle English expletives to go along with those attempts, my uninvited guest pressed his weight against the door and it popped open, nearly smashing me in the process, but also fortuitously causing him to fall down. Without even thinking, I dashed out from my hiding place, bonked the filthy sailor on the head hard enough to keep him unconscious for a while, but hopefully not hard enough to kill him. Then I dashed out the door, pulled it closed and forced the large brass key—which was still in the lock—to turn. I slipped the key inside my little net bag. I didn't want anyone to get back into the room for a long time.

The Archangel was watching over me because I didn't see anyone in the dark passageway. The odors of mold, unclean bodies and rancid oil nearly gagged me as I stopped to determine which way the ship was moving. The captain's quarters, I realized were in the rear of the ship. I knew nothing about fifteenth century ships, but I definitely knew I wanted to slip into the water at the back of the ship, so that it would go on sailing past me as the tide carried it in to shore.

Now, I just had to get up to the main deck without being detected, and I had no idea how many decks this ship had. When I spotted a ladder and hatch, I hesitated for just an instant. Once I opened that hatch, my fate would be sealed.

Gritting my teeth, I inched the forward section of the double-door hatch open, hoping to use it to keep the crew from seeing me. I dared to peek out and look around for just an instant, before I lowered the door back down again. The hatch opened onto the main deck of a small three-masted ship, with an afterdeck rising up behind me. That half deck would make it nearly impossible to slip off the back because the added height and visibility of the deck would make me an easy target. Even if I managed to scale the afterdeck without being seen, it would still leave a high jump from the ship into the water.

However, the good news was that the railings on either side of the main deck were low to the water. I decided to slip over the side of the ship and hope I could hang on unseen until it was time to go into the water. Two longboats stored on either side of the hatch would help shield me from view while I ran for the railing. But I needed to make a quick decision. Should I go to the right or left side? From my vantage point, I couldn't see Mont Saint Michel, but something told me to go right and I felt the assurance that I would be able to see the island from that side so that I could best gauge when to jump ship.

Reluctantly, I abandoned the candlestick, but I knew I would need full use of both hands to make the difficult maneuver over the ship's cap rail. After taking three deep breaths to calm myself, I pushed the hatch up just enough to slip through and then scurried like a monkey on my hands and feet. I hoisted myself over the side and miraculously, my bare feet found purchase on a narrow ledge on the outside of the ship's hull. The rigging lines were fixed to the ledge by a system of wires and screws. By pressing my toes onto the ledge and grabbing the rigging lines, I was able to crouch down and remain well below the level of the deck. As long as nobody looked over the side of the ship, I wouldn't be seen. Once I felt secure in my position, I looked up and saw Mont Saint Michel up ahead in the distance to my right. I had chosen correctly. Or the Archangel had given me the impression of which side to choose.

When no alarm sounded, I allowed myself to exhale a sigh of short-lived relief, but I knew my danger had just begun. This was a light, swift moving craft, rather than the heavy lumbering ship I had imagined. It was designed to sail in shallow waters and I feared it was more easily maneuverable than I'd originally calculated. The tide was a force to be reckoned with, but this ship might be able to change course and come back after me if I was spotted. I tried to judge which direction the wind was coming from, but it was impossible to tell.

Added to those concerns was my quickly deteriorating physical condition. The ship's draft whipped water into my face making it hard to see or breathe. My fingers were virtually frozen to the lines and my feet were like blocks of ice, threatening to slip off my precarious perch at any moment. My totally inappropriate 'swim wear' was soon drenched and clung to me like grasping fingers of death. I was grateful for the thick mist, which would limit the sailors' visibility when I finally dropped into the water, but its iciness threatened to hammer the nail into my already watery coffin. I needed to be at full strength for swimming, but I felt my strength being sucked out of me like lemonade from a straw in one hundred degree weather.

Just when I thought it couldn't get any worse, I heard a sailor yell at the top of his lungs. "A vast ye!"

I didn't know what those words meant, but I knew it wasn't good. Shouts and the sound of running feet only confirmed that conclusion. My absence had been discovered. I looked at the mount. It was still several miles away. Would I have the strength to ride the violent tide in? I wasn't sure.

"Hard alee," was the next command. The ship jerked, ramming me so hard into the metal bolts on the rigging pulleys that they sliced through the flesh on my upper right arm and already-bruised right thigh like a newly sharpened knife. Salt spray hitting my wounds brought a second wave of pain and I nearly blacked out. Then the yelling on deck intensified and shocked me back to reality. I faced the grim fact that the time had come. I had no choice but to drop into the water before the ship turned and put me on the wrong side for my escape, and before every hand on deck began searching the waters for me. My only hope was to get as far from the ship as I could and hope the mist would shroud my swimming form.

It was an alarming realization. I was freezing, weak and now injured and bleeding. I briefly wondered if there were sharks in these waters. But, I'd already decided to die trying to escape rather than experiencing a more horrific death at the hands of Abdon. Sharks or Abdon? Violent waters or Constable Collins? I let go, allowing myself to fall into the turbulent water.

My body hardly made a splash, and yet it was as if I'd been slapped with a block of concrete. I didn't think I could get any colder, but I soon found that my frigid perch was child's play compared to the glacial grasp of the vicious tide waters. Trying to find a glimmer of hope in my desperate situation, I processed the fact that the freezing water masked the pain from my cuts. It also probably slowed my bleeding. But before I could get my arms and legs to respond to the signals my brain was frantically screaming at them, I sank below the surface.

The water was teeming with sand. It was a roiling cauldron. For that instant underwater, everything happened in slow motion. I kicked my feet, but it took an eternity to move them through the water. My arms and hands, trained to respond automatically from years of swimming workouts and sprinting drills, took a millennium to move an inch. From under the water, I could hear the cries from the ship, but they were drawn out into low distorted sounds like the calls of a pod of whales.

I don't know how long I was below the water, but I do know that my disorientation probably saved my life. Just before my head surfaced, time returned to normal and I felt a speeding shaft skim my hair. The seamen were shooting arrows at me! Adrenaline kicked in and suddenly, my limbs responded. Here was the fight or flight mechanism I had lacked in Notre-Dame-Sous-Terre.

I took a deep breath and then dove below the surface as far as I could go, allowing my body to be carried along by the tide, but still attempting to veer to the right, towards the mount and away from my captors. Five seconds became ten and ten became twenty, and then twenty were forty and still I didn't surface. I felt engulfed by a euphoria that breathed for me and swam for me. My near-helpless body was just along for the ride. I happily gave in and waited for the warmth of the light that filled me. But then, something tickled at the edges of my cognitive awareness. Maybe this is what it feels like to die.

Gradually, the warmth wasn't enough and the need for oxygen outweighed the euphoria. I drove my head to the surface, coughing and struggling to get my mouth out of the water. The tidal waves did all they could to keep me down, to keep me from breathing, but my will was stronger. I gasped for a single breath of life-giving oxygen and dared to hope. Between the sea, sand and mist, it was difficult to see, but the shadow of the mount was still in front of me.

I pushed my head out of the water and turned so I could see over the waves to spot the ship. Although the sailors had attempted to turn their vessel, the tide and winds were in my favor, and the ship was well ahead of me and far to the left. If I had a hard time seeing the outline of the ship, it would be virtually impossible, even with a spyglass, for the sailors to focus on my bobbing body. Although exhausted, freezing and wounded, I managed to keep my head above water and allow the tide to do the work for me. I offered up a prayer of fervent thanks.

And then I felt the powerful bump of something large against my bleeding thigh . . . something large and terrifying in the water beside me.

Chapter 29

HE'D ALMOST GIVEN UP hope. And yet he still believed Katelyn was alive. He knew she hadn't drowned. He knew she hadn't tried to escape. No, Katelyn had been taken and Nicolas prayed that it hadn't been by Abdon.

When Robert le Boiteux pounded on their door that morning before dawn, Nicolas and Jean were sleeping soundly. Although Nicolas usually awoke early, he'd found a haven of peace in his deep slumber that morning. The violent banging turned the peace into panic in an instant. Nicolas bounded down the stairs and practically pulled Robert into the dark, cold salon, noting that the frail fisherman's distinctive limp, which gave him his name, was worse than usual. But when the young man saw what Robert extended to him, Nicolas forgot all about the man's limp.

"Where did you find these," he asked frantically as he grabbed Katelyn's shoes and robe. He felt the color draining from his face as Jean entered the room.

"I was digging for cockles in the sands along the southeastern shore," the fisherman explained. "You know, before dawn. Before the English make it impossible." The tiny cockles left two telltale holes in the sand after the tide went out, and with a long-handled pronged tool, a skilled collector could dig up buckets-full of the life-giving shellfish. If they knew where the sands were safe. And if the English didn't fire on them.

"I found the garment on the rocky stretch of beach just below the sycamore tree," Robert continued. "But it was the shoes that made me bring the clothing to you. My wife told me about your bride's odd footwear. I was certain they were hers."

Before Robert even finished his sentence, Nicolas bolted back up the stairs to Katelyn's bedchamber. He pounded loudly on her door while calling her name. When there was no response, he flung open the door to find her bed empty.

"Papa, she is not here," he shouted down to the two men as he began rifling through her knapsack. Inside, he found her clothing and other odd twenty-first century possessions. The clothing gave him initial relief. He didn't think she'd leave dressed only in his course robe, but what he was more intent on finding was her enseigne.

Finally, he dumped all her belongings onto the bed. But there was no enseigne. He felt all through her knapsack and discovered a number of oddly-fastened pouches. He could actually feel the round hardness of the enseigne in one of those pouches, and he finally figured out that by tugging on the tiny piece of metal, he could pull the fastener open. He breathed a sigh of relief when his hand touched the cold metal. She had not tried to return to the future. But where was she? He ran into his bedchamber, which he was now sharing with Jean, grabbed his clothing, then hurried back down the stairs. Nicolas briefly flashed the enseigne he clutched in his hand to his mentor.

"Nicolas," Jean said, "I fear it is my fault. I believe she went to bathe. She desperately wanted to bathe before the wedding, but I told her it was not possible. I should have found a way to make it happen."

"The tide went out late last night, so that means she has been gone for many hours. She has been pulled out by the tide," Nicolas cried out in anguish. As much as he thought he resented Katelyn Michaels, he suddenly felt a degree of fear and loss he'd never known before. Not even when he'd left his family in Brittany.

Jean turned to Robert and said, "Sound the alarm, Robert. Gather the villagers and soldiers. We must search every inch of the shore. Send the sharp of eye to the ramparts to search the sands and sea. The tide will be coming in soon, and perhaps . . ." Jean did not finish his sentence. Nicolas knew why. It was not very likely, in fact impossible for Katelyn to have survived being pulled out to sea and then being brought back in by the tide. No one could survive being in the cold, fast-moving water for that long. Robert turned and hurried from the house, heading up the street to the village church where the bell would be rung to assemble the Montois.

"There is another possibility," Jean said, as he reached toward Nicolas. His face looked gray and his hands shook. "She could have been abducted by the English."

"No—not Abdon," shrieked Nicolas. "No, surely it is not possible." Both he and Jean knew exactly what Katelyn's fate would be if Constable Collins got his hands on her.

Nicolas pulled on his breeches and shoved his bare feet into a pair of sabots by the fireplace. "I am going to the beach," he cried as he bolted out the door.

And there, several hours later—at the exact time he should be getting married—Nicolas le Breton sat beneath the sycamore trying his best to commune with higher powers. The Montois had searched every inch of the island and shore. There was no trace of Katelyn Michaels. The women wailed to think of the young bride dying on her wedding day. Everyone left Nicolas alone to grieve beneath the tree.

Surely, this was not how Katelyn's mission was to end? The young man felt thoroughly helpless—and hopeless. And it wasn't just a sense of hopelessness for Mont Saint Michel and its inhabitants. He finally admitted the truth to himself. In spite of her taxing temperament, in spite of her vitriolic tongue and her impertinent attitude, Nicolas could no longer deny the fact that what he felt for Katelyn Michaels was not animosity. It was not hostility or contempt. It was not abhorrence or rancor. It wasn't even disillusionment or disappointment. It was a feeling he'd never felt before. Aggravation, yes, but also attraction, affection and . . . even more surprising, ardor. Yearning and longing. And now, it seemed as if he'd lost the object of his affection before he even had the opportunity to tell her how he felt. If this pain is what love caused, then he finally had a glimpse of the agony his beloved mentor must have felt when he had lost Marie. It was unbearable.

How can I just sit here and do nothing? he thought.

But what was there to do? It was not as if he could walk across the sands to the English bastille at Ardevon and demand that his bride be returned. The only possibility for her survival was for Katelyn herself to somehow find a way to fight back. Having had some experience with her fiery temper actually gave him a miniscule breath of hope. She would fight to the death before she allowed Abdon to touch her. But would it be to the death?

Nicolas looked up, and through the mist he saw the silhouette of an English ship approaching. The tide was coming in and he knew he should take cover inside the ramparts. The English didn't hesitate to aim their arrows at any Montois who was unlucky enough to be caught outside the walls. But something kept him there at that spot. He stood up and melded his body into the tree trunk. He remained perfectly stationary but his eyes were anything but stationary. He scanned the incoming waters. Although he knew it was an impossibility, something in his head, and more importantly, something in his heart told him to remain exactly where he was.

The ship was nearly abreast, about a quarter of a league from the bank. Through the thickening mist, he could actually see his enemies on deck with their bows. He could hear them shouting and yelling. Something was happening, and *he* wasn't the cause of the commotion. No arrows came in his direction. As he squinted to get a better view, he realized they were aiming aft of the ship on their starboard side. They were shooting at a target while trying to turn the ship against the tide. That is when the adrenaline started coursing through Nicolas's body like a lightning bolt. And he knew. They were shooting arrows at Katelyn. She had been taken prisoner by the men on that ship and somehow, the amazing Katelyn Michaels had managed to escape.

When he finally saw a dark object bobbing up and down in the approaching waters, he nearly shouted in jubilation, but the jubilation was short-lived. It was only a seal. The marine animals were frequent visitors to the Bay of Mont Saint Michel. They loved riding in on the fast moving tides. If only Katelyn could be like that seal—an air-breathing creature that not only survived the violent tides, but flourished in them.

And then, as the tidal waters and the seal got closer, and the English ship got carried into the mainland, Nicolas gasped. He saw *two* heads bobbing out of the water together, and one was human. It was Katelyn's.

Without hesitating, he ripped off his shirt, jumped out of his sabots and ran towards the incoming water, taking no thought to watch for his English enemies or for the quicksand that could pull him under. At the speed he was running, his weight barely skimmed the surface of the sand, and he felt invincible. When he reached the point where the water began lapping at his feet, he could see that Katelyn actually had her arms wrapped around the seal's head and the seal didn't seem to mind. Nicolas plowed into the water at full speed and just before he could reach the seal, it twisted in the water quickly ejecting its passenger, as if to say, "I have brought her back to you, but I'm certainly not going to stick around to become a meal for the village."

As Nicolas enveloped the barely conscious girl in his arms, her unconventional traveling companion lifted its flipper in a gesture of adieu, and headed back out to sea.

Chapter 30

I GUESS BY THE TIME Nicolas pulled me out of the water, I was pretty much frozen and barely conscious. I don't remember much of what happened after that except his warmth as he wrapped my waterlogged body in his shirt and pressed me close to his bare chest. Then I checked out.

When I came to, I was in some type of sleeveless sheath, covered by rough linen sheets. Something heavy covered my sopping hair, and I had so many covers over me I actually felt hot after having nearly frozen to death during my swim. Except for my right arm. My arm was freezing, and as my thoughts came into focus, I realized that a tonsured monk was leaning over me holding my bare arm. It scared me to death until Nicolas hurriedly jumped in to explain that the monk was acting in his capacity as doctor of the mount. Witch doctor, more likely. Nicolas explained that Doc Monk had prepared 'curative plasters' for my arm and leg. As Doc lifted up the horrid mud and leaf gunk to apply the putrid-smelling mess to my upper arm, I cried bloody murder. The monk was so startled by my sudden reaction that he jumped backwards, fell on the floor and plastered himself with his so-called cure. Nicolas was trying to sop up the blood dripping from my arm with a dirty rag.

"Nicolas," I whispered contritely, "no offense, but no way is he putting that stuff on me." I tried to sit up, but I was so dizzy, my attempt at bravery didn't last long. I didn't want to let him know how crummy I felt because I knew my life depended on remaining coherent, so from my prostrate position, I added, "Listen to me. I'm from the twenty-first century, and I promise that mud isn't gonna cut it for my cuts. I know more about medicine with an eleventh-grade education than your very best doctor in France, so please just ask your monk" (I wanted to say 'monkey,' but I refrained), "to leave, and I'll let you and Jean take care of me. Judging by the fact that I'm in dry clothing, you've already seen me naked, so let's just confine the displaying of my bare limbs to the two of you. Okay?"

I'm not really sure if Nicolas understood a word of what I said, but he left his rag over my wound, helped the monk up from the ground, attempted to clean Doc's face, and then escorted him from the room, all while the muddy man protested vehemently. A few moments later, Nicolas returned with Jean.

There was so much I needed to tell them—about my kidnapping, my escape, and especially about Constable Collins' plan to attack the mount—and yet the first words I said to Jean were: "Did you undress me or was it Nicolas?"

I guess it was a pretty stupid question seeing as how I'd just managed to escape death and still might bleed to death. Concern for modesty should've been pretty low on my priority list, but it was a question I wanted answered. I might be from the twenty-first century where modesty is no virtue, but it is to me, and no man, not even a doctor, has seen me completely naked. Except when I was a baby in diapers, but that's not exactly the same thing, now is it? They've seen me in my Speedo, but that's my limit. I wasn't about to break that rule with my pseudo-husband. It might give him ideas and I wasn't in the mood to fight off any more males. Just the thought of Captain Raspy-Voice and his motley crew touching me made me gag.

"Do not worry yourself, Katelyn," Jean said. He had a smile on his face and his eyes crinkled up in a tender sort of way. I guess he was happy to see me conscious and talking, but I think he was just as happy to realize I had such, well how should I put it? Puritanical notions? I mean, let's be honest. I'm not a Hester Prynne wannabe. Nicolas had probably given Jean an earful about how women dress in the twenty-first century and Jean seemed pleased that I did not happen to be of their persuasion. I valued my privacy *and* my body, and so did my host.

"The villagers," Jean continued his explanation, "were so elated when Nicolas came through the gates carrying you that a gaggle of frenzied females followed him all the way here. After Nicolas brought you to the bedchamber, Madame Mercier and her cohorts shooed us away and they stripped off your drenched clothing. Madame Mercier dressed you in one of her beloved daughter's undergarments."

I have to say, at that moment, I felt pretty darn grateful for the Widow Mercier and her beloved daughter's undergarments. "Please, Monsieur Jean, will you get her for me, and I will instruct her how to treat my wounds." Then I realized I couldn't instruct her to do anything since I didn't speak enough French to instruct her. "Oh forget it," I said. "I don't care if you two see my arm and leg. After all, I spend half my life in a swimming suit. I might be a prude, but I'm not that much of a prude. And I trust you guys."

He knit his brow together, and so I simplified my message: "please tell her thank you. I will instruct the two of you how to care for my wounds, and she can assist you. Anyone else would question where such strange practices came from, but I will not have to explain to you."

"I understand, Katelyn," Jean said. "What shall we do?"

My head was spinning and I felt pretty sure that I was going to vomit, but I forced myself to remain motionless and calm. "We need to assemble several items. First, two basins. One I need by my side right now, because I'm going to vomit, and the other to clean my wounds. For that I need boiling water—clean water. Then, can you and Nicolas find clean fabric that could be used for washing and bandages? Muslin like this," I said, touching my chemise. "Maybe Madame Mercier will allow you to rip up some of her daughter's other undergarments. But please, it needs to be as clean as possible." I lifted the filthy rag from my arm and saw blood oozing out, but with no other choice, I pressed it back down on the wound. My heart sank and a wave of nausea hit. I knew the symptoms of shock, but it was impossible for me to succumb now, or I'd end up with monk mud plasters.

Nicolas disappeared for an instant and then returned with a pewter bowl just in time to catch the contents of my stomach. He patted my back as a second wave hit.

"Just in the nick of time," I gagged. "Sorry you had to see that. Can you start working on the boiling water? And make sure that boiling water isn't sea water," I added.

This time, Jean left the room, leaving me alone with Nicolas for the first time since I'd regained consciousness. For some reason, I felt embarrassed and awkward, like a school girl face to face with her first crush. But there were some things that needed saying, like how I didn't think I'd have made it if he hadn't been there when I hit the shore. I still wasn't certain how I'd made that swim. Everything was fuzzy. But seeing his face was the one pure memory I had. His face and the warmth of his arms around me infusing me with life and breath.

"Nicolas, thank you for being there," I said, not able to put into words everything I meant. "I mean . . . on the beach. How did you know where I was?"

"I did not know and I was frantic with worry. I thought you had drowned or been abducted by Abdon. I think the Archangel guided me there. Katelyn, did they . . ."

He paused, but I knew what he wanted to ask. "No, Nicolas. Other than punching me in the thigh, they didn't hurt me. They were saving that privilege for Constable Collins, and I knew I couldn't let that happen. I cut myself on the rigging during my escape. I'll tell you about it later. But just in case I don't survive—and I am fully expecting to, so don't get any ideas—but just in case, I have to let you know what I learned. Collins is planning an all out attack on the mount. At dark moon. We," (I was surprised at how easily the 'we' slipped out), "have got to prepare for them. To resist. I have some ideas." When had the ideas come? Suddenly they were just there in my head, as if the swirling waves and sand and mist had infused them into my soul. I wanted to get them all out, but I could feel my strength ebbing away.

"Do not to speak of that now," he said as he took my hand. His touch electrified me, in spite of my condition. "We shall speak of it later. But I want you to know, I was wrong about you Katelyn Michaels. I was very wrong. You are the bravest, most amazing woman I have ever known. And . . ." I could tell he wanted to say something else, something more, but he stopped. Then, kneeling by my side so that I could feel his breath upon my cheek, he said, "now, you must tell me what to do for your wounds."

My heart started beating faster, and that was not a good thing. That just meant more blood pumping out of my arm. I was pretty sure that the freezing temperature of the seawater had kept me from losing too much blood up until now, but I knew I'd be in trouble if I didn't get this bleeding stopped, and stopped soon. And then I began to feel the pain in my thigh. Since I was holding the rag over my arm, I couldn't check on my leg. I had no alternative.

"Nicolas, you need to look at my thigh. Will you remove the covers, please?"

He looked at me and I nodded. Reluctantly, he began peeling away the layers until just the thin barrier of the muslin chemise separated his hand from my thigh.

"Pull up the chemise, Nicolas. You've got to help me. I can't do it."

I felt the blood drain from my face, and I felt clammy all over. I was struggling to keep from passing out, but I managed to shift my weight off my right buttock so that he could uncover my wounded thigh while at the same time keeping my left leg covered. I was glad he didn't argue with me. I managed to lift my head slightly to see how bad the damage was. Someone, I guess Madame Mercier, had wrapped a rag—equally as dirty as the one on my arm—around the wound. It was saturated with blood.

"How bad is it," I asked. "Is the cut as deep as the one on my arm? Unwrap it. Is the flesh split open?"

I could see the color drain from Nicolas's face as he removed the bandage. It wouldn't do for both of us to go into shock.

"Nicolas," I repeated. "Describe the wound to me."

"It is just as deep," he said, "but even longer than the cut on your arm," he said lifting up his thumb and index finger showing me a length of about four inches.

"Is it still bleeding?" I asked.

"Yes," he replied, with his already ashen face looking even paler.

"Listen," I said, "and make certain you understand what I'm saying because I may lose consciousness before this is over."

I was grateful that just then Madame Mercier and Jean entered the room with a pot of boiled water, the basins, and a stack of muslin strips. It was none too soon, because I was going to need several pairs of hands.

I was blessed to be able to get through my careful explanation of how they needed to wash and sanitize their hands with my hand sanitizer, then apply direct pressure with clean rags to one wound, while working on the other so I didn't bleed to death. I knew they had no concept of sterilization in the Middle Ages, so I explained the importance of thoroughly cleaning the wounds with the sterile water and then disinfecting them with the last of my hand-sanitizer. Hey, it was either that or their alcohol they called cider. At least the hand sanitizer didn't have globs of apple gook in it!

Then I instructed them how to sterilize a needle and the nylon thread from my travel sewing kit, and then how to sew me up. I thought Madame Mercier would be better at the sewing business, but probably wouldn't have the fortitude, so I said, "Nicolas. You have to do this. You have the best eyes, and your hands don't shake. You can do it. I trust you. Just make sure the wounds are very, very clean. And try to pull the edges together like a tight seam."

He looked at me with trepidation, but I honestly had full confidence in him. I knew he had seen much worse things in his life. I even managed to have them find the Neosporin from my first aid kit to cover the wounds before applying the muslin bandages. And I did all that after I vomited again and before I lost consciousness.

No, I think I first prayed for one of Mont Saint Michel's healing miracles, threw up second, and then lost consciousness as Nicolas began the process of stitching up my leg and arm with the steady hands of a master stonecutter.

Chapter 31

IN SPITE OF THE UPCOMING invasion, Nicolas insists we go through with the wedding.

"The Montois will be more likely to listen to what you have to say if they feel you are one of us," he argues. "And our wedding will help. After the celebration is over, we'll plan our defense."

And so, today is my wedding day and I get to bathe after all. And in hot water! The Montois not only agreed but insisted that after what I'd been through, and how I'd managed to survive, I deserved extra rations of fresh water and the fuel necessary to heat it. And Nicolas agreed. He didn't even argue. In fact, he helped several of the village men lug the largest cast iron pot I've ever seen into my bedroom. It looks like a witch's cauldron, but then I think the Montois actually believe I'm a witch. But a good witch. You know, like Glinda, the Good Witch of the North. I think it's because of Madame Mercier. She was Nicolas's surgery assistant and kept him supplied with threaded needles. She told everyone that I had magic healing potions and that my bravery was beyond incredible. But let's be honest. It's not too hard to be brave when you're unconscious. Then somehow, the story got out about my being brought to shore by a magic seal. I'm going to have to ask Nicolas about that one, because I don't remember anything about a seal. Or do I?

So now, just two days after my ordeal, Madame Mercier and three of her cronies are here to help me bathe, because it's a bit tricky with my right arm and leg bandaged. With clean bandages, if I do say so myself. And with a carefully dispensed dose of Neosporin on each wound. I actually feel good. Sore, but good. Maybe the mount really does have mystical healing properties like Jackson told me.

But most of the credit goes to Nicolas. He was amazing at his nipping and tucking. I guess the artist in him took over, and like a true craftsman, he pulled my flesh together in perfect plastic-surgeon precision. I don't think I'm even going to have much scarring. Jean told me that Nicolas's hand held steady, even though his face was as white as a turnip. With that kind of a steady hand, I think he'd make a darn good surgeon in the twenty-first century. Maybe I should take him back to apply to medical school.

But back to my bath. First of all, I ask the women to wash my hair. I kneel over the pot as they pour hot water over my tangles, and am I ever glad my shampoo (and cream rinse and soap and bath gel) survived my abduction. Can I even begin to explain how incredibly magnificent it feels to have clean hair? No, it's simply impossible to put into words. Unless you've traveled back in time six hundred years, been abducted by filthy despicable sailors, escaped those sailors by jumping into icy, sandy water, and then swum for several miles with deep cuts in your arm and leg, I don't think anyone can understand.

I feel kind of like Botticelli's *The Birth of Venus* as I try to maintain my modesty. Only I'm standing in a giant cauldron, not a clamshell. With my bath pouf, the women gently scrub the body parts I can't reach, while protecting my wounded limbs. Then they rinse me with gloriously hot water. I feel like a new person. But I get just as much enjoyment from watching them oooo and ahhhh over my bath products. They find them miraculous. I try to concoct some story about how advanced society is in *La Bretagne Profonde.* I hope they buy it, because otherwise Jean and Nicolas have more explaining to do.

I pretty much give up the idea that I'm going to get away with wearing the simple gown I'd chosen from among Madame Mercier's offerings, and I allow the women to dress me as they see fit. And that means about ten layers including under-underwear, underwear, inner-wear, on-top-of inner-wear, under-outerwear, outerwear, and over-outerwear. I learn that Madame Mercier and her husband were wealthy merchants before the war. The clothing I'm wearing was prepared as part of their daughter's dowry, but she died before her nuptials took place. Madame Mercier seems happy to share these garments with me, and I have to admit, they are beautiful. I'm too exhausted to fight, and frankly, I'm happy to provide her and the other women with a moment of joy. Their lives are filled with so much heartache that I cannot deny them this moment of happiness.

With all these layers, I feel like I'm the Pillsbury Doughboy, but hey, that just makes it all that more difficult for my bridegroom to get any ideas about stripping the clothes off me! At least the women don't dress me in white. Somehow the fact that I'm wearing a ruby-red velvet gown makes this seem more like a funky prom date than a wedding. I mean really. A bride in red velvet? Maybe in Las Vegas. It all feels like make-believe. And of course, it is. The marriage, I mean. I just hope Nicolas remembers it's a make-believe marriage.

Not only do these endearing women take over the role as my personal fashionistas, but they are my hairdressers as well. I guess they don't think a giant thunking braid is appropriate for my wedding day. So I give them total freedom with my hair, which they finally manage to get dry and coerce into a few curls, topped with a wreath of autumn leaves and a few wilted yellow chrysanthemums.

I even provide further entertainment for the women by allowing them to watch me apply a hint of mascara, lip gloss, and blush. And I even curl my eyelashes and brush my teeth. I'm not sure why I want to put on any make-up for Nicolas, but, heck, that's a bride's prerogative. I know it's wrong for me to be exposing these women to my modern toiletries, but I just can't help it. It's just so darn fun to watch their expressions of complete and total bliss.

They primp and prance, tug and pull and view me from every angle, sighing with satisfaction. And then one of them comes in with a large crude mirror, obviously a prized possession. Just to please them, I admire their handiwork with appropriate appreciation. And quite honestly, I have to admit, I've never seen myself look quite so . . . how can I put it? So Renaissance-fairish. But Renaissance-fairish in a good way.

The women pronounce their work complete and lead me limping the short distance up the hill to the parish church. The foggy mists have dissipated and it is a clear and sunny, but cool day. It appears the entire village is present. My stylists are proud to show me off to the younger women, who surround me and fawn over me like I'm a rock star. Actually, I feel more like a museum display than a rock star or bride. I can just hear French Sheldon saying, "And here ladies and gentlemen, we are having an exhibit of the marriage rituals of the Middle Ages. As you are seeing, the bride is dressed not in white, but in red, and she is looking more like a giant Valentine than a bride." But a bride I am, French Sheldon.

As I finally approach the wedding venue, I notice that the women are all standing together on the left side of the church, facing the doors, and the men are on the right. I look anxiously for my groom among the men. Why do I care? I guess I just want to get this over with as quickly as possible so I can get on with the business of winning a war, saving the mount, and going 'back to the future.' You know, the typical thoughts occupying the mind of every bride on her wedding day.

Then I see Nicolas emerging from the group of men. It appears he too has bathed. His freshly scrubbed face looks so young and naïve, and yet I know he has already lived a lifetime of experiences. Nicolas has lived more life than any guys I know and I'm pretty sure I wouldn't have trusted any of them to sew me back together. The sunlight reflects off his damp golden curls, shooting out tiny prisms of rainbow colors. Oh, for heaven's sakes, it looks like my groom actually has a halo around his head! I hear the younger women sighing in unison. Hey gals, sorry, this one's mine. And then I realize the truth. He isn't mine at all, and for just a brief instant—a miniscule millisecond—I almost wish this is a real marriage. Then I think of my mother and I'm appalled. How can I even consider getting married at age seventeen? Especially without the people I love the most in the world there to support me?

Nicolas approaches and as he inspects me from head to toe, I see him actually blush. I thought that's what the bride's supposed to do, but no, Nicolas is the one blushing. He clears his throat, takes me carefully by my injured right arm, and leads me to the bottom step of the church. I stumble a bit as I hesitate putting weight on my right leg, but heck, who cares? I could be dead.

"You look . . . beautiful, Katelyn. *Très, très belle.*" he whispers to me as he takes my right hand in his.

"Aren't we going in?" I ask, ignoring his compliment. He looks pretty fine himself dressed in a clean linen shirt, and a pair of I guess what you would call breeches, which hit him below the knee. His legs are covered with woolen stockings and he is actually wearing a pair of pointy-toe, soft-leather ankle boots. I dare to look him in the eyes and I discover for the first time that his eyes are brown. Deep brown. A nice contrast to his golden curls.

"The actual marriage ceremony takes place here," he whispers to me in English, "and afterwards, we go inside to celebrate the nuptial mass."

The parish priest steps out of the church and onto the front steps to face us. The smile on his face says it all: he is happy to officiate over something other than a funeral.

"Why are all the men on the right and the women on the left?" I whisper, trying not to notice how Nicolas's eyes refuse to break contact with mine or that his hand refuses to release my hand. Surprisingly, I don't want him to release it. I feel safe with him by my side. And, I feel a slight flutter in the pit of my stomach. It's a feeling I've never felt before and I pray that I don't throw up all over Madame Mercier's daughter's ruby-red, velvet, Valentine gown. Vomit on velvet is not a good thing. Especially where there's no water to clean it.

"T'is a symbol that Eve was formed from a rib taken from the left side of Adam."

Well, the Women's Movement obviously hasn't hit fifteenth century France. In spite of what Ms. Carson would say, I'm not offended. I think it's actually kind of sweet.

The priest begins by asking if anyone knows any reason why Nicolas and I should not be married and when no one speaks up, he turns to us and asks us that same question. It's amazing, really, because I'm starting to understand quite a bit of French. Must be the Archangel who has enlightened my mind or given me the gift of tongues. I'm half tempted to answer, "Heck yeah," but Nicolas squeezes my hand at just the critical moment.

Then the priest looks at Nicolas and recites in French, "Nicolas le Breton, wilt thou have this woman to thy wedded wife, wilt thou love her, and honor her, keep her and guard her, in health and in sickness, as a husband should a wife, and forsaking all others on account of her, keep thee only unto her, so long as ye both shall live?" to which Nicolas replies, "I will."

Okay, now I'm getting a little freaked out because the priest's words aren't all that different from a twenty-first century ceremony. Somehow, I expected it to be so different that it wouldn't seem real. But it does. Nicolas can feel my panic. He squeezes my hand even harder and looks me straight in the eyes in a sort of plea. I remember when I first noticed his eyes. I'd called them earnest. And that is exactly what I'm seeing. His earnest eyes. It stops me cold in my tracks, and I know I can't back out now. I'm not even sure I want to, and that's even scarier.

"Katelyn, daughter of Michel," the French version of my last name, "wilt thou have this man to thy wedded husband, wilt thou love him, and honor him, keep him and cherish him, in health and in sickness, as a wife should a husband, and forsaking all others on account of him, keep thee only unto him, so long as ye both shall live?"

I pause just long enough to throw some fear into Nicolas, but then answer, "I will."

Then comes the part that Nicolas practiced with me in French, where we exchange our vows. I whisper loud enough for him to hear over his own nearly identical words: "I, Katelyn, take thee Nicolas to my wedded husband, to have and to hold from this day forward, for better, for worse, for richer, for poorer, in sickness, and in health, till death do us part, if the holy Church will ordain it: And thereto I plight thee my troth." I actually kind of chuckled at this part because nobody has even bothered to ask me if I'm Catholic. And I'm not. Just one more reason why this marriage can't be legally binding. I hope.

After that, the priest calls for the ring. I guess only the bride wears a ring in 1424. Surprisingly, Nicolas is equipped with a narrow band that actually looks like real gold. I have a sinking feeling that it's Jean's ring. Nicolas has told me a little about Jean and his beloved Marie. If it is her ring, I know it has been offered at great sacrifice. He slips the ring onto my left ring-finger. It's a little snug, but it goes over my knuckle. Marie must have been pretty thin because my fingers were thin even before I started starving to death. Again, it spooks me that the ceremony, down to the ring, is so similar to a 'real' marriage ceremony.

Then we bow our heads for the priest's blessing. He announces to everyone that we are now man and wife, and I'm pretty sure he includes something about a gaggle of children. A gaggle of geese would be just great right now. We could feed the entire population of Mont Saint Michel. But the children? Not gonna happen.

As husband and wife we enter the church, followed by the villagers. The monks aren't here, but I guess they have better things to do like . . .ummm. Why can't they be saving Mont Saint Michel if they're too busy to come to my wedding?

We kneel before the altar and the priest gives a prayer and another blessing, and then we sit through an entire mass. The best part about the wedding ceremony? No "you may now kiss your bride." I can handle the hand-holding, but I'm not going as far as the kissing bit. Kind of like the grandson in the *Princess Bride* not wanting it to be a kissing book. I don't want it to be a kissing wedding. I guess public displays of affection in the fifteenth century are frowned upon and I'm not complaining.

Now, I'm informed, comes the feast. But of course, it isn't really a feast since there's no food. Unless you consider Robert le Boiteux's cockles with steamed seaweed and Jean's apple ale a feast. But the Montois are pretty happy with that, and after trying to politely down my ration of those chewy, sandy little shellfish, I graciously thank the kind fisherman— who I'm told sounded the alarm about my disappearance—for his generosity. These people have treated me with such gracious kindness that I'm starting to understand what Nicolas meant about going through with the wedding. Not only has this been a means to provide the Montois with a cause for celebration, but it has served to unite our little community and I think they accept me. I hope they'll be ready to implement my plan.

But before that can happen, I must give the entire population the satisfaction of escorting us back to our 'wedding chambers,' while the women titter nervously and the men hoot and holler. I just hope they're the only ones hollering tonight.

Chapter 32

THE THEATRICAL PERFORMANCE was over, and he'd been the consummate actor. When they returned to the house—without Jean, thanks to the marital customs imposed by the Montois— Nicolas lit a candle and escorted Katelyn up the stairs to her bedchamber. He opened the door for her and handed her the candle. He could see the trepidation in her eyes. As much as he would have liked a different outcome from this, his wedding day, he fully understood his role.

"It has been a long day, Katelyn. We shall speak in the morning—of the attack and of your plans," he assured her. "Now, it is important for you to sleep."

"Thank you, Nicolas . . ." she said. Her eyes did not break contact with his. He could feel and smell her sweet breath upon his face, and there was nothing he wanted more than to taste that breath with his mouth. He thought she was about to say something more, but then she turned, and pressed the door between their bodies. "Good night," she said looking at him from behind the door. And then she added in French, *"bonne nuit."*

"Bonne nuit, Katelyn." He turned dejectedly and made his way to his own bedchamber.

"What do you expect, idiot?" he said aloud, but not loud enough for Katelyn to hear.

Aided only by the light of the moon streaming in through his window, he began stripping off the items of clothing Madame Mercier had given to him. They belonged to her late husband and she'd insisted that Nicolas keep them to 'be pleasing for his new bride.' The generous widow had done a fine job of making the bride pleasing to her new husband. Much too pleasing. As he removed the stockings and boots, he stubbed his toe, and swore under his breath. He was not in the habit of swearing. This dangerous girl-woman was turning him into something he'd never been before. First he'd detested her, and now he couldn't get her image out of his mind. He didn't understand what was happening to him.

And then he heard her call out his name.

"Nicolas? Are you still awake?"

Dressed only in his knickers, he ran to her room. She had the door opened a crack and looked out at him.

"I'm so sorry to disturb you," she said, "but . . ." She stopped and looked at his bare chest and turned her eyes away. Then, as if she was measuring her words carefully, she said, "I . . . I need your help."

"What is it?" he asked, trying to maintain self-control. The thoughts in his mind ranged from fear to elation. Why had she called him?

"With my injuries, I can't get out of these clothes," she said. "I tried, but I simply can't do it. There are too many fasteners and too many layers. I hate to ask, but . . . well, you've seen me in my undergarments before. For heaven's sake, you pulled me out of the ocean, and you sewed up my leg. I'm afraid you're gonna have to help me undress. And change my bandages."

This was simply asking too much! Katelyn Michaels was a temptress. He would never compromise her virtue and yet he couldn't get past the fact that they were married in the eyes of the world, and more importantly, in the eyes of God. He'd be justified . . . but their marriage was for appearances only. It was a parody. But, *zut,* it was still legal! Where was Jean when he needed him? Why had his mentor caved in to the demands of the Montois and agreed to stay at Robert's home for the night? Surely he must have understood the precarious nature of the situation?

Katelyn had removed her head wreath and pulled her hair up on top of her head so that her neck was exposed. Nicolas could tell she was in pain, because she cradled her right arm, and she was wobbling, trying to balance her weight on just one leg. It was a sobering reminder of her ordeal, and it only served to increase his desire to protect her, like a true husband should. This girl he'd originally viewed as a whining, coddled female was anything but. Yes, she could be peevish and quarrelsome. She could caterwaul with the best of them. But when it really counted, she had risen to the occasion. She'd exhibited true bravery and courage in the face of deadly peril, and he hadn't heard a word of complaint about her wounds. She was valiant in every way that truly mattered.

He stepped into the room and she turned her back to him. The shadows from the flickering candle minced about the room like a duo of woodland fairies setting out for a midnight tryst. There was just enough light for him to see the rows of crisscrossing ribbon that curved down below her waist. He lifted his hands and allowed one index finger to graze her bare neck before he began the work of untying and loosening the garment. As he pushed the gown forward off her shoulders, he heard her gasp at his touch. The simple functions of his body began accelerating. He knew his breathing was speeding up and yet he was powerless to stop the escalation. His thoughts were racing just as fast as his heart. He untied the full underskirt around her waist, and as she attempted to step out of the underskirt and gown, she stumbled.

He caught her in his arms, supported her weight, and then turned her gently—avoiding any pressure on her injured arm—so that she faced him. Although the room was chilly, he was anything but cold. Her body heat against his bare chest warmed him to the very core. He could hear her breathing and see the rise of her chest that matched his own. He looked into her eyes, and she returned his gaze. Her eyes were as pale as the early morning sky, and yet flecks of dancing fire in them spoke of the burning noonday sun.

The instant became a moment, the moment a minute, the minute an hour, and the hour an eternity. Neither of them uttered a word. And only the sound of their beating hearts and their labored breathing interrupted the silence of the night.

Nicolas inched his mouth forward slowly. He would stop if she resisted, but her gaze remained firm, and she did not pull back. In fact, she tightened the grip her left arm had on his shoulder. Only the width of a chrysanthemum petal separated their lips. Then Nicolas heard a creaking sound on the stairs. It echoed through the heated silence like a cannonball from the English bombards. He immediately shifted Katelyn's body so she could support her weight, and left the room to see who this untimely intruder could be.

"Jean," he cried when he saw the old man hobbling up the stairs. "What are you doing here?"

"I heard your pleas to return, Nicolas. In my mind," the tired old man said, running his eyes up and down Nicolas's bare torso. "And so I slipped out of Robert's house. I thought you might prefer to have some company tonight."

Zut alors! I must be more careful about what I pray for, he thought.

"Yes, you are right, Papa," he finally said. "I am . . . glad you returned. And Katelyn has need of us both. Madame Mercier and her assistants did a fine job of corseting the poor bride. She is tied up like a proper prisoner. She requires our assistance."

When Nicolas returned to Katelyn's chamber with Jean in tow, Katelyn was sitting at the dressing table preparing a clean set of bandages for her wounds. He was amazed at her ability to act as if nothing had just happened between them. Which it hadn't. If only . . . but life was full of 'if onlys,' and it served no purpose to dwell upon what couldn't be changed.

"Monsieur Jean," she said in what seemed to be a spontaneous display of pleasure, "I'm so glad you're here. We could use some extra help."

Was Katelyn really glad that Jean returned? Was he glad? He realized he would probably never know the true answer to those questions.

After the two men had assisted Katelyn in removing the remainder of her cumbersome layers, and after Nicolas had wisely allowed Jean to change her bandages, the young man begged for the mercy of sleep to overcome him. But to no avail. He tossed and turned, trying to find a comfortable position on his straw pallet as the moonlight highlighted specks of dust motes wafting about the room.

It seemed as if he lay there in silence for hours and yet suddenly out of the darkness, Jean said, "Nicolas, if it is of any consolation, I know how you feel. Marie was Katelyn's age when I first met her. And . . . I was completely and totally smitten."

Nicolas was stunned to hear the old man's steady voice. He thought Jean had been soundly asleep.

"But *your* marriage was authentic," Nicolas said, not trying to deny what Jean already knew about his feelings for Katelyn.

"Yes, that is true. But my calling as a Watchman ultimately caused me to lose the woman I loved. And so shall it be for you."

"But Papa, at least you had the opportunity to build a lifetime of happy memories with Marie."

"Which made her loss, and my son's death, all the more painful. When Katelyn leaves, your pain will be but a few weeks, a few months. You are a young man. You will find another to stand in her stead. My pain has endured for years."

It was unlike Jean to complain that his suffering was any worse than the suffering of others and Nicolas found it unsettling, and almost insulting.

"Who are you to say your pain is greater than mine?" he replied almost belligerently. "Who are you to judge between me and thee?"

"My son, my son. I speak by way of reassurance, not by way of judgment. I have seen visions of your future. You shall find love again. Of that I am certain. I cannot tell you from which quarter it will come, but be of good cheer. You shall not be left comfortless. I know this is of little consolation to you now."

"Papa," Nicolas said. "I did not expect to feel this way. You know how exasperating she can be, and yet there is something about her. She is so strong. How many of the women on this mount could have done what she did? Escaped from the English. Braved the unforgiving tides. She is amazing. I do not know what to do."

"What you do, Nicolas, is assist her in saving this island. That is what you have been called here to do. Unfortunately, your personal feelings are secondary to that."

"I know, Papa. But it hurts so much to think of losing her forever. I . . ."

"I know, my son. I know. But now you must sleep. You need your strength. After all, you have a world to save."

Chapter 33

WHEN I WAKE UP THE next morning, I know what I have to do. Playing dress-up is over. I'm not an adult, I'm not old enough to be a bride, and as much as I was tempted to consider myself a bride last night, I have to face the truth. I will be going home and Nicolas will be staying here. Facts are facts, and I don't see any way to change them.

Besides, I have more important things to do. It's time to focus on what needs to be done so that I *can* go back home. After Nicolas left last night, I couldn't sleep, so to push thoughts of him from my mind, I spent the night contemplating war strategy. I even got up in the middle of the night and started doing a word search of the Bible—my inspirational military handbook—which I just happen to have on my laptop. Yeah, I know, it sounds ridiculous. Take off bridal gown, put on military uniform, *et voilà:* General Katelyn Michaels. I'm not old enough to be a bride, but somehow I've got to conquer the English Army. But amazingly, I actually have some pretty good ideas, thanks to Jackson and his overzealous role as my Mont Saint Michel tour guide. Now I just have to convince the Montois that these are good ideas without putting the fear of God in them.

It is also clear to me now exactly why I had been inspired to load all of my electronic equipment into my backpack before Jackson and I went exploring—in fact, why I had brought it all to France in the first place. I would need every single item for the plan to work, including my father's iPod, which is loaded with some impressive orchestral works.

After I dress in my twenty-first century clothing, I awkwardly braid my hair with my sore arm and brush my teeth. I don't bother to change my bandages. Jean changed them last night, and I am amazed at how well my wounds are healing. No sign of infection. No redness. It's pretty miraculous. I guess the genies of the mount are doing their work. The stitches will have to come out in a few days, but that should be a piece of cake compared to them going in. And honestly, who happens to have clear nylon thread in their sewing kits? Was that just a fluke or what? Or divine providence.

I'm still amazed I managed to stay cool-headed enough to think through the whole 'what on earth should I do about these giant cuts?' business, after escaping from an abduction and swimming for my life. The Archangel must have helped me. It gives me a new sense of empowerment. I *can* do this, because I *know* I'm receiving divine assistance. And for the first time, I'm finally starting to figure out why I'm here.

I'm glad to see that, like yesterday, this will be a sunny day. Right now, I need the sun, and a lot of it. I sling my backpack over my good shoulder and brace myself to face Nicolas. I can't put off the inevitable. The longer I avoid him, the harder it will be. Might as well just get it over ASAP. I walk downstairs planning to act as if nothing out of the ordinary happened yesterday. Or last night.

My stomach growls, and I know how sparse my morning meal will be, but there's no use complaining. *I've* been hungry for days. The Montois have been hungry for months and even years. I'm grateful Nicolas managed to bring some food from my world, because that's what we've been living on. Pretty basic stuff, but at least edible stuff. I know Nicolas views our meals as luxurious. My only luxury is fresh drinking water. Jean knows I cannot abide his apple ale, and the Montois have consented to exchange a ration of fresh water for my ration of cider.

Jean eats very little, but I know it's because he's so unselfish. He wants Nicolas and me to have as much strength as possible to fight this war. I haven't been here long, but I see Jean becoming weaker each passing day. I want to be with him every minute and learn as much as I can from him. But I can't afford the luxury. Nicolas and I have much to do in the next week and a half before dark moon, and there's no time to waste.

I have to be honest, I'm surprised by the new me. I'm more confident and less whiney. Oh don't worry, I'm still good old Katelyn Michaels, but I guess something changes inside when you face death and stare down the grim reaper. I still feel angry but now, the object of my anger isn't Jean or Nicolas, and miraculously it's not even my father's trophy wife. I'm not saying I've learned to love her or anything, but the anger towards her in my heart is gone. I've come to understand she's probably doing the best she can to build a relationship with her new husband's children, and I haven't made that easy.

The truth is, marriages fall apart. I know that. I don't like it, but I must accept it as part of mortality. Divorce doesn't mean I can't go on. It doesn't mean my mother can't go on, and it doesn't mean I have to hate my father. I finally accept the fact that my parent's divorce is not one hundred percent my dad's fault. There are always two sides to every story and I've never even considered that he might have a side. Until now.

Anyway, now my anger is focused on a truly evil being: Abdon in the host body of Constable Richard Collins. *He's* the one standing between me and my life. *He's* the one who's ready to viciously attack and kill hundreds of innocent people, including women and children. *He's* the new object of my fury. And this time, I have to act upon that fury. I'm fully aware of the fact that I may be responsible for people losing their lives. It's a sobering thought for a seventeen-year old girl who has never worried about anything besides her parents' divorce. I'm woefully unprepared. But I have no choice.

When I get downstairs, Jean and Nicolas are sitting at the table. They greet me, and Nicolas immediately gets up to serve me my rations: a glass of water and a quarter of a bowl of canned peaches. Better peaches than pears. Yeah, I hate canned pears. But my gourmet breakfast can wait.

I'm glad Nicolas has also decided to face me, because I don't have time to go chasing him down. We must begin planning immediately to be ready for Operation Dark Moon. That's the name of my battle plan. I plop my backpack down on the table and take out my pen and battle plan notebook. Then, one by one, while Jean and Nicolas watch me in silence, I begin to remove my electronic devices, praising God that I actually had them in my backpack the day Nicolas brought me back to 1424. But then, I guess that was all part of the Archangel's plan. He inspired me to bring my gear. Anyway, I still have about an hour left on my computer's battery.

When I see my digital camera, I actually laugh. I wish I'd thought to get pictures of me as a bride. They'd be priceless. Unbelievable, but priceless. And to be honest, I really did look pretty darn good!

Oh well, too late for that. And honestly, do you think anyone in my world would believe what I've been through? Even with pictures? Nope.

Not even my gullible little brother. I guess the fact I'm a married woman will have to be my dirty little secret for the rest of my life. Not to mention the fact that I'm a time traveler.

"These," I say to my fellow Watchmen, "are our weapons against Constable Collins and his army."

They look at me in astonishment and wait for my explanation. I think they believe my electronic devices might be some type of actual weapons. I hope they won't be disappointed. I boot up my computer and get right to the point. "You believe I was sent here by the Archangel Michael because of certain abilities or knowledge I have that you don't have. Is that correct?"

They both agree.

"Then you're going to have to convince the Montois and the monks that my plan is ordained of God and will not in any way bring down God's condemnation. They must understand that and give their full support, or this will never work."

They reluctantly agree, still not knowing what I'm about to propose.

When I show them the documents I've been working on, and then give them a broad overview of my plans, they're doubtful, so I have to give them a few demonstrations. But, I don't want to waste my batteries. Even with the solar battery charger, I have no idea of how much sun there will be on a tidal island off the coast of northern France in the month of October. I explain about that, and although I know they don't understand how my stuff works off of solar energy, they don't ask questions. They take my word for it. They don't understand how my stuff works, period. And I don't even bother to try to explain electricity.

Jean suggests placing the unfolding solar panel on the roof. He assures me it's the sunniest spot on the property and it will be out of sight from neighbors who might ask questions. We all traipse upstairs and Jean and I watch nervously as Nicolas climbs out the window and maneuvers his way up to the roof. It won't do to have him fall before the battle has even begun, but he seems pretty nimble. I call out instructions to him so he's certain to get the solar cells facing up. After that's taken care of, we head back to the table to talk logistics.

With or without seeing my solar panel, the Montois will have plenty of probing questions. And so will the soldiers and monks. I'm thinking the explanation that I'm an angel sent by God with special powers will probably be easier to sell than the actual truth. But I guess that almost is the actual truth. Not the being an angel part, but the being sent by God part. Anyway, that story will be Jean's department because Nicolas and I are going to be busy with other things. But Jean's got to come up with a good explanation, and we all agree it shouldn't include time travel. The good news is that the Montois will be highly motivated to go along with us, in spite of what they think about my mysterious powers. Their lives depend upon our success.

Although my plan is a wild gamble and will be dangerous, we have no other, and these are dangerous times. Neither Jean nor Nicolas tries to dissuade me. They know, as do I, that this is our only hope for survival. Nicolas came to my time to get me to go back to do something they couldn't do, and so here I am, doing something they can't. But without the help of every single Montois, my plan will fail.

First, there're a few questions I need to ask. "You've already explained that Abdon is one of Lucifer's fallen angels and that his current host is Constable Richard Collins."

"Yes," says Jean.

"Earlier, you told me that there might be other fallen angels. Do you know of any others in Collins' army?"

"No, as far as we know, he is the only one at this time."

"And so the English soldiers, though they may be evil—and I have a personal witness of that fact—are still just mortal men?" I ask.

"Oui," Jean says. "That is what we think."

"Does Abdon have any special powers?" I ask. "I mean, I know he can't travel in time. You already told me that, but can he go in and out of Collins' body and go into other hosts? Or as a spirit, can he be here on the mount unseen? Could he know what we're planning right now?"

"No, he does not go in and out of Collins, for if he did so, he would lose the control he has over his host," Jean explains. "And Lucifer's angels cannot know our thoughts. God alone knows our hearts and minds. And as for your other question, you are essentially asking if the fallen ones can spy on us. Is that what you want to know?"

"Yes, that's exactly what I'm getting at."

"If they could do that, there would be no purpose for our existence. For the Watchmen, I mean," Jean says. "They would know . . ." He stops and looks at Nicolas. It seems they are exchanging a non-verbal message, but I don't know what it is. I wonder if there's something they're not telling me. "They would know," he continues "our exact situation here on the mount, our weaknesses and how to destroy us, how to destroy the mount. Just the simple fact that Mont Saint Michel still exists is an indicator that the fallen angels have no power to spy upon us without bodies. They cannot interfere in our lives, in our activities."

"So you're saying that unless Abdon or other fallen angels inhabit mortal hosts, they have no interaction with us as mortals. They do not see us, they cannot hear us, they cannot read the plans I've written in this notebook, for example?"

"They have no interaction with us unless we willingly invite them into our realm. Unless we turn to Lucifer through our evil actions, we cannot be influenced by them and they cannot be a part of our world. Lucifer has power, it is true, but because we have the physical bodies so desired by the evil ones, we have greater power to repel both Lucifer and his minions."

"Okay," I say, "that's the first bit of good news I've heard since I got here." I look up and see Nicolas studying me intently. He has hardly said a word this morning, and I don't know if he's furious with me, or what. I feel my cheeks begin to go red. I lower my eyes and begin doodling on my notepad as I ask my next question.

"So you believe Abdon is the only fallen one we have to deal with? The only one who will be intent on actually destroying the mount?"

"As long as I have been alive, and that has been a long time," Jean says, "I have never had any dealings with any fallen one other than Abdon. The only way he can know what is happening here on the mount is through strictly mortal means. He needs to see for himself as Collins, or have one of his English soldiers get inside the ramparts and report back to him."

I'm relieved. I don't need to worry about Abdon having non-earthbound spies on the mount. And mortal beings are more powerful than Lucifer and his evil ones. I have more power than Abdon, because I have my own physical body. Abdon's is just a loaner. And there are probably no other fallen angels in host bodies that I need to worry about. It's reassuring.

"Tell me how you know that Richard Collins is Abdon's host?" I ask.

"Because I have come face to face with him," Jean explains. "And Nicolas has seen Collins often enough to recognize Abdon's characteristics. That's why he knew your Gothman in the future was Abdon in another host." I look at Nicolas. He doesn't say anything, but he gives a nod of confirmation.

Then Jean tells me of his long history with Abdon. Evidently, his hosts don't tolerate his presence well, and after a few years, they either die or become catatonic. Consequently, the fallen angel is required to change hosts often. And each new host knows that Jean is the mount's Watchman.

“But how do you recognize Abdon when he enters a new host?” I want to know.

“It is difficult to explain, Katelyn, because obviously all of his hosts look and sound different. However, over the years, I have come to identify certain things. Regardless of the host, it is Abdon’s voice I hear, Abdon’s eyes I see, and his mannerisms I recognize. Let me reiterate the fact that it is a very difficult task for a fallen one to successfully inhabit a mortal body. Abdon has been one of the few who has been successful, but in order to succeed, his essence has to assert itself with such force that he actually changes his mortal host’s physical attributes.”

“When did you first come into contact with his most recent host, Richard Collins?” I ask.

“When the Godons—that’s what we call the English—first attempted to conquer the mount. Before their ships came to create the blockade, Collins led an attack at low tide. He forced his soldiers to cross the sands on foot. Many of them died before they even made it to the island, sucked into the quicksands. That attack ended in hand to hand combat with the soldiers sent by King Charles. When it became apparent our soldiers were failing, the men of the village joined them. I was one of those men and I fought Collins face to face. He knew exactly who I was, the Watchman of the Mount, and I knew exactly who he was. We even spoke about it as we fought, and he laughed as he told me how he was not only going to kill every single Montois, but destroy the mount as well, taking it apart stone by stone. That is not the English agenda. That is Abdon’s agenda. The English wish to keep the mount intact, to claim it as their own. To make it *their* rallying cry. But if Collins’ succeeds in breaking through the ramparts, his men will obey his orders. They fear rather than respect him. The mount will be destroyed, and everything in and on it will be obliterated.”

I can tell this discussion is taking a toll on Jean. I wish I could give him a break, but unfortunately, time is not a luxury we have.

"And so what happened? When you met Collins face to face? You obviously both survived that encounter."

"Katelyn, I wish I could have killed Abdon's host that day, but I am an old man, and Collins is young. I could not match his strength. I stumbled and fell onto my back, and just as Collins brought his sword down to end my life, my dear friend Robert jumped him from behind, allowing me to regain my footing. We managed to force him to retreat but unfortunately, Robert did so at the expense of his leg. He received a nasty wound from Collins, which resulted in his distinctive limp—and his name. I owe Robert le Boiteux my life."

I see Jean's hand shaking as he wipes the beads of sweat from his forehead. It's cold in the house, but Jean is sweating. This dauntless man has seen so much suffering, I'm surprised it hasn't cankered his soul. But it hasn't. He epitomizes all that is good and valiant and merciful.

"And so the Montois actually fought off Collins' army?"

"Yes," Jean says, "but the only reason we won that battle is because the Constable did not have enough soldiers. And we weren't starving to death at the time. Unfortunately, the bastille at Ardevon has now been reinforced with more soldiers. Abdon will not be so foolish this time around. He has four times as many Godons under his command and he knows they will face a decimated, starving band of Montois. He knows the blockade has taken its toll."

"How can you be certain about their numbers?" I ask.

Jean looks at Nicolas and nods his head.

"Because I've counted them," Nicolas says. They're practically the first words I've heard him speak all morning.

"What do you mean?"

"That has been my assignment since I came to the mount, Katelyn. That is why I was called. To gather information, and to help obtain enough food from the mainland to keep the Montois from total starvation. You see, I come from an area of Brittany where we have tides and sands exactly like in the bay here. I have a gift. I can read the sands. I know where it's safe to walk and where it is too dangerous. And I can read the water. I know every fluctuation of the tides. So, I have crossed the sands at night and visited the enemy camp," he said, "on many occasions. I know exactly how many Godons there are."

I'm stunned. This is the first time I've heard about his role. Nicolas is a spy. An intelligence gatherer. It takes my breath away. It's one thing to hide behind the ramparts and plan a defensive stand against a distant enemy. It's another to infiltrate the enemy camp and put one's life in danger on a repeated basis.

"Katelyn, I know a great deal about Richard Collins . . . and Abdon. I have never gotten close enough to kill him and fortunately, he has never gotten close enough to me to know who I am, but I have seen and heard him in action. The one thing I did not know, however, was about the attack at dark moon. Collins has done a good job of keeping that a secret. If it were not for you overhearing it on the Godon ship, we might not have learned about it in time."

He looks at me and this time, I do not look away. He extends his hand across the table and presses his hand briefly over my own, and then draws it away quickly. My heart thumps so loudly I'm certain both men can hear it. That small gesture means more to me than Nicolas will ever know. He is not angry with me.

"I was wrong about you, Katelyn. You may be able to save us after all," Nicolas admits.

"But I can't do it alone," I say, not even trying to express false humility at his unexpected expression of confidence in me. We have no time for word games. We're dealing with life and death. "I need your help. I need everyone's help."

"I will do whatever you need me to do," he says.

His offer completes the missing piece of Operation Dark Moon. Everything falls perfectly into place, but it comes at a high cost. I am about to put him in grave danger, and it could cost him his life. My heart drops, because this spy also happens to be . . . my husband, and as much as I want to deny it, the decision I've just made to put him in danger forces me to accept the truth.

I am in love with Nicolas le Breton.

Chapter 34

FIRST ITEM OF BUSINESS: we need a really fat pig and a gazillion sheets.

Okay, I know that sounds completely off the wall. Well, actually that's pretty accurate. They pretty much will be off the wall. Let me explain about the pig part first. I remember the story my stepmother (I can finally call her that) told me and Jackson as we were driving from Paris to Normandy. While setting the stage for our visit to Mont Saint Michel, she told us about Carcassonne, another medieval city in France that was under siege by the English in the Hundred Years' War. Its citizens, like the Montois, remained strong, and their fortifications proved impenetrable.

"But," she told us, "zee *first* siege of zat city, many centuries earlier eez much more interesting." Although I tried to act like I wasn't listening to her, it was such a bizarre story I couldn't *not* listen. And in my wildest dreams, I never thought I'd actually be using her story to help me win a battle in the Hundred Years' War!

It's the story of how Carcassonne got its name. It's a walled city somewhere in Southern France. Don't know where exactly, but the 'where' isn't important. It's the 'how' that counts.

In the ninth century or so, if I remember correctly, the city was under siege by the Emperor Charlemagne and his armies. Legend has it that the good citizens of the great city were starving to death (hmmm, that sounds familiar), when a certain Madame Carcas proposed a radical idea. There was just one sickly pig inside the city walls that hadn't been gobbled up. She proposed they feed it from the remaining stores of food to fatten it up. Can't you just imagine how happy the townspeople were with that idea? That's why I need a pig that's already fat. Besides, we don't have time to wait for a skinny pig to get fat. And frankly, we don't have any stores of food left.

Anyway, to finish the story, when the Emperor's troops attacked again, attempting to scale the walls with ladders and grappling hooks, the townspeople threw the fat pig over the ramparts in the guise of a bonking weapon! You know, 'ye old flying pig ploy.' I'm sure it's in the annals of military history somewhere. And it worked (or so goes the legend). Charlemagne believed that if the besieged townspeople still had fat pigs, and if they could afford to use one as a weapon, they must have an inexhaustible supply of food. So he and his troops abandoned the siege. And my stepmother's punch line—over which she giggled in that high pitched wheezing of hers—was this: the bells of the church rang (*sonner* in French) to announce the incredible victory. So the city was renamed in honor of Madame Carcas and the ringing bells: Carcassonne! I guess it could have been named after the flying pig carcass as well. I don't know if it's true, but that hardly matters. Desperate times call for desperate measures. I just hope the Godons aren't familiar with the legend.

So that's why I've added 'fat pig ammo' to my list of needs, and some apples would be nice too. Nicolas and I will be working on that one in a few days.

Now on to the sheets. Here's the deal: we're going to cover the entire mount with bed linens sewn together by the women of Mont Saint Michel, and then with my magical witch sorcery, I'm going to make the whole island disappear à la David Copperfield. Okay, just a joke, but a little humor is good in times of stress, and I'd say these are pretty stressful times.

But I actually do have a pretty awesome use for the sheets. After presenting my plan to Jean and Nicolas this morning, Nicolas and I set out on an inspection of the mount and find the perfect wall for my plan. The south front of the abbey, above the village, is a flat, crenellated wall along its entire length. I don't remember it looking like that in the future, but in the fifteenth century, it's perfect. And it needs to be covered.

So, with Madame Mercier's help, Jean is gathering every piece of white or cream fabric on the island, and getting the women busy sewing some of them together into a long single piece, and others into robes. For now, I'm just asking everyone to take this one on faith. They'll discover why I need the sheets soon enough.

Then we've got to gather every man, monk, soldier, woman and child on the crest of the hill below that abbey wall. It's the longest piece of uninterrupted real-estate on this island. Oh, and they each need to be there dressed all in white, either in their own clothing, or in our sheet robes. That ought to be interesting. That will happen as soon as the robes are ready.

But I'm not planning on the pig and sheet tricks alone. I've got a multi-pronged attack going here, like Kevin in *Home Alone,* all neatly diagrammed in my little war games notebook. And the thing is, it's not enough for us to just win this particular battle, because the English will just keep coming back. No, we've got to completely scare them off so they never, ever want to come anywhere near Mont Saint Michel again. That's why my strategy is a bit over the top. But, since I don't plan on staying around here for the next sixty years fighting battles against the English, I really need to go out with a bang!

So I'm going to use plenty of conventional methods as well. One of them is to start digging a trench from the southwest to the northwest side of the mountain, just where the mountain meets the beach. Since the ramparts on the lower part of the island don't extend all the way around to the west side, which is just a rocky cliff, invaders could scale the cliff and get over the abbey's less challenging ramparts on that side. We're going to try to stop that from happening with fire.

I've put Jean in charge of working with the Montois on this, giving him all my specs. First of all, it's pretty important for them to remove anything flammable above the ditch, or I will single-handedly be responsible for burning down Mont Saint Michel. That would be a good one for the history books! Girl from twenty-first century makes giant gaff and destroys France's number two tourist destination. Yeah, I'm hoping to avoid that kind of fame.

The Montois will gather tinder, wood shavings, parchment, paper, fabric, you name it, anything flammable to fill up the ditch, arranging the larger pieces of wood on the bottom. The only things I agree to exempt are personal documents of value and the collection of books and illustrated manuscripts in the abbey library. This one's for you Jackson, because I remember you telling me all about the fabulous abbey manuscripts, which in our time are in Avranches (along with the skull of the town's bishop). Wow, I hope I get back so we can go visit the collection. Can you imagine being able to tell my little brother that he's responsible for it being saved? I guess I'll never really be able to tell him that, but it makes me smile just thinking about it.

Anyway, as far as the fire trench goes (or the Fire Swamp as I've named it in English), everything else is fair game to burn. This fire will have to sustain itself for a long time to be effective. The Montois may have to sacrifice their last pieces of furniture and clothing, but if I'm right, they'll soon be doing commerce with the mainland again, and let's face it, the pilgrimage business will be brisk with the siege over. The Montois might have to start from scratch, but at least there will be a scratch to start from if we succeed. And their homes will still be intact. If my plan doesn't work, then they'll be dead anyway, so either way, the gamble's worth it.

We'll need an accelerant to douse the fuel in the ditch so the fire starts burning instantaneously. I know that ale and wine don't have a high enough alcohol content to be flammable (I did a science fair project as a kid about flammable and combustible liquids and their flashpoints). We need distilled alcohol. I wasn't certain if it exists in the fifteenth century, but Jean informs me that it does and that he's pretty certain Abbot Jolivet left behind plenty of distilled alcohol in the abbey's off-limits wine cellar.

Okay monks, there's nothing off limits anymore except your library. For heaven's sake (no pun intended), your abbot has done everything he could to betray you. His treachery with the Duke of Bedford has nearly resulted in the abbey falling into English hands, so grow some . . . uh, hair and start being part of the solution!

We'll gather up any other combustible liquids on the mountain as well. Jean's in charge of that project and I suggested he use the monks for labor. During the attack, some of the monks will be stationed on the West Terrace to drop stuff on any of the Godons who make it through the Fire Swamp, including the stones being used for the abbey church rebuilding project. If they have to dig up the stones paving the terrace, then get busy digging.

There're a lot of them there. I know. I checked out every one of them looking for jobber's marks. Incidentally, I forgot to ask Jean or Nicolas what my symbol means. I've got to remember to ask them another time. Now, I've got to keep focused on the best way to stop or kill an invading army. Ugh!

The rest of the monks will be stationed at various windows and terraces in the abbey complex. I've got some tricks up my sleeve for them, too. I've also asked Jean to gather any materials that could be used to produce noise. I'm hoping there's some thin copper or lead sheeting. I remember my humanities teacher saying that cathedral builders poured melted metals into large flat frames to produce sheeting for the church roofs. We'll test those items out later.

Nicolas and I visit the garrison to meet with the acting commander and his soldiers. There're only a couple dozen soldiers left on the mount, but Nicolas does a good job of getting them fired up about Operation Dark Moon. And they are the valiant ones, the ones who didn't abandon their posts in the face of terrible odds. They've remained committed to protecting this island sanctuary, and they won't abandon us now. General Nicolas (since he reminds me there are no female officers in medieval armies and they wouldn't take too kindly to receiving orders from a strange Breton girl-warrior), assigns them the responsibility of handling the city gates, drawbridge, and the lower ramparts. He assures me they'll fight to the death before they allow the enemy to breach the city walls. I hope he's right.

The village men, under the direction of Robert le Boiteux, will handle the mid-level ramparts, and the women and older children will be stationed on the upper ramparts. The children are assigned to gather buckets of small pebbles along the beach. Their parents are asked to gather larger stones, blocks, or other heavy items to be used as munitions. Metal serving trays, leather hides, and tableware will be used to fabricate makeshift shields and body armor to protect them from enemy arrows. Axes, daggers, knives, swords, clubs, lances, and spears will be gathered and distributed equitably among the defenders.

Every basin, pot, tub or watertight receptacle will be gathered, placed throughout the village in strategic places and filled with sea water. These will be used to douse any fire the Godons try to send in by air with their longbows or catapults or any blaze spreading up the mount from the Fire Swamp. One can never be too careful. We've also planned some fireballs of our own to hail down on the English soldiers in strategic locations, so we'll be playing with a lot of fire.

In short, every man, woman and child will use every imaginable item on the mount to push back the attacking English army. We have all this to do without the Godons getting any hint that we know they're coming and are prepared for them.

And except for Jean and Nicolas, the Montois still don't know anything about my little sound and light show. But they will. We'll have to explain it to them after I make Jean's recordings and when I film my little army of Montois angels.

Chapter 35

NICOLAS WAS ANGRY that Katelyn hadn't told him the complete truth.

He fully believed he would be going to the Godon camp alone. But then the truth was revealed the night he planned on leaving for Ardevon, as the three Watchmen sat at Jean's table. She insisted that both of them know and understand how to use her astonishing little boxes. She carefully went over each step again and again, and each time she reached over to correct his hand placement, Nicolas delighted in her touch. He reveled in her smell and hungered for the lips he had all but tasted the night of their wedding. He wished he could have used his Watchman's key to stop time all together in that one instant, so that he could savor the moment for eternity. But it was not to be. He still wasn't certain if Jean had been a life saver or a life destroyer that night. Those were questions he would consider at a later time. If there *was* a later time.

Now he had to focus on the task at hand. There had been no time to speak of personal things. He, Katelyn and Jean had to invest their entire concentration to protect the mount and its people. And its secrets. Secrets that Katelyn herself didn't even know. He admitted that he'd probably made a mistake about not telling her the truth, but hopefully, he would have time to remedy that later. For now, he decided, Katelyn Michaels should not have any additional worries to complicate her already difficult situation.

The three of them had spent the past several days working on the preparations and planning, and none had broached the subject of what had happened the night of the wedding. They were playacting, pretending that night had never happened, just as the entire population of the mount had playacted for Katelyn's little theatrical production on the crest of the hill below the abbey wall.

And now that dusk had fallen, Katelyn made her revelation. But not until she'd combined everything she'd been working on into the talking, moving-pictures on the big magic box, the one she called a computer. And not until both Nicolas and Jean had demonstrated their mastery of her contraptions.

"By George, I think you've got it," she said in a funny English accent.

Nicolas didn't understand her words, but from her tone, he assumed she meant they had performed each step correctly. He couldn't help but beam at her proudly. Then she added the unexpected caveat.

"But let's pray you won't need to finish the movie or operate these puppies by yourselves, because that'll mean I'm out of commission."

He turned to Jean for a translation, and Jean just shrugged his shoulders.

"What puppies?" asked Nicolas. "I do not understand what you are saying. And what is 'out of commission'?"

"Well, you'll only have to take over my magic boxes, as you call them, if I'm injured or . . . dead."

"But I'm to use these in the Godon camp," Nicolas insisted, "and you will not be with me."

"No," she said, "*I'm* going to use them in the Godon camp, and *you're* going to try and keep me alive! And then if I don't make it back, you've got to add the footage we take there to our little movie. I'm gonna show you how to do that now."

"*Absolument pas!* You are not coming with me, Katelyn. It is too dangerous. Besides you will be needed here to oversee the preparations," and then because there was a distinct possibility that he might not return, he added, "and the battle."

"No, I think I've pretty much made all the assignments," she said. "Even if we don't succeed with our mission, Jean will be able to implement the remainder of my plans. He knows what to do if we don't make it back. It will still be a spectacular show."

Nicolas was furious. "I shall not allow it," he said, and she actually laughed.

"What do you mean you won't allow it? I'm the war strategist here, Nicolas. You came to get *me,* remember? Not the other way around. I'm in charge here, and I will be a far better choice to infiltrate Collins' inner sanctum than you. I hear he prefers *jeunes filles.*" She placed her hand seductively behind her head and swung her hips.

"Katelyn, that is not even remotely humorous. Everything is not a *plaisanterie,* you know," he said, so angry he was fuming. "Abdon is an evil, evil being, and in his host Collins, he could rape or kill you on the spot and I might not be able to stop it."

"Don't worry, Nicolas. I'm planning on being well prepared," she said as she pulled out the dagger she'd taken from the Godon ship. Madame Mercier had stitched up an ingenious holster for the dagger, which fit inside her inner thigh. It was uncomfortable, but it was the only way she could think of to get the weapon inside the English Bastille at Ardevon. Nicolas's baggy trousers had been fitted with a hidden opening to allow her to reach in to retrieve the knife.

"Even if you manage to get close enough to hurt or kill Collins, you'll never be able to escape," Nicolas insisted, upset that Jean was not trying to dissuade her as well. The old man seemed too tired to react. "He is surrounded by his own private guards."

"Well then, it's a good thing that's not why we're going, isn't it? But I've gotta say, if I get a chance to kill him and can get away with it, I'll do it," she said, almost hissing.

Nicolas was surprised at her vehemence, but then he couldn't imagine what it had been like to be abducted by the Godon sailors and to overhear her captors talking about Collins' sexual excesses. Besides, he knew that if he got a chance to kill Collins, he would do it as well. It wouldn't stop Abdon from wanting to destroy the abbey, but it would delay his ability to influence the English army in the immediate future. Abdon alone, Nicolas could handle, but Abdon and the entire English army? Neither he nor Jean could contend with that. And, consequently, Katelyn had been summoned. As much as he wanted to prevent her from going with him to the enemy camp, he knew it was not his place to dictate to her. But he owed her the truth.

"I must warn you, Katelyn. The crossing is very difficult, and I worry about your wounds. They are not entirely healed yet. T'will not be easy."

"What can be so hard about walking across the sands? I'll be safe as long as I have you as my guide."

"I think you cannot understand how difficult it will be," he repeated. "And I am speaking just of the crossing."

"The crossing will be the easy part, Nicolas. Hello! Remember me? Katelyn Michaels who just escaped from a ship full of English soldiers? I can do it. I promise."

He could see it was of no avail to argue with her, and as he looked at his mentor, the frail man nodded his head slightly and then excused himself to go and prepare supper.

"Okay," he said using her favorite word. He liked saying it because each time he used it, she involuntarily smiled. And Nicolas loved nothing more than seeing her smile. "I'll follow your instructions, but if I ever feel that your life is in jeopardy, I will get you out of there any way I can. You have to obey me, no questions asked? Will you do that?"

"It's a deal, Westley. And why don't you just call me Buttercup while you're at it?" Nicolas didn't know who Westley and Buttercup were, but he assumed that meant yes. "Now, let's get our supplies ready," she added. "You're the tide expert. What time do we leave?"

"We will leave at one in the morning. By then, the tide will just be pulling away from the southern side of the mount. Katelyn, this is also very important. You must follow my exact instructions as we cross the bay. Any deviation could result in our deaths. Do you agree?"

"Yes, I agree," which she said to the clackity clack sound Jean was making in the kitchen.

"It is impossible to wear shoes because the sands pull them in, so you must plan to cross barefooted. The sand and water will be cold, but it is the best way. It is a waning crescent tonight and the skies are clear, so it is imperative that you be completely covered by the robe I gave you."

"A waning crescent?" says Katelyn. "What in the heck is that?"

"It means the moon is becoming smaller, but it is still just slightly less than half visible. Generally, I would never attempt a crossing except at dark moon. But since that is when our enemy is attacking, we have no choice."

"But shouldn't we be dressed all in black?" she asked. "Isn't your robe too light in color for the night?"

"If we were dressed in black, we would be visible crossing the sands. The English have sentries watching the bay all night long," Nicolas said. "No, we need to be dressed in a color as close to the color of the sand as possible. Besides, the wool robes will give us protection. When we reach the mainland, we must . . ." he couldn't find the words to explain, ". . . slide on our stomachs. We will place our supplies in my knapsack, which I shall carry under my robe."

"Okay. Then maybe it would be a good idea to get some sleep until just before it's time to leave. I can set an alarm on my phone to wake us at twelve-thirty," she said as she lifted up one of her magic boxes.

"But first," said Jean, as he re-entered the salon and brought two plates with the most delicious-looking omelets Nicolas had ever seen, "you must eat, and eat well. The villagers brought these eggs for you."

Katelyn looked as if she were going to faint dead away.

"Oh Jean, this looks incredible!" said Katelyn as she knelt over her plate and drew in the odor of her omelet. "But I will not eat without you."

"No, Katelyn. You will both need all of your strength and wits about you. I shall eat something from one of your tins, but the omelets are for you.

Katelyn finally acquiesced, and took a bite. "This is the best thing I've tasted in my entire life," she said. "How did you get it so puffy? It looks like you used a dozen eggs."

"The secret is whipping the eggs in a copper bowl, my dear. It's a secret known only to the Montois. Nicolas has never had one of our Mont Saint Michel omelets because we've had no eggs."

Katelyn had the oddest look on her face, and she said "Hmmm, have you ever thought of opening a restaurant called *La Mère Poulard?"*

"Sometimes you say the strangest things," Nicolas said to her, "but while we are savoring this feast, I would like to know exactly how you plan to infiltrate Constable Collins' garrison."

And so she told them.

Chapter 36

BESIDES HIS KNAPSACK, Nicolas is carrying a stick with a large flat bottom when we leave Jean's house. I wish it was a rifle, but no such luck. I'm not sure a stick is going to really help.

Then as we walk towards the city gate, he explains that the stick is his tool to assist him in reading the sands. He pushes it into the sand, and depending upon how the sand reacts, he can tell if it's safe.

He has also brought an additional piece of homespun fabric, which he explains we'll put over our heads so that our faces are covered, and also so we move as one unit.

"I want you to walk behind me with your arms around my waist, following each step I take with your corresponding foot," he explains. "This will also make us a smaller target."

"But how will you be able to see," I ask. I have my headlamp in his knapsack, but he already told me we won't be using it.

"With the moon, t'is far more light than I usually have," he says. "Do not fret, Katelyn. I will be able to see, and as long as you do as I say, we will be safe. We cannot go straight across the bay to the English camp. We must walk far to the west side of the island so that the Godons do not see our silhouette against the mount as we are out in the bay. We will get to the shore and then work our way inland to an abandoned farm I know. The Godons have sentries all along the shoreline, so one more thing. Do not say a word. Sound is magnified a hundredfold across this bay. Not a word. Do you understand?"

"My lips are sealed," I say.

The French soldiers have been informed of our sortie and there will always be two on guard until we return. I think it means they'll be ready to attack anyone who tries to pursue us if we're discovered. The English have arrows, but so do the French. Just not as many.

We slip out the same camouflaged entrance I used to exit the village a few days earlier. That escapade nearly resulted in my demise, but I don't regret it. How can I? It provided the invaluable information about the Godons' attack plans. Nicolas would not have made another crossing to Collins' headquarters until dark moon, and by then, it would have been too late. That crazy obsession I had to take a bath just may have saved the mount. And then I remember that it really had been a crazy obsession. An obsession inspired by the Archangel.

I wish Jackson could see me now. He'd be so proud. Hey, I'm proud of myself. How on earth did I get so brave all of the sudden? Actually, I'm not brave. I'm scared half out of my wits, but I am highly motivated. I don't see that I have any choice, and I really do feel as if I have divine assistance. When Nicolas told me that I'd been brought into shore by a seal after my escape from the Godon ship, I could hardly believe it. He told me I had my arms wrapped around the seal, and the little guy brought me straight to him. I don't remember putting my arms around a seal. The last thing I remember from that horrible morning is thinking I was being attacked by a shark. So, I believe in miracles and I pray there will be more. Plenty more.

Once outside the city walls, Nicolas covers us with the large square of itchy fabric. It feels about as comfortable as burlap and I feel like a giant potato sack. From the ramparts, we move quickly to the sand, because the rocky beach is painful on our bare feet. That's when Nicolas pulls my arms around his waist and brings me in close to his back. In spite of my freezing feet, my proximity to his body starts a fire in my heart. It feels good to have my body pressed against his, but I have to stay focused.

Nicolas turns to the right and hugs the shoreline of the mount some distance around the island before he heads out into the open sands. I match him step for step. I understand what he meant about the sand pulling shoes in. In some spots, I can hardly pull my feet out of the goo. Nicolas is walking quickly, confidently, not using his stick yet.

After about twenty steps, I feel the coldness of water and the heavy tug of a current. This must be the Couesnon River, which has cut a shallow channel in the sands, and is being pulled out to sea with a tremendous amount of force. Without his stable strength, I would fall. The water comes up to our knees, but we get through it quickly. Then when we reach the other side of the channel, Nicolas begins to use his 'divining rod.' It's a slow, methodical process as he bends slightly to inspect each stick placement. From that point onward, every foot closer to the shore is a victory. At times, we're forced to move sideways. As we zig and zag, attempting to make forward progress, Nicolas pats my hands clenched around his waist, as if to reassure me that all is well.

I can no longer feel my feet, but I still match his every step. At one point, he stops completely, and I feel the whistling of something close to my ear. An arrow! I recognize that unhallowed sound from my escape from the English ship. But unlike that experience, there is no shouting, no sound of angry Godons. We remain standing stationary like that for at least a half an hour, and all the while, Nicolas squeezes my hand. I don't even want to know what just happened, but I trust him.

The sound of our breathing under our makeshift tent is the only sound I hear. And the staccato clogging of my heart begging for relief because I can feel my feet again, and they're a pulsing mass of pain. I want nothing more than to move, sit down, or run. Just standing there without moving an inch is one of the most painful things I've ever experienced. I feel the throbbing in my arm and thigh as the blood pumps against my stitches, threatening to explode. I think I might die if I have to stand immobile for one more instant but I can't let Nicolas down. I promised I would do exactly as he says. And so I do.

Finally, he shifts slightly to the side and I breathe out in relief at being able to move, but he stops again. I bite my lip to keep myself from screaming out in agony. And then slowly, step by miniscule step we continue. However this time, he stops after every step and waits for what seems an eternity, but is probably only about five minutes. Now I really know what it means to cross the Fire Swamp, avoiding the flame spurt, fighting the Rodents of Unusual Size, and navigating the lightning sands, and it is by far the most difficult voyage I've ever made.

When my feet touch a different texture, I don't even realize it at first because they are so numb. Not until Nicolas pulls me down to the ground do I realize we've made it to the mainland. We're in the salt marsh, the tufts of salty grass I remember from our drive to the island. I'm hoping we might find some of those salt marsh sheep. They'd be just fine in place of a fat pig.

After we remain flat on our stomachs for another eternity, Nicolas finally sits up. He pulls my shoes and socks out of his knapsack and hands them to me. I can hardly get them over my swollen, frozen feet, but I finally begin to feel some relief. I'm grateful they're dry. Nicolas puts on his sabots. He won't find any warmth from them, but they will provide some protection. He indicates that we're going to move along the marshy land on our bellies. The ordeal is not over. I'm beginning to wish I'd let Nicolas go alone after all.

It takes us at least another two hours of working our way over the damp, bumpy terrain. Now, it's not only my feet that are cold and wet, but every inch of my body as well. I'm grateful that Nicolas's course robe is between me and the ground, because it provides some protection for my wounds. Now I know why the Montois are starving. I'd just as soon starve as go through the Fire Swamp ever again. And then the reality hits me: I've got to go back the same way I came.

Finally, we make it to a dilapidated farmhouse. Nicolas pulls me to my feet and we press ourselves against the wall as we work our way around to the door. It hangs askew, and creaks as he attempts to open it. Inch by inch, he creates enough of a gap for us to slip inside. When we finally make it, I collapse with fatigue.

Chapter 37

I WOKE UP JUST AS the sun began to filter in through the gaps in the roof of our sanctuary. The warm light danced across my face like the slippered feet of wood nymphs. The smell of decaying wood, mold, and dark earth assaulted my nostrils and made me sneeze. It took me a few minutes to figure out where I was. I was covered with what seemed to be a network of crisscrossing branches, and I was lying on a pile of damp straw. I could hardly move. Every muscle of my body screamed out in protest. What kind of ordeal had I been through? Then everything fell into place.

I was on the mainland of Normandy. Nicolas le Breton and I had successfully crossed the Fire Swamp. But where was Nicolas? As I pushed the branches off me, I looked frantically around the deteriorating shelter in pure panic. I was all alone. But he was Westley, wasn't he? And he had promised to always come for me.

I gritted my teeth and with one of the branches, I managed to push my body up to a standing position. My arm and thigh were on fire. I prayed there was no infection, but I didn't have time to worry about that now. When I finally made it to my feet, I felt as if I was going to pass out, and so I plopped back down to a sitting position, and put my head between my knees. How could I be successful with Constable Collins in this condition? But then I remembered my cover story, and I figured I'd be pretty convincing after all.

I felt some comfort at seeing Nicolas's knapsack hidden under the branches. He must be out scouting. Or pig hunting. Or answering nature's call. I needed to do that as well. I took my time getting to my feet again. I was still covered by Nicolas's heavy robe, and underneath, I wore the other clothing he'd given me. His shirt and trousers. I was wet, dirty and injured. In other words, in perfect condition to visit Constable Richard Collins. I removed the robe and quietly made my way to the door. It was open just enough for me to maneuver through the space without having to push against it any further.

I was surprised to see that not thirty steps away from my derelict shelter was a spectacular deciduous forest. Although some of the leaves had already fallen, it was still a canopy of vibrant oranges, reds and yellows. Dew on the leaves reflected the morning sunlight like tiny prisms, and gave the illusion that a myriad of precious gems had been generously scattered by a legion of forest fairies. It was not only beautiful, it was perfect for my needs. For a minute, I debated about crossing the clearing between the farmhouse and the forest on my stomach, but then decided against it. After all, I was in English-occupied territory, and if the Godons discovered me now, I was ready to play the role I had devised. With the help of Nicolas and Jean, I was prepared for the charade. Except for the shoes. I knew I should change my shoes and put on the flimsy fifteenth century boots

Nicolas had brought for me, or there would be questions. But nature's call was rather urgent, so I bolted across the clearing.

Just as I was completing my unpleasant little task, I heard the whinny of a horse.

In spite of what I'd told myself about being prepared for possible capture, that horrid rush of adrenaline from my over-active fight or flight mechanism kicked in. I wanted to run and hide, and I chided myself for not having changed my shoes or prepared my gear. If the English came upon me now, I wouldn't be prepared. And if they went through Nicolas's knapsack, I was dead meat. Just where was my wingman when I needed him?

And where is the confident Katelyn of yesterday afternoon? I wondered. Oh yeah, that's right. She's trying to recover from her ordeal in the Fire Swamp. And my one true love, Westley, is nowhere to be seen. And the neighing is getting closer.

I found a large tree to crouch behind that offered me an unimpeded view of the clearing, and as the horseman rode up to the farmhouse, I nearly died of relief. It was Nicolas riding bareback on a skinny brown mare. He held the horse's mane in one hand, and in the other, he grasped a wiggly, squealing pig.

I had never been so happy to see anyone in my entire life. No, I'm not kidding. Never. I rushed headlong towards him and as he dismounted, I embraced him, pig and all.

He started laughing and carefully untangled the pig's feet from my ratty mass of hair, and then handed me one end of the rope tied around the horse's neck while he hauled the pig, also with a length of rope around its neck, into our little farmhouse sanctuary. I secured the horse to a tree, and followed Nicolas into the shack.

Once the horse and pig were safely secured, Nicolas turned to me and returned my fervent embrace.

"I was so worried when I woke up and you weren't there," I said with tears welling up in my eyes. "I didn't know where you'd gone." A lone drop worked its way up and over my bottom eyelid and coursed its way down my grubby cheek.

"Katelyn," he replied as he held me in his arms, "I am so sorry my absence frightened you, but I had to take care of a few things before we continued our journey, including pilfering your fat pig from the inland village of Pontorson. While I was at it, I thought the horse would lend more credence to our story. You were sleeping so soundly and I could not bear to disturb you. But all is well now."

Yes, all was well. I continued to cling to him as if I couldn't get close enough. I could feel his heart beating against my chest, and I marveled at how my own thumping heart borrowed his tempo, creating a perfect duet. He saw my tear, and tenderly wiped it away with a calloused finger. Then he pressed his lips to my forehead, and I melted as I felt them moving their way along my temple, then down to my cheek, in the pathway blazed by my tear, and then to the corner of my mouth. I drew in my breath sharply. It was a magical moment, as if all the wood imps, pixies and fairies of the forest had joined together in perfect twelve-part harmony to create a musical masterpiece of epic proportions. (Yeah, I know, Mrs. Hunter. Those are all pretty bad metaphors, but it's the best I can come up with. Woops, just ended that sentence with a preposition.)

I turned towards him, wanting his lips to claim mine, but he turned away his head.

Oh now I've really blown it, I said to myself. I looked up at him with a question in my eyes, and he said, "Katelyn. There is nothing I would like more than . . ." He stopped and brushed my lips with his fingers. "But I cannot, for I fear I would not have the strength to stop. And unfortunately, we have more pressing matters to take care of today. If we succeed in carrying out your plans, then we will have the time later to consider the nature of our . . . relationship."

My heart dropped to my toes, but frankly, I couldn't dispute his logic. But come on. Just a kiss? Just one? But I wasn't going to be the pathetic begging female. No siree. Not Katelyn Michaels.

"Okay," I said. "You're right." He was *so* wrong, but I wouldn't give him the satisfaction of knowing how hurt I felt. "It's about time we got this show on the road, anyway."

And so we tied up the pig inside the farmhouse so he couldn't make a mess of our belongings. Nicolas had scavenged some wormy apples to keep the noisy swine content and to take back as ammunition, but he handed me the least offensive apple of the bunch. Even with its wormholes and bruises, the fruit tasted sweeter than anything I can remember. It renewed my spirits.

It was time to prepare. I changed my shoes, forced myself not to gag as I stuffed my hair up into the smelly old hat Nicolas had procured for me, and removed my watch. We placed all the items we would not be taking on this leg of the journey back into Nicolas's knapsack, hiding it carefully beneath the damp straw, and covering the straw with the branches. With our gear divided up according to plan, we took a moment to review our strategy and consider every contingency.

"Nicolas, I agreed to do exactly what you said while crossing the sands, and I did. I also promised you that I would allow you to extricate me if you feel my life is in danger. But now, you must make me a promise."

"What promise?" he asked.

"You must promise me not to overreact. Allow me to play my role. Even if you believe I'm in danger, trust in my intuition on this one. We'll have a code." I tried to think of some words that fifteenth century Englishmen would not understand, and actually smiled at my first choice. "If I say 'okay,' it will be a warning for you to back off, that I am in control of the situation. If I say 'dork,' it means run for our lives.

"Okay. I understand that one," he smiled at me. "And the other one is . . . dork." He repeated it slowly several times.

"Then I shall have a code word as well," he said. "Because I am not to be allowed to speak, two grunts means: I am in charge, no matter what you say!"

We laughed, and I couldn't help but wonder if that would be the last time we ever laughed together. Then Nicolas hesitated for just a second and touched my lips gently with his fingers before pulling the door shut behind us as we left our sanctuary.

Part Four

. . . and the king of the south shall be stirred
up to battle with a very great and mighty army;
but he shall not stand: for they shall
forecast devices against him.

Daniel 11:25

Chapter 38

AS WE APPROACH THE English fort at Ardevon, I prepare for the greatest role of my life. I wish I'd been more active in my high school theater program, but as a movie geek, I've heard plenty of English, Irish and Scottish accents and dialogue. I just pray I can get the fifteenth century colloquialisms down. My only hope is to plead ignorance of the intricacies of Richard Collins' English because of my long isolation in the Isles of Zetland.

Let me explain. When I was in primary school, every sixth grader was assigned a country at the beginning of the year, and throughout the year we did research on every aspect of our countries. Mine was Scotland. The year culminated in the school's popular "World Fair," at which every student exhibited the totality of his or her work throughout the year. Visitors to the fair were asked to judge the exhibits, question the students to test their level of expertise, and then to vote on a grand prize winner and two runners-up. In the true spirit of the times and 'to make every child a winner,' awards were also awarded in just about every sub-category imaginable. I was devastated at not winning one of the top three prizes, but I did win in the language category, having diagrammed the early roots of the various dialects of the Scottish language.

While working on that project, I'd been particularly fascinated with the isolated Shetland Islands off the coast of Northern Scotland. Although the early name of the Norwegian-settled islands was *Inse Catt,* meaning the 'Isles of Cats,' if I remembered correctly, I was pretty certain that by the fifteenth century, they were known as the Zetlands and were under Scottish control. I was also pretty certain that the language they spoke in 1424 was Norn, the evolution of the Norwegian-inspired old Norse. I decided that my chances were pretty good that no one in Collins' camp would be from the Shetland Islands or know this obscure language. I could blame all my English language inadequacies on my 'exotic background.'

I wish I had that good of a memory about everything I've learned over the years, but I have a very selective memory. I tend to remember every word of the poems I learned in primary school, but I can hardly remember what my last math test was about.

I even have a Zetland name to use for my charade. As part of that sixth grade assignment, we had been asked to choose new names for ourselves representative of our countries. I chose a Gaelic first name to symbolize Scotland, and a Norwegian-inspired surname to represent the Shetlands, both of which were close to my own name: Kallan Mikkelsen. However, I remember that in the fifteenth century, the surname would have been Mikkel's 'daughter,' not son, hence my new name for our charade: Kallan Mikkeldatter. And then I remember something else, which in Sixth Grade meant nothing to me but now takes on a whole different significance. The name Kallan, which I had chosen only because it was the closest Scottish name to Katelyn, had an unusual meaning: *Powerful in Battle.* The coincidence (or non-coincidence) of it hits me like a ton of bricks. It is as if every experience I've ever had in my life, even back in primary school, has prepared me for my role as a Watchman. There are basically two ways to look at it: either I'm calling on every bit of knowledge or every ability I have to fulfill this role, or every bit of my knowledge I've acquired and every ability I've developed were to prepare me for my calling. I don't know quite how to look at it, but it is a bit unnerving.

Anyway, if Collins questions my English, I'll use the ole 'Zetlander' defense. I just pray there's no true Zetlander in the camp. Oh, and another important little detail. I also happen to be the great-niece of the Duke of Bedford, the English-appointed Regent of France. You know, the one who is the brother of the recently deceased King of England, Henry V? I've learned a lot of history from Jean, which will hopefully help me be convincing. And hopefully, my 'kinship' to the Duke of Bedford, whose headquarters are in Rouen, will protect me from Collins' evil intentions.

Looking as if I have every right to ride into the English encampment with my mute Zetlander manservant, Ivarr, leading my horse, I call out to the guards in the best Norn/Scottish/English brogue I can produce. The gates of the Bastille are closed and two guards block our entrance.

"Kind sirs, is this the headquarters of Constable Richard Collins? I pray that it may be so, for I have come from Rouen with an important message from the Duke of Bedford, and our journey has been perilous. Please announce our arrival to him immediately." I nudge the skinny mare forward, not allowing myself to show even a smidgen of fear.

"Stop where you are," the guards call out in unison. The older-looking guard is short and pudgy with a ruddy complexion, and the younger one is acne-faced and tall and skinny. He can't be any older than me. "Dismount immediately," says Ruddy-Face, "or you will receive an arrow instead of an announcement."

I stop the horse's forward progress, but I don't dismount. I'm praying Nicolas will play his part and not react to their insulting treatment. I'm relieved that the guards seem to understand my phony-baloney Scottish-English.

"Nay, I shall not dismount until you guarantee my safe passage to your commander," I insist. "I am in no mood for your inquisitions. Three of my men have already been killed along the route by the dastardly French rebels and I am left with only Ivarr and this sickly horse we conscripted in Caen. We have been without a decent meal for over a week," (which except for Jean's omelets, is pretty darn true) "due to the inhospitable nature of these French barbarians, and I am wounded," (which is also pretty darn true). "As you may ascertain, I am in no mood for further impediments. Now, once again, I repeat: I bring news from the Duke to be delivered in person to Constable Collins."

"Then you shall give us the missive, and be gone," says Acne-Boy, trying to give the appearance of self-assurance and authority, but he's just a kid, for heaven's sake.

"That, my fine fellows, I cannot do, for my message is not one that has been committed to parchment, but rather a message that has been inscribed in my head," I say as I tap my forehead, "and as I have been instructed, it shall be given to one man only, and that man is Constable Collins."

I can tell that the soldiers are puzzled. This is not a typical occurrence at the Bastille. They are clearly fearful of being punished by their commanding officer if they dare to make the wrong choice, but they just can't decide what the right choice is.

"Be gone with you, lad," Ruddy-face utters, but it is not said with much gusto. "Do you think us so addled as to believe the Duke of Bedford would send a boy as his envoy?"

"Certainly not gentlemen," I say. "I do not believe you are that addled, but I do find you remarkably unobservant," I add as I remove my hat, and allow my hair to tumble out upon my shoulders. "Now, will you please announce the arrival of the Duke of Bedford's niece, or would you have me return to Rouen and report that the sentinels of Ardevon are both addled *and* blind?"

I see the color drain from their faces and they immediately open the gates of the fortress and allow us to enter the courtyard. Another gate stands in front of us. My audacious bluff has succeeded. So far.

"Milady, we . . . we had no idea that, well. Why are you dressed as a male?"

"Would you consider it safe for a woman to be traveling through enemy territory?" I ask. "Would it be wise for me as my uncle's envoy to ride through the French countryside dressed in female finery?"

"Ahhhh, yes, you have a compelling argument indeed. We offer our sincere apologies," says Ruddy-Face. "But, we still cannot allow you entrance unless you allow *us* to relieve you of your weapons. By order of Constable Collins himself."

"As you wish," I reply. "Please excuse me as I explain your request to my man. I'm afraid he is dumb and cannot utter more than a few grunts and he only understands the language of his and my homeland." I lean over and speak complete gibberish into Nicolas's ear, making certain to include the word 'okay.'

I am pleased that Nicolas remains so calm. He is playing the role of half-wit to perfection. Clumsily, he steps forward and hands over a heavy stick and an old knife to the two guards. This goes as planned. As we also planned, the guards pat him down thoroughly. They find nothing else on him, because there is nothing to find. That is because I have both my digital camera and my iPhone attached to the top of my feet with hair elastics, hidden by Nicolas's oversized, floppy-leather boots.

"Mademoiselle," Ruddy-Face says reluctantly, as they shoo Nicolas ahead, "we must examine you as well. You must understand, we have no means of knowing who you really are. You could be a French infiltrator for all we know."

"Gentleman, do I sound like a French infiltrator?" I ask.

"No, you certainly don't sound French, but you don't sound English either. You have an unusual fashion of speaking," replies Ruddy-Face.

"If you gentlemen had been paying attention, you would have deduced that I am not primarily of English origin."

"But you said you were the Duke of Bedford's niece," says Acne-Boy.

"Actually," I reply, "I have not been entirely forthcoming. I am his great-niece. And I am not in the habit of giving a personal genealogy to strangers, but since you two are so slow to understand, I shall give you a brief explanation. My mother, the Duke's niece, married a Zetlander. I was consequently born and raised in the Zetland Islands off the coast of Scotland." It is clear they have no idea what or where the Zetland Islands are.

"Then how is it that a young helpless lass like yourself is here in France being bidden by her powerful uncle to deliver his missives?" asks Ruddy-Face.

I am ready to tell them more of my planned, story, but then I stop. TMI. I don't need to justify anything to these men. If Constable Collins pushes me, then I will be more forthcoming.

"That, gentlemen, is a long story, and one which I am not prepared to share with you. It shall be for Constable Collins' ears, and his ears alone."

"If you are who you say you are," persists Ruddy-Face, "then you will not resent being asked to deliver your weapons."

"You are absolutely correct," I say, "and if I had any, I would relinquish them, but I am unarmed. The men my uncle sent as bodyguards were armed, but as I told you already, they and their weapons fell prey to enemy attacks. Only my personal servant, Ivarr here, survived to protect me. But I am happy to allow you to verify my words," I say as I dismount, "within certain appropriate limits." I notice out of the corner of my eye that the expression on the face of my simpleton servant has changed. Nicolas is completely alert and ready to pounce if needed.

I stand with my legs slightly apart and my arms extended, and the extremely nervous guards pat around my waist and briefly down the outside of both legs, but they don't even get close to my inner thigh. I wince as they pat my injured upper arm, and I think they can see I am in real pain. Acne-Boy dares to shove up my shirt sleeve, and when he sees my bandaged wound, he pulls away and discontinues the search. I limp as they usher us to the inner gate.

"I suggest you resume your male masquerade," Ruddy-Face says. "I cannot guarantee your safety among these female-starved soldiers." It doesn't take much convincing for me to shove my hair back into the disgusting cap.

They take the horse from 'Ivarr' and attach her rope to a hitching post. Then Ruddy-Face pounds on the inner gate. It opens inward and we're ushered inside the enclave. Ruddy-Face assigns the sentry to take his place outside the fortress, and he becomes our private escort to Constable Collins.

Men are rushing back and forth inside the compound, and I sense an unusual level of activity, almost organized chaos. It's evident that preparations are underway for the attack. Nicolas keeps his head lowered but I can tell he's taking in everything he can without appearing to be too observant. My heart is racing so fast I'm afraid it will bounce right out of my mouth, but I order myself to maintain an attitude of haughtiness. After all, I am the grand-niece of the Duke of Bedford and I have little patience for these inferior, meddling soldiers.

Ruddy-Face stops in front of what I gather are the headquarters of Constable Collins. More sentries are stationed before the stone structure, a well-maintained manor house. The English have simply appropriated what was once a Norman village and have built a fortress around it. I can't help but wonder what happened to the original occupants of the hamlet. It's a chilling thought.

Nicolas and I once again face a rigorous interrogation and examination, but finally one of the sentries, a man with pox-marked skin, escorts us inside the building along with Ruddy-Face. We find ourselves in a receiving foyer with two guards standing at attention, dressed in full military regalia. On their heads they wear oddly-brimmed, round metal helmets that pretty much look like flying saucers. I mean pretty dopey. They're also equipped with metal breast plates worn over short leather tunics, and both are gripping seven-foot-tall battle axes. Intimidating to say the least. This has now changed from an officially scary mission to one that's petrifying. A single misstep and Nicolas and I are history. This part is going to be tricky.

Poxy instructs us to wait. He knocks on a heavy mahogany door, and then goes inside with Ruddy-Face. I was hoping to have a moment alone to retrieve my gear from my boots, but no such luck with the battle-axe guards watching us like hawks. Nicolas keeps his head faced downward, but he shifts his eyes toward me and makes a brief movement with his hand. He's warning me not to do anything rash. I pray that the opportunity will present itself to do what I've come here to do. I know that this is the point where for the first time, Abdon will see our faces. From this point on, Nicolas and

I will no longer be incognito. The thought is sobering, but it is unavoidable for my plan to work. It is also inevitable for we can't avoid the reality that in the future, Abdon recognizes both of us, which is probably a result of this very visit.

Poxy and Ruddy finally come back out and Ruddy leaves the building. I'm certain he has repeated every detail of our conversation to Collins. Poxy signals for us to follow him inside the room were Collins waits. Then when he stops Nicolas short of the door, I realize he's giving permission for me, and me alone, to enter the inner sanctuary of my mortal enemy.

"Only you, Miss," he says. "The Constable will see you in his receiving hall, but you must come alone, without your servant."

"If the Constable wishes to see me, than he will see me with my man," I say, wondering if this is going to fly. "Ivarr stays with me at all times. You yourself searched him. You know he is unarmed, and as a female, I refuse to be alone in the presence of any male without my bodyguard."

Poxy starts to argue with me but he can tell I won't budge, and so he goes back inside for a moment, and then returns.

"The Constable will allow your man to come with you Miss, but only in the presence of his personal guards."

"As he wishes." Nicolas and I follow Poxy into the large frigid room to be followed by the two armed henchmen. They take their places on either side of the door and Poxy exits and closes the door behind him. The room is nearly devoid of furniture except for a sideboard and a massive rectangular table with a chair on each of its four sides. There is a fireplace large enough for me to stand in, where wood is laid out but no fire is burning. This is clearly not Collins' office, if a medieval army commander has such a thing. What had Poxy called this? A receiving hall? There's a door behind the table, and I see a key in its keyhole. The room behind *that* door is the room I want to see.

Standing at the window is Constable Richard Collins. He doesn't look at us as we enter, but remains focused on something outside. I brace myself to look him in the face because I know that behind those mortal eyes lies an even more frightening adversary. Abdon.

"Welcome to Ardevon, Miss. I hear you have an enthralling story to tell me," Collins says as he finally turns towards us. His voice is overbearing and has an unusual quality to it. Although not identical, it does have the same unique characteristic as Gothman's voice. Now I understand what Jean meant about being able to recognize Abdon's hosts. Collins doesn't look anything like Gothman, but I'm familiar with his voice and mannerisms.

I involuntary shudder as my eyes make contact with his. I recognize those piercing eyes from the Abbey refectory where I first faced Gothman. I'm in the presence of evil. This being is a master of deception and craftiness. I'm not certain I can match wits with him, but I'd rather die than not try.

"I assume your guards have informed you of my identity," I say with as much confidence as I can muster, although I feel anything but confident.

"Yes, they tell me you are an envoy of the Duke of Bedford. But, Miss whatever your name is, I find that very hard to believe. I have had dealings with the Duke for many years, and never has he sent a female envoy, so I await your explanation."

Rather than the belligerence I expected, Collins speaks politely. But his eyes convey his true character. He's a cold, calculating devil. He *is* a devil. I keep reminding myself of Jean's words: 'but because we have the physical bodies so desired by the evil ones, we have greater power to repel both Lucifer and his minions.' I may not be physically stronger than Richard Collins, but I'm stronger than Abdon.

"Do you wish to converse about my identity or about the Duke's message?" I ask as I stand my ground and look him straight in the eye.

"Both," he says. "But first, I understand you've had a long and treacherous journey and that you bear wounds from your ordeal. Perhaps you will join me in some refreshment?" he says and ushers me to a chair pulled up to the massive table. I make my limp noticeable but not obnoxious. He says nothing, but waves his hand. One of the guards leaves the room. Collins then takes a seat in a chair on the opposite side of the table. My feet are not visible to him. Nicolas moves up and stands behind me but slightly to my right, blocking the view of my right leg from the remaining guard.

This may be my only chance. I've practiced this step over and over for both speed and accuracy.

"Thank you," I say, rubbing my right arm and then bending over ostensibly to rub my leg which I lift as high as I can. "I have received wounds in both arm and leg, and I fear I am faint from the loss of blood and want of food, but I promised my uncle I would not fail," I say as I manage to slip one hand inside my boot and remove the cell phone and a bloody handkerchief from my pocket with the other hand.

My iPhone camcorder app is ready to record and requires just a single touch of my finger. The bloody handkerchief is to distract Collins from what my right hand is holding, and to make me as repulsive as possible to the lecherous man. After starting the recording, I begin coughing into the handkerchief. Nicolas slaps me on the back to add to the confusion.

"I beg thee forgiveness, sir. I fear I have been suffering of late from coughing fits, but I can assure you it is not the King's Evil," I say as I carefully allow a few drops of the blood on my handkerchief to show.

When I had earlier explained my plan to Jean and Nicolas, I told them I needed a contagious disease to make myself as unappealing to Collins as possible. I had no desire to have to fight off his advances along with everything else I had to endure during our visit. Jean suggested the 'King's Evil,' which the people of this era superstitiously believe could only be cured by the touch of a newly crowned king. From the symptoms Jean described, I think it must be tuberculosis.

Anyway, whatever the disease is, it works. Collins shrinks from me in involuntary horror, and the camcorder is working. At this point, I will probably not be able to get any shots of the constable, but I will get his loud distinctive voice.

"Perhaps we should delve into the heart of the matter," Collins suggests. He doesn't ask me again why the Duke of Bedford has sent his niece. He just wants to be rid of me as quickly as possible. I don't think I'm going to run the risk of his finding me appealing in any way, shape or form.

"Pray tell, what is the Duke's message that is of such great import that he would send his niece?" I don't think he really buys my story, but he acts like he does.

"The Duke has learned of your imminent attack upon Mont Saint Michel and has some important stipulations by which you must abide."

"Since there is no such imminent attack being prepared, I do not see that you have any message to deliver. I fear your perilous journey has been in vain."

"I understand your reluctance to be forthcoming with me, Constable Collins. However, I assure you that you have no reason to fear me. I would surely die before I allowed my knowledge of your plans to fall into the hands of the French. I have nearly lost my life already, and were it not for the fact that I have vowed to return to my Uncle with your assurances, I would have perhaps already perished. However, my will, if not my constitution, remains strong. Now do you wish to know his message or should I return and inform His Grace that you refused to receive it?" My foot is shaking so hard I have to will it to stop, but I refuse to allow Collins to see my fear. I will not give in to this monster.

"I am beginning to understand why your uncle entrusted you with his missive," he said. "You are a rather tenacious young woman." I feel the blood flow through my face in relief. It appears he may have bought my story. Hopefully, he'll think I'm blushing because of the King's Evil.

"I am indeed," I say and then wait for him to continue.

"May I ask you your name?" he says.

"My name is Kallan. Kallan, daughter of Mikkel. Mikkeldatter, if you wish. My father, now deceased, was of Norwegian descent. I am certain your guard told you I was born in the Zetlands."

"Kallan, that's Gaelic, isn't it?"

I start coughing again and once again, Nicolas pounds me on the back. I have no time for this man's games.

"May I address you as Kallan?" he asks, to which I give my permission with a nod. "So how is it that your uncle knows of an attack of which even I have no knowledge?" He's trying to bleed me for information. I'll give him something to think about.

"The Duke knows everything there is to know about his realm," I say.

"How so?" he persists with that voice that is as cutting as a razor blade.

"My Uncle has eyes and ears throughout the land. I am one of them, but there are many others."

"Are you saying he has spies in my camp?"

"An odd choice of words," I say. "In actuality Constable, this is not your camp, but his. While we are fighting this war to have his nephew rightfully crowned King of France, the infant Henry's uncle is not only Senior Regent of the Realm, but Regent of France as well. May I remind you that you are his servant?" My boldness must have surprised Nicolas, because I see his fist clench. I may have gone a teensy-weensy bit overboard.

"You are a little vixen, aren't you," Collins says with a forced smile. "So proceed with the Duke's message."

"His message is this: if and when you conquer the mount, after the battle is over, you are not to kill any surviving inhabitants. Not the townsfolk or the monks. No one. And you are not to destroy anything on the mount. Not the village and especially not the abbey. That is his message."

Constable Collins starts laughing. "Your uncle has sent you all this way to bring me that message? That is it?"

"That is it," I reply and add nothing more.

"And why is this so important to the Duke, if I may ask?"

"In the great victory over the French at Agincourt, Duke John's brother, our dear departed monarch, Henry the Fifth, made a grave tactical error," I say. "The Duke does not want that error to be repeated. Not on his watch."

"And that error was?"

"You know the history, Constable. You know of what I speak."

"No, pray tell. I am all ears. I find it invigorating to be taught the intricacies of military strategy by a lass who was but a child in 1415. Why, you must have been sewing at your dear mother's knee up in the Zetlands when Henry eradicated the French army on its own soil."

"It is unimportant where I was in 1415, sir. It is only important where I am at this instant."

He laughs again, and flicks his hand at me. "Go on, please do tell. What was Henry's great error?"

"As you well know, sir, King Henry's reputation was tarnished when he made the decision to put to death all the French prisoners taken at

Agincourt. Though he won that battle, the price may have been too high. His decision continues to galvanize the French, even though the French pretender Charles is so weak."

"Nonsense. If Henry's reputation was tarnished, it wasn't because of what the French thought about his decision, but because of what his own supporters thought of it. We felt he had killed many illustrious prisoners who could have been held for very profitable ransoms."

"As you wish, sir, but nonetheless, the Duke does not want to see this mistake repeated."

"I find little justification for this request," and then it is as if the floodgates open. "If and when I conquer Mont Saint Michel, my plans are to destroy the mount and everything on it." He is becoming more and more animated and his voice, which is already loud, now booms across the room. "I intend to kill every living human, every living creature, and destroy every inanimate object on that accursed mount. I intend to raze it to the ground until the remnants of it are washed away by the tides, never to rise again. We shall once and for all be free of that wretched French bastion." His face is now blotchy and I see red veins bursting out in the whites of his eyes. Constable Richard Collins shares Abdon's long-standing hatred of Mont Saint Michel. He wants nothing more than for this symbol of freedom to be obliterated.

"If you find no justification for the Duke's request, then you are . . ." I hesitate. I want to say 'blind,' but I don't want to enrage this devil so much that he kills me and Nicolas here on the spot. We have to get the video back to the mount. I cough again until I come up with the right words. "You are perhaps ill-advised," I say. "As you well know, Mont Saint Michel continues to be a rallying cry for the French rebels. Were you to destroy it, their rebellion would be greater, not less. The Duke wishes for a gesture of good will to be expressed by the English, to facilitate our eventual union with this country. Furthermore, as you are undoubtedly aware, the abbot, Robert Jolivet, has thrown in his allegiance with the English. He has given us important information about the defenses of the mount and he is a close personal friend of the Duke. To repay such loyalty," I wanted to say treachery, but my acting was impeccable, "there is a certain expectation that my uncle will return the favor. The Duke insists that the mount remain intact," I continue, "so that Jolivet can return to his abbey as befits the patriot. And furthermore, in and of itself, the abbey is a treasure for the entire Western World. It is a pilgrimage center for God-fearing peoples of all lands. It is the repository of an incomparable library, including the writings of the ancient Romans and Greeks, and the early Saints. If destroyed, those writings could never be replaced. And were the mount itself to be destroyed, the English would be vilified for generations to come. Surely, you see the wisdom in this request, Constable?"

"Yes," he says too easily, but his eyes tell me no. "Now, I am beginning to understand."

Just at that moment, Collins' guard enters the room with a tray of food and places it on the side board. The smell of it makes my mouth water.

"My dear Kallan," Collins says, "I'm afraid your message now requires me to confer with my officers, so I cannot sup with you." He stands up, walks to the door to his inner sanctuary, turns the key, and then pockets it. "However, I invite you and your manservant to remain here and partake freely of this meal. I shall return shortly with my response for the Duke. My guards shall leave you in peace, but they will be outside the door should you need their assistance."

In other words, they will be there to prevent our exit from this room.

"Thank you Constable. Your thoughtfulness and consideration will be dutifully reported to my uncle," I say as I actually gag, covering it by coughing again into my soiled handkerchief.

Collins and the two guards exit through the same door by which we entered and leave us alone in the room. Nicolas grunts at me twice. I look at him questioningly and he kneels by my side and whispers into my ear, "We must escape, Katelyn. Immediately. Collins is planning to kill us when he returns."

Chapter 39

"HURRY AND GRAB THE food," Katelyn whispered as she continued to direct her little black box around the room. "I'm not about to leave that behind, but don't drink anything. I bet Collins poisoned the ale. And find me a weapon," she said as she handed him the dagger from her thigh holster, "because this is yours now. I can hit, but I don't think I'm ready to stab."

Nicolas pulled out the thin drawstring bag Katelyn had stitched up from the Godon ship captain's underclothing. She had attached it to the waistband of his trousers so that it allowed him to carry contraband while leaving his hands free. After he'd gathered the foodstuffs, he looked quickly through the side board drawers. Except for the pewter jug and mugs brought with the food tray, there were no eating utensils or knives. Of course Abdon was not foolish enough to leave them in a locked room with knives. Nicolas emptied the ale from the jug into the mugs. The heavy jug would now be Katelyn's weapon.

"I shall attempt to pry open the inner door," Nicolas said, pointing to the door behind the massive table while Katelyn crossed to the wall next to the window and carefully inched her body next to the casement to peer outside. Then she held her magic box out with her right arm to capture whatever moving pictures she could outside in the encampment while Nicolas focused on the locked door.

"Okay, that battery's dead," she whispered. "On to the camera." She sat down, removed her boot and switched the magic boxes, taking the larger silver box into her hands.

"What do you think? Can you break the lock?" she asked. They continued to communicate in whispers.

"If we are fortunate enough to have a few more minutes. Arm yourself with this." He handed her the jug. "Stand by the outer door and don't hesitate to use it if anyone tries to enter."

She stood just as he instructed and waited patiently with the jug held high above her head while he continued to gnaw away at the metal and wood. Katelyn had been absolutely brilliant today. He was amazed at the poise she'd displayed when forced to come face to face with the most evil being Nicolas had ever known. He was fairly certain that Collins had believed Katelyn's story. However, it made no difference in Collins' attitude. It had been immediately clear to Nicolas that even if Collins believed the story, he would never allow 'Kallan Mikkeldatter' to leave the fortress alive. Collins would simply plead ignorance of the Duke's instructions, claiming the Regent's messenger had never arrived.

At this very moment, Collins was probably disposing of the two guards who had interrogated Katelyn so there would be no witnesses. His personal bodyguards, standing outside the door, would defend him to the death, knowing their very lives depended on it. They would deny ever having seen the female courier.

Yes, Katelyn had done her part. Their success in saving the mount now depended entirely upon his ability to get her out of the Bastille, and to get her out quickly. He felt that if they could escape the manor house, they had a fighting chance. After all, he had created a hidden entrance through the fortress wall, which he routinely used during his scouting expeditions. It was a false wall he'd fashioned behind a large gorse bush. Scratches would be added to their list of woes, especially if they had to move quickly to get through the prickly shrubs, but that very characteristic kept his entrance completely hidden from the English soldiers. Especially since a second gorse bush on the outside of the timbered wall camouflaged the passageway from the exterior. No one would ever consider looking behind the spiny branches.

The other advantage Nicolas had, which the English didn't know, was that he knew the layout of this encampment almost as well as he knew the village on the mount. He'd been here often and could navigate even in total darkness.

He finally felt the door yielding, and when he was assured that no one was inside what he assumed were the Constable's private quarters, he motioned Katelyn to come. Together they slipped through the door and once inside, Katelyn handed the pewter jug back to Nicolas and aimed her magic box all around the room. Nicolas stuffed the jug into his bag, shut the door behind them and propped a chair up under the door pull to provide a few extra minutes of grace time.

Where the receiving room had been nearly devoid of furnishings, this room was so filled with bookcases, desks, tables and chairs that there was barely any space to maneuver. A fire burned in a small fireplace, and the welcoming warmth was deceiving. This was Richard Collins' library, the war room where he was planning his massacre of hundreds of innocent people. There was nothing welcoming about it. Katelyn clicked away with her box at the array of books, maps, tide charts, lunar phases, handwritten documents, and drawings spread out on a table nearly as large as the one in the receiving room.

Nicolas grabbed a large cutlass propped up on one of the bookshelves and returned Katelyn's dagger to her. Now they were both armed, even if she was uncomfortable using the knife. While Katelyn was capturing her images, Nicolas scouted out their escape route. There was an unlocked door leading into Collins' bedchamber, and the bedchamber had a large window with a view looking out onto the private grounds behind the manor. Nicolas let out a sigh of relief. They were on the ground level and this window opened. They could simply climb out the window and avoid the guards.

"I've found our means of escape," he whispered to Katelyn, who was still busy with her magic box. "Come, we must leave."

"Nicolas, what do you think about starting the library on fire? Would it hinder or help our escape?"

"As much as I would like to destroy everything about this man, I think it would hinder our escape. It would just give him more ammunition to hunt us down and kill us. We want him to continue to believe that you are on the English side in this conflict, and that you really are the Duke's niece. If we set fire to the English commander's quarters, he will doubt your story."

"You're right," said Katelyn as she picked up a quill pen and dipped the tip into the ink well sitting on the Constable's writing desk. "So, I think I'll leave him a little note."

She found a sheet of writing paper, composed her message, and read it to him out loud as her quill scratched across the absorbent paper.

"Constable Collins," she read. "I sensed your extreme discomfort over my uncle's directives and as I do not wish to linger while you debate the merits of his advice, I have made the decision to leave immediately. However, I wish to leave you with the assurance that although I will be returning to Rouen post haste, I will report back to my uncle that I was unable to deliver his instructions because of a French ambush on my company. With my regards, Kallan Mikkeldatter."

"Hopefully this will soften his anger at our escape just a tad," she said. "He'll know we were perceptive enough to pick up on the fact that our lives were in danger, and that to stay on his good side, I'm not going to snitch on him."

"Snitch?" asked Nicolas as he pulled her out of the library where she had left the letter prominently displayed on Collins' writing desk.

"You know . . . tattle, tell, inform? Oh, I know he'll still try to find us and kill us, but hopefully, he'll also still believe I am who I said I am. If he thinks we're from the mount, he might attack now before we're completely ready.

Nicolas assisted her out the window and said, "Follow me and do not make any noise. I know a way out of the compound. As soon as they discover our absence, Collins will sound the church bell. And he will release the dogs. We must get as far from here as possible. No more talking." He closed the window behind him and got in front of Katelyn to lead the way.

The two escapees hugged the wall of the house until they reached its corner. Then inching forward on their stomachs as they had done to cross the salt marshes, they headed for a hedge that ran along the back border of the property. Nicolas aimed for an area of the hedge that had a slight opening, and they wriggled their way through it. They found themselves in a long narrow strip of ground that separated the hedge from the massive log spikes of the Bastille's defensive enclosure. Since the hedge was higher than Nicolas, he stood and grabbed Katelyn's hand and the two fugitives ran as fast as they could until they reached the end of the hedgerow.

They were now faced with the necessity of crossing an unprotected stretch of ground, about the length of the nave of the village church, in order to get to their next cover, a row of stone buildings that backed up next to the enclosure wall. Nicolas's gorse-bush passage was behind the last cottage in that row of buildings. It was broad daylight and if anyone happened to be looking towards the log wall, they would surely be seen, even lying flat on the ground. But Nicolas knew they had no other choice.

He once again lowered himself to his stomach and looked through the less dense foliage near the bottom of the hedgerow towards the village square. He could not see anyone walking about. This is where Collins would muster his soldiers once he discovered Katelyn's absence. In spite of their total lack of cover, they had to cross quickly before the alarm sounded.

Nicolas indicated for Katelyn to go first, while he stood watch with his cutlass, ready to attack if needed. She lay flat on the ground and pulled herself across the space as quickly as she could without making any noise or abrupt movements.

When she reached the safety of the first cottage, he gestured for her to stand up. There were no windows along the back walls of the stone cottages, so they would be safe standing upright. Just as Katelyn got to her feet, a bell started ringing loudly and continuously.

Katelyn looked across the gap at Nicolas, and he could see the panic in her eyes. In the multiple times he had visited this military installation, he'd never felt the fear that now threatened to choke his breath. He knew it was not fear for his own safety, but for that of Katelyn. She did not know where the secret passageway was and without his assistance, she would be a helpless target inside the compound. From his vantage point behind the hedge, he could already see men running into the square, but the lot had been cast, and he had no choice. If he hesitated even for a second, their escape would be hopeless. He lunged out into the open and squirmed his way across the gap without looking anywhere but forward. Towards Katelyn. He could hear the bellowing voice of Constable Collins just as he reached her, grabbed her hand and began running at full speed.

He had no way of knowing whether he'd been seen, but he didn't think so. As Collins shouted on about capturing the enemy spies, Nicolas heard the dogs being released. They had only seconds. Nicolas had already encountered Collins' guard dogs, and they bit to kill. It didn't help that Nicolas was carrying a bag full of food, including thick slices of mutton.

After what seemed like an eternity, they finally reached the gorse bush. Nicolas whispered to Katelyn, "I know it doesn't look like it, but there is a hidden passageway behind the bush. I will go first and get it open, but follow me immediately afterwards. It is not easy and you will get scratched, but there is safety on the other side.

"Here," said Katelyn, handing Nicolas her two magic boxes. "I have a bad feeling about this. You take them, and if I don't make it through, you know what to do." She reattached her knife into the makeshift holster inside her thigh.

"Nonsense," Nicolas whispered back. "We've just about made it." But rather than argue, he stuffed her boxes into his linen bag with the food, and maneuvered his way through the lower branches of the prickly gorse as quickly as he could. His face, which he usually protected when using this passageway, took the full brunt of the thorns, because he refused to go slowly. He had to get the wall opened and pull Katelyn through to safety.

Months earlier, Nicolas had spent hours and hours hidden inside the corresponding gorse bush on the enclosure's exterior sawing his way through the bottom of three thick logs until they fell away. The remaining portion of those logs, above the opening, were held firmly in place by the pressure of the surrounding logs and the bindings tightly connecting the spiked tops together. Nicolas had removed the lower section, and replaced it with a much thinner panel of wood brought from the mount. But in order to move that panel to uncover the opening, he had to wiggle it out from its wedged position, and then slide it along the inside of the wall through the branches of the thick gorse. The cramped quarters did not allow more than one person to pass through at a time.

Nicolas finally managed to remove the panel, wedged deeper than usual by weeks of rain and softened soil. He slid it aside and then maneuvered his body around so that he could exit feet first. Then he heard the dog approaching.

“Hurry, hurry, Katelyn,” he whispered frantically as he stretched to grab her hand and pull her through the gorse and into the wall opening. “Forget about the thorns. Just come.”

Nicolas had almost succeeded in getting her into the protection of the gorse bush, when he heard the sickening sound of snarling, of teeth crushing bone, and of Katelyn’s involuntary shriek.

Chapter 40

I THINK I'M DEAD. Honestly, I must be. But then the wave of pain in my foot kind of refutes that theory. Aren't you supposed to be free of pain on the other side? Isn't it supposed to be glorious and light? Maybe that's just in heaven, though. Maybe I didn't make it to heaven.

And then I hear a voice calling me back to earth. It's a gentle voice, a soft voice, a beloved voice. It's Nicolas's voice.

"Katelyn, Katelyn, *ma chérie. S'il te plaît, reveilles-toi.*"

And then when I open my eyes, I'm not looking into Nicolas's face, but the face of the largest dog I've ever seen. And this face, with its drooping sad eyes and its hanging slobbery jowls, is actually licking me. That's why my foot hurts, I remember now. This is the dog that just munched my foot. I recoil in total horror.

"Nicolas," I cry. "Get him away from me. He just tried to kill me. Are you crazy!"

"Katelyn," he says. "Don't worry. This is my friend. He didn't try to kill you. He just may have saved your life."

Nothing makes sense because I'm pretty darn sure that the reason my foot is throbbing is because it has deep marks in it that correspond to this dog's teeth. And then I remember trying to escape from the Bastille. Where are we, anyway? Have we been captured? I try to lift my head to see, but everything starts to spin, and I hurry and lie back down. I'm also shivering.

"Katelyn, you are safe. We are at the farmhouse," Nicolas says. Now I realize we really are at the farmhouse, because I can hear Porky Pig squealing away. I think he must be as terrified of the dog as me.

"Can you sit up?" he asks me.

I think I just showed him how much I definitely can't sit up. So I just lie there until the wave of nausea passes. Man, I'm really batting a thousand here in 1424. Except for some scratches on his face and hands, I don't see any major wounds on Nicolas, but I've got plenty to pass around. I mean really. Can it get any worse? Yeah, I guess it could. I could be dead.

"What happened?" I finally manage to say, although I'm not really certain I want to know. "How on earth did we get away from there?" As my eyes focus, I realize that Nicolas is shirtless. This is the second time I've seen him without his shirt, and in spite of my condition, I want nothing more than to feel the warmth of his smooth skin.

"I had a friend on the inside. Gaspard here," he says as he pats the giant beast.

"What do you mean?"

"In my many sorties to the English camp, I have been forced to deal with the guard dogs. When I could, I would bring pieces of game I killed in the forest to appease them. These mastiffs can be pretty intimidating. They have been bred as guard dogs and used in battle for centuries, but I learned that they can actually have a soft side. Eventually, Gaspard and I became friends. Very good friends, in fact. He's the dog on duty in the sector where my hidden entrance is located. He actually became my protector against the other dogs. When one of those dogs clamped down on your foot, Gaspard saw and smelled me and knew you were with me. He attacked your attacker until that poor dog limped away in pain. He paid for his crime. But at that point, you lost consciousness. I knew I needed help to get you out of there quickly, so I got you and Gaspard through the opening, sealed it back up, and voilà, he got you here."

Gaspard's slobber doesn't seem so disgusting now.

"But how did he get me here? It's not like I could ride him like a horse. I mean, he's a big dog, but not that big. Besides, I was unconscious."

And what on earth is all this passing out business? I have never passed out until I came to Mont Saint Michel—in 1424, that is. It's getting ridiculous. But then, I've never had the kind of injuries the fifteenth century has brought me. And without painkillers. I guess it's my survival mechanism kicking in to block the pain.

"No, you didn't ride Gaspard," he says in response to my question. "I carried you as far as I could run with you into the forest and then when I could run no more, I cut some branches and wove them into a sort of bed for you that he could drag. I tore strips from my shirt to tie the branches together and harness it to Gaspard."

"You are amazing, Nicolas. You saved my life. You and your buddy, here," I say as I lift my hand to pat the gentle giant. "But are we safe? Won't the soldiers find us?"

"This farmhouse is in the opposite direction as Rouen, so if they continue to believe your story, they will concentrate their efforts to the northeast. However, I do not wish to stay here any longer than necessary.

We must leave when it gets dark so we can cross the sands at low tide. Now, I need to examine your foot. But first, I will get our robes. It is very cold in here."

Of course it's cold, you knucklehead. You hardly have any clothes on!

I gaze at his muscular back and shoulders as he digs out his knapsack from under its hiding place. His pure beauty takes my breath away. I want to lie in his arms and forget that an army of English soldiers is trying to kill me. I wonder if there'll ever be a moment just for us, when we don't have to worry about killing or being killed, where we can actually touch our lips. If only just for a moment. But if we don't get out of here alive, that'll never happen.

Nicolas pulls on his robe, and then helps me sit so he can pull the coarse fabric over my head. He also hands me my watch. It's six o'clock in the evening and it's already getting dark.

"Now lie still, Katelyn. I am going to remove your boot."

"It's a good thing I gave you my phone and camera," I say as he props up my leg on a few branches and gently begins removing the floppy leather boot, "or at least one of them would have teeth marks in it." I'm trying to keep my sense of humor and stay brave even though his manipulation of my right foot is killing me. Hey, at least I have all my major injuries on the same side! My left arm, leg and foot are doing just fine. Then a horrible thought floods me with more panic. Does rabies exist in the fifteenth century?

"Is the skin broken?" I ask when he finally gets the boot off. I know the skin has to be punctured for a rabid animal to get its saliva into your blood stream.

"The Archangel is watching over you, Katelyn. Your ankle is red and very swollen, but the leather prevented the dog's teeth from breaking the skin. But I fear there are broken bones. Do you think you can put weight on it?"

I sure don't feel like putting weight on it, but I feel even less like getting caught by Collins' men.

"I'll try in a minute, but first, do you have any fabric left from your shirt?" I remember my pediatrician's instructions when I sprained my ankle ice skating two years ago: the acronym RICE. Rest, ice, compression and elevation. I'm going to have Nicolas bind my foot tightly. The RIE will have to wait until we get back to the mount. If we get back to the mount. Of course, this is not exactly a sprained ankle. But if it's broken, it will still be good to keep it immobile.

He pulls what remains of his massacred shirt out of his knapsack, and uses its sleeves to rip some wide strips. I instruct him how to wrap my ankle tightly, and then I manage to sit up.

"I believe we should take sustenance before we go," Nicolas suggests, as he hands me the drawstring bag. "It will give us both strength to face the journey back to the mount."

For the next half hour, Nicolas and I forget our troubles as we share a meal courtesy of our enemy, ironically the best I've had since arriving in 1424. He leaves me briefly to go to a nearby stream to fill Collins' pewter jug with cool, refreshing water. Just what the doctor ordered. I'm not just starving, but I'm also severely dehydrated. I never get enough to drink on the mount, and I am finally able to fully quench my thirst.

I show Nicolas how to make a sandwich, placing a thick slab of lamb and a hunk of cheese on a piece of dagger-sliced bread. It is the best sandwich I've ever eaten. We savor each bite, and lick our fingers of each tiny crumb. I just hope I haven't changed history, because I don't know if the Earl of Sandwich has been born yet.

There's still some food to take back to the mount, although Nicolas and I do share one of Richard Collins' apples. Delicious, firm and un-wormy, unlike the apple I had yesterday. Was it yesterday, or two days ago? I've completely lost track of time. Anyway, the apple is heavenly. Heavenly. Oh, and Gaspard and Porky also get handouts. Gaspard deserves it, but it's kind of wasted on Porky, who will soon be sacrificed to the gods of war. It does keep him quiet, though.

After our meal, I try to stand. Honestly, I'm trying so hard to be brave, but it's torture. I don't want him to see me cry, but I can't stop my tears. I think Nicolas may be right. Gaspard's cousin did some damage. I cannot put any weight on my foot. If it's not broken, it's got some nasty tendon or ligament damage. I don't know how Nicolas is going to get me across the sands, unless it's on my belly. Or unless Gaspard pulls me. But who is going to get Gaspard through the Fire Swamp?

We've got plenty of tree limbs to make crutches. They won't help in the sand, as their tips will just sink into it, but they'll help on land. So that's our next project. We manage to find two perfect candidate branches and Nicolas whittles away until he's got the perfect length and some fairly decent underarm support, which he then pads with the remnants of his shirt. Although I'm wobbly, the make-shift crutches actually work quite well. At least I'm partially mobile.

"Katelyn," he says, "I am sorry that we cannot stay here until you are stronger, but we must leave now. We will not go back the way we came—the long way across the salt marshes—as we have neither the time nor the ability. I will have Gaspard pull you through the forest directly to the coast, and then we'll see if that will work to cross the sands as well. My prayer is that the usual coastline sentries will be involved in Collins' search for us to the north. And we have Gaspard on our side. He will be our protector. Any ideas on how to keep our pig from squealing?" It's now pitch black and I can hardly see Nicolas, but I can tell that he's nervous. He's more worried than he lets on to me.

We don't want the pig dead yet, as we still have a week before dark moon, and throwing a putrid pig off the battlements doesn't give quite the same impression as a fat healthy one.

"Cut up a couple of the apples into small pieces and let me hold on to the pig's rope as Gaspard is pulling me. That way, you won't have a squirming, squealing pig in your knapsack. I'll give him a bit of apple whenever I sense a squeal coming."

"That's as good an idea as any I have," Nicolas says, as we gather our gear and leave our sanctuary behind. It's just after ten o'clock at night, and the waning moon comes in and out of a slight cloud cover.

We must paint an unusual picture, the four of us, as we set off through the forest. Nicolas with his knapsack bulging from underneath his robe, guiding Gaspard, who's pulling me on a makeshift toboggan, while I'm pulling the pig and dishing out tiny morsels of apple every so often. An odd moonlit silhouette framed against the midnight blue sky. Wish I could take a movie of us, but Nicolas has my camera, and besides, it would be an unwarranted luxury. But wow. Imagine showing that one to Jackson! It's the stuff dreams are made of.

Our journey takes much less time than our belly crawl across the marsh. I don't think Nicolas would be so reckless if I were mobile. As it stands, he really has no other choice than to move quickly and directly back to the mount.

When we reach the edge of the forest, he halts our little circus parade and sits down.

"We must wait here until the tide is just right," he says. "And then we'll run like the wind because we have no other choice. We will be a visible target from the shore. I haven't seen any sentries, but if there are any along the beach, they will see us. Our only chance for survival is to outwit and outrun them. I know the safest path to take through the sands from this direction, even without testing each step. The English have a dreaded fear of crossing the quicksand, so I'm counting on that. They will shoot arrows at us, but I doubt they will come after us in the bay. And, we've also got Gaspard with us. He is a good ally to have."

So he knows the safest path through the sands, does he? What about the fact that every time the tide comes in and out, it pulls and twists the sands, changes the channels and adds new hidden dangers? I think Nicolas is just saying he knows the safest path to give me hope. He knows what the dangers are. For heaven's sake, I know what the dangers are. I was with him when we crossed over the first time, and we moved inches at a time. I recognize his words for what they are: a full-out sprint across the bay is a move of total desperation. Dang my foot. The dog bite may not have killed me, but it may just have cost us our lives.

Chapter 41

AFTER THE ALMOST interminable wait, I was almost relieved when Nicolas whispered "it is time." As we had discussed, I took his knapsack on my lap with Porky inside. It was my only job. Stay low and hold on to Porky for dear life. Surprisingly, the pig didn't squeal. He was probably too scared to squeal. Just like me. I laid my new crutches beside me on my stretcher as well.

We made it to the beach without any trouble, and without any alarm being sounded. Good, we're going to be okay.

But the minute we hit the sand, I heard shouting behind us and to my left. Since I was lying on my back looking towards the shore, I could see the forms of two men running from opposite directions and converging upon us.

"Run faster, Nicolas," I whispered. I didn't want the men to know there was an English-speaking woman on the stretcher, or they'd figure out pretty quickly who we were. And that would not be good. "There's two of them and they're going to chase us onto the sands."

Nicolas began to sprint without the luxury of being able to examine where he placed his feet. He still didn't head in a direct course to the mount, however, which led me to believe that he *did* have a general idea of the best path to take. When I saw the soldiers stop and hold up their bows, I held Nicolas's knapsack up in front of my face and offered up poor Porky as a sacrificial lamb . . . ah, pig. If they were going to shoot arrows, better a punctured pig than me.

"Stay low," I cried softly. "They're starting to shoot."

"Hold on. I am going to make some evasive maneuvers."

I nearly fell off my stretcher when Nicolas jerked Gaspard sharply to the left. It was a good thing he did, too, because I felt and saw an arrow fall exactly where my body would have been if we'd stayed on a direct course. Nicolas continued to dash us about erratically until finally our pursuers gave up on trying to aim at us. However, they didn't give up on pursuing us. Our gamble had failed. They were ready to sacrifice their own lives to stop us. I watched as they followed in our exact footsteps, and with no burdens to carry, they were catching up quickly.

"Nicolas," I cried. "They're going to catch us. You've got to leave me behind and run for it. The only way to save the mount is for you to get back with my gear and carry out the plans."

"Then we shall fight to the death," he said as he stopped short. "Get your dagger out and prepare yourself for battle, because I will never abandon you, Katelyn. Never. Get up!"

I managed to roll off the stretcher with knapsack and pig. I fell to my knees in the sand, and worked on standing up while Nicolas untied the make-shift harness from Gaspard and propped up the stretcher in front of me with one of the crutches, like a shield. I managed to grab the other crutch and put the under-arm support down onto the sand, thinking it wouldn't sink in as far as the tip. With one hand on the crutch tip for balance, the other holding the dagger, and with Nicolas's toboggan shielding me, I faced our assailants.

The sentries were now close enough for us to hear their breathing, and I could also see the flash of their daggers in the moonlight.

"Attack, Gaspard, attack," cried Nicolas to the mastiff. The obedient dog bounded away and tried to attack both men at once, but they immediately separated, forcing the canine to make a choice. He chose the one on the right, and I saw the soldier plunge in his dagger as Gaspard leapt on him. Gaspard yelped, but still went for the soldier's jugular. There was nothing we could do to help the dog. The soldier on the left kept running towards us, and with precision aim and power, Nicolas threw his cutlass at him. But at the last second, the soldier slipped to his knee, and the cutlass flew over him, landing useless on the sand about ten yards away from us.

"Katelyn, your dagger," Nicolas cried as he grabbed it from my hand and pounced on the soldier. I could hear the clash of metal on metal. Without a weapon or mobility, I was helpless.

Then it became clear what I had to do. I knew it was going to be unbearable, but I dropped my crutch and ran for the cutlass, almost passing out from the agony that seared through my ankle like a thousand bullets. Not that I really know what bullets feel like, but I imagine a thousand of them would feel like my ankle. The pain from my earlier cuts was nothing compared to this, but Nicolas's life depended on my being able to reach that cutlass.

I could hear grunts and the continued metallic clashing behind me as the two men fought in the sand. Finally, I reached the cutlass and as I turned back to go to Nicolas, two things happened simultaneously: my foot gave out completely and I was tackled from behind. The wind was knocked out of me as I landed chest first on the damp, hard sand and the cutlass went flying again. The soldier Gaspard had attacked had obviously won that contest. As my assailant jumped on my back, he gripped his powerful hands around my throat. I jabbed at him blindly over my head with my hands and fingers, trying to find his eyes, as he attempted to strangle me, but I couldn't get him off me. I wondered how long I could survive without air.

As gray spots started fuzzying up my brain and I began to lose focus, I heard the most appalling hissing noise. It got louder and louder, and my brain emptied itself of all thought and became filled with nothing but that ghastly sound. Then, with one moment of remaining clarity, I recognized it. I had heard that sound when Grandpa Michaels was dying in the hospital. It was a sound I knew I would never forget. It was the death rattle. Was it my own death rattle? Was this how my sojourn in the fifteenth century was going to end? Being strangled to death in the sands of Mont Saint Michel Bay? Then having my body pulled out to sea to become fish food?

Just when I reached the point where my world was turning black, my attacker released his hold. It was as if every cell of my body was clamoring for air with grasping fingers, and I pulled that air into my lungs from the sand, from the sky, and from the water. I pulled in every ounce of oxygen that existed in the universe, and then when it filled me up with life, I offered it back. As I coughed uncontrollably, I felt a warm liquid seep through the coldness of the night, through my robe, onto my back, down my sides. At first it felt like a healing liquid, until I smelled that distinctive coppery odor. And then I was horrified.

I twisted to the side and the dead weight on my back rolled off. When I got to my knees and turned around, I discovered where both the death rattle and the warm liquid had come from: the first from Gaspard, who with his dying breath had dragged himself across the sand to save my life, and the second from the dead English soldier, who had Gaspard's large jaws clamped around his neck.

However, there was no time to process this gruesome scene because I could hear Nicolas still struggling with the other sentry. I tried to stand, but this time, as much as I willed it, I couldn't put any weight on my foot. Not just because my foot hurt, but because it was completely non-functional. It just flopped around uselessly. When I looked down at Nicolas's make-shift bandage around my ankle, there was a huge bulge, and blood was now seeping through the fabric strips. It could have been the blood from the dead Englishman, but somehow, I didn't think it was.

I realized with horror that I had completely snapped the bones that held my leg to my foot, and they were poking through my skin.

Too bad. I'd have to deal with that later.

I crawled to the cutlass and then dragging it, hopped towards Nicolas and the other sentry. But when I finally reached them, I realized the cutlass wouldn't help Nicolas. The two men were no longer fighting with each other, but were fighting against a more insidious enemy. They were being drawn deeper and deeper into a bottomless pit of smothering, choking sand. The soldier was deeper into the sand, but he would not let go of Nicolas.

I scrambled back around to find one of my crutches and screamed for Nicolas to take hold of it. Just as he reached for it, I watched in horror as the Englishman's head was pulled beneath the muck. For a brief instant, I felt the tension release on the branch as the soldier finally released Nicolas, and I thought we were safe. But then the loathsome sand kept clawing away at Nicolas, pulling, pulling, pulling like an obscene black hole.

"Nicolas, don't let go," I screamed at the top of my lungs. "Stop fighting the sand. Relax your body completely, and let me pull you out. But whatever you do, don't let go of the branch!"

"I'm trying but I will not pull you in with me," he gasped. "I can't fight it much longer."

"Don't you dare give up, Nicolas. Do you hear me? Don't you dare. I will never, never, never forgive you if you let go of this branch. Do not let go!"

By that time, I was sobbing hysterically and uncontrollably, because I realized that rather than my body pulling his towards me, he was pulling me towards him. And I knew what that meant. I knew what he was about to do.

"Katelyn Michaels," he said in a soft, resigned voice. "I love you."

And then he let go of the branch.

Chapter 42

TONIGHT IS DARK MOON. At least, I think it is. I think that's what Jean keeps trying to tell me. He keeps asking questions, but I've told him and the others all of this before. Why do they keep asking? I'm so tired, I just need to sleep. Can't they leave me alone? Sometimes they ask me questions about my 'magic boxes,' as they call them. Sometimes I can answer their questions, but other times I'm too tired and can't open my eyes. Besides, I thought I taught them how to do everything before I left with Nicolas to go to Ardevon.

Ardevon. Something unspeakable happened at Ardevon. Or was it on the way back?

Home. Where is home? Lemon bars and Chicken Divine. Mother scolding me for being mean to poor little Jackson. Jackson just doesn't appreciate my sense of humor.

"He's just a boy, for heaven's sake, Katelyn. Can't you give him a break? Just for a day or for a measly little hour?" says mother.

But that's not really home, is it? I'm not sure. Or is home with Jean? In his cold but welcoming kitchen where just the hint of a flame burns in the large fireplace, and where he always gives me more than my portion of food. Or in his bedchamber, which he willingly turned over to me so that 'poor traumatized Katelyn' could have some privacy in the household of men.

I wish I could be in that funny straw-pallet bed again, and then sometimes I think that's where I am. I just don't know. I'm not sure. But I do know that my foot hurts and I hear them talking about it. Sometimes in French, sometimes in English, but the two languages are so intertwined in my mind that I don't know which is which.

"How did this happen? I have never seen such a horrific break."

"The wound is unclean. There is too much poison."

"We must do a venesection in her arm, and drain the toxins out of her body."

"But she has already lost too much blood. We do nothing. We wait until we can ask her. But we must keep the wound clean. No bloodletting."

"Whatever you do, no bloodletting," I scream as loudly as I possibly can, but I don't hear my voice.

Occasionally Madame Mercier comes to see me. She sits by my bedside and holds my hand or washes the sweat from my head, because it is so hot in here. Why is it so hot? I don't think it's summer because yesterday, or two days ago, or last week it was October, I think.

Anyway, Madame Mercier says things to me in French. I don't always understand, even though my French is so much better. She says things like, "*O pauvre petite fille. Quelle dommage. Elle est si jeune, si jeune,*" after which Jean usually shoos her from the room because she is crying, and he doesn't want her to disturb my sleep.

But I'm not always sleeping. Sometimes I wake up for my other guests as well. Like Nana Suzie. She tells me stories about when I was a little girl and then she tells me how proud she is of the woman I've become. She tells me how astounded she is at my bravery. Grandpa Michaels comes as well, but not as often, and I'm usually too tired to talk to him. But it's comforting to know he's sitting by my bed watching over me and holding my hand.

But my favorite visitor is Nicolas, and he holds my hand as well. He comes every night after the sun goes down so I won't be afraid, because when it gets dark, I see Richard Collins' eyes, and they make me scream. But Nicolas is there to comfort me. He kisses my forehead and rubs my arm. Then he tells me how much he loves me and that he's waiting for me. He laughs when he tells me how much he despised me at first. How he thought I was a spoiled little brat. He doesn't use those exact words, but I get the picture.

Then he tells me how amazing I am. How courageous I've been. How wrong he was about me and that he regrets he made Jean promise not to tell me about the secret. He thanks me for everything I've done to save the mount. Then he speaks to me about Michael and the War in Heaven, about the fallen angels, about the stones, and about the secret of Notre-Dame-Sous-Terre. He teaches me how to use my key, my Watchman's enseigne, but I'm just so tired. I keep forgetting what he says about the keys and the stones and the chapel. And Michael. And Adam. But I remember when he tells me he loves me. And he assures me that I'll be going home soon.

It's getting dark now, but I know Nicolas will come. He always does. Just like Westley always comes for Buttercup. In fact, here comes my Westley now. He sits down beside me and takes my hand in his. He kisses my brow, and then he tenderly moves his fingers down my face, and gently touches my lips. I wish he would kiss me, but I wouldn't have the strength to kiss him back. I'm so tired. I wish I could tell him how much I love him, as well. I try to talk to him. I try to tell him, but all he says is, "I know, Katelyn. I know. You do not have to tell me because I already know." It's comforting.

Then he says something else that's comforting. "Tonight is your last night, Katelyn. Whatever happens, tonight I will take you home."

I'm glad. I'm just so tired, and so I close my eyes and fall asleep.

Chapter 43

A sound of battle is in the land . . .

Jeremiah 50:22

And the Lord shall utter his voice before his army:
for his camp is very great: for he is strong that
executeth his word: for the day of the Lord is
great and very terrible; and who can abide it?

Joel 2: 11

IT WAS NEARLY MIDNIGHT. The tide was coming in, and it was dark moon.

Every man, woman and child on the Mont was in place. They were manning their stations on the ramparts, behind the gates, in the village streets, on the West Terrace. Everyone except Jean. His station was at home, in the bedchamber he now considered to be Katelyn's. The bedchamber he'd shared with Marie so many years earlier.

His post was at Katelyn's side. His assignment was to watch over Katelyn and to make the ultimate decision as to her fate. If the fever broke and it looked as if she would recover, then she would remain here to see the completion of the task she had started. At least for a few more days. It could not be much longer than that because even if the fever broke, there was still the matter of her broken ankle. But Jean knew how angry Katelyn would be if she were sent home before the battle she herself had planned was over. And Katelyn's anger was becoming legendary on the mount.

However, if she hovered on the verge of death, then Jean had a decision to make. He knew that in Katelyn's world, they could save her from the fever's grasp. Make her completely whole again. When she had sustained the cuts during her escape from the Godon ship, she'd told him and Nicolas of the poisons that entered the body through broken skin and polluted the blood.

Then she had told them of the miraculous medicines in her time—antibiotics, she had called them—which destroyed the very poisons that were threatening to take away her life at this moment. She'd also spoken of machines, bigger than her magic boxes, which could take pictures inside the human body so that doctors could knit bones back together with metal pins. She'd told them of wondrous things, marvelous things, things of which Jean could only dream.

If only he could see Katelyn's world, but it was too late now. He'd already made his decision. His body was tired and he wanted to go home to his maker . . . and home to Marie. And Michel. If they would accept him, that is. He thought of Michel, and of the dark truth he had kept buried for so long. The impossible choice he'd been forced to make. It was something he'd not told Katelyn or even Nicolas, because he had seen how the truth had destroyed Marie. How it had taken away her will to fight, her will to live. Her ability to support Jean in his calling.

"We are doomed," she had said when years after Michel had died, he had finally told her the truth about their beloved son's demise. "How can we fight against Abdon? He will always be stronger than us. It doesn't matter who his host is. It will always be the same. I understand that you must be true to your calling, but I cannot do it, Jean. I cannot do it any longer. I will be his next victim, and that will kill you. So what is the point in pretending any longer? I will leave in the morning."

Jean had cajoled, pleaded, cried and begged. But in the end, it had been no use. She could no longer live with him knowing what he'd been forced to do and knowing that she would be next. Like Abraham of old, Jean had been obedient. But Isaac had been spared. Michel had not.

Marie departed the next morning before Jean awoke, leaving the simple gold band, which symbolized to him their union for eternity, and Jean had never seen her again. Marie had died that day for him, and so had a part of Jean.

After Marie's 'death,' he came to understand how difficult it would be for anyone to live this lifestyle without having heard the Angel's voice. And even if you heard the voices, it was still difficult. Katelyn was a case in point. Look at how resistant she'd been to her calling, even though she *had* heard the voices. And so after Marie left him, he vowed never to speak again of that sunny afternoon in October, so long ago. An autumn day much like today had been. Months ago, he'd told Nicolas that Michel had died in an accident while visiting the West Terrace work site with his father. And that part was true. But it wasn't the entire story. Jean's thoughts returned, unbidden, to those last hours with his son.

The rest of the workers had gone home that afternoon, but Jean remained because his son was so eager to learn his father's craft, and Jean decided it was as good a day as any to begin Michel's apprenticeship. Not as a Watchman, but as a carver of stone. The stonecutters were paving the terrace, so Jean placed one of his perfectly cut blocks into the prepared space, and then showed Michel how to turn the chisel just so, to make the curved lines in his jobber's mark. Jean had chosen this particular jobber's mark for himself because it was the symbol on his Watchman's key.

"It is easy to pound in the straight line with the chisel," he explained to the eager boy, "but only a master carver can manage the curved lines perfectly."

That day, he allowed Michel to hit the hammer onto the chisel to produce the curved lines, and the two laughed as each chip of stone flaked away correctly. They were so engrossed in their work and in the joy of being together as father and son that they didn't see or hear their enemies approaching.

Abdon's host and two of his human lackeys had scaled the cliff below the West Terrace, and before Jean realized what was happening, he was being held prisoner by the two henchmen, while Abdon grabbed Michel and rushed with him to the edge of the terrace overlooking the cliff.

"You have a choice to make now, Watchman," Abdon seethed. "It is a simple choice, really. You tell me the secret of the mount, and your son lives. You refuse, and I throw him off the terrace. And do not think you might save him by lying to me. We shall keep him until we learn if your words are true. And so you see, it is not so difficult a choice to make, is it? It is either yes or no."

Jean looked into his son's eyes. Those eyes showed the complete faith that Michel had in his father. Then suddenly Jean could read his son's actual thoughts. Michel was frightened, yes, but knew his father would never let him die. No secret was worth the sacrifice of his only child. No secret. Those were Michel's thoughts.

Michel didn't cry. He just looked at his father with total confidence. He still had faith when Jean broke down and sobbed, and he didn't even cry as his father begged him for forgiveness, told him how much he loved him, and explained to him that if he betrayed God, they could never be together again. Michel didn't cry when his father promised him that God would keep him safe until Jean could come to him on the other side. Michel didn't even cry as Abdon threw the courageous little boy over the cliff of the West Terrace. He didn't cry as his little body crashed onto the stony islet below, the little islet attached to the main island by a narrow rock-covered beach.

But Jean cried. He wept for days and weeks and months and years and so did Marie. Jean wept as he asked the abbot if he could bury his son beneath the stones on that little islet. He wept after Michel's funeral and burial. He wept when many years later, he asked the abbot for another favor. Could he please build a chapel dedicated to his son on that little islet? A simple chapel. It would not take him away from his work at the abbey's construction site.

He wept when the abbot gave his permission, but requested that the little chapel be publically named after Saint Aubert. But privately, it could be consecrated to Michel. Jean wept every time he cut and laid a stone on the tiny chapel, every time he chiseled in his jobber's mark, and most of all, he wept when after he'd finally told Marie the truth and she had left him, he had been unable to finish the work.

Jean wept as he heard the legend that began to grow up among the villagers about the mysterious unfinished chapel: that it was built on a stone that had miraculously fallen from the summit to the sea during construction of the abbey. It was true. A mighty stone *had* fallen. His son. The foundation stone of Jean's life with Marie. And he wept when once that foundation stone had been broken and shattered, the rest of his house had crumbled as well.

And finally, Jean wept when he told Nicolas about the islet, about Michel's burial place, and about the chapel that would never be completed.

As the tired old man began to hear the sound of battle all around him, he began weeping again. This time, he wept for the tragedy of love lost for Katelyn and Nicolas. Katelyn still wore Marie's ring on her finger and Jean had no intention of removing it. It was Katelyn's now. Perhaps in some small way, it would bring her joy as a reminder of two men who had loved her: one like a father, and the other like a suitor. As he touched his cheek to Katelyn's forehead, his worst fears were realized. Katelyn's fever had spiked, and she lay lifeless on the bed. It was time for Katelyn Michaels to return home.

Jean wept as he gathered all of Katelyn's belongings—minus her magic boxes which were still in use—and then placed everything carefully in her knapsack. She would have to go home without her boxes. But he folded up all the cords used to charge her batteries. The solar battery charger was still on the roof, and without Nicolas to get it, it would remain on the roof. He also placed the dagger she'd pilfered from the Godon ship, along with the captain's room key.

He wanted her to always remember the amazing strength and courage she had displayed in her brief stay with them. Hopefully one day, the memories associated with those items would help her get through even more difficult times.

Then Jean remembered something else he wished to give Katelyn besides Marie's ring. He no longer had any need of it. Perhaps it would jog Katelyn's memory about the sacred things that had been discussed during those days and hours when she had been so delirious. He placed the object inside a pouch of her knapsack, placed the bag on top of her stomach, and then wrapped her up in a worn blanket, since all of the bed linens had been conscripted. Jean's body was wasted and weak, but the Archangel infused him with the strength necessary to lift her and carry her down the stairs.

He managed to get the door opened, and as he exited the house that Katelyn had helped to make a home—as it had once been with Marie—Jean heard his own voice booming out over the village.

Yes, this day of the Lord was truly great and very terrible. Jean had been given the strength to execute God's word, but that strength was ebbing, and he knew he would not be able to abide the day. He knew it was to be his last.

Chapter 44

And I John saw the holy city, new Jerusalem, coming down from God out of heaven, prepared as a bride adorned for her husband.

The Book of Revelation 21:2

IT WAS NEARLY MIDNIGHT. The tide was coming in, and it was dark moon.

John was nervous but excited. It was the young English soldier's first experience in siege warfare and he knew it could end in hand-to-hand combat. And it was to come on the darkest night of the month. He was used to peering out into the darkness. His shift was as a night watchman, guarding the shoreline, watching, always watching for anyone coming or going to the mount. But he had never seen a single soul trying to cross the treacherous sands of the bay. Consequently, it had been very unusual when two of the English sentries had disappeared a week earlier. Many of the soldiers blamed it on the sands. For some reason, the soldiers must have ventured out into the bay at low tide and had been sucked up by the sinister shoals. Their disappearance caused a feeling of malaise in the camp. The soldiers were superstitious and many of them viewed it as an evil omen for their upcoming campaign. Some feared their attempt to take Mount Saint Michael was doomed.

John had heard many strange things about the infamous pilgrimage destination and its mysterious bay. The soldiers in the enclave shared tales, but never within earshot of Constable Collins. Collins didn't abide any of what he called 'such nonsense.' Some soldiers claimed the mount was indeed watched over by Saint Michael, the great dragon-slayer himself, and that when he was present, strange lights could be observed at night. Others said Mount Saint Michael had a direct connection to both heaven and the underworld, and that while God and Michael had power over the tidal island, Satan had jurisdiction over the seas and sands of the bay. Several soldiers even told John that the mount was the site of the New Jerusalem, which at the great and terrible day of the Lord at the end of times would descend out of heaven dressed as a bride, and signal the coming of the bridegroom, Jesus Christ.

John didn't know what to think about all of these stories, but he put them out of his mind as at high tide, the frigate began its silent journey from the shore to the mount. He hoped he would be able to actually enter the village and the abbey and see firsthand this unique place of pilgrimage before they burned it, for the orders had been given by the Constable himself. Every living creature on the mount was to be slaughtered. Every building burned, and every stone crushed. There had been grumblings among the troops saying such extreme measures were unwarranted, but Constable Collins had then gathered all the soldiers before their departure and read the missive from the Duke of Bedford in which these orders had been clearly laid out by the deceased king's brother.

"They are not my orders," Collins had underlined. "These are the orders of our Regent. It is as if these orders come from the King himself."

The soldiers had cheered then, and vowed to carry out the Duke's royal command.

As one of the elite troops selected to join Collins' own battalion in attacking the city gates, John had also cheered. But now, as he climbed aboard the frigate, just one of the many crowded English vessels taking his comrades-in-arms to the battleground, he felt more uncertain. He was a God-fearing man and the thought of killing helpless women and children was appalling to him. He hoped he wouldn't be called upon to commit such atrocities.

The ship had barely left the shore, when to John it appeared that a giant portion of the invisible abbey before them suddenly turned white. The stark white was the only thing visible against the blackness of the sky.

Unbidden, a story popped into John's mind. It was the tale of a wealthy royal princess who had chosen to wear a simple white frock on her wedding day, rather than an elaborate gown of red, purple or blue. Such bold, vibrant colors were always chosen by noble women to show they could afford such expensive dyes. When asked why she had chosen such a plain white dress, the princess replied, "to symbolize my purity before God and my husband, and to show that possessions and wealth do not measure up to the wealth of love I shall pour out upon my husband and the wealth of obedience I offer up to God."

John didn't know if the story was true or not, but it got him thinking. A bride dressed in white. That is what the abbey appeared to be! He pointed out the phenomenon to his neighbor, who passed it around until every soldier on the frigate was staring in astonishment at the abbey.

As the ship scraped the bottom of the sands close to the mount, Collins motioned for everyone to remain as quiet as possible as they disembarked. No one was to make a sound until all of the soldiers were in position. Vessels, unseen in the darkness of the night, had been dispatched all around the island, so that infantrymen would literally surround the mount. Attacks were to come from the cannons onboard the vessels as well.

And then with a single blow of a horn on the far side of the mount where the last of the soldiers had disembarked, the signal was sounded for the English to commence the attack. But for John and every other soldier around him, that signal was also the beginning of complete and utter terror that ripped through the English battalions like a bolt of lightning. It was as if by the simple sounding of the trumpet, the wrath of heaven or hell—or both—was released down upon them.

Seven bright lights appeared in the upper-most windows of the abbey, and a sound of thunder shook the skies, even though they were clear. A beam of light shot up from the steeple of the abbey church into the heavens, and then suddenly it was if the hosts of heaven, clothed in white, appeared on the abbey wall. Amidst the thunder, their voices could be heard shouting in unison, *Alleluia: for the Lord God omnipotent reigneth. For the Lord most high is terrible; he is a great King over all the earth.*

Many of the soldiers around John began to panic. Some even turned back towards the water, from whence they had come, trying to reach the ships that had pulled away from the shore. John cringed at their screams, as their heavy armor and equipment pulled them under the accursed waters. A few of the cannons had been discharged, but then they fell silent, as the terrified sailors beheld the spectacle as well. Then drops of hail fell upon the infantrymen, only this hail was as hard as stone, and gradually the size of the hailstones increased. Collins and his officers screamed at the unorganized chaos that had become their well-trained army.

The sound of powerful threads of music, unlike any John had ever heard, assailed their ears, as if the angels themselves were strumming their harps and blowing their trumpets. A few of Collins' valiant legionnaires managed to send flaming arrows over the ramparts. But in return for their efforts, huge balls of fire were cast down upon them as punishment for their audacity. And still the Constable screamed orders at them to continue the attack and not to break ranks.

John helped his comrades place the scaling ladders against the ramparts but then cried out in agony as scalding liquid burned his arm and hand. As he fell to the ground, he saw Collins strike down one of the fleeing English soldiers with his sword, and then another.

"Cowards," Collins cried. "This is nothing but an illusion. Stand and fight, you hopeless cowards. I say fight!"

But no one was listening to Collins, because they were being pelted with every type of projectile imaginable: dishes and mugs, stones and garbage. Apples and fish. Even sewage. Collins gathered a few of his closest bodyguards and began scaling the single ladder that had been secured in place, but he and two of his men were knocked off the ladder and back to the ground by of all things a pig. A fat pig that was alive and added to the chaos by squealing in terror and knocking down soldiers.

John was stunned. He didn't know whether he was fighting against a heavenly army or a mortal army, but whichever it was, he knew that Collins had lied to his soldiers. He had ensured them that the Montois were weak and starving to death. That there would be little if any opposition. Not so! If they were using foodstuffs and even a fat and healthy pig as ammunition, then surely they had an endless supply of food. Perhaps their food was heaven sent. Perhaps this truly was the New Jerusalem that had descended out of heaven signifying the great and terrible day of the Lord!

Then a piercing voice echoed from the ramparts, saying: *Behold, I know your thoughts, I see your acts, I know your hiding places, and I know the devices which ye wrongfully imagine against me.*

Simultaneously, high up upon the abbey wall appeared images of their Encampment at Ardevon, images from within the enclosure, and even more shocking, images from what were clearly Constable Collins' private quarters, his office and bedchamber, including clear views of maps, tide charts, lunar phases, handwritten documents, and war plans.

The voice of Constable Richard Collins spoke simultaneously saying, "Pray tell, what is the Duke's message that is of such great import that he would send his niece?" And yet, Constable Collins was lying at the foot of the wall being helped to his feet by his private bodyguards. The voice did not come from him, and yet it was his voice.

A female voice, speaking with a strange but understandable accent, answered: "The Duke has learned of your imminent attack upon Mont Saint Michel and has some important stipulations by which you must abide. Now do you wish to know his message, or should I return and inform His Grace that you refused to receive it? Constable, this is not *your* camp, but his. May I remind you that you are his servant?"

At this point, every soldier around John stopped dead in his tracks, while Collins screamed out unheeded orders. John looked around him, and even Collins' officers had stopped trying to rally their men.

"So proceed with the Duke's message," said Collins booming voice.

"His message is this: if and when you conquer the mount, after the battle is over, you are not to kill any surviving inhabitants. Not the townsfolk or the monks. No one. And you are not to destroy anything on the mount. Not the village and especially not the abbey. That is his message."

The sound of Constable Collins sinister laughter rang out through the night sky, and it sounded more evil than the most evil sound John had ever heard. "Your uncle has sent you all this way to bring me that message? That is it? I find little justification for this request. If and when I conquer Mont

Saint Michel, my plans are to destroy the mount and everything on it. I intend to kill every living human, every living creature, and destroy every inanimate object on that accursed mount. I intend to raze it to the ground until the remnants of it are washed away by the tides, never to rise again. We shall once and for all be free of that wretched French bastion."

"If you find no justification for the Duke's request, then you are . . . ill-advised. Mont Saint Michel continues to be a rallying cry for the French rebels. Were you to destroy it, their rebellion would be greater, not less. The Duke wishes for a gesture of good will to be expressed by the English, to facilitate our eventual union with this country . . . the abbey is a treasure for the entire Western World. It is a center of pilgrimage for God-fearing peoples of all lands. It is the repository of an incomparable library, including the writings of the ancient Romans and Greeks, and the early Saints. If destroyed, those writings could never be replaced. And were the mount itself to be destroyed, the English would be vilified for generations to come."

And then the booming voice of thunder said: *"Thou hast not lied unto men only, but unto God. For this is an heinous crime; yea it is an iniquity to be punished by both God and man."*

A simultaneous shout arose from the soldiers as they turned on their officers, but even more significantly, turned on Constable Richard Collins and his bodyguards. John could not see what happened to Collins, because his guards closed ranks and fled around the southwest side of the mount, but one thing was certain. The English soldiers at Ardevon would never again be fooled into attacking this holy sanctuary, for this mount was surely protected by the Archangel Michael, and even by God Himself.

Chapter 45

And out of the throne proceeded lightnings and thunderings and voices: and there were seven lamps of fire burning before the throne . . .

The Book of Revelation 4:5

The Lord also thundered in the heavens, and the Highest gave his voice; hail stones and coals of fire.

Psalms 18:13

IT WAS NEARLY MIDNIGHT. The tide was coming in, and it was dark moon.

Nicolas had been reluctant to leave Katelyn's side earlier in the evening, but there was no other choice. He had to man the magic boxes, and he had enlisted three of the more enlightened monks from the abbey to assist him. Although Jean le Vieux knew how to use them, Nicolas felt much better about leaving Katelyn knowing that Jean would remain at her side. Her condition was precarious. The poisons of which she had been so afraid had entered the open wound of her mangled foot. If she hadn't been trying to save Nicolas's life out in the bay, she would never have broken the bone in her foot so badly that it punctured through her skin.

He and Jean had debated back and forth about when to send her back home so that she could receive the treatment she so desperately needed. As long as she remained semi-lucid, they agreed she should stay. Not out of selfish motives, not because Nicolas feared he could no longer live without her, but because they knew her so well. And they knew her temper.

"Can you imagine how furious she'll be," said Nicolas to Jean, "if we send her back before she knows the outcome of the battle? She will never forgive us for that. Never."

Katelyn had already told Nicolas she would never forgive him for releasing the crutch out on the sands of the Mont Saint Michel Bay, but he'd had no choice. He was so afraid she would slip and be pulled into the quicksands headfirst before the French soldiers could reach them, that they wouldn't be able to save her. She had been so concentrated on holding onto that branch, that she had neither seen nor heard the entire garrison from Mont Saint Michel running towards them, oblivious of the deadly shoals.

It had been a gamble for Nicolas to let go, but he'd felt confident that with that many hands, the soldiers would be able to pull him out before his head went completely under. And they had. Just in time. He was pretty sure Katelyn had forgiven him for that, but she wasn't ever completely coherent enough to say so. But Nicolas had heard the words he longed to hear from her. "I love you Nicolas, I love you."

Though she may have forgiven him for letting go of the branch, she would honestly never forgive him or Jean for sending her home before the battle was over. And so, they played a precarious waiting game. Jean was wise enough to know if and when to take her back to Notre-Dame-Sous-Terre. Nicolas just prayed it wouldn't happen without his being able to say goodbye to her. And so much more.

During the preceding days, Nicolas had worked untiringly to prepare the Montois for the upcoming invasion. He'd used the images from Collins' office—which revealed Abdon's exact attack plan—to place the Montois defenses. And as Katelyn had instructed, he'd even been able to complete her sound and image show by adding the images and voices from their incursion into the Godon Bastille. Everything had gone like clockwork and every single person on the mount had been cooperative when it had been explained that Katelyn had brought power from God to save them.

But when darkness fell each night, Nicolas had gone back to Katelyn. And there, in the bedchamber where Jean had spent decades with his beloved Marie, Nicolas had crammed a decade into each night.

Night after night, he sat with Katelyn, caring for her, reassuring her, and talking to her. He told her about his childhood, about his parents and siblings and about his calling by the Archangel. He apologized profusely to her for not having been forthcoming about the true role of the Watchmen. He told her everything. About the stones, about the chapel, about the secret they were sworn to prevent Abdon and the other dark angels from ever learning.

Although sometimes she seemed to understand what he told her, other times she seemed completely delirious. At those times, she thought he was dead and that he had come down from heaven to take her home. All he hoped for, all he dreamed of was one moment with her of complete lucidity, so that she knew the truth. And so that she knew of his eternal and undying love for her. That is what he asked of the Archangel: a single moment of clarity with Katelyn. He knew she had to go back very soon because her life and health were in jeopardy. He couldn't change that. But he also dared to ask just one more thing of the Archangel. If Katelyn had come back in time once, couldn't she come back to him again? Or could he go forward to her world? All he knew is that he could not live a lifetime as long as Jean's had been, without more time with Katelyn Michaels.

The trumpet sounded. Nicolas, stationed behind a strategically placed rock on the open crest of the hill below the abbey's rampart wall, took the time to pray that all of their preparations, all of their sacrifices, and all of their efforts would not be in vain. He knew that similar prayers were being offered by every Montois, every monk, and every French soldier on the mount.

But Nicolas knew this battle was not just about the English versus the Montois. This was a battle to protect a gift and solemn promise made many centuries earlier. This was a war against Lucifer's fallen angels who wanted all of mankind to be miserable. This was a war against oppression and unrighteous dominion, a battle to symbolize freedom for all of God's creatures.

And yes, Katelyn, he thought to himself, *this is a war to plant the seeds that will blossom into your great country of freedom in future years.*

Nicolas adjusted the projector just as Katelyn had shown him, and pushed the play button on the magic box. Immediately, the giant screen of sewed-together bed linens—which had been dropped by the monks above from the abbey's southeastern rampart wall a few moments earlier—lit up. It would be visible to anyone approaching from the east and south, whether on land or sea.

When Katelyn had first tested her moving picture show on the abbey wall (without the sheet screen), the sound hadn't been loud enough, but she'd found a way to remedy that. She had what she called 'pop-up speakers' that she connected by wires to her moving picture box. Then, before they'd left for Ardevon, they had fashioned two large cones from some heavy parchment in the abbey's library. These were attached at the small end of the cones to the speakers.

Then Nicolas and Katelyn had tested the best positioning of the cones to take advantage of the natural acoustics of the Mont Saint Michel Bay. In fact, they hadn't been able to do much of a dry run because it had been so loud, and they didn't want the Godons to hear anything prematurely.

Before the Ardevon incursion, Katelyn had completed her moving picture, complete with majestic background music somehow added in from her little white box, and Jean's voice powerfully quoting the ancient sacred writings. However, Nicolas had added the last part, the sounds and images from Collins' quarters. Katelyn had painstakingly taught Nicolas and Jean every detail of how to add that portion, 'in case she didn't make it back.' It was a good thing too, because even though she had made it back, she had not been in any condition to do the work herself.

He reflected on that chaotic afternoon when she had gathered all of the Montois onto this same hill crest, all dressed in white. First she had taught them all to chant together loudly and clearly, one single English phrase: *Alleluia: for the Lord God omnipotent reigneth.* She had captured the sound on one of her magic boxes—she called it recording—and then by some process he didn't understand, she kept re-recording with another magic box while playing the recording and having the people chant simultaneously until she had succeeded in making a recording that sounded like thousands of voices, instead of hundreds of voices.

Then Katelyn had divided the group into three sections, and had clustered them all on the right side of the crest, with just enough space behind them and in front of the abbey wall for people to pass through. As she panned her magic moving-picture box from section to section, the previous section members ducked behind the next group, going to the far end, and this pattern repeated itself until everyone reached the left side of the crest. It increased the number of people appearing in the moving picture by many times. All the while, they chanted their single English phrase while she played the sound recording along with them, which was then recorded onto the moving picture box. They had practiced over and over, until she was finally satisfied. The end result was a moving picture that captured what looked like thousands and thousands of white clad 'angels' chanting in unison. This she then put on what she called a loop, so that it played over and over, complete with background music.

On the other side of the abbey, on the West Terrace and in the cloisters on the north side of the island, Nicolas's three hand-picked monks were simultaneously using Katelyn's other boxes and computer to broadcast the audio portions of her creation down the hill above the fire trench, with similar amplifying cones. It wasn't as loud, but with three separate stations, there wasn't a spot on the island that wasn't bathed in sound. All of the batteries had been charged as Katelyn instructed, and she had determined they'd be able to continue their broadcast for a couple of hours.

Other monks had tended carefully stoked fires that were hidden behind cloaked windows in the uppermost parts of the abbey and church until the battle trumpet had been sounded, and had then uncovered their windows to represent the seven lamps of fire spoken of by the Apostle John in the Book of Revelation. One monk had even shimmied up the church spire to turn on Katelyn's headlamp directed straight up into the night sky like a beacon to heaven.

But judging from what Nicolas now saw happening below him, he didn't believe it would take hours to convince the Godons they were fighting against God himself. He watched as hundreds of English soldiers attempted to get back to their ships, some even choosing to drown in the waters of the bay rather than stay in the safety of the mount's shores. It appeared that the entire English army was in total chaos. He couldn't see exactly what was happening directly below the village ramparts, but there had been no successful English attacks by fire, catapult, or cannonball, and no incursions of men over the ramparts on the south and east side of the island. He prayed the same could be said for the northwest, west and southwest sides.

His projection machine was self-sustaining, and he decided to check on the efforts on the West Terrace. Taking his cutlass, he worked his way around the hill to his right to reach the set of stairs that led directly up to the West Terrace. He bounded up the steps. When he reached the wide flat terrace, he immediately realized that something was amiss and he moved back into the shadows of the guardhouse.

Although Katelyn's magic boxes were still broadcasting their messages out over the back of the mountain, the monks were not at their defensive stations along the terrace wall. As he made his way around the corner of the guardhouse, he saw why. Three grappling hooks were lodged into the corner of the terrace wall that abutted up to the guardhouse. English soldiers must have scaled this narrow section of the rampart—which sat at a right angle to the rest of the West Terrace rampart—sight unseen by the defending monks. But how many were there? Surely, they could not have killed all of the monks defending the abbey?

Then as Nicolas carefully peered out around the next corner of the square structure, he saw the monks pressed against the wall of the abbey church. Three English soldiers stood before them in front of the terrace wall. At first Nicolas couldn't understand how only three soldiers had managed to subdue dozens of monks, and then his heart dropped in horror. These were not just any soldiers. Richard Collins was standing behind two of his henchmen, and each of his brigands held a figure in front of him as a shield against any possible missiles or weapons that could be thrown by the monks. Those human shields were Jean le Vieux and Katelyn. Katelyn was unconscious, but the monster held her body full length in front of him.

Nicolas immediately pulled himself back behind the protective cover of the guardhouse. He could be seen by the monks, but not by the Englishmen. He had to think, and he had to think quickly.

He heard Abdon in Collins' voice shout out to the monks in perfect French: "If you do not tell me immediately who this female is, we will throw her over the mountain. I have already asked Monsieur Jean here, but he is not cooperating. Unfortunately, he has a long history of non-cooperation. He doesn't seem to like answering my questions. And just to convince you that I am not making empty threats, the last time Monsieur Jean refused to answer my question, I threw his son over this very same cliff. So you see, I doubt he will be forthcoming, but you are men of God. Surely you would not allow this beautiful young woman to die? So, who is going to answer my question?"

One of the monks looked over and spotted Nicolas. Nicolas gestured for him to speak to Collins and to let the other monks know Nicolas was there, without arousing Collins' suspicion.

The brave monk stepped forward into the middle of the terrace, so that he was directly in front of the line of monks, and as he started speaking, he simultaneously gestured with his finger behind his back, pointing in Nicolas's direction so that only the monks could see the gesture.

"This woman is the wife of Nicolas le Breton," said the monk, giving only the most basic information.

"And who is Nicolas le Breton?"

"He is a stonecutter." During this succinct conversation, Nicolas was scaling the wall of the guardhouse. His plan was to slide up to the peak of the roof until he was in a perfect position to hit the soldier holding Katelyn with his cutlass.

"Is he a young man with curly golden hair?" asked the astute Collins.

"Yes," replied the spokesman as Nicolas tried to pantomime his plan to the monks. He wasn't certain if they understood that he needed them to rush the English soldiers after his attack. Hopefully, in the resulting chaos they could save both Katelyn and Jean. It wasn't a very good plan, but it was the only plan he had.

"And does he happen to be an apprentice to our friend here, Jean le Vieux?" asked Collins, as Nicolas, nearly in position, pleaded for the Archangel's divine assistance.

"Yes."

"*Eh bien,* Jean, I see you have your replacement well-trained. Another Watchman for me to deal with, *n'est-ce pas?"* As Collins turned to look at Jean, Nicolas crested the roof, took aim, and then let his cutlass fly. It sliced deep into the shoulder of the English soldier barely missing Katelyn's head. Both the soldier and Katelyn fell to the ground, and Nicolas leapt from the roof as the monks charged in unison.

Nicolas managed to grasp Katelyn and pull her to safety behind the guardhouse, while the monks struggled with Collins and the other English soldier.

When the scuffle was over, both of Collins' cutthroats had their own throats cut but Collins himself held Jean in front of him, with a knife to the old man's throat.

"I will kill him," said Collins. "Do not come one step closer."

Once Nicolas had made certain Katelyn was safely out of the mêlée, he emerged from behind the guard house.

"I am the one you want," he said to Collins.

"Oh, yes, my fine boy. You play the role of idiot nicely. So, are you going to tell me who you really are and who your so-called wife is? I am growing tired of this game, and I am tired of old Jean here." He pressed his knife into Jean's neck until he drew blood.

Not even flinching as his neck was cut, Jean cried out to Nicolas in French, "do not tell him anything, Nicolas. You know what you need to do and we both know it is my time."

Collins dragged Jean closer to the edge of the terrace as Nicolas and the others looked on helplessly.

"Stop," said Nicolas. "I will tell you what you want to know." Nicolas had no intention of telling Abdon anything, but he was buying time until he could think of a solution.

"No," Jean said, more quietly now as Collins pressed his neck harder. "I have taught you everything you need to know. It is time for me to go home. My only regret is that you will know how *I* felt when Abdon murdered Michel, but you will do the right thing."

The old man looked at Nicolas with such love and devotion in his eyes that his young pupil could not stop the tears from welling up. His chest hurt as if he'd been hit by the enemy's cannonball, and there was a lump in his throat that threatened to choke him.

"No, Papa. I cannot allow you to die." The tears spilled over his eyelids, and then flowed freely down his cheeks.

"But you must," said Jean before he was interrupted by Collins saying: "Now isn't this a touching scene. Like father like son—only the roles are reversed this time, Jean."

"You will never understand what it is to love a son," said Jean, "or a wife. You will go throughout your miserable existence and never know love or happiness. You might think you are strong, Abdon, but you are just a miserable, pathetic creature." At this, Abdon pressed against Jean's throat until blood started dripping down onto the terrace.

"So my friend, I guess this is goodbye," Collins said to Jean, as he pulled the frail man, knife still at his throat, towards the wall of the West Terrace. Then Collins stopped for a moment and said, "And to prove you wrong about me, I will even show you some compassion. I will allow you to offer any words of farewell you may wish to leave."

"Nicolas, get her home," pleaded Jean. "She will not survive if you don't get her home immediately. And Nicolas . . ." the old man paused and looked up to the heavens, "will you finish Michel's chapel for me?"

"Papa, you know I will," Nicolas said through the sobs.

And then a cry rang out over the terrace: "Stop. Stop! I'll tell you."

Katelyn had regained consciousness and was crawling out onto the terrace from behind the guardhouse. "Let him go and I will tell you who I am."

"No Katelyn," cried both Watchmen simultaneously.

"Katelyn, don't say a word," pleaded Nicolas as he helped her to a standing position and supported her body. "If you don't say anything, Abdon will never . . ."

"Now this is an interesting development," Collins said in English. "I didn't count on you coming back to life, my little vixen. I feared you were too far gone. I know you are not Kallan Mikkeldatter, the Duke of Bedford's niece, but I do know you are the one responsible for this fine little display tonight. Yes, you are the one who ruined what should now be my victory celebration! So pray tell, who are you and how is it that you have such remarkable powers?"

"Release Jean and I will tell you?" Katelyn begged, as Nicolas pressed her body to his chest and tried to quiet her. "You cannot let him die, Nicolas," she pleaded,

"We must, Katelyn. It is the only way to keep you safe."

And keep the secret safe.

"As a gesture of good faith, I will remove the knife from his throat," Collins said to her.

"Nicolas, we know that this must be," she whispered. "It is in my future for Abdon to come for me. You know it, and I know it. I cannot let Jean die."

"We can change your future, Katelyn. Abdon doesn't need to know," Nicolas tried to convince her.

But without allowing him to finish his sentence, she cried out to Collins: "my name is Katelyn Michaels."

"That is a good start wench," said Collins. "And from whence do you come?"

"Let him go and I will tell you," she insisted as Nicolas tried to put his hand over her mouth, but in true Katelyn fashion, she kneed Nicolas in the groin with her bad leg, which dropped him straight to the ground in agony. Collins hurriedly released Jean and took a step backwards.

"My name is Katelyn Michaels, and I am from America in the . . ." but as she said these words, Jean turned and charged Collins head first. The force of the head butt sent both men flying over the enclosure wall just as Katelyn finished her sentence, ". . . twenty-first century."

She let out the most agonizing wail as she watched Jean disappear from sight, and with that cry of despair, her strength gave out, and Katelyn Michaels collapsed. For the second time as a result of Abdon's treachery, Katelyn fell to the cold, hard stones of the Western Terrace. And for the second time, Nicolas le Breton stopped her fall with his body.

Chapter 46

WHEN I OPEN MY EYES, I realize I'm in a hospital room, but I have no idea where the hospital room is. My right ankle is throbbing. My leg is bandaged and elevated on a pile of pillows. Thoughts are tumbling around in my head like a huge load of laundry in the dryer. They pass by so quickly that I can't focus on any one of them. I just get a flash of their colors and textures as they pass by the window of my mind. White muslin sheets and deep red velvet. Brown woolish home-spun and cream-colored linen.

The one thing I do know is that it isn't 1424.

1424? What on earth? Why would the thought of 1424 come into my mind?

"Katelyn," I hear my brother say. "Katelyn, you're awake!"

"Jackson," I say. "Where are we? Where's Mom?"

"Mom? In America," he says. "We're in France, Katelyn. Don't you remember?"

Do I? I'm not sure.

"Let me get Dad," says Jackson. "He'll be so relieved. And so will Adèle. They have been frantic with worry, and Adèle feels so guilty." He turns to leave the room. "They're getting a bite to eat in the cafeteria. I'll go get them."

Adèle, Adèle? Abdon? I think. Yes, I know who Adèle is. Yes, yes, yes. She's the Frenchwoman who stole my father. I hate her . . . don't I? I'm supposed to hate her and yet I don't feel any hatred for her. But I certainly feel hatred for Abdon! But I can't quite remember who Abdon is.

"Jackson," I call. "Wait a minute before you get Dad and Adèle. I need to ask you some questions first. Please? I'm kinda confused."

"Wow, Katie, you must be really, really confused. I think that's the first time I've ever heard you say Adèle's name."

"Yea, well. I just . . . Jackson, who is Abdon?"

"Abdon? Never heard of anyone by that name."

"Where are we?" I ask again.

"I just told you. We're in France. Have you forgotten already?'

"No, I mean where in France?" I press my fingers into my forehead with as much pressure as I can, as if I can somehow push my lost thoughts back into place.

"We're in Rennes."

"Rennes? I've never heard of it. Where is Rennes?"

"Rennes . . . in Brittany. It's the closest big city to Mont Saint Michel. You needed a good hospital, Katelyn, because of your . . ."

"Yes," I cry out. "Mont Saint Michel! I remember. Adèle took us to Mont Saint Michel and then . . . What happened there, Jackson?"

"That's what we're all trying to find out. You think *you've* got questions? Well, we've got like a million. The last thing that happened before you disappeared is that we jumped that Goth guy who stole your enseigne and . . ."

"Abdon!" I cry. "That was Abdon."

"Okay, well I never heard what his name was. Katie, he threatened to kill you and he sure wasn't afraid to hurt me! Did he push you down the stairs or something?"

"Oh, yeah. He's the one," I say, and then notice the bandage on Jackson's chin. And then I remember how terrible I felt about abandoning my bleeding brother. My brother who fought to defend me. "That's right, he whipped you with his chain. Are you alright, Jackson?"

"Are you kidding? I'm a heck of a lot better than you are. I just don't get how you could have gotten such injuries! As for me, a couple of stitches did the trick."

"Jackie, I didn't get a chance to tell you how amazing you were. You know, in the refectory. I'm so sorry I left you . . . but . . ." I can't finish the sentence. I can't explain why I left him, but fortunately, he jumps right in, not waiting for an explanation.

"Yeah, I was pretty miffed," he admits. "Remember our friend Sheldon? He called Adèle for me, but then it got pretty scary when we couldn't find you. I thought the Goth guy, what's his name . . . Abdon? . . . had gotten you. And we were looking for that other guy who was helping us . . . you know, the one in the monk robe? What happened to him?"

"Nicolas," I reply automatically, without even processing my words, "Nicolas saved me." As if by the simple repetition of that name, that beautiful, wonderful name, the colors and textures and smells of my spinning laundry thoughts fall into place. One by one, they are all neatly folded and arranged in the drawers of my mind. But one drawer is completely empty, and there's no more laundry to fold. Not a dress, or a shirt, or even an odd sock. It's the drawer with the memories of what happened after Nicolas let go of the crutch out on the sands of the Mont Saint Michel Bay.

Frantically, I look at my hand. For my ring. Nicolas's ring. Jean's ring. My finger is bare. I'm frantic. Who stole my ring?

"Jackson, I had a ring. Who took my ring?" I say almost in tears. "And what about my enseigne? Where is it?"

"Jeez, Katie. Calm down. All of your belongings . . . well, almost all of your belongings 'cuz some of your stuff got stolen . . . are in the locker. When we found you, you were holding the enseigne in your hand. I put it in your backpack. And the nurses removed your watch and ring for surgery. I think it's in the drawer in a plastic bag. But where did that ring come from? I mean, I've never seen it. And you were wearing it on your left hand, like a wedding ring. What's that all about, huh?"

I reach for the drawer, but I can't quite get it open. "Can you get it for me?"

"Sure," he says as he opens the bedside table and rummages around. Finally, he pulls out a Ziplock baggie.

"Voilà," he says as he hands it to me. The ring is inside, along with my watch and a hair elastic. I pull the bag to my chest and breathe out a sigh of relief. I want to put the ring back on my left hand, but I know there will be too many questions, so I decide to keep it out of sight for now.

"Will you bring me my backpack, Jackson? I want to see what got stolen."

"Oh I can tell you exactly what got stolen: your battery charger, your movie camera with that built in projector, your headlamp, your pop-up speakers, Dad's iPod, and . . . I think that's all."

"You mean my laptop, phone, and camera are in my backpack?" I ask.

"Yep," he said. "We thought it was really odd that some of your electronics were stolen, but not all of them. And it was even weirder that the clothes you were wearing when you disappeared were in your backpack. What the heck? The police have a lot of questions for you."

"The police?" I say, surprised.

"Ah, yeah," he says, drawing out the 'yeah.' "I mean you disappear, and I'm bleeding all over the place. Sheldon called Adèle and abbey security, and when we couldn't find you, we thought you'd been kidnapped, so the abbey security guys called the local gendarmerie in Avranches. They looked everywhere for Abdon . . . and for the other one. Nicolas? Is that his name? But they had both completely disappeared from off the face of the planet. And then, we find you three hours later unconscious and practically dead! You were dressed in a weird muslin smocky thing, and we were so afraid you'd been, well you know . . . but the doctors said no.

"And you had a pretty horrific break in your ankle and a raging infection. The doctors say that infection nearly killed you. If the medics in the ambulance hadn't gotten you on I.V. antibiotics immediately, you might not have made it here to the hospital. And that's the deal no one can figure out, Katie, because how on earth could you get that kind of infection in just a few hours? From the time you ran down the abbey steps until we found you in Notre-Dame-Sous-Terre? It just doesn't make sense.

"And then, when we got you to the hospital, they found you had some oddly stitched-up cuts on your thigh and arm. I mean, they were stitched up with nylon sewing thread! None of it makes sense. I know you didn't have those cuts when we got to Mont Saint Michel, and yet the doctors say they're healed? How do you explain that one, huh?"

"Jackie. I'm just as confused as you are," I say, wondering how on earth I'm going to explain my way out of this mess. I finally add. "And the sad thing is, except for knowing that Gothman is responsible for my broken foot, I don't remember a darn thing."

That's my story and I'm going to have to stick with it because there are no logical explanations for Jackson's questions. Except the truth, and who would believe that? But I do remember. Not everything . . . but I do remember Nicolas letting go of the branch.

Chapter 47

I WAS SO RELIEVED when Dad, Adèle, and Jackson finally left. And they didn't press me for answers after I insisted I couldn't remember anything. Dad wanted to sit with me through the night, but I told him I was tired, and that I needed sleep, not company. I knew he and Adèle were exhausted, because Jackie told me they hadn't slept in a couple of days.

I also talked to my mom on the phone and assured her that I was okay and that she didn't need to fly to France. Dad's going to fly home with me and Jackson as soon as I get out of the hospital.

I guess my ankle is pretty bad, but the French doctors put it back together with a slew of pins, and the infection is clearing up. Thank heavens for antibiotics! The 'stitches' have been taken out of my arm and thigh, and the scars are surprisingly non-repulsive. Nicolas did an extraordinary job. But there is still no way to explain those wounds . . . or those sutures.

When the nurse came with my pain pill, I kept it under my tongue but didn't swallow it. There would be plenty of time for sleep later. I asked her to bring me my backpack, and surprisingly, I asked her in French. It just kind of came out naturally. She told me I needed to sleep, but she still brought my bag, put it on my bed, and then dimmed the lights in the room before she left me. I was alone with my thoughts for the first time since regaining consciousness.

The first thing I did was cry. Oh, not about all the trauma I'd been through. Not about my bionic foot or the scars on my arm and thigh. And certainly not about Dad and Adèle (see I *can* say her name). No, I cried about Nicolas. And about Jean.

The last memory I had was of being on the sands of Mont Saint Michel Bay. I was desperate to find out what had happened. Who had rescued me? The tears flowed as I remembered those last minutes as Nicolas sank into the quicksand. I had loved him and lost him before I'd even been able to tell him how I felt. How was it possible to feel so much pain about losing someone I'd only known for, what was it? I didn't even know how long I'd been with Jean and Nicolas. A couple of weeks? A month. I had no idea. I tried to smother the sounds of my sobbing with my pillow because I didn't want the nurse to come back in and scold me.

I was also desperate to learn about the Godon attack and Operation Dark Moon. I prayed that Jean had left me a note or message in my backpack, but as I rummaged through my belongings, I discovered that my notebook was missing, and there was no letter or written message of any kind.

Then I had another thought. I had taught Jean how to use my 'magic boxes.' Maybe he had been clever enough to leave me some type of message electronically before sending me back.

One by one, I pulled out each item from my backpack. Jackson had been right. My clothes were there, so were my travel and first aid kits. I was dumbfounded to find Raspy-Voice's dagger and the key to his cabin, which Jean had obviously wanted me to have. Souvenirs of my incredible escapades outwitting the Godons. I also found my iPhone, digital camera and even my laptop. It didn't make sense that Jean had put in some of my stuff, but not all of it. Was that a good or bad sign? Did it mean my plan had worked or failed?

I tried to turn on my computer, but the batteries were dead. As I dug deeper, I found the electrical cords were all there, as was the plug adapter to make my dual-currency gear with American plugs fit into the round-pronged French sockets. I also found the cord for my missing movie camera. Strange. That means without a way to recharge the batteries, Jean couldn't use it again, so why send back the cord and keep the camera and the solar battery charger? Maybe the battle had been fierce, and the missing items had been destroyed.

As I maneuvered around to find an electrical outlet I could use, I remembered my enseigne. Jackson told me he'd put it in my bag. I dumped everything out. It wasn't there. Then I remembered the zippered pocket inside the backpack. Of course.

When I opened that pouch, I found not only my enseigne, but another one as well. I turned it over, and on the back was one of the jobber's marks I remembered from the West Terrace because it had looked like a squiggly X. In fact, I'd taken pictures of it. I placed the two enseignes side by side:

ם א

The new symbol didn't mean anything to me. The enseigne must have been placed in my bag by Jean. Could it possibly be Jean's key? I quickly turned it over and read: *Aultre ne Veut Que J.V.* It *was* Jean's key. I didn't know why he'd given it to me, but it obviously meant he wouldn't be using it ever again. I smothered back another crying fit.

And then I remembered something else. I remember standing with Jackson in front of the famous omelet restaurant in the village, *La Mère Poulard,* watching the girls whipping up eggs in their copper bowls. I'd snapped a photo of the window reflecting Nicolas's face, and then a movie with my digital camera of Abdon chasing Nicolas up the street. That was before I knew who either of them were. I prayed that the photo of Nicolas had worked. I needed to be able to remember his countenance. I needed to touch his face and tell him how much I loved him . . . how even at only seventeen years of age, I would always consider him to be my husband.

I checked to make sure the SD card was still in my camera. It was. Both the battery in the camera, and the extra one in the pouch were dead. But if my laptop worked, I could look at the photos on it.

I finally managed to twist and turn until I got the laptop plugged in and turned on. Before looking at my photos, I quickly scanned through all the documents, but I didn't find any message from Jean. I did, however, find my Operation Dark Moon movie. I'd used my computer to add all the sound effects and music to what I had filmed, and then transferred it back to be played on my movie camera. I watched it with the tears flowing when I saw that Jean had been able to add the footage I'd filmed in Collins' camp in Ardevon. He had obviously remembered how to transfer the filming from the SD card as I'd taught him, and I was grateful he had added this segment to the computer for my benefit.

But I was watching the movie to catch a glimpse of the faces of Nicolas or Jean. I wanted to see them, wanted to have something to hold onto, something to touch. Unfortunately, neither Jean nor Nicolas were in the 'Hallelujah Chorus' scenes. I remembered they'd been on the sidelines when I filmed that segment, helping me direct traffic. Why on earth hadn't I taken photos of them? . . . Of my marriage? Of Jean's cottage. Of the village? Of the abbey? How stupid could I be? I guess I was so overwhelmed trying to save Mont Saint Michel that I never thought of taking souvenir photos. My one strong point, and I'd blown it.

I watched the movie over and over and over, wondering how the Godons—okay, I need to get back to twenty-first century political correctness—how the English had reacted to my little theatrical production. I would probably never make another movie of such importance in my entire life. I prayed that it had put the fear of God into Collins' army and that his soldiers had fled in panic or turned on him. Why, oh why hadn't Jean told me?

Even though I was completely exhausted, I finally placed the SD card from my camera into the camera card port, transferred the photos to my laptop so I would have a back-up copy of them, and looked for the pictures I'd taken in front of *La Mère Poulard*. And there it was! The clear reflection of Nicolas's face in the front window of the restaurant. Although the colors were muted, the image was clear. His golden curls, and those eyes . . . those eyes that had mesmerized me from the very beginning.

I enlarged the image and touched the reflection of his cheek, as my tears once again flowed freely. It was as if by stroking his face, I could somehow stroke away the six hundred years that separated us, as if I could bridge the gap between life and death.

And then the corners of my mouth began to turn up as I thought of how aggravating I must have been to him, how he and Jean had found me to be a spoiled brat when I'd learned I'd been whisked back in time, how much the Montois women had enjoyed preparing me for my 'wedding,' how nervous I had been the night of my wedding when I'd had to ask Nicolas for assistance, and yes, the conflicting feelings I'd felt when Jean had interrupted that moment. Myriads of emotions fought for validation. What would have happened that night if . . . Jean hadn't come? Was I relieved . . . or disappointed?

I thought of escaping my English captors after having been kidnapped and of infiltrating Richard Collins' headquarters. I thought of how amazed Nicolas had been at my ability to assume the role of Kallan Mikkeldatter. I actually smiled as I thought of the entire population of Mont Saint Michel cooperating as I transformed them into God's heavenly hosts. Oh, how I would love to tell Jackson about how I, his unenlightened sister, had become Commander in Chief for Operation Dark Moon.

More and more thoughts played out in my mind in vivid Technicolor. I had managed to make a lifetime of memories in a period of a few weeks—memories that would have to sustain me for the rest of my life. Memories I could never share with anyone. And memories that were incomplete because of my ignorance about the outcome of Operation Dark Moon.

Then I thought about my iPhone. I hadn't checked my iPhone! Even with the battery dead, I had the charging cord. I unplugged my computer and plugged my iPhone cord into the adapter. The phone lit up like a Christmas tree on Christmas morning. I checked several apps, and then went to the movie app.

I cried out in glorious, heavenly elation as I heard Nicolas's voice coming to life. At first, I thought he'd filmed this before we had left for Ardevon, but then the truth was announced. It was unbelievable. Amazing. Nicolas was alive! At least he was alive in 1424. Buttercup *and* Westley had survived the Fire Swamp and the lightning sands.

"My dearest Katelyn," he said, "I do not know if you will remember anything from this past week, and so I will tell you everything that has happened. First, because I fear the batteries on your box are almost dead, be assured that Operation Dark Moon was successful beyond our wildest dreams."

'Hallelujah,' I felt like crying out for everyone to hear, but whispered instead, 'for the Lord God Omnipotent truly reigneth.'

"Now, I will go back. When I let go of your crutch out on the sands of the bay, I did so because I could see the French soldiers coming to our rescue. I was dragging you towards me and I was afraid you would be pulled into the sands head first, and then you could not be saved. The soldiers pulled me out but you were unconscious by then. You had tried to run on your already-broken foot to save me, and the bones snapped and broke through your skin. T'was a terrible sight. Thank you, my darling, for your courage and sacrifice in trying to save both me and the mount."

Yes, I remembered running with that horrible pain, but I would have done anything, anything to save Nicolas. Nicolas panned the iPhone camera around so that I could see we were in Notre-Dame-Sous-Terre. It was Nicolas, and not Jean, who had sent me home. The chapel was lit only by a single candle, like when I'd first arrived in 1424, but I could see my body lying on the stone wall next to my keyhole. Then Nicolas turned the phone to capture his own face. I gasped at the clear sight of him and kissed the screen with tears streaming down my cheeks.

"Although Jean and I cared for you the best we could," he continued, "you remained delirious. Sometimes you seemed to be awake, and we talked of many things, but other times, I think you believed I was dead and that I was from heaven coming to take you back with me."

Try as I might, I could not remember any of that.

"I managed to complete the moving picture with the sound and images from Ardevon and then I transferred it to your moving image box. Your images of Collins' plans were invaluable in setting up our defenses. When the Godons came, it didn't take long for them to give up the fight.

The soldiers fled in total panic, and I do not think they will return. But Collins and his bodyguards did not flee. During the battle, Jean remained with you in the upstairs bedchamber, but you became so feverish he knew if he did not send you back home for your twenty-first century physicians to care for your wound, you would die."

I hoped beyond hope that Nicolas had captured Jean's voice or at least his face in this movie as well, so I waited for the next portion with anticipation. Unfortunately, his next words brought only more tears of anger and grief, rather than happiness.

"Katelyn, I am grieved to tell you this part, but you deserve the truth. While Jean was taking you to the abbey to send you home, Collins and his men captured you both. You told Collins who you were to try to save Jean's life, but Jean then sacrificed himself to protect you by killing Collins. He pushed Collins, and they both fell over the West Terrace wall and were killed."

I paused the recording, gasping at the realization that Jean had sacrificed himself to protect me. He had given his life for me. I began sobbing, thinking of how many things I had learned from my beloved tutor, and of how many questions I still had for him. My training had not been long enough. I had not spent enough time with the wisest man I had ever met. I had not been adequately prepared to be a Watchman. I felt Jean's loss as keenly as I had felt the loss when my own father had left us.

Finally able to continue, I pressed play again. However, just hearing Nicolas's voice added to my intense anguish.

"I also learned then that Abdon had murdered Jean's son, Michel, in the same manner—by throwing him over the wall because Jean would not betray the secret of the mount. I will bury Jean with his son in the little Saint Aubert chapel below the West Terrace, and I will finish building the unfinished chapel as Jean requested me to do. That is where they will lie,

Katelyn. I hope one day, you can return to Mont Saint Michel and pay tribute to them there."

I remembered that first day with Jackson, peering down at that tiny Saint Aubert chapel from the West Terrace and having that overwhelming feeling that it had been built in honor of a lost child, not of Saint Aubert. Now I knew it was true. I covered my sobs with my pillow as I thought of the heartache Jean must have felt for all those years, knowing that because he had remained true to his calling as a Watchman, his son had been murdered.

But I didn't understand what Nicolas meant about 'the secret of the mount.' Would I ever know what he was talking about? I finally came to the realization that there were certain things about being a Watchman that Jean and Nicolas had not told me, important things they had not dared share with me. I couldn't blame them, at least in the beginning. After all, I had given them the initial impression that I was a spoiled twenty-first century brat who couldn't care less about my so-called 'calling.' But hadn't I eventually proven my worth? Hadn't I confirmed to them that I could be trusted? Those thoughts just increased my heartache.

"Katelyn," Nicolas continued, "Abdon knows who you are, and you must always be wary of him. For the rest of your life, you must be vigilant."

A sinking feeling hit as I realized that Nicolas was warning me that for the rest of my existence, I would have to watch. To watch for Abdon. It was a sobering thought. However, his words also gave me a tiny glimmer of hope. Perhaps my responsibilities as a Watchman had not been completed with the success of Operation Dark Moon. Perhaps, just possibly I would be able to go back to Nicolas again. And prove my worth to him.

I continued listening to this emotional message sent through six centuries of time.

"Knowing your condition was critical, I gathered the magic boxes I had and put them with your other belongings in your knapsack, which had already been packed by Jean. As you will see, I was not able to get everything, since the moving picture was still playing on the rampart wall and the sound was being played from your white box on the West Terrace. I could not risk taking the time to retrieve all of your belongings. I will protect them from fifteenth century questions, but I cannot destroy them. They are my only reminders of you. And then I brought you here to Notre-Dame-Sous-Terre where you see me now . . . and I sent you home. It broke my heart."

He then held the phone so that it captured him bending over my still body and kissing my lips with such love and tenderness, I could hardly bear it. Our only kiss, and I couldn't even remember it! It was the most heart-wrenching thing I have ever witnessed. By this time, Nicolas's face, like mine, was covered in tears. And then he continued talking while filming his face. A fifteenth century selfie for me to cherish for eternity.

"As I sat with you in those days before the battle, I told you the secret of the Mount Katelyn, but I cannot repeat it here in case someone else takes possession of this box. Go deep into your soul, and you will remember what I said. I know you will. You need to know, you must know, because, like me and Jean, you are a Watchman. You have proven your worth."

He *had* trusted me! He *had* told me the secret! I *had* proven my worth to him, but try as I might, I couldn't remember what he had told me. But that was okay. My brain was still so fuzzy from having been so sick. I had plenty of time to think. Plenty of time.

"And now, you must go, my darling. Although our marriage was for show only, I want you to know that I consider you to be my wife. I will always consider you to be my wife. I love you, Katelyn Michaels and I shall love you forever."

I sobbed and sobbed as he spoke those last words. My heart felt as if it would break into a million pieces and that I would die of grief.

And then, my beloved Nicolas, my dearest Westley, gave me the slightest glimmer of hope in my now otherwise bleak existence when he pronounced his final sentence before turning off the camera: "My darling, beautiful Katelyn, I cannot conceive of life without you. I will find a way. I do not know how, or when, but you must know this one thing. I will always come for you."

Author's Note

While this is a work of fiction, all of the historical background given about Mont Saint Michel is factual. As a tidal island and religious site, Mont Saint Michel has endured for 1,300 years despite wars and revolutions. Its fortifications, village, and abbey have evolved throughout that period. During the Hundred Years' War (1337-1453), the French house of Valois was pitted against the Plantagenets of England (who originated in the French province of Anjou), both of whom laid claim to the throne of France. Many townships and fortresses in Normandy fell into English hands and were governed by the Duke of Bedford, the brother of Henry V. However, Mont Saint Michel never capitulated. The English made one of their most determined assaults on Mont Saint Michel in 1424. The siege was ultimately unsuccessful and the mount was never conquered until the German occupation of France during WWII, when the Nazis used it as a shelter.

The information about the tides and the hazardous sands of the Bay of Mont Saint Michel is also factual.

Mont Saint Michel is one of the most visited sites in France.

www.ingramcontent.com/pod-product-compliance
Lightning Source LLC
Chambersburg PA
CBHW020509260626
47156CB00006B/1940

9780692342855